THE
BUTCHER

Center Point
Large Print

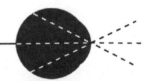

**This Large Print Book carries the
Seal of Approval of N.A.V.H.**

THE
BUTCHER

Jennifer Hillier

CENTER POINT LARGE PRINT
THORNDIKE, MAINE

This Center Point Large Print edition is published
in the year 2014 by arrangement with Galley Books,
a division of Simon & Schuster, Inc.

Copyright © 2014 by Jennifer Hillier.

The text of this Large Print edition is unabridged.
In other aspects, this book may vary from the original edition.
Printed in the United States of America on permanent paper.
Set in 16-point Times New Roman type.

ISBN: 978-1-62899-391-2

Library of Congress Cataloging-in-Publication Data

Hillier, Jennifer.
  The butcher / Jennifer Hillier. — Center Point Large Print edition.
  pages ; cm
  Summary: "Thirty years after police chief Edward Shank killed
Seattle's infamous 'Beacon Hill Butcher', Shank's grandson, Matt, and
Matt's girlfriend, Sam, pursue leads that prove that the real Butcher is
still alive"—Provided by publisher.
  ISBN 978-1-62899-391-2 (library binding : alk. paper)
  1. Serial murders—Fiction. 2. Family secrets—Fiction.
    3. Large type books. 4. Psychological fiction. I. Title.
PS3608.I446B88 2014b
813'.6—dc23
                                                         2014033224

For Darren

THE
BUTCHER

APRIL 25, 1985

It had once been a lovely apartment building, but the crackheads had changed all that. Graffiti covered the old brick walls and the front doors were badly in nccd of a new coat of paint. Most of the windows—the ones that weren't broken—had mismatched bedsheets as curtains, and the courtyard in front of the building looked and smelled like a garbage dump.

The light Seattle rain drizzled down steadily, covering Captain Edward Shank's face with a fine mist that felt good. Twenty feet away from the apartment's entrance, he stood still in the dark, feeling secure, if a little warm, under the weight of the Kevlar vest hugging his torso. Several other police officers flanked him on either side, and though they weren't touching, he could feel the tension in their bodies cutting through the cool night air.

He spoke to them in a low, commanding voice and gripped his weapon tighter. "Nobody moves till I move."

The only light in the area was weak and yellow, seeping from a bare bulb over the doorway to the building. A striped cat with missing patches of fur moved quietly through the shadows and into the walkway light, pausing to sniff the air. The front door to the apartment building opened and the cat scampered away. A middle-aged man, potbellied and wearing a too-tight wifebeater-style tank top and a pair of saggy denim shorts, stepped out.

Edward Shank moved forward, aiming his weapon at the man's chest. "Rufus Wedge!" His voice, strong and authoritative, carried easily into the quiet night. "This is Captain Edward Shank from the Seattle Police Department. Don't move. You're under arrest. Get on your knees and place your hands in the air."

Startled, Wedge turned in the direction of Edward's voice. His left hand crept toward his back pocket.

Without hesitation, Edward fired. So did the four other police officers beside him.

The gunfire propelled Rufus Wedge backward. The man hit the door hard before slumping to the ground, bright spots of blood immediately appearing in several places across his torso, stark against the white cotton of his shirt. The man's grizzled jaw went slack, the few stray hairs from his comb-over falling across his pink, shiny forehead in moist wisps. As the light went out of his eyes, the dull yellow bulb above him cast a golden, almost angelic glow on his face.

An interesting contradiction. Edward almost felt guilty.

Almost.

"We got him, Captain," someone said. Edward recognized the voice but didn't turn to look. He couldn't bring himself to take his eyes off Rufus Wedge, so he nodded without averting his gaze. "We finally nailed the Butcher. Thank fucking Christ."

From somewhere in the dark, the striped cat yowled.

The officers around Edward rushed forward to check the man's vitals, as was protocol, guns still drawn. Their captain stayed behind, unmoving, under the cover of the darkness, his eyes fixed on Wedge's dead body.

Rufus Wedge, otherwise known as the Beacon Hill Butcher, had been the most wanted man in the Pacific Northwest for a long time. The manhunt was now over.

Holstering his weapon, Edward let out a long, slow breath. Wiping his brow, slick from the rain, he stepped forward into the light toward the dead man. Wedge stared up at him with blank, glossy eyes.

"No more now," Edward said quietly. He wasn't speaking to anyone in particular, except maybe himself. "No more."

11

1

PRESENT DAY

The ornately carved 1890 Mathushek upright piano was the only thing left in Edward's house, and here it would stay. There was no way to bring it with him to the old folks' home, because the goddamned piano had to weigh at least five hundred pounds.

He would miss it.

Once upon a time, the Mathushek lived in a saloon somewhere in Texas. It was originally a player piano that could belt out seventeen different tunes without anyone's help, which must have seemed like magic back then. The saloon closed after a Mexican gang shot the place up, and the piano was brought to the owner's house, where it stayed until he died of a heart attack while fucking his mistress, a former singer in the saloon. The mistress then inherited the piano, and it stayed in her family until her adult grand-children decided to sell it at auction. By then, the Mathushek was in terrible shape, dented and scratched and out of tune, and it had taken almost a year to restore it to its original beauty.

Or so the story went, according to the man who'd refurbished it and sold it to Edward Shank thirty years ago for twice what it was probably worth. The guy could have been lying, as most salesmen did. Anyway, who gave a rat's ass? It didn't matter now.

The bay window in the living room where the piano sat had a clear view of Poppy Lane, and Edward stood in front of it, smoking a cherry-flavored cigar, watching, waiting. He didn't have much time left in this house, and after fifty years as its sole owner, the thought wasn't pleasant. He didn't want to move out, but at eighty years old, the house was becoming harder to keep up. He was still in good shape, but the fall that had bruised his hip badly a month ago hadn't helped anything. All good things had to come to an end, and while this was something he understood well, it was also something he dreaded. He could see a faint reflection of himself in the clean window. Some days he simply didn't recognize the thinning mop of white hair and leathery lined face staring back at him.

His hand, still strong but dotted with sun spots, stroked the burl walnut wood of the antique piano lovingly. He traced the rose carvings with a finger that ached from arthritis, his bad hip throbbing slightly, though he refused to sit down. Edward would miss this house. He would miss this piano. Memories of his late wife and daughter were everywhere, and he could still recall the fresh smell of their apple-scented shampoo when he kissed the backs of their heads as they played "Heart and Soul" on the beautiful Mathushek. A lifetime ago. In just a few hours, he would be an official resident of the Sweetbay Village Retirement Residence, and from then on the most exciting thing in his life would be bingo tournaments on Saturday afternoons, and Mac 'n' Cheese Wednesdays.

He didn't know whether to kill himself, or someone else.

He sighed. Maybe he'd go for a drive later this week, and go hunting. Hunting used to always cheer him up. He still had his old cabin down in Raymond, though he hadn't been there in years and had no idea what shape it was in. One day those two hundred acres of densely wooded forest in Raymond would be Matthew's, too.

But not yet.

Moving away from the window, Edward glanced at the wall above the piano. It was bare now, save for the little scuffs left behind from the various framed photos that used to hang there. He'd already brought all of his pictures over to the old folks' home—sorry, *retirement community for active seniors*—but he knew the exact spot where his favorite photo used to hang. It was taken the day the mayor of Seattle awarded him a medal for taking down the notorious Beacon Hill Butcher back in April of '85. The day Captain Edward Shank had become a hero and Seattle legend. The case, nationally known, had almost single-handedly made his career. You didn't become chief of police for writing speeding tickets and catching petty thieves. The Butcher had been the case of a lifetime, and he still got requests for interviews about it every now and again.

Though he was alone, Edward grinned, running his tongue over the smooth white dentures that made up his smile.

There was a sizable dent in the corner of the piano, and his sore finger traced the rough edges where the wood had chipped and cracked. The dent hadn't been there long, and it was a damned shame it existed at all, because otherwise the instrument was in wonderful condition. Marisol, his late wife, had seen to that. She'd been diligent about keeping the Mathushek in tip-top shape, moisturizing it regularly with wood polish and hiring a professional piano tuner once a year.

The ivory keys were slightly worn in places, but still soft to the touch. Edward could play the piano a little, though the arthritis was making it harder. Taking a seat at the leather bench, he rested his cigar on the ceramic ashtray on top of the piano and flexed his fingers. He made it halfway through Beethoven's *Moonlight Sonata* before his aching fingers forced him to stop.

Disappointing, but not a big deal. Marisol had been the musician in the family, a graduate of Juilliard and a pianist in the Seattle symphony for a few years. She'd also taught piano right up until the day she died, and Edward had always been content to be her captive audience. Their daughter Lucy had been talented too, only she hadn't lived long enough to develop her mother's skill.

His hip burned and he rubbed it gingerly. He stood carefully by the window once more, watching, waiting, six-foot-four frame erect and ready. If anyone strolling down the sidewalk looked up, he or she would see a sprightly eighty-year-old man standing ramrod straight in the window, dressed in a plaid button-down shirt and pressed trousers, cigar smoke swirling around neatly combed silver hair. One must always present himself well. First impressions mattered.

But Poppy Lane was quiet on this rainy Sunday afternoon, at least until his grandson Matthew arrived with the U-Haul and his friends. Matthew was moving in today, and Edward knew his job would be to stay out of his grandson's way until the young men had unloaded everything. Then he would take the boys out for burgers before heading over to the old folks' home for good.

Watching. Waiting. Edward had been a police detective for close to forty years, and patience was indeed his virtue.

The white U-Haul truck finally rounded the bend, bouncing down the street, another car following behind it. The boys were here. Soon it would be time to go.

At best, it was bittersweet.

Taking one final look around, Edward's gaze once again lingered on the antique piano. His eyes misted as memories of Marisol came rushing back. God, how he missed his wife. The house hadn't been the same without her these past few months. Reaching out, he once again touched the dent on the side of the Mathushek, left there from when he'd smashed her head into it four months ago.

At least he'd managed to get all the blood out of the carved roses before calling 9-1-1, despite his arthritic hands.

One must always be careful cleaning up after a kill.

2

There were three things Matt loved most in the world: *adobo*, the Seahawks, and Samantha. He didn't think it made him a dick that his girlfriend was third on that list; at least he was honest about it. Most guys weren't, and that's why so many relationships ended (in his not-so-humble opinion).

Adobo was a traditional Filipino dish infused with vinegar, soy sauce, and garlic. Every family —hell, every individual Filipino—had their own unique recipe, and no two dishes ever turned out exactly alike. Matt's recipe was based on the version his Filipino grandmother—his *lola*—used to make as he was growing up, which included brown sugar, bay leaves, peppercorns, and a secret ingredient that Matt would take to his grave. After all, *adobo* was his signature dish, the dish that had made his food truck the most popular stop at the Fremont Food Fair every Sunday, and the dish that had ultimately allowed him to open up his own restaurant in the heart of Seattle. Appropriately named, of course, Adobo.

Matt had inherited his grandfather's height, build, and personality, but his love for food and cooking was all from his grandmother. Marisol Perez had met Edward Shank in 1962 when the Chief was in the air force and stationed at Clark Air Base in the Philippines. When recounting the story of how they'd met, the Chief liked to joke that Filipino women were their country's greatest export. Kind of an awful thing to say, but his *lola* had always laughed it off. She'd always believed that her husband was complimenting her, and Matt had never had the heart to tell her that his grandfather was not.

The restaurant had been his lifelong dream, and Matt had busted ass to make it a reality. And finally, his hard work was paying off. The food truck was still kicking ass at the food fairs every week, and he'd been profiled in *Seattle* magazine and *Bon Appétit*. Several of his recipes (not his *adobo*, of course—that was sacred) had been published in *O* magazine, *People*, and *Martha Stewart Living*. His food truck had also been featured on the popular Food Network show *Diners, Drive-Ins and Dives*.

Which was why the Fresh Network, the Food Network's prime competition, wanted to produce a reality show about him. And why wouldn't they? When you were on fire, everybody wanted you, and Matt had no problem claiming credit for his own success. There was no place for insecurity in this business, or in any aspect of life, for that matter. His grandmother, may she rest in peace, had always believed in him, even when the Chief—perpetually disappointed that his grandson hadn't chosen a career in law enforcement—hadn't. Matt only wished his *lola* had lived long enough to see him shine. She would have been the proudest Filipino grandmother ever.

And now, inheriting his grandparents' house was just the icing on the cake. He'd been born and raised in that house, and everything about moving back into it felt exactly right.

When Matt had told his girlfriend about his grandfather's decision to move into the old folks' home and give him the house on Poppy Lane—a real house, with a backyard, a working fireplace, and four large bedrooms—Sam had started decorating it in her head. She'd automatically assumed that her boyfriend of three years was taking their relationship to the next level, and that she was included in Matt's grand plan to give up the bachelor pad he rented in Belltown to move into the gorgeous old Victorian in the prestigious neighborhood of Sweetbay, where the grass was greener, the incomes higher, and everybody was married with a couple of kids and a dog.

She couldn't have been more wrong.

First, Matt wasn't ready for kids anytime soon. Hell, he barely had the time to spend with Elmo, his five-year-old Abyssinian cat.

Second, he wasn't ready for cohabitation. Matt didn't want to live with anybody right now, not even Sam. He'd had roommates in college, and had been utterly turned off to having other bodies sharing his living space. He couldn't wait to spread out, cook for himself in a proper kitchen, and buy an obnoxiously large stainless steel barbecue for backyard get-togethers. He most certainly didn't want pastel bedsheets, a living room that smelled like vanilla candles, and long strands of brown hair all over the bathroom floor.

And lastly, doing this on his own was just really important to him. He'd always been this way, and he was getting tired of having to explain it to people. The Chief had refused to take a dime from Matt for the house, citing that it was his inheritance anyway, but Matt would happily have taken out a mortgage if that's what his grandfather had wanted. He didn't ever want to feel like someone had given him a handout. He didn't believe in taking shortcuts to the finish line.

Maybe he was being a bit overzealous about it, but it was honestly how he felt. His explanation to Sam, of course, was much more subtle.

"There are things I need to do on my own, and this is one of them."

This had hurt Sam, probably more than she was letting on, but she said she understood and let it go. For a while, anyway. But as the weeks passed, and she listened to him talk about the house and all the renovations he was planning, she became more and more vocal about why it was *exactly* the right time for them to live together, and how she was certain they were ready to take the next step.

"We love each other and we've been together for three years. I'm clean, I'm financially responsible, and I still have sex with you three times a week," Sam said. They were lying in her bed, naked and sweaty. "I don't understand what you're so worried about. I'm not even asking for a ring."

Her timing was irritating. She knew damned well she'd just drained him of all usable body fluids, and now she was hitting him up with this conversation yet again.

"I'm not worried." Matt was careful with his tone. He was in no mood to argue. Frankly, he didn't have the strength. "It's not about you, or us. It's about *me*. I need to do this. After ten years of

21

busting my ass with nobody's help, things are finally going in the direction I want them to. I need to keep doing things on my own."

"So I don't get a say at all?" Sam's hair was plastered to her face, her cheeks still flushed. Despite her aggravation, he thought she looked sexy as hell.

"Honestly, I don't see why you would." Matt hated the wounded look on her face, but he felt cornered and vulnerable. He pulled the sheets over his exposed body. "Don't take it like that. That's not what I mean. All I'm trying to say is, this doesn't change anything between you and me."

"But what if I want things to change?" she said in a small voice.

"You're still my girlfriend. I'm one hundred percent devoted to you. But there are things I need to do first before *we* change things."

"It's always about you." Sighing, she turned away. "I don't know why I'm even surprised."

He flinched. She wasn't wrong, and he wasn't sure how to respond. "Just be patient," he finally said. "We'll get there."

Pushing the sheets off her naked body, she headed to the bathroom. "I'm already there."

A few days later, Sam had brought Jason into the ongoing argument, and that was the last straw. Jason Sullivan was Matt's closest friend, but Sam had known him longer; they'd been friends since childhood, and he was like a big brother to her. A big, overbearing, intrusive brother. She'd told Jason everything, and of course their mutual friend, who at times wasn't so mutual, agreed with Sam. Jason, normally a laid-back and open-minded guy, seemed awfully opinionated about Matt and Sam's relationship.

"There are a lot of financially good reasons why you guys should move in together." Jason sounded infuriatingly reasonable. They were in their usual fifty-yard-line seats at CenturyLink Field, courtesy of Jason's three years playing quarterback with the Seahawks. Though his friend had retired from the NFL four years ago, football fans still recognized Jase, and going anywhere in public with him was always an ordeal. The Hawks were down 17–14 to the Niners, and Matt could not believe that Jason Sullivan, of all people, would initiate a conversation about his relation-ship during a football game. *The sacrilege.* He munched on garlic fries and tried to drown out the annoyance of his friend's well-meaning voice.

"She's got cash on hand for the renovations you want to do, she can pay half the bills, and she's almost as good a cook as you are," Jason said, using his fingers to tick off each point as he went. He sounded a lot like Sam. "And she's a neat freak, so you can finally fire your weird cleaning lady. Think of the money you'd save. That could mean another food truck next year, my friend, maybe even another restaurant. How about *that.*"

Matt sipped his beer, squeezing the plastic container so hard it warped. He didn't care if his friend was a famous ex-quarterback and that people all around them were surreptitiously snapping pictures of him with their cell phones, he was seriously considering dumping his beer over the guy's head. If it hadn't cost nine bucks, he might have. "No. And I don't want to talk about this with you anymore."

"I'm just saying, think about it. Everything in your life is falling into place. The food trucks are hot, the restaurant's doing well, you've got those people from the Fresh Network calling, and now you're moving into the big house. Don't you want someone to share all that with?"

"I already have someone to share all that with."

"Elmo doesn't count."

"He would beg to differ."

"Consider how Sam feels."

"Let it go, Jase."

Jason sighed. "You've been with her for a long time. You haven't asked her to marry you, which, okay, I get, because marriage doesn't exactly appeal to me right now, either. But you don't even want her to live with you? In that big-ass house? Have you stopped for a second to think that maybe you're being a tiny bit of an asshole here? You gotta throw her a bone, man. Relationship Advice 101. You don't give a little, they leave."

Matt said nothing.

"Is it even an option at some point?"

Matt scraped up the last bit of garlic from the bottom of his paper cup, wishing his friend would shut up. "I don't know. But don't you fucking tell her that."

"Why not? Why waste her time then, man? She's paid her dues."

"She knew the drill when we first hooked up."

"She thought you'd come around."

Matt was a quiet for a moment. "I love her. She knows that. I don't get why that's never enough." He thought about saying something else, but decided against it.

Jason shook his head and took a long swig of beer. Belched loudly. The woman in front of them in the Russell Wilson jersey turned around and glared at them. Jason flashed her a grin and winked. It seemed totally obnoxious to Matt, but it worked; the woman's dirty look melted into a smile.

"Oh my God, you're Jason Sullivan," she said.

"Yes, ma'am."

"Can I take a picture with you?"

"Of course."

The woman handed her phone to Matt, who refrained from rolling his eyes even though he wanted to. This kind of thing happened all the time. He took their picture and the woman turned back around, squealing to her friend beside her.

"Sam's a good girl," Jason said, jumping right

back into the conversation. "Just, you know, give it some more thought. All I'm asking. Not that I'll ever get what she sees in you, anyway."

"She's with me because I'm a swell guy," Matt said, his jaw tight. The crowd roared as the Seahawks made a first down. "And hey, I don't see you putting a ring on Lily's finger."

"It's *Lilac,* you asshole, and we've only been seeing each other for three months. Completely different thing."

"And Rachel?"

"Fling. Never destined to go anywhere."

"What about Susan?"

"Suzanna. And she was already married. With two kids."

"She was?" Matt couldn't help but laugh. It was hard to stay mad at his friend. "I didn't know that. Who's the asshole now?"

"You are. Sam's one of the good ones. And you're going to fuck it up."

Instantly Matt's face flushed, and he clenched his fist. Jason glanced down.

"What, you gonna hit me?" his friend said quietly. "Thought we were all done with that shit."

Matt forced himself to relax. "We are."

"Good, I'm glad those classes you took weren't just for show."

Gritting his teeth, Matt didn't respond. Truthfully, there was nothing he could say. He'd lost his temper one too many times in the past, and after a bar brawl and a night in jail, had been forced to undergo a three-week anger management course over a year ago. The Chief had had to pull strings so he could avoid jail time. It wasn't something he was proud of.

Finally he said to Jason, "I thought you were on my side."

"I'm on both your sides." Sighing, Jason finally threw up a hand. "You know what? I tried. And I'm done, I'm out of it. Buy me a beer and I'll shut the hell up, because God knows we both want me to."

And that, for the most part, had ended it. He didn't know what Jason had said to Sam after the game, but she'd backed off once and for all, and for that Matt was grateful.

3

His grandfather's house was in the center of Sweetbay, one of Seattle's oldest neighborhoods, and also one of the most desirable. A little to the north and west of downtown, Sweetbay was situated on a small tip of land that jutted into Puget Sound, and quite a few of the homes had water views. The houses were a mix of Tudor, Victorian, and Craftsman, and they all had perfect green lawns dotted with bright flowers and trimmed shrubs. Trees decades older than Matt lined the streets, and on a summer day when the wind from the ocean rippled the leaves just right, the whole neighborhood seemed to smell of good fortune.

If you asked one of the old-timer residents where they lived (and there were a lot of old-timers in this neighborhood), they would answer "Sweetbay," not Seattle, as if the place was a town all by itself. And in some ways, it was. It was completely self-sufficient. It had its own little shopping area complete with a Whole Foods, a movie theater, and an assortment of cafés and coffee shops. There was even a farmers' market on Saturdays (not quite big enough for Matt to justify a food truck, but it was cute nonetheless). Most everything was within walking distance, and the best part of all? Sweetbay was only a ten-minute drive to downtown Seattle, making it the ideal yuppie neighborhood for those who could afford a house in the city.

Though he'd moved out of the Belltown apartment and into the Sweetbay house a few days earlier, Matt had just bought a new bed from Restoration Hardware, and that was what was inside the second U-Haul truck he'd rented this week.

The truck was brand-new and not too big, easy enough to maneuver through leafy Poppy Lane. Jason and another friend, PJ Wu, who was also his assistant head chef at the restaurant, were following behind him in Matt's utility van, because the bed was heavy and would be a bitch to unload. Matt took his time driving, minding the signs posted everywhere that said speeding endangers our kids, which was interesting considering there were hardly any kids in Sweetbay. It would make more sense to change the signs to speeding endangers old farts.

He pulled up to the house and reversed, backing the truck halfway into the Chief's long driveway. Smiling to himself, he wondered how long it would be before he stopped thinking of the house as his grandfather's. The paperwork had been completed the day before and the house was officially in Matt's name. It felt absolutely right; he'd grown up here, after all. His grandparents had raised him after his teenage mother had died when he was just an infant.

Stepping down out of the truck, he looked up at the old Victorian and felt a sense of peace wash over him. He was almost there. He almost had everything he wanted. The house was another piece of Matt's personal success puzzle. *Home sweet home*.

His utility van pulled up beside the curb and Matt turned to see Jason and PJ laughing about something.

"Not too shabby, buddy," PJ Wu said, stepping out of the van and snapping his gum. It was an irritating sound, and Matt could see the wad of pink rolling around on his friend's tongue. Stepping onto the grass, PJ clapped Matt on the shoulder with a grin. The two looked up at the house together. "Jase said this was a gorgeous place, but I didn't realize it was so damned huge. What are you going to do with all this space?" Snapping his gum one last time, PJ hawked, and the gum flew out of his mouth and landed on the grass.

Matt frowned. The sight of that bright pink wad of chewing gum resting on top of his perfectly manicured green lawn was ugly. "Seriously?" he said, not bothering to hide his annoyance. "Don't you have any manners? Pick that shit up."

"What?"

"Don't spit your goddamn gum out on my grass. I said pick it up."

PJ blinked and took a step back. "Dude. Chill." He bent down and picked up the gum, holding it gingerly between his thumb and forefinger even though it was his own. Turning, he flicked it into the sewer grate beside the curb. "It's just gum. You can ask nicely."

"I don't have to ask nicely. I shouldn't have to ask at all."

"Hey." PJ's dark eyes furrowed. "Don't talk to me like that. I'm not working for you today. Shit, dude, I'm here as a friend, not your employee. I'm helping you out, remember."

Matt snorted. "Helping me out is what friends

do. Cooking at my restaurant is what I pay you to do. Spitting your nasty-ass gum on my clean lawn is what assholes do."

"Did you just call me an asshole? Are you kidding me?" PJ squared his shoulders and took a step toward him. "What the fuck is your problem?"

Matt laughed, but there was no trace of humor in the sound. PJ was eight inches shorter and probably weighed forty pounds less, and Matt would pound him. "You're my problem, asshole. Don't ever leave your shit on my lawn."

"Wow." PJ's mouth hung open, but before he could say anything more, Jason intervened, stepping in between them and slinging an arm over each of their shoulders.

"Come on now, boys, simmer down." As usual, Jason's tone was easy with a side of snark. "What are we fighting about? My delicate ears don't appreciate such rated-R language. Today's a happy day, isn't it? Please tell me we're not arguing about gum. What are we, little girls?"

"Talk to your boy, Jase," PJ said, his face still hot. He shrugged off Jason's arm. "He's the one who needs the attitude adjustment."

"From where I'm standing, you could all be little girls." The gruff voice, naturally loud and commanding, carried across the lawn, and all three guys looked up in surprise to see Edward Shank standing in the open doorway. A lit cigar was in one hand, and the aroma of smoke and cherries wafted over. "Bunch of pussies you are, standing around crying over a little bubble gum. You boys trying to embarrass me in front of the neighbors?"

On cue, they all straightened up. Jason dropped his arms from around their shoulders and smoothed his hair. PJ made sure his shirt was tucked into his pants. The Chief had that effect on people, whether they realized it or not.

"Chief." Matt took a step away from PJ and Jason. "Didn't realize you were here."

"Walked over. It's a nice day. And I still have my key." The old man took his key chain out of his pocket and shook it. "Should I have called first? Maybe I should have; looks like you boys are gearing up for a fight."

"Of course not." Matt exchanged looks with Jason and PJ. PJ dropped his eyes and looked away.

Jason let out a laugh, but it sounded forced, and it was obvious he was trying to break the tension. "Good to see you, old-timer," he said, giving Matt a stern look before bounding up the porch steps to shake Edward's hand. "Still got your iron grip, I see."

"I could still kick your sorry ass." The Chief's eyes were alight with good humor. He punched Jason in the shoulder, then winced and rubbed his knuckles. "Goddamn it, I think you're bigger than when I last saw you. You juicing or what? And

32

what do you need all those muscles for, anyway, champ? You don't play football anymore, and it won't do you a bit of good when I get my foot up your sphincter. Mind you, you'd probably enjoy that, though I'd hate to muss up that hair."

"You must be looking forward to moving into the old farts' home." Jason's grin was equally wise-ass. "I hear they got tuna casseroles and backgammon going on every night. How will you possibly handle all the excitement? You might keel over if you're not careful."

"Son, I haven't been excited in twenty years. Not since my wife surprised me on the night of our thirtieth anniversary."

"Oh God, I didn't just hear that." Finally relaxing a little, Matt shot one last glare at PJ before stepping onto the porch to give his grandfather a hug. "Chief, I think my ears are bleeding. That's my grandmother you're talking about, for God's sake. May she rest in peace."

The old man ruffled his hair fondly. "Ha. So what? And how did I manage to raise such a pussy?"

"Same question I'm asking myself," PJ muttered as he pushed up the sleeves of his sweatshirt.

"Oh let it go, already," Jason said, rolling his eyes. He looked pointedly at PJ, who sighed and turned away. The two of them headed back to the U-Haul, opening the back door to reveal Matt's

33

new bed frame, headboard, and mattress set.

Clapping Matt on the shoulder, Edward leaned in to whisper in his grandson's ear. Sweet smoke curled up toward their faces from the Chief's cigar, which he held down at his side. "You know, I always thought that PJ kid was an idiot, too, and you can bust his balls when you're at the restaurant tomorrow. But right now you need his help, so it doesn't do you any good to get in his face. Always pick your battles. You got me?"

Matt had to smile. His grandfather always knew the right thing to say. "Yeah, I got you, Chief."

"I understand, though," Edward said, taking a drag on his cigar. His voice was low. "If this had still been my lawn, I'd have ripped his face off. Disrespectful little shit."

4

First order of business: build a deck and buy a hot tub. Matt loved the outdoors, and he had big plans for his new backyard.

Though tired from a long day at the restaurant, he was exhilarated to see that work had begun. As he stood alone at the back door, surveying the progress, a light rain drizzled over him. At present, the yard was a giant mess. Holes and piles of dirt marred what used to be a neatly manicured lawn, but unlike the gum incident, it didn't bother Matt. He could envision the end result—a stained wood deck, the hanging lanterns, the giant barbecue grill, and the hot tub. He had initially wanted an inground pool, but Jason had put the kibosh on that idea, reminding Matt that the weather in Seattle was only conducive to swimming between July Fourth and Labor Day. Eight weeks of summer was hardly worth the thousands it would cost to build a pool.

His cell phone rang in his back pocket and he pulled it out. Recognizing the name and number, he answered quickly.

"Hey, Matt." The raspy voice of Duncan Hastings, the contractor Jason had recommended, was in his ear. "Just wanted to check in. We made good progress today. Tomorrow we'll start pouring the cement for the deck, so long as it isn't raining too hard."

"Looking good so far, man." A speck of rain landed on Matt's brow and he wiped it away, moving back under the bright yellow awning covering his back door. "Can't wait to see the finished product."

"If all goes well you'll be having a party to celebrate in two weeks. Anyway, the reason for my call." The contractor cleared his throat. "We dug something up in the backyard, almost ripped right through it."

"You dug something up? What was it, a dead body?"

Hastings chuckled. "The crate wasn't big enough. I didn't know what to do with it, so I moved it to the side of the house. Beside your raspberry bushes."

"I have raspberry bushes?"

Another laugh. "Anyway, hope we didn't cause any damage. It was buried pretty deep. Seems like it's been there awhile, as the soil was pretty settled around it. I'm guessing it was the Chief's?"

Everybody knew who Matt's grandfather was, and everybody knew that Edward Shank had been the chief of police of Seattle. Like everyone else, the contractor was referring to the old man by his nickname, as a matter of respect.

Matt started walking toward the side of the house. "I see it." A large plastic crate, measuring four feet by two feet by three feet, sat innocuously beside a bare bush. He knelt down to examine it. The crate was sealed with two locks, one on each side, and there was a long crack down the side of one wall. Matt ran a finger over it. The crack was probably where Hastings had hit it with his equipment. "Wonder what it is."

"It's buried treasure, of course. Loot from a high-end robbery case your grandfather worked. Illegal guns. A million dollars in cash." Hastings paused. "No, make that two million. It was a big crate."

"If only." Matt laughed. "Thanks for calling."

"Send the Chief my apologies if we damaged

anything. We weren't expecting to find anything buried that deep."

"Will do." Matt disconnected and slipped the phone back into his pocket. Reaching forward, he attempted to lift the crate. It didn't seem that heavy, but it was more awkward than he expected, especially with one side of the plastic cracked. Taking a moment to position himself, he knelt down and hoisted the crate up, hauling it carefully toward the back door that brought him into the kitchen. He sat it down on the rectangular wood table with a harder thud than he intended.

Elmo appeared out of nowhere, nudging and winding around Matt's legs, his long tail vibrating as it always did when Matt first came home. Then he jumped up onto the kitchen table and proceeded to sniff every inch of the crate.

"Any idea what's in here, buddy?" Matt said, stroking the cat's fur thoughtfully. With his other hand, he fingered the locks. "Should I call the Chief? It's obviously his crate, so he probably has the keys."

Elmo didn't have an answer, but he did continue to smell the crate, bumping up against it, his little pink tongue eventually darting out to lick a bit of moisture off the sides. As Matt headed to the fridge to grab a cold beer, the cat bumped the crate again with his head. This time, the bump was a little too hard, and the crate slid off the edge of the table before Matt could stop it. The crate hit the floor with a loud shatter.

"Shit!" He put his beer down on the counter. "Elmo, goddammit!"

The cat scampered away.

"Oh, hell," Matt said again, kneeling down. The crate had landed on its side and the locks were still intact, but now the lid was cracked at the joints. He wouldn't need his grandfather's key to see what was inside now, because the box was open. And whatever was inside didn't smell too good. He wrinkled his nose at the odor emanating from the crate. Something inside had broken and was now oozing a greenish liquid. A puddle was forming on the white kitchen tile.

"Just awesome," Matt said to himself. "And what the fuck is that smell?" Whatever the liquid was, it smelled like rotten eggs. Probably sulfur. Grabbing a paper towel from the counter, he mopped it up. Then he lifted the broken lid and took a look inside the crate.

The contents were jumbled, and it took Matt a moment to process what he was looking at. He'd assumed, like his contractor, that this was the Chief's crate, but the first thing he saw was a ladies' hairbrush. He turned it over in his hands, curious. There was nothing particularly interesting about it, except that it was filled with strands of very long, dark hair. His grandmother's, before she'd turned gray? He pulled a strand free and examined it. No, he didn't think so. The hair was

38

too long, and his *lola*'s hair had always been short.

Putting the brush aside, he sat on the floor and began picking through the rest of the crate's contents. Various items of clothing lined the top, all ladies' stuff, mostly smaller sizes. He pulled out a black T-shirt, well worn and clearly well loved. Size small. He recognized the iron-on picture of the eighties alternative band on the front right away. The Cure. *Nice.*

Under the T-shirts were also a half dozen brassieres. Amused, Matt picked up a pink lace bra and looked at it closely. It was cheap and frilly, but still kind of sexy, the kind of thing Sam would never wear. Had his grandfather had a mistress or something back in the day that nobody ever knew about? There were a dozen or so pairs of women's underwear in the crate as well. Curious but a little uneasy—Matt had loved his grandmother and the thought of the Chief having an affair was unpleasant—he scooped one of them up, only to drop them like they were on fire a second later when a thought occurred to him.

Good Lord, could these be his *mother's* things?

It seemed entirely possible. Lucy Shank was a drug addict, and had died in 1985 of a drug overdose at the age of sixteen, when Matt was only a baby. He'd only ever seen a handful of pictures of her, and none of them had been taken past the age of fourteen. Lucy was a super-touchy subject with his grandparents, and whenever he'd tried to ask them questions about their only child, they'd murmur vague comments like "She was always a troubled girl," and "She'd be so proud of the man you've become," as if that somehow explained the person she was. It was frustrating, so he'd stopped asking questions about his mother a long time ago. And it was useless to ask questions about who his father was, as his grandparents simply didn't know.

Taking a deep breath, he continued to pick through the crate, sorting through the clothing. Maybe he'd find pictures of Lucy, maybe even a diary. At this point, he'd take anything. He'd spent his entire life being hungry for information about his mother, and the more he sifted, the more certain he became that this stuff had to belong to Lucy. Why else would the Chief have locked it all away?

Matt's fingers touched something hard. Peering into the crate, he could see the tops of a dozen or so large glass Mason jars sitting at the bottom, the kind of jars his grandmother used when she made fruit preserves. He reached in, then hissed when something sharp pricked his finger.

Swearing under his breath, he peered closer. He'd forgotten that something had shattered when the crate had fallen, and he'd just discovered what it was. Reaching in again, slowly this time, he grabbed hold of one of the jars and took a good look.

And almost dropped it. What was inside the jar was most definitely *not* his grandmother's fruit preserves.

Staring at the glass container, his brain seemed unable to process exactly what he was looking at. A human hand appeared to be floating, sort of, in a greenish, murky liquid. The skin was super-pale, almost white, and two of the fingers looked partially decayed. It was a small hand, but definitely an adult hand, and female. Looking a bit closer, he could detect some kind of sparkly nail polish on two of the fingers.

Confused, he placed the jar gently on the floor beside him, where Elmo, who'd come back, immediately began to sniff it. His mind sifted through a variety of explanations for what it could really be, because surely it wasn't an *actual* human hand. A quick glance into the crate again confirmed that there were more hands inside more jars.

But they couldn't be human. Of course not, because that would be, like, totally and com-pletely fucked-up.

Movie props. Of course. When Matt was a teenager, his grandparents had taken him to Universal Studios in Orlando, Florida, and they'd watched some live presentation on special effects, props, and movie makeup. Maybe his

41

grandfather had bought a few of these hands for shits and giggles, and forgot to tell Matt. Maybe these hands were supposed to be . . . a gag gift. For . . . horror buffs.

Neither of which fit Matt, or his grandparents.

Still, his brain struggled to find some logical reason why the hands could in no way be human.

Never mind that the skin was beginning to separate from the muscle and bone.

Never mind that some of the fingernails were beginning to detach from the fingers.

Never mind that it all looked so completely real, Matt thought he might throw up.

And the other jars in the crate were the same. Hands. Hands. And more hands.

And they were all *left* hands.

Okay, so they were real. Matt sat on the floor, stumped. But there could be reasons for that, too.

Maybe his grandfather had kept evidence from a crime scene he'd worked years ago before he'd retired from the Seattle PD. Cops did that, didn't they? While Matt couldn't really understand the appeal, clearly the Chief had enjoyed his job, and maybe these were some kind of souvenir, kept here to remind the old man of his glory days, when he'd been the most famous hunter of killers that the city of Seattle had ever seen. While Rufus Wedge was by far the most famous killer that Edward Shank had caught, he most certainly hadn't been the only one. Edward had been a homicide cop for a long time before becoming chief of police; murder had always been the old man's specialty.

Swallowing the sickening feeling welling up inside him, Matt put the jars slowly back in the crate. Realizing after a moment that the tops weren't level, he pulled them back out, and peered into the plastic once again. At the bottom of the crate in the corner was a worn leather scrapbook and a VHS videocassette. Moving aside the tape, he stared at the scrapbook, running a finger over the scratched reddish brown leather cover. He wasn't really going to open it, was he? Whatever was inside was bound to freak him out even more, but still . . . how could he *not* look? He needed an explanation.

The glue that bound the pages together was old, and the scrapbook made a cracking sound when he opened it. It was filled with newspaper clippings . . . and hair.

Ignoring the newspaper articles for the moment, Matt examined the swatches of hair that were taped into the pages. Unlike the hairbrush, which contained tangled strands from actual use, the scrapbook contained bunches of hair that were neatly trimmed. All brunette, ranging from medium to dark brown. Neatly taped.

Neatly labeled, too. First names only. Rebecca. Joan. Sandy. Gwen. Sarah. Lori Ann. Jasmine. And on and on. Touching the strands lightly, he knew this wasn't doll hair. The swatches felt real.

The newspaper articles were dated from 1978 to 1985. There were over two dozen clippings, and the last one, dated April 26, 1985, was one Matt had seen before, because it had been framed above the piano when he was growing up. The headline, in thick black letters an inch tall, screamed BUTCHER DEAD!

Matt closed the scrapbook, stuffing the articles back inside, relieved. Thank God, it all made sense now. His grandfather had kept a crate of stuff from the Butcher. Bringing down Rufus Wedge had made the Chief's career, and he'd obviously wanted souvenirs to remember it by. Was it weird? Hell, yes. But catching killers had been his grandfather's job. Nothing about that had been normal. Edward Shank had never been the warm, sparkly-eyed grandpa who read bedtime stories and tucked him in. The job had always come first, and the Chief had been damned good at it. Matt may not have understood that as a kid, but he sure as hell understood it now.

The VHS tape was still lying innocently amid the pile of clothing, and Matt picked it up. A standard black Memorex, no label. Curiosity getting the better of him, he stood up, leaving everything else from the crate on the kitchen floor.

A few steps later, he was in the living room, where his brand-new fifty-five-inch high-definition TV was set up with an old DVD/VHS combination player he'd been meaning to replace with a Blu-ray at some point. Not that he ever had the time to watch movies. He'd bought the TV so he could watch the Seahawks.

Slipping the tape in, he pressed play. The VHS player groaned to life, and the soft whirring sound of the tape rolling filled the quiet room.

His grandfather appeared on the TV screen, looking younger than Matt could personally remember. The Chief's hair, completely white now, was still salt-and-pepper in the video, and the lines on his face were less prominent, the shoulders a little broader. He was standing in what looked like . . . the garage?

On the Chief's decades-younger face was a grin that stretched from ear to ear. The setting behind him was a tad fuzzy, but Matt could make out the long work table. That table was still in the garage, and it was huge, measuring eight feet long and almost five feet wide.

And on it was a female body. Totally nude. From the distance of the camera, it was difficult to tell how exactly old she was, but she was definitely young, probably a teenager. Canvas straps were fastened tight around her shoulders, torso, and ankles, and though she couldn't move too much, she was squirming. A cloth had been stuffed in her mouth. She couldn't make a sound, but her eyes, huge and terrified, were screaming.

"It's showtime," Edward Shank said directly into the camera. He was smoking a cigar, and Matt didn't have to smell it to know that it was cherry-flavored. The Chief's voice sounded exactly the same as it did now—deep, authoritative, almost melodic. It was like he was speaking to Matt personally, and every inch of Matt's body was rock solid with tension as he watched his grandfather on the large TV screen. The Chief winked into the camera, then reached for something beside the woman's bound feet.

A cleaver. Stainless steel with a wood handle. Super-sharp.

The Chief picked it up, and never had a kitchen tool looked so deadly. In fact, Matt had a similar cleaver in the kitchen right now, minus only the wood handle. It had been a graduation present from his grandfather when he'd finished culinary school. A shudder ran through Matt's entire body.

Holding it up, Edward grinned, the cleaver gleaming under the garage's fluorescent lights. Then, without a word of warning, he chopped off the young woman's left hand. Her body writhed in agony, as much as it could under the restraint of the straps. The severed hand fell to the floor noiselessly, and blood from the stump of her arm gushed onto the sealed concrete.

"Now that that's out of the way," the Chief said, "let's get to work."

Matt's insides, already Jell-O, went cold.

Over the next two minutes, he watched. He couldn't seem to look away, and he wasn't sure he could even blink. So he watched. Even in grainy, dulled-out color, the sickening images of his grandfather torturing the poor young girl seared into his brain like a cattle prod. He watched, stone still, as his grandfather did things to her that he'd only ever seen in horror movies. But the difference was, this was real. There was no scary music, no special lighting or effects. Just her pain, and her screaming.

Edward burned her with the cigar. Cut her with the cleaver. Climbed on top of her and raped her. Then strangled her, his face making almost no expression until the end, when he looked directly into the camera and smiled.

The screen faded to black. Then a cardboard white sign appeared, containing words written in thick block letters. Unmistakably his grandfather's handwriting. Unmistakably his grandfather's fingers holding the sign.

AUGUST 22, 1974. JESSICA. AGE 14.

Edward Shank, former chief of police of the city of Seattle, had been the Butcher.

Feeling something tickling his face, Matt touched his cheek. It was covered in tears.

5

Samantha Marquez did not like the word *obsessed*. It suggested a lack of control, which she greatly resented. She much preferred the word *determined*. She frowned into her phone even though Detective Robert Sanchez couldn't see what he referred to as her "Kermit Face."

"I'm not obsessed, I'm researching," she informed him. "It's a lot of work to write a book, Bobby."

"I don't doubt that, my sweet," Sanchez said with a chuckle. Sam could make out the not-so-faint sounds of laughter in the background. The Seattle PD detective had called her from his home, and his three teenage sons made a lot of noise. "You've published two books already, so you clearly know what you're doing. But you gotta have a life, too. How's that boyfriend of yours? He move into the new house?"

"He's all moved in and renovating the back-yard."

There was a small silence as Sam waited for the inevitable next question. But Sanchez, who'd known her for over twenty years, seemed to know better. Instead of asking why she wasn't living with Matt, he said, "Lunch this week?"

"Of course."

"I'll call you. Don't work too hard. It's not healthy to be obsessed."

"Shut up, Bobby."

"Don't you Kermit Face me," he said before disconnecting, and she laughed.

Although, looking around her messy living room strewn with newspaper clippings, photographs, and scribbled notes on random pieces of paper, it wasn't hard to understand why he would think she had an obsession. A lot of writers were obsessed when they worked, and usually Sam was able to separate her job from the rest of her life. But this time, the project she was working on was personal.

So far, she'd published two true-crime books on specific murderers who lived in the Pacific Northwest. The first was called *Enraged: The Killer Next Door.* It was about a Vancouver, Washington, man named Harold Bunch, a mild-mannered accountant who'd come home early, sick with stomach flu, only to find his wife in bed with another man. He stabbed both his wife and her lover to death, and was currently serving back-to-back life sentences at the Washington State Penitentiary, a place where Sam had spent considerable time conducting interviews with Bunch.

Her second book was about the serial killer Ethan Wolfe, also known as the Tell-Tale Heart Killer. He'd been a graduate student at Puget Sound State University, Sam's alma mater, and the homeless shelter where he'd volunteered had become his hunting ground. The book, aptly titled *Hungry Like the Wolfe*, was currently sitting at number nine on the nonfiction bestseller list for the Northwest region. Not too shabby for a sophomore effort.

Despite her success, Sam's publisher hadn't been too keen on her third proposal, which was to write about the Beacon Hill Butcher. The Butcher had been a huge case, yes, but it was old news, a story that had been big nearly thirty years ago. The publisher had changed their tune, however, when they learned of Sam's possible personal connection to the killer. Sam's theory was that her own mother, Sarah Marquez, had been a victim of the Butcher . . . which meant the Butcher wasn't Rufus Wedge at all.

Her mother's case, still unsolved, had long gone cold, and Sam was determined to get Detective Robert Sanchez to put it back onto the burner. After all, it was how she'd met Bobby. Just a rookie back in 1987, Sanchez was the police officer who'd first responded when her mother's body had been found.

Sam had only been two years old then, and what few memories she had of that time were foggy at best. Her mother, Sarah, had been young, only seventeen when she was murdered, a high school dropout and full-time employee at McDonald's. Sam owned exactly one picture of the two of them, and it now sat framed on the side table beside the sofa. Looking at it always filled Sam with a sense of loss she couldn't quite pinpoint; it didn't feel exactly like grief, but it ached nevertheless. It wasn't that she missed her mom—she couldn't really remember her mom— or that she felt particularly sad. It was more like a sense of . . . longing. There was a hole inside her that never seemed to fill up, no matter how much Sam tried to stuff it with friends, relationships, work, and wine.

Sam had no idea who'd taken the one and only picture, but she knew it was snapped in front of the very first Starbucks, in Pike Place market, on a hot summer day. Her mother, dressed in a patterned halter top, cutoff denim shorts, and a pair of Converse Chucks, looked even younger than seventeen. Two-year-old Sam was dressed identically, her chubby arms wrapped tight around her mom's slender waist. Both mother and daughter had thick dark hair, big brown eyes, and toothy, genuine smiles.

It was an Instagram photo before there was Instagram, perfectly square in shape, worn at the edges, and slightly yellowed from age. Sam had multiple copies of it on her laptop, home desktop computer, and iPhone. She didn't remember that day, but the image filled her with warmth nonetheless.

In contrast, the pictures spread out in front of

her now on the coffee table were not nearly as pleasant. Unlike Instagram, crime scene photos had no filters to blur out the details, and every spatter, speck, and wound was clearly visible on the victims' bodies. There were fourteen dead women in total—all young, like Sam's mother had been—ranging in ages from fourteen to nineteen. Each one had been brutally raped vaginally and anally, sometimes with a blunt object, and then strangled to death. Each one had been missing a left hand that was thought to be chopped off with a cleaver just below the wrist bone (thus earning the Butcher his moniker). Each one had been burned with a cigar and found in a wooded area, buried in a shallow grave loosely covered with leaves. The bodies were found all over the Northwest, from as far south as Eugene, Oregon, right through Washington State, all the way up to Langley, British Columbia.

The Butcher's kill zone.

And Sam was determined—not obsessed, thank you very much—to prove that her mother was one of the Butcher's victims. There were several similarities. Sarah Marquez had also been raped vaginally and anally, both with and without a blunt object, and strangled to death. She'd been found in the woods a few minutes outside Olympia, Washington, buried in a shallow grave covered with leaves. In Sam's professional—yet determined—opinion, this was more than enough to explore the Butcher as Sarah's murderer.

Unfortunately, Seattle PD disagreed with Sam, and for two good reasons. The first was that Sarah, unlike the other Butcher victims, still had both hands intact. And the second reason was even stronger: Rufus Wedge was shot and killed by Edward Shank's team in 1985. Sarah Marquez's murder didn't happen until 1987.

While Sarah's case was still technically unsolved, the last theory was that she had been killed by a homeless person, as she'd been seen interacting with a homeless man outside her workplace a few hours before she was murdered. However, the cops never made an arrest, citing lack of evidence. And since the Butcher case had been so sensational, anyone could have copied the Butcher's tactics.

The thing that had always bothered Sam, though, was *why?* Why copycat an MO from a *dead* serial killer? What was the point of that, when everybody would know it couldn't possibly be him? The fun of being a copycat killer was to capitalize on the publicity, to create further panic and mayhem in a city that was already scared. Or so Sam thought.

Unless, of course, it *was* really him. Sam didn't believe that Rufus Wedge was the Butcher, and this theory was the basis of her current book, *Butcherville.*

Her intention was not to criticize Seattle PD and

their investigation. All she wanted was to open up the possibility that maybe someone else could have committed the murders. After all, the cases had never gone to trial. Rufus Wedge had never had the opportunity to defend himself. And nobody, not even the Chief, could deny that the charges against Wedge were based on strong circumstantial evidence only. There were no fingerprints, no DNA, and no trace evidence that definitively put Wedge at any of the crime scenes.

But neither was Sam intending to sanctify Rufus Wedge. The man was certainly no angel. He'd had a long criminal history that included sexual assault, larceny, drugs, and statutory rape long before he'd ever been accused of murder. Sam was fascinated by criminal profiling, and Wedge certainly fit the textbook definition of a serial murderer. He was a white male, loner, early forties, with a history of violence. He'd had no family and no friends, and so there'd been nobody to stand up for him after his death and insist that it *couldn't* have been him. It had been easy to accept Rufus Wedge as the Butcher.

Sam wanted *Butcherville* to document the mass hysteria that had taken over Seattle during the height of the investigation. From what she'd read and from what Edward had told her, women under the age of thirty were instructed not to go anywhere alone after dark, and many businesses were allowing their female employees to leave work early so they could be home by sundown. The city had been on the verge of imposing a curfew. Sam wanted to explore the extreme pressure on the Seattle Police Department to hunt the Butcher down. But she also wanted to point out that the main reason everybody believed Rufus Wedge to be the Beacon Hill Butcher was that the murders stopped after Wedge's death.

Or had they? Sam had theories on that, too. If the real Butcher had never been caught because some other guy had been nailed for his crimes, wouldn't it make sense to change his MO after Wedge was killed?

She had, of course, discussed all this with former police chief Edward Shank, who'd generously answered all of her questions. The Chief wasn't buying her theory, of course, but neither did he disapprove of Sam's current work in progress. In fact, her boyfriend's grandfather seemed to be very interested in what she came up with, and often called to ask how the research was going. He'd even bought her a textbook for Christmas called *Practical Homicide Investigation: Tactics, Procedures, and Forensic Techniques*, which was the same textbook police officers used to study homicide before taking the detective's exam. It was complete with graphic color photos of actual crime scenes and the methods used to investigate. Sam had been ecstatic. Edward had also offered to write a foreword for her book, which she believed had ultimately been the reason she'd been able to sell the book to a publisher.

Matt, on the other hand, had thought the homicide textbook to be an extremely disturbing Christmas gift, but her boyfriend had resigned himself to her "strange hobby" a long time ago. Mind you, Sam wasn't crazy about the word *hobby,* either, but she vastly preferred it over the word *obsession.*

Sam picked up a picture of Rufus Wedge and stared at it for what seemed like the thousandth time. It was taken right after he'd been shot outside his apartment, and he was covered in bullet holes and blood. He certainly made for an interesting villain, as far as criminals went. So far, there hadn't been a definitive book about the man believed to be the Beacon Hill Butcher, and Sam could only assume this was because there was so little information about him other than his arrest record. From his birth to his death, Wedge had lived life mostly off the grid. He'd never had a driver's license (not in his real name, anyway), had never filed a tax return, and had never voted. He'd never had a bank account. He'd never had a steady job that lasted longer than three months. What Wedge did have was a conviction for third-degree sexual assault (for which he'd served three years), a series of arrests for petty drug possession and larceny (for which he'd cut deals), and a charge for the rape of a sixteen-year-old, which never went to trial because the girl refused to testify. It was Sam's theory that had Wedge not been shot and killed, and had the case gone to trial as it should have, the prosecution may not have won a conviction. Yes, underwear and other personal items belonging to the victims had been found in Wedge's apartment. Yes, Wedge had been in every single city at the time one of the Butcher's victims was killed. But that was really all they had. Police hadn't even been able to find the cleaver that had been used to chop off the victims' hands.

Moving the photos aside, Sam traced a finger over the photocopy of the front page of the *Seattle Times* from April 26, 1985. BUTCHER DEAD! screamed out in thick, black letters, and underneath was a close-up of Rufus Wedge's face. It was his old mug shot from the sexual assault arrest, and of course he looked every bit like a serial killer should, with his greasy hair, doughy face, and dead eyes.

So easy to believe that he was the one.

And then, of course, the murders had stopped.

A ping from her laptop broke her thoughts, and Sam turned her attention to her computer. She was currently logged into a website called TheSerialKillerFiles.com, and okay, she could agree that the amount of time she spent on this particular site might potentially be considered a little obsessive. But where else could she chat with other site members about murder, serial killers, weapons, victims, and forensics? The website was originally owned by a teenager named Jeremiah Blake, who blogged about serial killers, and it was now owned and operated by someone else who'd purchased the domain name and turned it into an active forum for people who liked to discuss all things murder. And that was a lot of people.

The ping meant she had an instant message. When Sam clicked on it, she wasn't surprised to see it was from someone she'd been chatting online with a lot recently, someone who went by the username "KillerRed." She knew nothing personal about KillerRed, just as KillerRed knew nothing personal about Sam. You didn't ever want to give people you'd only ever chatted with online (about serial killers, no less) your personal information. All Sam had ever let on was that she was doing research for a book she was writing. No specifics.

However, Sam had been enjoying her conversations with KillerRed, someone who seemed a little more levelheaded than the other conspiracy theorists she'd run into on the site. They'd had several discussions about different Northwest serial killers, and of course they'd talked about the Butcher quite a bit. Sam had been delighted when KillerRed agreed with her theory that

Rufus Wedge was the wrong man. Anonymous or not, it was finally nice to talk to someone who didn't think she was full of shit.

KILLERRED: Are you still doing research for ur book?

SAM_SPADE: Yes, I am. It's coming along slowly. Any new theories for me? :)

KILLERRED: No, but I was thinking it was time we met IRL. Maybe go for coffee?

Sam blinked. Great, she wasn't expecting that. "IRL" was online speak for "in real life." She frowned at her computer screen and contemplated how to respond. She'd been hit on a few times online—that was how it was with the Internet and social media. She sighed. So KillerRed was a guy, then. And coffee with a guy she'd never met before, who was a serial killer aficionado? *Hell, no.*

SAM_SPADE: Appreciate the invite, but probably not a good idea. Anyway, aren't you in Sacramento?

KILLERRED: Will be in Seattle this week for a job. Ur interested in the Butcher, right? I think we should meet, I have info for u that will help ur book.

SAM_SPADE: I appreciate that, but can you send it to me some other way?
KILLERRED: U don't want to meet?
SAM_SPADE: I have a boyfriend.
KILLERRED: LOL! That's ok! I'm female!
SAM_SPADE: Oh sorry, haha! I just assumed you were a guy. Still, I'm not sure it's a good idea.
KILLERRED: Because ur worried I'm some kind of crazy person, LOL?
SAM_SPADE: Pretty much, haha.
KILLERRED: We could meet in a public place. Bring a friend if u want. I made a decision. I need to reveal what I know. I promise u I'm not a psycho.

Yeah, right. Sure, you're not. And I'm not obsessed with the Butcher, either.

SAM_SPADE: What do you know?
KILLERRED: I know the Butcher's real identity.

Sam snorted. She certainly hadn't been expecting *that*. Maybe KillerRed was a freak, after all.

SAM_SPADE: Tell me.
KILLERRED: Not online. IRL only.
SAM_SPADE: Sorry, wish I could.

KILLERRED: U don't believe I know who the
real Butcher is?
SAM_SPADE: I believe that you believe it. :)
KILLERRED: I know of a victim that the police
don't know about. They don't
know she was killed by the
Butcher.

That makes two of us, Sam thought.

KILLERRED: I have a picture. It's me with the
victim. Do u want to see it?
SAM_SPADE: Sure.
KILLERRED: Gimme a sec and I'll upload it.

Rolling her eyes, Sam waited, though she
couldn't deny that she was a little curious to
see whatever it was KillerRed wanted to show
her. She hoped it wasn't a picture of himself, or
worse, his penis. That happened sometimes with
guys online, too, and it was always gross and
unwelcome.

After a moment, a square thumbnail—a mini
picture—appeared in the chat exchange. Sam
could make out two faces in the photo. Definitely
not a nudie shot. More curious now, Sam clicked
on it.

And almost choked.

One of the faces was her dead mother. There
was no mistaking that the young woman on the

left was Sarah Marquez. Wearing a bright smile, her dark eyes lit up Sam's computer screen. In one hand was a strawberry ice-cream cone that was just beginning to melt. The other face belonged to a young woman Sam didn't recognize, someone with green eyes and red hair.

KILLERRED: That's me on the right. With the red hair. This was a long time ago, I was only 16.
SAM_SPADE: Who's the woman on the left?
KILLERRED: Her name was Sarah. She was killed in 1987 by the Butcher.

Sam suddenly found it hard to type. Her fingers were shaking too badly.

SAM_SPADE: How do you know?
KILLERRED: Because the Butcher tried to kill me too. I got away. She didn't. The police think a homeless guy did it because Sarah was killed after Rufus Wedge was shot. I want them to reopen the case. Maybe they will if I tell u what I know, and u write about it. U said u were published before, right?
SAM_SPADE: Yes.
KILLERRED: Then maybe they'll listen.
SAM_SPADE: How did you even know Sarah?

KILLERRED: She was my best friend. She lived
with me for a while. Her and her
daughter.

Sam didn't know what to say. Her heart was
pounding so hard she thought it might burst. At
this point, she almost didn't care that the woman
had information about the Butcher. KillerRed
had known her *mother*. Sam had been put in foster
care at the age of two. She had never met anyone
who'd known her mother. Ever.

SAM_SPADE: Where do you want to meet?
KILLERRED: I'll message u when I'm in
Seattle in a few days.
SAM_SPADE: Ok. I look forward to meeting
you.
KILLERRED: I hope UR not a psycho, LOL!
SAM_SPADE: Ha, touché. Talk soon.

KillerRed logged off and Sam finally exhaled.
She felt light-headed, slightly unable to process
what had just happened. What an incredible
coincidence, some random person online
knowing her mom, and believing that her mother
had been murdered by the real Butcher.
Or, maybe it wasn't? Maybe this random person
wasn't so random, and had somehow figured out
Sam's IP address and knew exactly who she was.
Maybe this random person was an actual serial

killer who used the site to lure his victims into meeting him, so he could perform unspeakable acts of violence.

Goddammit, it was totally crazy. Beyond crazy. It was insane.

Nevertheless, she was still totally going.

Sam picked up her iPhone and called Jason.

6

Edward Shank didn't like candy asses, and Jay Leno was a total candy ass.

He changed the channel to David Letterman, settling back into his recliner in room 214 of the Sweetbay Village Retirement Residence. He enjoyed Letterman. Unlike Leno, the man wasn't afraid to make his guests squirm. And Edward enjoyed it when people squirmed, because they didn't do it like other creatures in the animal kingdom. Human beings didn't wriggle or try to get away. They shifted uncomfortably in their chairs, they averted their eyes, they sweated, they stammered. And it was fun as hell to watch. Interrogations had always been Edward's specialty.

He missed making people squirm. He missed working. Doctors liked to say that stress killed, but Edward had decided that boredom was the real killer. The only visitor he'd had since he'd moved here had been Matthew's girlfriend, Samantha, and she'd visited twice. His grandson seemed to be too busy to stop by, but that was all right. Edward understood. The kid was working hard, as he should be.

Edward's room was small, but it had everything he needed, including a kitchenette and small washer and dryer. He didn't mind it. He really didn't mind much about the place at all, except for the fact that it could get a little noisy. During the day there was always a lot going on, what with all the card tournaments, bingo, lawn bowling, and movies playing endlessly in the recreation room.

And the chatter. Oh, the chatter. It never stopped.

But after 10 p.m., the retirement home quieted down. By midnight, Edward's favorite time, it was a ghost village. Hell, of course it was, since they started serving breakfast at seven, which meant the place was up and at 'em by six. The food really wasn't half bad, if you liked gourmet omelets made with egg whites and low-fat turkey bacon (which wasn't bacon—if it didn't come from a pig, it wasn't bacon), and Edward was mostly fine with it, as it wasn't any different than what Marisol used to make him eat. His late wife had been more concerned about his cholesterol than he was.

And there were a few nurses on staff that were diddle-worthy, not that his pecker worked anymore (it had died around 2001, and only that marvelous drug known as Viagra could raise it from the dead now), but it was still nice to ponder. Certainly the female residents were nothing to get excited about. Most were halfway to dying, and the ones that weren't were so damned wrinkled you couldn't tell their pussy holes from their belly buttons.

He had a few buddies here, old-timers like him who enjoyed admiring the nurses' asses as much as he did (discreetly, of course—making open comments about women's body parts was seriously frowned upon nowadays, and could be construed as *harassment,* though in his day they called it *making a pass*). He liked his Monday and Thursday night gin rummy games. The macaroni and cheese they served on Sunday nights was better than edible. And on the first Wednesday of every month, a busload of them got to go to the Tulalip Casino, where they had an All You Can Eat Buffet and five-cent slot machines and cute little Indian waitresses who served watered-down cocktails with umbrellas in them. Good times, indeed. It's how they kept the old folks busy. Sweetbay Village might be fancy, but it was still essentially a storage unit for elderly people with nothing but time to kill until death came for them.

It could be depressing. While the brochures for the place showed smiling, happy seniors enjoying their retirement in the luxury of the Village, the real message was that you lived here because you were old and could no longer risk living on your own. When Edward had bruised his hip, he knew it was time to move on, but he still missed his house. He missed the spaciousness, the way the floors creaked, and the backyard filled with berry bushes. He especially missed the magnolia tree in the front yard, which he'd planted a few days after he and Marisol had moved in, which was now full grown.

He drove by the house regularly in his old Seville, usually when he was bored, which was often. He hadn't been surprised to see that Matthew had begun renovations on the house. His grandson had talked about building a huge deck out back, and work had started, judging from the giant piles of lumber stacked at the side of the house, and the holes dug deep into the dirt.

Had they found the crate? Edward thought he had buried it pretty well, and though it wasn't likely, it was still a possibility that the workmen had dug into the ground in the exact spot where he'd hidden it all those years ago. If they'd had found it, Matthew hadn't said anything about it. Yet.

But if and when it ever happened, Edward was ready for that conversation. Part of him hoped Matthew would say something. Part of him hoped he wouldn't. Every man wanted to pass on his legacy, and Edward was no different. It just wasn't quite the legacy Matthew would be expecting.

But Edward believed the kid would understand. Matthew reminded Edward so much of himself. The ambition, the aggression, the darkness that seethed just below the surface . . . it was all there, just waiting to be unleashed.

He'd seen Samantha's little white Mazda parked in the driveway a couple of times, but not lately, and he wondered how those two were doing. Edward approved of Sam. She was a sweet, respectful girl, and he could appreciate her intellectual curiosity. They talked often about Edward's career in law enforcement, and he was happy to regale her with stories of rapists and murderers and, of course, the Butcher. Who didn't like having a captive audience? One day, when Matthew was ready, she'd make a good wife and a good mother. She was a bit of a free spirit, maybe spoke her mind a little too much, but Edward had always liked his women spirited. He liked it when they fought back.

Yes, he liked Sam. She reminded him of Marisol. He wondered how much he would tell his grandson's girlfriend, when the time came. Maybe everything. It would certainly make for a bestseller. The Butcher would make her career, just as the Butcher had made his.

Glancing at the clock on the wall, Edward sighed. Twelve fifteen a.m. It was official. He was restless. What he wouldn't give for a cigar, but

Sweetbay Village had a strict no-smoking policy. If he wanted to smoke, he'd have to go outside.

He didn't sleep much. He'd never needed much sleep, even in his prime, and at his age now, he felt like he needed it less than ever. While the body was beginning to shut down—bad hip, arthritic hands, creaky knees—his brain was as sharp as ever, maybe sharper. Christ, had it really been fifteen years since he'd retired? He'd done some consulting for the department for a year afterward and then a little private sector stuff, but he hadn't worked in a very long time.

And goddammit, he was bored.

The itch was coming back.

He'd managed to squash it after Rufus Wedge was put down. He'd gotten rid of his souvenirs, burying everything but the cleaver in a safe spot he thought nobody would ever find until he was ready. But the itch hadn't gone away overnight. In fact, he'd slipped a few times. Okay, more than a few, but then he'd managed to quash it until Marisol.

But now the itch was beginning to come back. That damn itch, screaming out for relief, consuming him with desire. It was like being horny, only a hundred times more amplified. And he knew that soon, it would be time to scratch it properly. He would need the release, and there would be no other alternative. There never had been.

Lucy. How he missed her.

A noise in the hallway brought him out of his chair, and he winced at the dull pain that bloomed in his hip as he stood up. Stepping toward the door, he leaned into the peephole. Old Greg Bonner was shuffling by, using his cane. Though the sound was mostly muffled on the carpeted floors, Edward could still hear him.

His old plaid robe was hanging on the back of his chair, and Edward slipped it on, tying the belt tight around his waist. Where was old Bonner going this time of night? Every room had its own full bathroom, so the only place Bonner could be headed was to the kitchen for a late-night snack. The Village kept a pantry and a fridge stocked with readily available snacks of all varieties—fruit, yogurt, cookies, crackers, cheese. Residents could help themselves. Bonner was probably hungry.

He opened the door and peeked down the hallway. Bonner was gone, and Edward stepped out, shutting the door quietly behind him, not bothering to lock it. He made his way down the short hallway to the elevator and pressed the down button.

A second later he was on the main floor, and sure enough, he could hear Bonner's cane thumping from somewhere close to the kitchen. Moving soundlessly over the carpet in his socked feet, Edward found Bonner in the kitchen, cane resting against the center island, bald head buried deep inside the massive stainless steel refrigerator.

Three strides and Edward was behind him. Looking back in surprise, Bonner's mouth had barely opened to say hello before Edward grabbed the man by the throat. One deep breath, then Edward banged the man's head into the granite counter. Forcefully. Authoritatively. With a satisfying thud. In a moment like this, there was no room for half-assedness.

One hit was all it took. Bonner immediately sank to the tiled floor, blood streaming out of the wound in his right temple. Edward stood still, ears cocked for any strange sounds, watching as the life seeped out of Greg Bonner's face. His eyes were wide open, his mouth a flat O of surprise.

It didn't matter who it was—old, young, male, female, healthy, sick—people always looked the same way when they died. Bonner stared up at him with rheumy eyes, and then slowly his gaze became unfocused. And then blank. It was like someone had turned the lights off inside.

Greg Bonner was dead.

Edward exhaled. Quietly, he rested Bonner's cane on the floor beside him, then turned and headed back to his room.

He felt so much better. It wasn't quite enough, but it would have to do. For now.

7

Was it so hard not to be a dick? Sometimes Sam wondered. And then wondered about herself that she put up with it.

Adobo was bustling, typical for a Saturday night, and there were a dozen or so patrons waiting at the entrance for their tables. The bar area was even busier, and Sam squeezed in between a redheaded beauty and her much older husband. The husband gave Sam a lingering look as his wife ignored him in favor of her iPhone.

She recognized the bartender but couldn't remember his name. Smiling, he gave her a wink. "Hey, Sam. Usual?"

"Please." She smiled with pleasure. As Matt's girlfriend, she was always treated well here. The Adobo staff always went out of their way to make sure she had whatever she wanted, and she couldn't deny she enjoyed it. Her mojito—extra simple syrup, extra mint—was ready in two minutes while others around her waited impatiently for their drinks. The bartender slid it over with a grin.

"Thanks," she said. "What do I owe you?"

The bartender gave her a look. "As if."

She slipped him a five-dollar bill, anyway. "At least let me tip you. Matt around?"

Another look, but this time it was an expression Sam couldn't read. "Yeah, he's out back. I'd wait a few minutes, though. I heard he was cussing someone out."

"Really? Who?"

He shrugged, throwing a dish towel over one shoulder as he wiped down the bar with a wash-cloth. "Wait'll you see. If *he's* getting in trouble, we're all in trouble. What I will tell you is that the dude got into a fender bender on the way here, which made him almost an hour late, and I'm sure you know how Matt is about punctuality. He's not being very understanding about it."

"I do know, but . . . you're kidding. It was a car accident."

The bartender leaned in. "You didn't hear this from me, but the boss has been in one helluva shit mood the last few days. Screaming at every-one, difficult to talk to. Everyone's been tip-toeing around him and nobody wants to set him off. Any idea what's going on with him?"

Sam hesitated, not sure what she could say. She didn't know anything, and it made her feel stupid. "I'm sure it's just stress."

"What does he have to be stressed about? This place is kicking ass, the food trucks are making mad money, and he's going to be on a reality show. The guy's about to blow up." The bartender stopped, his face reddening. "Oh shit. I shouldn't talk about it. You're his girlfriend."

Sam downed her mojito and patted his arm. "We'll keep it between us. Thanks for the drink."

She maneuvered her way through the busy restaurant with its cappuccino walls, distressed wood tables, and cream leather chairs. Matt had done a great job of creating a warm and cozy, yet slightly upscale, ambience. Adobo had been open for less than two years, and thanks to the popularity of the food trucks strategically placed at all the big farmers' markets and food fairs around the greater Seattle area, the restaurant had become quite successful. Pretty impressive considering how competitive the Seattle food business was.

Adobo was a tribute to Matt's Filipino grand-mother's cuisine, and had long been her boy-friend's dream.

She ordinarily wouldn't drop in this close to the dinner rush, but Sam hadn't heard from Matt in almost two days. He hadn't returned her calls or texts, and while Sam was trying not to take it personally, she was irritated. The whole world didn't revolve around Matt Shank, despite what he liked to think, and his arrogance was the one thing about him she truly disliked.

But he got like this sometimes, especially when under pressure. He was the most ambitious person she'd ever known, and she couldn't deny that his drive was one of the things she was most attracted to. She never doubted that he would be extremely successful at anything he wanted to do, and so far, she was right.

Their relationship was going on three years now, certainly not the longest in the history of relationships, but long enough that discussions of the future and "Where is this going?" were happening a little more frequently. She knew Matt loved her. Of course he did. She loved him, too. But unlike Matt, Sam knew what she wanted. Marriage. House. Kids. Preferably in that order, but she was learning to be flexible.

You had to be, if you were Matthew Shank's girlfriend. Nothing was ever linear with him, and his career always came first. But it wasn't sitting well with Sam anymore. She was twenty-nine years old. She was ready. Matt was thirty-two, and he still wasn't.

She entered the kitchen. Heads looked up and several of the kitchen staff smiled at her. Raoul, Matt's head chef, caught her eye.

"Out back, mama," he said, flicking his head toward the back door. "I'd wait a few minutes, though. He's having a . . . discussion." He said the last word distastefully.

"I heard," Sam said, squeezing Raoul's arm as she passed. Crossing the kitchen, she pushed open the door and was met with a cool breeze and loud voices.

"I run a restaurant. A *busy* fucking restaurant." Matt was barking and Sam didn't have to see his face to know her boyfriend was enraged. "If you're going to be late, you *call* me. You're my assistant head chef. You don't leave me short for a half hour on a Friday night when we've got a lineup waiting for tables."

"I already told you, dude, I got held up because this kid rear-ended me—"

"Did he rear-end your phone, too?"

"No, but dude, he—"

"And stop calling me dude. When we're at work, I'm your boss, not your friend."

Sam peeked through the door and was shocked when she saw who it was Matt was yelling at. It was PJ, his old college friend, someone they'd both known for years. The same PJ who'd just been through a terrible divorce, and who'd been working with Matt since day one when Matt only had a food truck and a dream.

"You know, *dude,* I don't need this shit, okay?" PJ said, sounding scarily close to tears. "Sharon cleaned me out, my apartment is shit, and now my car is fucked. You could have a little sympathy. We've been friends for a long time, man. I always have your back."

"And I haven't had yours? I brought you in from the beginning, didn't I?" Matt's face was red. "I made you an assistant head chef. I give you advances on your pay when you blow all your dough on poker and sports betting, which is every other month. I've let a lot of things slide over the years, *dude,* and you still can't get your shit together."

Under the dim lights of the alley, PJ's face went dark. "Wow. Thanks for making me feel even worse, bro."

"You don't need this job, you say the word." Matt's tone was icy. "I mean it."

PJ opened his mouth to respond, but then seemed to think the better of it and snapped it shut.

Matt jerked his head toward the door. "Get back inside. You're closing tonight. You're the last one to leave."

Sam moved aside as PJ pushed past her. Giving her a look that was half despair, half anger, he said, "Talk to your boy, Sam. He's losing it."

Before Sam could think of what to say, Matt was in her face. "What are you doing here? Can't you see I'm busy? I've had a shit day."

"I was worried about you. You haven't returned my texts and I called you this morning."

"You don't have to check up on me. I do actually work, you know."

He made as if to move to past her, and she grabbed his arm. "Hey. You don't speak to me like that. Ever. I don't work for you. Got that, *dude?*"

Matt sighed and ran a hand over his face, suddenly looking very tired. "Fuck. I'm sorry, babe. I've had a busy few days, and I haven't been sleeping, and I'm not feeling well. There's just . . . there's been a lot going on."

Sam softened and touched her palm to his forehead. "You feel okay. Want me to stay over tonight? I'll wait up, have a little food ready for you when you get in, and I can make you breakfast tomorrow."

Matt checked his watch. "That won't be until at least one a.m. Mario has to leave early so I have to—"

"Doesn't matter. I'll wait up."

He smiled. Leaning down, he kissed her on the tip of her nose. "Okay. I'll try and get out as fast as I can."

"I'll need your key."

He stopped. "Oh. Right." He cleared his throat. "Um, you know what, I'll just come over to your place. My house is a disaster, and I didn't go shopping so there's nothing in the fridge . . ."

"You don't want me at your place?"

"It's just really messy." An uncomfortable pause followed, and then he said, "What are you up to tomorrow?"

"Meeting Jase for coffee." Sam hesitated, unsure how much she wanted to tell Matt. Another look at his face told her that in this case, less was more. "I'm bouncing some ideas off him for the book."

It was Matt's turn to stiffen. "Feeding your obsession, I see."

"Stop." Sam punched his arm. "It's my job, okay? I write about true crime. You knew that when we met."

"I guess I'll just never understand it."

"You don't have to understand it. You just have to support me."

"Like Jase does?"

She backed up a step and looked up at him. "What's going on with you? He and I have been friends for a long time."

"I'm well aware of that, thanks."

Sam waited a few beats, not sure how to respond. Matt had always been a little bit jealous of her relationship with Jason, not that he had any reason to be—after all, Jason was the one who'd introduced them to each other three years ago. She'd known Jason since grade school, and he was like family to her.

Finally she said, "I'll tell him you said hello."

"You do that."

"Don't be jealous." Sam kept her tone light. "He's practically my brother."

Matt smiled, but it didn't touch his eyes. "So you always say."

"He's your friend, too."

"He's your friend more."

There was no point in arguing, because they both knew he was right.

8

Sam loved Pike Place market.

It hadn't changed much since she was a little girl, other than that it was much busier than she remembered. Tourists from all over the world flocked in to watch the fishermen throw salmon at each other, which was happening right now. Sam stood, captivated, as a hunky twenty-something fisherman dressed in fish-blood-spattered coveralls expertly wrapped brown paper around a huge piece of fresh salmon in record time. He then threw it football-style to his coworker at the cash register, who was a good twenty feet away. The waiting customer, along with the rest of the crowd, laughed and clapped, and pictures on smartphones were snapped.

Inhaling deeply, she could appreciate the weird smell of raw fish and fresh-cut flowers mingling. And though the inner area of the market was noisy, she could still hear sounds from the street outside where a four-man doo-wop a capella group was performing outside the world's very first Starbucks. They were singing an oldie but goodie called "In the Still of the Night."

She so loved the ambience of the market. It never lost its appeal.

Someone bumped her and she stiffened.

Annoyed, she turned around, relieved to see it was only Jason. His usual wise-ass grin was present, and he held out a Starbucks cup. Before she could take it, he withdrew it, and offered his cheek for a kiss. She obliged. It wasn't exactly hard to kiss Jason Sullivan, one of Seattle's most eligible bachelors. He looked particularly handsome today dressed in a fitted button-down and a pair of dark jeans. His dark blond hair, always perfectly wavy, glistened in the late afternoon sun. Two young women walked by him, staring, though it was hard to tell whether it was because they recognized him from his time with the Seahawks, or if he was just *that* good-looking. If Jason noticed, he didn't act like it.

"I didn't see you coming," she said.

"That's because I have the stealthy moves of a jungle cat." He finally handed her the coffee cup, which she accepted gratefully. "As requested, madam, a soy chai latte with a shot of vanilla. You owe me four bucks."

"Seriously?"

"No, not seriously." Jason sniffed the air. "Yuck, it smells like fish in here. Let's go before it permeates my clothes."

"That's because we're in a fish market, in case you didn't notice. You're such a girl. But kudos on using *permeate* in a sentence. Fancy."

"Thought you'd appreciate that."

Sam took a long sip of her coffee, then grimaced

slightly. "It's hot. I should have changed my order to an iced latte. I'm going to overheat." She eyed his drink, which was so cold it was sweating. "Is that a green tea lemonade?"

"Yeah." He took a sip and then offered it to her. "Switch?"

"Yes, please."

They exchanged beverages, sipping in silence for a moment, people-watching.

"You know this is nuts, right?" Jason finally said. "Meeting this woman?"

"Yes, I know."

"You don't even know her name."

"She doesn't know mine, either."

"What if she stabs you with an ice pick?"

Sam rolled her eyes. "In broad daylight? In Pike Place?"

"Hey, killers are crazy. You of all people should know that. You can't assume they operate under the same logic you do." Jason raised an eyebrow, taking a long sip of the chai latte. He made a face. "Gross. How can you drink this? It's way too sweet."

"Fine, switch back."

They exchanged drinks again.

"So what does she look like?" Jason asked. "And how will she know who you are?"

Sam shrugged. "The only picture I saw was when she was a teenager, and she had red hair. Her username on the site is 'KillerRed,' though, so I'm assuming she's still a ginger." She pulled out her phone and showed him the picture she'd uploaded the other day. "She could look totally different now. Oh, and I told her I had dark hair and would be wearing a green jacket."

Jason leaned in, taking a closer look at the picture. "Oh wow. That is definitely your mom. No mistaking that."

Sam smiled.

"I only ever saw that one picture of you two," he said. "The one in your living room, that was taken here. Is that a coincidence, or did you plan it that way?"

"She picked the place."

"You look a lot like your mom, you know," Jason said with a smile. "Same dark eyes, same cute smile, same dark hair. That picture could have been you at sixteen. Except you were dorky. Whatever happened to those purple glasses you used to wear?"

"I still have them." She poked him in the ribs. "And you think I have a cute smile?"

He rolled his eyes and they shared a laugh. It was always so easy with Jason. His personality was the exact opposite of Matt's—light instead of dark, approachable rather than intimidating. He might not be the hardest worker right now, but Sam didn't hold it against him. He'd made good money during his years with the Seahawks, and had invested his money wisely, and still picked up endorsement deals. He enjoyed life, something she wished Matt knew how to do.

She pondered this casually for a moment until she spotted a woman coming toward her with an expectant look on her face. Light auburn curls framed a round face spattered lightly with freckles, and a shapeless black wool coat hid a fuller figure. Pretty, mid-forties . . . it had to be KillerRed.

"I think that's her," Sam said in a low voice, taking a quick sip of her latte. "In fact, it has to be. Stay here, okay?"

"You don't want me to come with you?"

"Just stay here and keep an eye on me. I'll go talk to her."

Jason looked dubious, but he didn't argue. "Don't stand too close to her. She could have a bottle of acid in her coat and she might throw it in your face."

"Oh my God, enough. Seriously, who would do that?"

"I told you, crazy people. Just be careful and keep your distance. I'll be right here. Shout if there's any trouble. Actually, no. Run first, and I'll follow."

"Shut up. You're not helping to quell my nerves."

Handing Jason her latte, Sam started walking toward the woman, who was about twenty feet away. She smiled, and the woman smiled back, but as they got closer, the older woman's face paled, and she staggered.

Sam made it to her just in time to catch her before she fell over.

"I'm sorry," the auburn-haired woman said when she regained her balance. Her hand flew to her throat, and she began to rub the pendant that was hanging on the end of the chain around her neck. The pendant was a little gold bear, but not cutesy like Winnie the Pooh. It was modeled after a real bear, and it seemed a curious choice for jewelry. Her green eyes were huge and they never left Sam's face. "I just . . . oh my God, I wasn't expecting this."

"You must be KillerRed." Sam kept a hand on the woman's arm until she was sure she wouldn't fall over again.

"Yes, I am. I mean, I'm Bonnie. Bonnie Tidwell." The older woman continued to stare at Sam in shock. "Pardon my language, but holy shit. I thought I was seeing a ghost. You look just like Sarah."

Sam nodded. There was no point in pretending. "I'm Samantha. Sarah's daughter."

Tears filled Bonnie's eyes and she blinked them back. "Of course you are." Reaching forward, she grabbed Sam in a tight hug. "Of course you are. Holy shit. This is incredible." She pulled back. "Do you know there hasn't been a single day when I haven't thought about you? Wondered how you were?"

Sam nodded, feeling a little emotional herself.

"That's sweet of you to say. You knew my mom well, I take it?"

Bonnie reached for her necklace again, rubbing the little gold bear. "We were best friends. I loved her very much. I helped take care of you, you know." The older woman smiled sadly. "You were a really good baby. God, I'm so glad to know you're okay."

"I'm okay," Sam said with a smile. "I promise. I don't remember you, though. I wish I did."

Bonnie nodded. "You were so little when she died. I wanted to keep you, but you were sent into foster care." She touched Sam's face briefly. "I understand now why you finally agreed to meet me. You must have been blown away when I sent you the picture of me and Sarah."

"That's putting it mildly." Sam looked around. Jason was watching them closely, and she gave him a little wave to let him know everything was all right.

"Your husband?" Bonnie asked.

"Just a really good friend."

"Wow, what a looker."

"Oh, he knows," Sam said with a laugh. "Did you want to sit down somewhere? Find a coffee shop, or a place to eat?"

"Of course. I'm sure you have lots of questions." They started walking toward Jason, who met them halfway, and Sam made a quick introduction as the two shook hands. Smiling at the two of them, Bonnie continued, "We lived together for about a year. You, me, and your mom. I used to babysit you whenever I wasn't working. You used to call me Baba, because you couldn't pronounce Bonnie."

A tingle went through Sam then and she looked at Jason, who cocked his head and grinned. Yes, that was right. While she didn't remember Bonnie, the nickname "Baba" was strangely familiar, and suddenly everything the woman was saying rang true.

There was so much Sam wanted to ask, but she didn't know where to start. *To hell with it,* she thought. "Bonnie, where are you staying?"

"The Sixth Avenue Inn."

"Why don't you come back to my place? I can make some dinner, and we can talk. Would you be okay with that?"

Jason cleared his throat. Sam ignored him.

Bonnie nodded, and another sad smile appeared on her face. "Sure, I would love that. I . . . there's a lot to tell you. I'm sure you have so many questions."

"I want to hear everything." Sam took a breath. "About my mom, the Butcher, all of it."

"And I'm prepared to tell you everything," Bonnie said. "I mean, you're writing a book about him, so I would have, anyway. But now that I know who you are . . . my God, if anyone deserves the truth, it's you, Samantha."

9

The only way Matt could handle it was to not think about it. Which wasn't working that well. Because even when he was able to put it out of his mind, his body reminded him. Acid was eating his stomach, knots had turned his shoulders into pretzels, and he was delirious from lack of sleep. He had no appetite, and the leftover pizza sitting on his plate tasted like cardboard.

So, he drank. It was his fourth Corona. By the time he went to bed tonight that number would be doubled . . . but who was counting.

Matt might not be an expert on serial killers the way Sam was, but it was common knowledge for anyone who'd lived in the Northwest during the eighties that the Butcher's MO was to chop off left hands. And in Matt's garage, inside an old crate, were jars full of left hands. There was no denying who his grandfather really was. Edward Shank, the former chief of police of Seattle, was the fucking Beacon Hill Butcher. It might have been impossible to believe had Matt not seen it with his own damn eyes.

He took another long swallow of his beer, trying to force out of his mind the mental images of that poor young girl being tortured.

His grandfather had always been the hero, a

legend, the ultimate good guy whose job was to catch the bad guys. Matt could still remember that day in seventh grade when the Chief had come to talk to the kids at his school for career day. It was a few years after he'd brought down Rufus Wedge, and everybody knew who the Chief was. His fellow classmates had been delighted. The teachers were in awe.

It had all been a lie. Not only was Edward Shank not a good guy, he was the villain. And not only was he the villain, he was a monster. A monster who had terrorized the entire Northwest for years because he tortured, raped, and murdered young girls.

Matt closed his eyes. *Jessica, age fourteen.* She'd been someone's daughter, someone's granddaughter, someone's friend. She'd been innocent. And now she was long dead, brutalized in the most horrific ways possible, at the hands (no pun intended) of his grandfather. The scene was tattooed in his mind; the shrieks and cries were a soundtrack that looped endlessly no matter how many times he tried to mentally turn the volume down.

He finished his Corona and reached for another.

Had his *lola* known? On the one hand, Marisol Perez Shank had been married to the Chief for almost fifty years—how could she *not* have known? But on the other hand, the Chief had lied to everyone. Why wouldn't he have lied to his wife, too?

Matt's first instinct had been to confront his grandfather. Maybe, just maybe, there was some kind of strange explanation for it all that Matt hadn't thought of. Maybe none of it was real. Maybe he'd hallucinated the whole thing. Maybe the tape was a fake, one of those fetish videos for people with really depraved sexual tastes. Maybe the Chief had tried his hand at acting, and the tape was just a re-creation of a crime he'd worked—

Shut up, stupid. Of course it was real. The screams had been relentless until they'd finally faded to whimpers. There had been blood. There had been begging. There had been a sick satisfaction in his grandfather's eerily distant eyes. You couldn't fake these things. Nobody could.

And what would he say to the Chief, anyway? More important, what was it he *needed* the Chief to say to him? Would it make a difference if the old man explained it to him somehow, explained that he was a psychopath and had murdered God knew how many innocent young girls because he couldn't help himself? And that he was now sorry for what he'd done? Was that what Matt needed to hear? Would an *apology* make him feel better?

Fuck, no. Nothing would make this better, except for Matt to hit the rewind button on his life so that he never looked inside the god-damned crate in the first place.

Matt had also considered going to the authorities. After all, he was a responsible citizen, and it was clearly the right thing to do. He could just drive over to the nearest police precinct and dump the crate on some lucky detective's desk. Let them wade through the contents, watch the tapes, test the hands for DNA, and find out the identities of the dead victims. Families would be notified and an arrest would be made. The Chief would be outed as the Butcher, and the trial would make national headlines. Reporters from all over the country would flock to cover the story of the hero who was really a monster. Books would be written, movies would be made. Edward Shank would die in prison, and everything Matt had worked so hard for would be gone.

Because yes, this was about him, too. In this case, the "all publicity is good publicity" adage would not apply. Nobody would want to eat at a restaurant owned by the grandson of man who tortured, raped, and murdered little girls. Adobo would go bankrupt. The food trucks would disappear. No more Fresh Network show.

Matt would be ruined.

He finished his beer and stood up. The room spun, but not too badly, which at this point was unacceptable. He reached for the cabinet and pulled out a bottle of Jameson Irish Whiskey. He couldn't remember who bought it for him, but it was disgusting stuff, not his usual thing. Didn't matter. He needed to shut his brain off and sleep, and a few shots of whiskey would be about the only thing that would make that happen.

The floor in the hallway leading to the kitchen creaked, and Matt whirled around.

"Got another shot glass?" Edward Shank said.

Matt stiffened as his grandfather approached. He hadn't heard the front door open, but clearly it had, and in the Chief's left hand dangled his key to the house. Matt had never asked him for it. Why would he?

The two men were identical heights, both six four, and it was easy to meet the old man's cool gaze.

"Sure, Chief," Matt said. "Have a seat."

"Don't mind if I do."

If the Chief was aware of the tension, he wasn't letting on.

"It's late," Matt said. He poured his grandfather a full shot of Jameson, then poured himself one, too. "I wasn't expecting you."

They raised shot glasses and tilted their heads back. The whiskey was like fire on Matt's throat, and he welcomed the burn. He poured them both another.

"Couldn't sleep. Decided to go for a drive. Saw your lights on, thought I'd say hello. I haven't seen you in a while."

"I've been meaning to come by sometime. See how you're doing."

"Sure you were." Edward grinned. "You're busy. I understand. You've got a business to run, a house to renovate. I saw that you ripped up the backyard. Find any buried treasure?" Edward's eyes fixed on Matt's face, steady and unwavering.

Matt met the old man's gaze with an equally steady one of his own. Never mind that his hand was shaking under the table. "No buried treasure. I wish."

"Dead bodies, then?"

"Something like that."

Edward appraised him, then tapped the side of his glass. Matt obliged, pouring another shot for each of them. "What's on your mind, kid? You're awfully quiet."

"Nothing. Just tired. And I wasn't expecting you."

"I believe that last part, but the rest of it . . . you've never been much of a liar, Matthew."

Unlike you, Matt thought, but he kept his mouth shut.

"Want to talk about it?" The Chief's voice remained cool, his eyes missing nothing, but he seemed to genuinely want to hear whatever Matt had to say. "I can listen. Sometimes I even give decent advice. I got nothing but time."

"Nope, I'm good."

Edward knocked back the shot, then pushed the

glass away. "Okay, then. How's the restaurant? I've been meaning to come by sometime."

"Sure you were," Matt said. "You're busy. I understand. You've got lots of bingo games and gin rummy to play over at the old folks' home."

The Chief snorted and pulled out a cigar from his breast pocket. "Mind if I smoke?"

"Have I ever?"

"Just checking." His grandfather shrugged. "It's your house now."

Edward bit off the tip of his cigar and then lit it. Matt recognized the lighter. His grandmother had given it to her husband when he retired, and it was sterling silver with fourteen-karat gold trim. On one side, it was engraved with the initials *EMS*. Which stood for Edward Matthew Shank. And on the other side, it said "The Chief." The smell of the cherry-flavored cigar smoke filled the kitchen.

"How's the restaurant?"

"Extremely busy."

"And the food trucks? My buddy Howard from the old farts' home said he stopped by your truck at the Fremont Market when he was there with his grandkids. They loved the *lumpia*, said they were better than Chinese spring rolls."

"That's because they are."

"You should be very proud. You've worked very hard. Your *lola* is beaming up in heaven."

"You must miss her."

There was a pause, and then Edward said softly, "Every day."

"Did she know?" Matt asked. After five beers and three shots of whiskey—or was it four? he'd lost count—on a mostly empty stomach, his words were beginning to slur, and it was hard to stay focused on the Chief's face.

"Know what?"

"Who you really are."

"And who is that?"

"I know you know what I'm talking about."

Edward sucked on his cigar, then blew out a long stream of smoke. "She knew only what she needed to know. Nothing more. Nothing less. She never asked questions. Wasn't her business. Your *lola* knew her place."

"And what's mine?" Matt said. "What's my place, Chief?"

His grandfather's gaze was steady through the smoke that swirled around his face. "It's whatever you want it to be. But you're a lot like me, Matthew. Always have been. I find it amusing that you fight it. You didn't want to follow in my footsteps and go into law enforcement; you wanted to do your own thing, run your own ship, excel at something that's just yours, all the while thinking that would make you less like me. What you don't realize is that it makes you *exactly* like me."

A silence fell between them as Matt tried to

process this through his drunken haze. Finally he said, "Why, Chief? Why'd you do it?"

Edward thoughtfully watched the smoke curl in the air before meeting Matt's gaze. "That's a deep question, kid. Why does anyone do anything? I do what I do because I want to. And because I can. Same as you."

"Who was Rufus Wedge?"

"He was a piece of shit."

"And what does that make you?"

The Chief leaned back in his chair, appraising him. "It makes me the former chief of police of Seattle. It makes me a hero who won commendations from the mayor. It makes me a man who kept the streets of this city safe by putting away hundreds and hundreds of criminals."

"It makes you a monster."

A pause. "I don't expect you to understand."

"How could I possibly?" The room was spinning and Matt's stomach was beginning to churn. The few bites of pizza he'd ingested suddenly didn't seem to be mingling well with the alcohol. "How could anyone?"

"Why do you eat?"

"What?" Matt said, confused. "What do you mean?"

"Answer the question." The Chief puffed on his cigar. "When you eat, why do you eat?"

"Because I have to. Because I'm hungry. Because I'll starve if I don't."

"Same thing."

Matt felt his face flush. "Not remotely. And you're a psychopath if that's how you feel."

His grandfather waved a hand. "You asked. That's my answer."

"It's sick."

"So what are you planning to do?" Edward asked. "You've obviously been thinking about it."

"I haven't decided."

"Sure you have." The Chief laughed, but he wasn't amused. "You won't do anything. Because you have everything to lose."

"So do you."

"My reputation." His grandfather shrugged. "My legacy. But who's to say which legacy I want to leave behind? We can all choose how we want to be remembered. I've been retired for fifteen years now. I'm on the downward slide to dead, kid. I'm forgotten. And I think about that every day."

"Ever consider turning yourself in?"

"Why would I do that?"

"Because it's the right thing. And I thought you, of all people, would understand the difference between right and wrong."

"They weren't angels, you know," the Chief said. "None of them were what you would call 'good girls.' They were the dregs of society. Drug addicts. Prostitutes. Teenage whores. A waste of good taxpayers' money."

"It was still wrong." Matt's hands began to shake as the nausea welled up in his gut. "You . . . you hurt them. You didn't just kill them. You made sure . . . you made sure they suffered."

"How is that any different from the spider you trapped when you were five years old?" Edward took another drag on his cigar. "You kept it in a jar for days until it died a slow and painful death. You watched it suffer. I remember that glint in your eye because I know how you felt. You enjoyed it."

"I was five, and it was a goddamned *spider*. Not a human being."

"Life is life, Matthew. We all play God in whatever way we can." The Chief pushed his chair back and stood up. "I would hate to see you lose everything on account of me. They're long dead, all of them. Telling the truth isn't going to bring them back."

"Did you want me to find the crate?" Matt asked. He could taste stomach acid, and he tried to swallow so the burning in his throat would go away.

"Yes," Edward said simply. "It's a big secret to keep. The older I get, the more I realize how important it is that you know me. And to know me, you have to know my secrets. You're the only family I have left."

"Your secrets are terrible," Matt whispered, looking up at him. "They're terrible, Chief. They're a burden." His head spun and he took a deep breath. In a stronger voice, he said, "I want that shit out of my house. I don't care what you do with it, but get rid of it. I don't want it here."

"Fine."

"None of this makes any sense."

"It doesn't have to," the Chief said. "The *why* doesn't matter. It never did. After almost four decades in law enforcement, that's one of the most important things I learned. It never matters why."

"So what will you do?" Matt looked up at his grandfather with bleary eyes. "What happens now?"

"Now? Now I'm going to do what I always do. Go back to the old farts' home. Go to sleep. And wake up tomorrow knowing it's a brand-new day, and that there aren't many of them left. So I'm going to make the best of it, and then, like all great men, go out with a bang."

Matt had no idea what that meant.

Edward looked down at him. "And what will you do?"

Matt poured himself another shot of whiskey with unsteady hands. "I'm going to finish this bottle of Jameson. Puke my guts out. And then pass out, hoping that when I wake up tomorrow, this will all just be a nightmare I've already for-gotten."

He closed his eyes and downed the shot, savoring the burn on his raw throat. When he opened his eyes again, the Chief was gone.

10

Sam liked Bonnie. A lot. Which was probably a bit premature since she'd only known the woman for two hours.

But Bonnie Tidwell was the closest thing to her mother Sam would ever get, and she wasn't about to waste the opportunity to learn everything she could about her teenage mom and her mom's best friend. It was almost too good to be true, but the Internet was an amazing place. You just never knew who was out there, and who would find you.

Bonnie had more photos of Sarah at home in Sacramento, but it obviously never occurred to her to bring them, as she hadn't known she would be meeting Sarah's daughter. The two women were now sitting on Sam's sofa, finishing off the last of the Pinot Grigio Sam had poured. In Bonnie's hand was the framed photograph of Sam and her mother, and the older woman stared at it, smiling, before putting it back on the table.

"Pike Place market. That had to have been . . ." Bonnie frowned, thinking for a moment. "August 1987. I still remember that day. You were so little. Do you remember my nickname for you?"

Sam shook her head.

"I called you Dumpling," Bonnie said, and

Sam laughed. "Because you were so cute and chubby. I wanted to eat you up."

"I don't remember." A wave of sadness washed over Sam. It was that feeling again, that sense of longing for something she couldn't remember ever having.

"It was me who took the picture, you know. I had this camera I'd saved up to buy." The older woman took a sip of her wine and smiled at the memory. "I knew back then I wanted to be a professional photographer, and there was a guy who had a camera he didn't use anymore. I can't tell you how many hours I worked at McDonald's to pay for it."

"Is that where you met my mom?"

"Yes. I found her crying in the bathroom at the end of my shift. She'd just learned she was pregnant and her boyfriend had left her. She didn't want to go home because she was afraid her parents—your grandparents—would make her give you up for adoption. I took her in and got her a job. I was already living in a house with two other girls, and I figured, what was one more? And then she had you." Bonnie smiled. "A lot of girls under one roof, and it was chaos, but we were like family. We looked out for each other."

"Do you know who my father is?" Sam held her breath.

"I wish I did, honey. Sarah never told me. All she said was that he was a boy from the wrong side of the tracks, and that the only good thing he ever gave her was you."

Sam worked at processing this. After years of knowing next to nothing, it was all a lot to take in. "You know, I tried looking for my grandparents after I aged out of foster care. They were both dead. Grandfather had a heart attack; grandmother died of cancer."

"And of course Sarah was an only child." Bonnie squeezed her arm. "You must have felt so alone."

"Still do sometimes."

"That friend of yours, Jason, seems to really care about you." The older woman's tone was sly.

Sam laughed. "I've known him since the fifth grade. I was living next door to him with a foster family, and so we were neighbors for two years. Then the foster family moved out of state, and of course I couldn't go with them, and so Child Services placed me with a new family. Jase and I kept in touch, though. He'd write me from time to time, and I'd write him. But he's a couple of years older than me, and we lost touch when he started high school. A few years later, we ran into each other at Puget Sound State, where we both went to college. By then he was a huge football star, and gearing up for the NFL. We reconnected and have been close ever since."

"But you never dated?"

"No way." Sam laughed again. "I always

thought he was cute, but in college, he was so full of himself, total ladies' man. And still kind of is. We're best friends, though, and he introduced me to my boyfriend, Matt. They were roommates in college."

"Ah," Bonnie said with a grin. "So you do have a boyfriend."

"Three years now. He owns his own restaurant. He's very successful." Sam smiled. It wasn't hard to brag about Matt.

"He sounds like a catch. But why I do a sense a *but* . . . ?"

"That's exactly it. *But.* Is it that obvious?" Sam sighed. "He's not ready for anything more. I have a feeling he never will be."

"If you feel that way, honey, then unfortunately it's probably true."

"So why were you on the forum?" Sam changed the subject. It was so easy to talk to Bonnie about her personal life, but there was still so much about her mother and the Butcher she wanted to know. "I assumed, like everyone else on that site, that you were just a nutty conspiracy theorist with an unhealthy interest in serial murder." Bonnie's eyes widened, and Sam held up a hand. "Hey, I'm guilty of it myself. Takes one to know one."

"I wouldn't say your interest is unhealthy. You write books about them. It's research." Bonnie hesitated. "For me, it's personal."

"It's personal for me, too."

"Because you believe the Butcher killed Sarah."

"Yes. I always have. So what makes you agree with me?" Sam asked. "My mother's hand wasn't chopped off. And you know she died two years after Wedge was shot."

"I can only guess why her hand was still intact," Bonnie said. "But I know for certain Rufus Wedge wasn't the Butcher."

"Are you going to tell me how you know?"

"It's because I met him."

"Rufus Wedge?" Sam was confused.

"No. The Butcher."

There was a small silence as Sam digested this. Finally she said, "Please tell me what happened."

"I noticed him at first because he was tall." The older woman's jaw clenched, but her eyes took on a slightly faraway look as she remembered. "Sarah took his order at McDonald's a couple of nights before she died. He seemed harmless; mainly he just watched her while she worked, but that wasn't anything unusual. Your mom was pretty; a lot of guys noticed her. This guy, though, he seemed to like brunettes. He complimented her dark hair a few times." Bonnie fingered an auburn curl. "After our shift was over, we saw him out-side the restaurant near the bus stop, sitting in his car, as if he was waiting for her. When he saw she was with me, he drove off.

"A couple of nights after that, she was killed. I was actually with you the night she died.

Babysitting. She was scheduled to be home around eleven, but she never made it. I called the McDonald's we worked at, but it was already closed for the night. I didn't know what to do. It wasn't like her to not come straight home, and I was worried. But I knew if I called the cops and reported her missing, it could put you at risk. She was only seventeen. Even if Sarah turned up okay, what if they thought she was unfit to raise you? So I waited." Bonnie closed her eyes. "And then the next morning, the cops showed up. Told me that she'd been found dead. She'd been seen giving water and french fries to a homeless man at the end of her shift, they said, and they thought maybe he was the one who'd killed her. They asked me if Sarah had any enemies, and of course I said she didn't. She was the nicest girl, always giving stuff to homeless people. I mentioned the man who'd been watching her before, and gave them a description, but nothing came of it. Then a social services caseworker showed up and took you away that same day. That was the last time I saw you."

"Wow." Sam didn't know what to say for a moment. Bonnie stayed quiet, allowing time to let everything sink in. After a long silence, Sam said, "Robert Sanchez was one of the police officers who notified you. He's the one who was first on the scene."

"That's right." Bonnie looked surprised. "How

do you remember that? You were just a toddler."

"He's kept tabs on me over the years. Made sure I was never mistreated at any of the foster homes I lived in. He's been a good friend, pretty much the closest thing I've had to a parent."

"It eats at me, you know," Bonnie said, her eyes moist. "The guilt. Wondering if I did the right thing. What if I had called the police right away? What if they'd found her before she was murdered? But I didn't call, and she died."

Sam wasn't sure how she felt about this, either, but it wouldn't help either of them to say so. Instead she put a hand on the older woman's arm. "You didn't call because you were protecting me. You weren't sure what happened, and you didn't want anyone to take me away from my mother. I understand."

Another small silence fell between them. Gathering her thoughts, Sam said, "How do you know the man at the McDonald's was the man who killed my mother?"

"Because he tried to kill me, too. Two days after they found your mom. He was waiting for me outside the restaurant, and he grabbed me. Stuck a rag over my face with something that stank really bad."

"Oh my God." Sam put a hand over her mouth, horrified. "Chloroform?"

"Whatever it was, it knocked me out." Bonnie shuddered. "When I came to, I was in the woods somewhere. I had no idea how much time had passed, but it was cold and dark, and when I realized he was on top of me, I tried to scream. But he'd stuffed something in my mouth and I couldn't make a sound. That was when he held up the cleaver, and he put it right in my face. The light from the moon caught it and I saw how sharp the blade was, and I wet myself." It took Bonnie a moment to catch her breath. "He didn't cut my hand off, though. Obviously. It's like he knew he couldn't, because the Butcher was supposed to be dead. It's probably why he didn't chop off Sarah's, either. But he sure as hell wanted me to see it. He asked if I knew who he was. I said I did, and he smiled."

"But you got away," Sam whispered. "Holy shit."

"Pure luck. If you can believe it, there was a bear."

"A *what?*" Sam wasn't sure she heard her correctly.

The older woman nodded, her hands moving to her throat. Finding her pendant, she rolled it between two fingers. "You heard me right. There was a bear, of all things. Not so crazy when you think about how we were in the woods, but crazy because of the timing. A giant black bear just came out of nowhere. I remember hearing the dried leaves crunching under its feet. It just came sauntering out, and then it stopped and sniffed a tree about twenty feet away. The Butcher, he froze when he saw it, and whispered to me not to move, that it would maul us if I did. But what did I care? I was about to be carved up anyway, and I started freaking out. I started kicking, squirming, screaming. It caught the bear's attention because it started walking toward us. That's when the Butcher rolled off me. And as soon as he did, I got to my feet and ran like hell."

Her eyes misted over. "I'm not religious, but sometimes I swear that bear was God." She held up the little gold bear and the pendant glinted in the soft living room light. The choice of jewelry now made sense.

Sam, who wasn't religious, either, nodded. "I don't blame you. I probably would, too."

"The Butcher didn't chase me. I wasn't sure what happened to him, but I prayed the bear had mauled him. I found the road and hitched a ride to a friend's house, because I knew if he wasn't dead, he'd come looking for me. I hid out there the whole next day, trying to figure out what to do. I was scared to leave the house, too scared to even go to the police station because I was sure he'd grab me again. And then . . . I saw him on the news. And that's when I learned the Butcher's real identity. Thirty minutes later, I was on a bus out of town."

"You saw him on the news?" Sam said, sitting up straighter. "So was he killed by the bear?"

"Oh no, he was fine. He was on the news for completely different reasons." Bonnie's lip curled up in disgust. "He was always on the news. People believed he was a hero."

"Tell me his name." Sam's phone buzzed on the coffee table. She glanced at it but made no move to pick it up. "Please. Tell me."

Bonnie hesitated. The phone continued to vibrate. "Answer your phone first."

Holding back her frustration, Sam reached for her phone and answered the call. "Hey, Jase. It's not a good time. Let me call you back."

"Wait, everything going okay?" Jason said. She could hear *SportsCenter* on in the background and it sounded like her friend was chewing something. Whatever it was, he swallowed it. "Just making sure the redhead hasn't poisoned you and you're not on your living room floor, writhing in pain."

Despite the intensity of the last few minutes, Sam couldn't help but chuckle. "With an imagination like that, you should be the writer. No, we're good here. Just catching up. Lots to talk about. I'll call you later, okay?"

"Want me to come by later?"

"Sure. I'll call you."

They disconnected. Bonnie smiled at her. "Sweet of him to call. Are you sure you're dating the right guy? Jason sure seems sweet on you."

Sam felt her face grow hot. "Now you sound

like Matt. Jase and I are just really good friends, I swear. So, about the Butcher—"

"What does Jason do now?"

Sam gritted her teeth, stifling a sigh. Obviously Bonnie wasn't going to tell her the Butcher's name until she was good and ready. She forced a smile. "A bunch of different things. He owns some real estate, and has a few endorsement deals. He guest commentates on ESPN once in a while."

"And it's Matt who has the restaurant?"

"Yes, he's a chef. He opened up his restaurant about two years ago, after he'd had a lot of success with his food trucks." Despite her anxiety, Sam felt herself puff with pride. "He's also about to star in his own reality show on the Fresh Network."

"Wow!" Bonnie was suitably impressed. "I should check out his restaurant while I'm in town. What's it called?"

"Adobo," Sam said, spelling it for her. "I'd be happy to take you there for dinner before you go home. And Matt's last name is Shank, if you want to look him up. He's kind of a local celebrity. Now, what was it we were talking about before—"

"I'm sorry, what?" Bonnie froze. "His last name is Shank?"

"Yes. You've heard of him?"

"I . . ." Bonnie looked pale. She set her wineglass down on the side table with a shaking hand. "Actually, the last name sounds very familiar. What does his family do?"

"He was raised by his grandparents, actually," Sam said, not sure why Bonnie seemed so freaked out all of a sudden. Then she slapped her forehead. "Jesus, I can't believe I didn't mention this to you earlier. Matt's grandfather is the former chief of police of Seattle, Edward Shank. The one who brought down the Butcher. Obviously you've heard of him. *Duh*. Everybody knows who the Chief is."

"Oh, I've heard of him." Bonnie's voice was tight. "I definitely know who he is."

"He'd probably love to meet you. Obviously he's long retired, but he still has a fascination with true crime."

"Bet he does." The older woman shifted uneasily on the sofa. "A man like that, probably can't get it out of his system."

"I can't believe I didn't tell you that right off the bat." Sam shook her head. "It's just that we got caught up talking about my mom, and somehow it slipped my mind. So you see, I do have connections. If I can prove Wedge wasn't the real Butcher, I know Edward will pull strings to reopen the investigation. He's not chief of police anymore, but he still commands a lot of respect around here. The mayor and current chief of police both used to work for him."

Bonnie smiled, but it didn't touch her eyes, and

every inch of her body seemed tense. "It's okay, honey. I don't blame you for not thinking of it. When we met on the forum, we were both trying to stay anonymous, and you telling me that your boyfriend's grandfather is the former chief of police might have given away your identity. And obviously, once you found out my relationship to your mom, it wasn't exactly the first thing on your mind." The older woman twirled a lock of auburn hair around her finger, and it appeared she was thinking very hard about something. Finally she said carefully, "So tell me, does Matt's grandfather know what you think? About Sarah and the Butcher?"

Sam nodded. "We've discussed it. A lot. And of course he thinks I'm full of shit, but he tolerates my questions, thank God. However, if I had a name to give him that he could check out . . ."

Bonnie took a deep breath and sat back. "Actually, Sam, I don't think I can tell you. I'm not sure it's a good idea."

"You're joking," Sam said in disbelief. "But I thought you came here to—"

"I think I've told you too much already. Dammit, had I known . . ." Bonnie stood up, looking flustered. "You know what, I should go. And I think you should let this go, Sam. Maybe write about something else." She looked around. "Now where did I leave my purse . . ."

"What in the hell are you talking about?" Sam

knew her tone was rude, but she couldn't conceal either her confusion or her frustration. Why was Bonnie freezing up all of the sudden? They were just about to get to the important part of the conversation, which was the Butcher's real identity. "You've told me everything else already, so why not tell me the Butcher's name? I thought you wanted justice. I can do something about it, you know. It's not just Edward. I have personal contacts at Seattle PD. I can call Detective Sanchez right now—"

"I changed my mind."

"You changed your mind?" Sam was on her feet now too, incredulous. She glared at the older woman. "Are you serious? That's incredibly unfair, Bonnie. You can't come here, to my house, and give me all this information about my mom, and then decide you've changed your goddamned mind. I need answers. I need to know who the Butcher is. It's not fair for you to keep that information from me." Sam crossed her arms over her chest. She was shouting, but at this point, she didn't care. "You don't have the right."

"I'm scared, okay?" Bonnie's face was white, a mask of anguish. It was obvious the woman was totally spooked. "I'm scared. Please, Samantha. Just let it go. I'm not ready."

"I don't care if you're scared, and I don't care if you're not ready." Sam's voice was tight. "This isn't about you. The information you have isn't yours to withhold. I need to know."

"The only thing you need to know is that your mother loved you." The older woman's voice broke. "With all her heart, she loved you, and she would be so proud of the woman you've become."

"That's sweet of you, but goddammit, who killed her?"

Bonnie ignored the question. Plucking her purse from the floor where she'd dropped it, she headed for the front door. "When I get back to Sacramento, I'll send you those pictures, okay? You should have them."

"Bonnie, who killed her, goddammit?"

The older woman shook her head and reached for the doorknob.

"Bonnie, don't go. Please." Not knowing what else to do, Sam burst into tears, more out of sheer helplessness than anything else.

The older woman turned back and grabbed her in a tight hug. "It's better this way, Dumpling. You need to trust me. Whatever I do next, I don't want you involved. Sarah wouldn't want that, either. You have to trust me."

"I don't understand any of this." Sam's voice was shaking. "Why now? Why'd you even want to meet with me if you weren't prepared to tell the truth?"

"Like I said, I changed my mind." Bonnie's eyes were moist but her tone was firm. "I'm sorry, sweetheart. I don't know what else to say."

Sam went over to her purse and fished around, then pulled out a business card. "This is Sanchez's number. If you won't talk to me, will you talk to him?"

"I don't know."

"Take the card, please. And just think about it."

Bonnie took it and slipped it into her purse. "I'll think about it. I should get back to the hotel."

"Just let me get my purse. I'll drive you."

Bonnie wiped away a tear. "Sam, I know I don't have the right to ask, but will you keep this conversation between us?"

"Who would I tell?" Sam said, more confused than ever. She grabbed her purse from the sofa. "You haven't given me anything to go on. Sanchez isn't going to want to hear from me unless I have an actual name to give him."

"What I mean is, I don't want you to say anything to anyone," Bonnie said. "Okay? Can you give me your word? Just wait for me to figure it out. I promise I will."

"I don't have anything to tell, because you haven't told me anything," Sam snapped, reaching for her keys. "But I won't mention to anyone that we met. Can you at least tell me one thing first?"

"Sure. What's that?" The older woman sounded relieved.

Sam looked Bonnie directly in the eyes. "Is the Butcher still alive?"

"Yes. Very much so." Bonnie's face darkened.

"You of all people should know, Sam. You've studied it enough. Monsters like that don't die unless they're killed."

Edward watched as Samantha left the house with the red-haired woman, the two of them getting into her car. After his conversation with Matthew, he thought it might be a good idea to drop in on the kid's girlfriend. While he didn't really think Matthew would say anything to anyone about the crate, he *had* been drinking a lot lately, and something could have slipped out. Edward wanted to be prepared. After all, Samantha had her own agenda. Didn't everyone?

He had been surprised to look through the window to see she had a guest. Thankfully he hadn't rung the doorbell, because what a guest she was. Time might have wrinkled her skin and expanded her waistline, but Edward never forgot a face. She was the only one who'd ever gotten away, and he'd looked for her for a good two years before finally giving up. No doubt she'd changed her name after she'd left Seattle, maybe even more than once.

But now she was back, and it was Edward's chance to finally tie up a loose end. And, of course, have a little fun in the process. He had no idea what the woman had told Samantha, but he would find out. Edward had always been an expert at making people talk.

Waiting a few seconds, he started the engine on the Seville, then slowly followed Samantha's white Mazda down the street. As he drove, his groin tingled. Looking down, his eyes widened in surprise.

Goddammit if there wasn't a tent in his trousers. Would wonders never cease. He had an erection, his first one in years. In the darkness, Edward Shank grinned.

Perfect timing.

11

If people would just do what they were fucking told, people wouldn't have to worry about losing their fucking jobs.

Matt knew he was in a bad mood, but for Christ's sake, he had good reason to be. Adobo had never been busier and yet he was under-staffed ever since two servers had quit without giving notice. Lauryn Kinney, his day manager, had been late twice in the last week due to some custody battle with her ex over her son (Matt didn't know the details, as he hadn't really been listening). And now his old college friend PJ Wu was asking for a few minutes to chat in private, no doubt to ask for another advance on his pay, probably because he'd gotten in too deep with his bookie. Again.

To top it all off, Matt had the Fresh Network people calling to try to schedule a time to meet with him, and they were pushing for him to fly down to San Francisco for a meeting at their offices. As if he had time for that. There just didn't seem to be enough hours in the day.

He was fucking busy, okay? And if people couldn't keep up, then maybe he needed to hire new people. Adobo was currently *Seattle* magazine's Best Restaurant in their Reasonably Priced/Casual Fare/Ethnic Foods category, and this was all due to Matt's blood, sweat, and tears. Nobody worked harder than he did because nobody had more to lose than he did, and he certainly did not have time for half-assed employees who thought they deserved to get paid for hours they hadn't even worked yet. Jesus Christ, the balls on some of these motherfuckers.

Matt inhaled and forced himself to listen to PJ's latest woe. Lately, his assistant head chef had been such a little shit, and Matt still hadn't quite forgiven him for the gum incident. But surprisingly, PJ wasn't babbling about how he needed money. Not even close.

"They asked me to talk to you, okay? Because we go way back. And your energy is just frantic, man," PJ was saying.

It was the in-between time and they were alone in the kitchen; the lunch crowd had died down and it would be another two hours before the dinner patrons started arriving. PJ was chopping onions with lightning speed, and Matt had to admit the guy was a natural. Unlike himself, his friend had never been to culinary school, but he had good instincts, which was the reason Matt had hired him to run his first food truck seven years ago.

"You're freaking out the staff," PJ continued, reaching for another onion. "You're like, impossible to approach. We don't feel like you're listening to our concerns. You're like a Nazi these days. Everybody is walking on eggshells around here. You explode over little things."

"*That's* what this is about?" Matt stifled a sigh and stuck a hand into his pocket, feeling around for his cigarette pack. He didn't find it . . . because he'd quit smoking five years ago. Goddammit. "Do any of you think we got to where we are—"

"It's not about that, man. I'm not trying to start an argument." The frustration in PJ's voice was palpable, even thicker than the scent of the onion between them. He put his knife down and rested both hands on the wood chopping block. "We all know how good we're doing, okay? And we're really proud of that. We're getting great press, everyone is excited about the Fresh Network thing, it's all fantastic and we're happy to be a part of it. It's just . . . it's you. You're different."

Matt opened his mouth to respond, but the kitchen door opened and two of his prep cooks

119

walked in. They stopped, saw the expression on Matt's face, and turned to leave.

"No, you guys stay. Get the *sinigang* going and we're low on *lumpia* wrappers, so make three hundred more." Matt looked at PJ and jerked his head in the direction of the back door. "We'll finish this outside."

"But the empanadas—"

"You just said I wasn't listening to your concerns, didn't you? Well, I'm listening now."

Sighing, PJ wiped his hands on his chef's coat and followed Matt outside. The air was damp and cool, and there was a light, steady rain. The odor of the overflowing dumpster a few feet away in the alleyway was pungent. It hadn't been easy securing a location for the restaurant in small, hipsterish Fremont, but the location couldn't be beat.

"So talk." Matt allowed the door to close behind him.

"I already said what I had to say."

"PJ, right now we're not friends, okay?" Matt said. What he wouldn't give for a cigarette. "Right now I'm the owner of this restaurant and you work for me, and you have concerns. So talk. What are the staff saying about me?"

PJ dropped his chin slightly and stuck his hands in his pockets. "It's like, nothing really bad, it's just they feel like the environment hasn't been fun lately. Obviously you're stressed, and you seem to be mad when nobody else is. Nobody can relax around you, man. And it's not healthy. Like last week, with the car accident, you were pretty hard on me. That was out of my control, man. I mean, that's why they call it an accident. I was shook up, I couldn't find my phone right away, and you didn't even . . ."

"Didn't even what?"

PJ rubbed his hair again, and it stood up in short black spikes. "You weren't even concerned. You didn't ask if I was okay. I work for you, I get that, and I know you sign my paychecks. But to yell at me because I got sideswiped by some kid who had his license for maybe two minutes? That was uncool. And then yesterday, with Lauryn? She was crying, man. Did you know her ex beat her? It took forever for her to leave him, and she's living with her mom right now, and she's trying to get her kid back—it's not a good situation, and you were a jackass. You weren't even listening to her; you just chewed her out for being late.

"We're people, okay? We're not robots. When we're here, we give a hundred percent, but we have lives outside of work. There isn't one person who works here who doesn't work their ass off for you. We love this place, and we absolutely feel a sense of ownership over what we do and over the success of the restaurant. But if things don't change . . ."

"If things don't change, what?" Matt's jaw was

tight. "Finish it. You've come this far. Don't stop now."

PJ took a deep breath, then looked directly at Matt. "If things don't change, you'll lose people. Good people. People who helped you get Adobo to where it is. You didn't do this by yourself, okay, man? You didn't get here on your own."

Matt laughed. He couldn't help it, because it was just so absurd, the things that were coming out of little PJ Wu's mouth. He stepped forward, moving into PJ's personal space, causing the smaller man to shrink back a little.

"I can hardly believe what I'm hearing. Are you seriously telling me how to run my restaurant? You all don't think I know how to run a business? You think the pressure of this is easy?" The need to laugh subsided, and Matt felt the heat rising in his cheeks, his heart rate accelerating with every word. "You're worried about Lauryn? Do you know what she makes? I pay her extremely well, my friend, and I pay her extremely well that so that she'll do her fucking job extremely well. I pay her to help me manage this restaurant, not hear her excuses. And I definitely don't pay you as well as I do—which is pretty goddamned well for a guy with no formal training—to come in late to work on a Saturday night crying like a little girl over a fender bender. The restaurant is where it is because of *me,* because *I* run a tight ship, and because *I* know what the fuck I'm doing."

PJ's face was red, and he shook his head, wiping a drop of rain from his brow. "Okay, you know what, forget it. I tried, but this is bullshit." He made to move past his boss toward the door, but Matt put a hand on his arm.

"I didn't dismiss you. We're not done."

"Dismiss me?" PJ blinked, his small eyes widening in shock. "Did you really just say that?" He raised both hands. "This conversation is going totally sideways. I'm going back to work."

"I said, we're not done."

"Please take your hand off me, Matt."

"Oh, this bothers you now?" Matt stepped even closer, getting into the other man's face. "This bother you, too?" Before he could think about it, he poked his friend in the chest. Hard.

Mouth opening slightly in surprise, PJ pushed back with his palm, with surprising force. Matt was propelled a step backward. Instantly, everything around him went hazy and quiet. All he could see were PJ's beady eyes glaring up at him, and the anger that consumed him was so raw he could almost taste it. Matt's fingers clenched into a fist, and before he could think about it, he punched PJ square on the jaw as hard as he could.

The sound of his knuckles connecting with PJ's round face was satisfying, almost ridiculously so. The smaller man went down instantly, his head slamming into the pavement with a dull thud.

The haze cleared. Blinking, Matt looked down.

Shit shit shit. PJ was out cold, not moving, and now Matt was going to jail, which was the last thing he fucking needed. Part of the agreement he'd made with the assistant district attorney when he'd been assigned community classes over jail time last year was that any further assault charges would result in a minimum one-year jail sentence. He'd gotten into a bar fight then and had beaten the other guy silly; his grandfather had smoothed things over.

But there would be no smoothing things over this time. When PJ came to, he was going to be mad, he was going to sue, and Matt would be going to county.

This was a fucking disaster.

Cursing himself for his lack of control, Matt took a deep breath, trying to remember the relaxation techniques he'd learned. When PJ woke up, he would apologize. He would offer him money. He would do whatever he had to do to make this go away. Like his friend had just said, they went way back. Surely PJ would forgive him and they'd be able to move on.

The rain was coming down a bit faster now, and he crouched down. "PJ. I'm sorry, dude. Wake up."

The man didn't move.

"PJ. Come on, man."

Matt put a hand on his friend's shoulder and shook him. PJ's head turned slightly on the pavement, and the next thing Matt knew, blood was seeping out. He recoiled, shocked.

Oh no. No no no.

Forcing himself to move in closer, Matt turned PJ over slightly, and that's when he saw the large jagged rock under his friend's head. PJ must have slammed into it when he'd hit the ground, and whatever injury this was, it was obviously more than just a concussion.

Matt touched the smaller man's shoulder gently. The blood continued to seep out from the side of PJ's head in a steady, warm stream of bright red. "PJ? Wake up. Wake up, buddy. Please try and wake up."

PJ didn't move, but his mouth finally opened and a small moan escaped his lips. Then his mouth closed and his whole body went slack.

No. No no no. You've got to be kidding me. This cannot be happening.

Heart racing, Matt felt for a pulse on the side of PJ's neck. If there was one, he couldn't find it. He checked PJ's wrist. Nothing there, either. He shook PJ harder, and the man's head lolled to the side.

He was totally fucking dead.

Shit shit shit fuck shit. How could this be possible? Matt had hit him, yes, but never in a million years had he meant to kill the guy. PJ was his friend. And now his friend was dead, and Matt would lose everything he worked for because of one lousy, out-of-control moment. *Now what?*

Matt looked up and down the alleyway. They were completely alone, and nobody had seen what had just happened. Thank God. And although it was the afternoon, there wasn't much daylight due to the rain that was coming down pretty steadily. The alley was just shadowy enough . . .

He made his decision.

PJ wasn't a big guy, about five foot eight, and he was very lean, maybe around 155 or so. Matt was in pretty good shape thanks to regular weight training and running, but none of that made it any easier when he hefted his friend's limp body up off the ground. There really was such a thing as dead weight—it felt like PJ weighed three hundred pounds.

Placing his wrists under PJ's armpits, he dragged the smaller man over to the dumpster. Heart pounding and scared as hell that somebody would come into the alley, Matt bent his knees and heaved. The adrenaline coursing through his veins helped; PJ was up and into the dumpster in a few seconds, his body landing on the bags of garbage inside with a soft thud.

Panting, Matt's knees buckled, and he fell back against the dirty metal of the dumpster, catching his breath. The rain was coming down harder now, and he lifted his face up to let the downpour cool him off. *Okay. All right. Step one complete.*

Step two was moving the body someplace new. PJ couldn't stay inside the dumpster for too long, as garbage pickup was tomorrow morning. And there was no way the boys from Waste Management would not notice a dead body falling into the back of their dump truck. Matt had no choice but to come back for PJ after the restaurant closed. No way around it.

How the hell did you get rid of a dead body? *Fuck fuck fuck.*

The back door to Adobo opened then, and one of the prep cooks appeared with a Hefty bag stuffed to the gills. Matt straightened up with a start, his lower back screaming out in pain. Dammit, he'd strained his SI joint, which was the absolute last thing he needed.

"I got that, Wayne," he said to the employee, stepping forward. He worked at keeping his posture erect so nothing would seem out of the ordinary. Risking a glance downward at himself, he was relieved to be reminded that he was wearing all black. If there was any blood on him, it didn't show. Another glance toward the spot where PJ had fallen confirmed that the rain had washed away most of the blood from the head wound. "I can toss it in, I'm already wet. If there's any more inside, go and grab it for me."

More garbage bags would cover up the body until Matt could figure out what to do with it.

Wayne seemed surprised. "Thanks, Matt, appreciate it." He looked around. "Where's PJ?"

"Sent him home," Matt said, sounding every bit like the boss, his tone leaving no room for argument. "He wasn't in the mood to work after our conversation."

The prep cook raised an eyebrow, but he didn't ask questions. Nodding, Wayne left for a moment, then returned with a few more bags of garbage. Then he closed the back door, leaving Matt alone in the alley once again.

Matt heaved the garbage bags into the dumpster one by one, back throbbing, hoping that PJ was totally buried. Then he pulled out his iPhone. Hesitating a moment—did he really want to make this call?—he found the number he was looking for.

His call was answered after two rings.

"Chief?" Matt said, his voice breaking. "I fucked up. I need your help."

12

Jason's black Range Rover was sitting in her driveway when Sam pulled up, and she couldn't help but smile. He was waiting for her on the porch, dressed in sweatpants and a T-shirt, dark blond hair comfortably mussed. She got out of her car and gave him a tired hug.

"Tacos?" Jason held up a brown paper bag covered in grease spots. "I also have a burrito and an enchilada if you can't make up your mind."

Tacos from Taco Time weren't quite in the same league as Matt's empanadas, but Sam had to admit they smelled damn good.

"I also brought wine," Jason said. "Tempranillo. I'm hoping it will make the food taste more expensive."

Sam raised an eyebrow. "Fancy. Hey, I thought you were going to call first."

"I did. Twice. When you didn't pick up I had visions of you lying beaten and bludgeoned to death on your kitchen floor, so I raced right over."

"And stopped for fast food and alcohol along the way?"

"Well, yeah. If you weren't dead, I assumed you'd be hungry."

Sam unlocked the front door. "As a matter of fact, I'm starving."

They sat cross-legged on the living room floor, the television tuned to the college football game in the corner. The Puget Sound State University Steelheads were playing against the Washington State Cougars, and of course both Sam and Jason were rooting for PSSU since it was their alma mater. They enjoyed the Tempranillo with the Mexican takeout and promised each other they wouldn't say anything to Matt, a food snob

129

who would have been horrified at the beautiful Spanish red wine being paired with cheap fast food.

"How'd it go tonight?" Jason asked, taking a bite of his taco. "Did Bonnie tell you a lot?"

"At first, yeah. But she stopped short of telling me the Butcher's real name." Sam gave him the rundown of everything she and Bonnie talked about. "I was so close. It's frustrating."

Jason raised an eyebrow. "So she came all the way from Sacramento to Seattle to *not* give you the most important bit of information? How does that make sense?"

"After we talked, she said she changed her mind." Sam sighed. The wine helped, but it wasn't enough. She was still aggravated. "Wish I knew why."

"You think she's on the up-and-up?"

Sam gave her friend a look. "Of course I do. She knew my mom, knew all about the night she died. She even remembers Detective Sanchez."

"Maybe you should call him, have her checked out, just in case."

"Not a bad idea."

"I think it's important that you find out what's in it for her." Jason finished his taco. "Something about it seems fishy."

Sam paused. "I wouldn't say fishy. It's more like she panicked. I get the feeling the Butcher is someone with some notoriety, someone who

130

might be recognized. She mentioned seeing him on TV. She's scared, Jase."

"Of what? Did you ask her?"

"Of course I asked her," she snapped. "She wouldn't say. She's being incredibly selfish." Her voice was getting loud, and she slapped the coffee table with her palm. It stung.

"Okay, okay." Jason softened his tone. "I'm not trying to upset you. I just want you to be careful. You met her online, remember. She has a picture of herself with your mom. She believes your mom was murdered by a serial killer that everyone else thinks is dead. It's just . . . weird, you know?"

Sam rubbed her eyes. "I can't disagree with you there. It's fucked-up. I fully accept that."

"Just remember that everyone—and I mean everyone—has an agenda. Including you. You want information about your mom, and you want to know who really killed her. What's Bonnie's agenda?"

"Justice? For Sarah? And herself?"

Jason smiled. "If it's that simple, and noble, then great. All I'm saying is, keep your eyes open. Be careful. Everybody wants something."

"I will." Sam sighed. She knew Jason was right. She couldn't deny that she'd been a bit blinded by her own awe in meeting someone who'd known her mother, but if she tried to look at the whole thing objectively, it *was* weird. Seriously, what were the chances of Bonnie finding her?

Or of her finding Bonnie?

Suddenly it didn't feel right at all. She made up her mind to call the Sixth Avenue Inn first thing in the morning. Sam needed answers, goddammit, and the woman was going to give them to her, whether she liked it or not.

"So how's *Butcherville* coming along?" Jason said, referring to her current work in progress.

"Right now, I'm stuck. I'm trying to illustrate the intense pressure Seattle PD was under to catch the Butcher, and how they might have wanted Rufus Wedge to be the killer a little *too* much. The evidence they had against him was purely circumstantial, and had Wedge not been killed, and had the case gone to trial, I can't imagine how they would have convicted him." Sam sighed again. "But how I do present that as a theory without making the entire police department, including the Chief, look bad?"

"It's just your opinion, right? It's not like they're going to sue you for publishing it?"

"No. At least I don't think so. I'm not accusing them of corruption. It's more like . . . incompetence." Sam grimaced. "God, even that sounds ugly."

"Pretty sure Edward Shank would agree with you. Never known a man who hates to be wrong more than he does."

"Except Matt."

They shared a laugh.

"Maybe you should talk to the Chief about it," Jason said, sipping his wine. "Tell him what Bonnie told you. See what he thinks."

"Can't. I promised her I wouldn't say anything. She knows who the Chief is, knows I'm dating his grandson. She doesn't want me to reveal anything about the Butcher until she's ready to talk. I'm hoping she'll call Sanchez soon."

"Let me ask you this." Jason paused, and it was clear he was choosing his words carefully. "Say the two of you are right and it turns out that Seattle PD got the wrong guy, and that some other dude is the real Butcher. Have you thought about what would happen?"

"They'd put the real Butcher away. Assuming he's still alive. Bonnie seemed sure he was."

"And then what?"

"What do you mean?" Sam said, confused.

Jason sat up straighter. "Think about it, Sam. If some other guy turns out to be the real Butcher, then that task force from Seattle PD shot and killed the wrong man. An *innocent* man. The task force that Edward Shank headed up."

"Right," Sam said with a shrug. "Of course it's going to be a shitstorm. It will be all over the news. But if that's the truth, then that's the truth, and the truth is all that matters. At least justice will be done."

"Justice for who?" Jason asked. "For you and your mom, yes. For Bonnie. For all the other

Butcher victims. But what about the Chief? He's a hero in this city. What would it do to him if it turned out he got the wrong guy?"

Sam shook her head. "I've already talked about this with Edward. It was a good shooting that night. Wedge was reaching for his pocket and they had no choice but to shoot him. The Chief doesn't seem worried."

"Come on, be realistic. You and I both know it would tarnish his reputation. No hero kills an innocent man. He'd go down in flames like Lance Armstrong. Didn't you once tell me that there were citizens groups that were outraged that Wedge was killed before he had a chance to go to trial? They'd be screaming murder, and they'd be right."

"The Chief will have to deal with it, Jase. That can't be my problem. And besides, Rufus Wedge wasn't exactly a fine, upstanding citizen. He was a recluse with a long criminal history, even without being the Butcher."

"Still, Wedge's family could sue for wrongful death or something."

"Wedge had no family. He had no friends. Wedge had nobody."

"Okay," Jason said, changing gears. "What about how this affects Matt?"

"Why would it affect Matt?" Sam was losing her patience. "Matt has zero to do with any of this."

"Think about it for a minute." Jason's tone was earnest. "He's a local celebrity of sorts. Mostly that's because he runs a damn good restaurant and is a damn good chef, but let's be honest here. In almost every interview he's given, it's mentioned that he's the former chief of police of Seattle's grandson. He's never made that a secret, and you and I both know Matt plays up on that all the time because it's good publicity. He gets asked all the time why he didn't follow in his legendary grandfather's footsteps and go into law enforcement. And you know how he always responds to that question."

Sam thought for a moment. "He says that he followed in his grandmother's footsteps instead. Because she was an amazing cook, and so his cooking is a tribute to her."

"Right. But who Edward Shank is has only helped Matt's celebrity, Sam. And if it turns out that the Chief fucked up, and the whole thing turns into—like you just said—a shitstorm, how would that impact Matt? It would be awful publicity that his grandfather killed an innocent man. Our boy is about to become the biggest thing since Emeril."

"So you're saying I shouldn't tell the truth so I can protect Matt?" Sam looked at her friend, aghast. "What about *my* truth?"

"I just want to make sure you know exactly what will happen here. It's one thing to discover that

Edward Shank killed an innocent man. You're right, the Chief can handle it, and besides that, he's long retired anyway. But it's a whole other thing how that information—which will be made very public—will affect Matt."

"So what are you telling me to do?"

"I'm not telling you to do or not do anything," Jason said. "I'm just trying to give you a dose of reality. I've known Matt for a long time. If you do anything—anything at all—that ends up affecting the success of his business, he'll never forgive you."

"I thought you were on my side." Sam's voice was tense.

Jason moved forward, close enough to reach out and touch Sam's leg. "I am always on your side, okay? And I always will be. That's why I want you to look at the whole picture. I know how much you love Matt. I know you want a life with him. But if you do anything that hurts him, I really don't see how you'd have a future together."

That stung. Because Sam couldn't disagree. She'd known since the day she'd met Matt three years ago that his career meant more to him than anything, and deep down, she'd hoped that would change someday.

Well, someday was here, and nothing had changed. If anything, the more successful her boyfriend became, the more they grew apart.

"He's never going to give me what I want, is

he?" Sam said, her voice heavy. "I'm an idiot, right?"

"Not if you're okay with how things are," Jason said. "If you're okay with it, then okay. Keep doing what you're doing."

"And if I'm not okay with it?"

Jason touched her cheek, his eyes kind. "Then you do what you have to do. But put yourself first. Because you know damn well that he does."

There was nothing Sam could say to that, because she knew her friend was absolutely right.

13

The Chief seemed a little put out, though for the life of him Matt couldn't imagine how he could have disrupted his grandfather's evening. The man was eighty years old and living in an old folks' home, for Christ's sake. What else would he have to do at one in the morning? Yet the Chief had seemed distracted when Matt called him a few hours earlier, and it still seemed like something was on the old man's mind.

Adobo was closed and the staff had finally left for the night. Matt had managed to restrain himself from letting everyone go home early, because everybody knew that the boss would never do the cleanup himself. Best not to do anything that would arouse suspicion, and being too nice would certainly do that.

The lights in the restaurant were off everywhere except in the kitchen, and his grandfather stood in silence as Matt wiped down the large marble island. He could feel the Chief's eyes on him and wondered how to even tell him what had happened earlier. He bought himself another minute by opening the huge stainless steel fridge and fussing around with its contents, before finally shutting the door and turning to face the old man.

The Chief raised a bushy silver eyebrow. "Well? What's got your panties in a twist?"

"I'm not in a twist," Matt replied, but even he could hear the tension in his own voice.

"I've got things to do, you know." His grandfather frowned. "You called, I'm here, but I ain't got all night."

"Really? Where could you possibly have to be at"—Matt glanced up at the large clock mounted high on the kitchen wall—"one twelve in the morning? Got a hot date?"

"Matter of fact, I do," the old man said evenly. "And don't be a jackass. I might be retired, but I still have a life, and places to go, and people to see. Not that it's any of your goddamned business."

"Sorry." Matt averted his gaze. "Didn't mean to offend you."

"Kid, if I was that easy to offend, I'd have keeled over three decades ago. Now are you going to tell me what happened, or do I have to coax it out of you?" The Chief looked at him expectantly. While his expression wasn't unkind, it was clear he was getting impatient.

"I did something really bad." Matt was horrified to realize he was dangerously close to tears. The last time he'd felt anything remotely this upsetting was when the Seahawks lost the Super Bowl to the Pittsburgh Steelers in 2006. This, obviously, was a million times worse. "I don't know what to do, Chief. I really fucked up."

"This about Samantha?"

"What?"

"You mess around on her?" His grandfather's tone was stern. "It's best to tell the truth, Matthew. Lying doesn't help. You'll have to come clean, no other way around it."

"No, I—"

"Not to me, to her. I don't give a rat's ass if you screwed someone else, though let me tell you, it's hardly ever worth it. But we're men and we're programmed by Mother Nature to fuck anything with lipstick and a pulse. But Samantha's a good girl, Matthew, and you should—"

"I killed someone," Matt blurted. "I killed someone, okay? You gotta help me, Chief. I don't know what to do."

A silence descended over them and for a

moment, neither Shank said anything. Edward stared at Matt, his eyes bright and searching, as if he were waiting for the punch line. Which, of course, didn't come, because nothing about this was a joke.

When his grandfather finally spoke, it wasn't the question Matt was expecting to hear. "Anybody see you?"

"No. I don't think so."

"You don't think so? Think hard, Matthew."

"Nobody saw anything, I'm sure of it."

"Where's the body?"

"Out back. In the dumpster."

"Show me."

"The body?"

"No, you dummy, the moon." The Chief looked irritated. "Of course the body."

Moving slowly past his grandfather, Matt pushed open the door that led to the back alleyway. Both men stepped out into the cool night air.

Fremont was dead this time of night, and it was absolute silence in the alleyway. The lightbulb above the restaurant's door burned a dim yellow, and the shadows seemed spookier to Matt than normal.

"In there," Matt said, pointing to the large black metal bin a few feet away. "I didn't know where else to put him."

The Chief looked toward the dumpster, scratching his chin. In the darkness the gesture seemed almost villainous, and Matt found himself shivering even though he felt hot. It was all so surreal, like it was happening to someone else.

"Give me a boost," his grandfather said. "I need to see what we're dealing with here."

"I can't, I hurt my back," Matt said. "It's killing me right now."

"Then go get me something to stand on," Edward snapped. "*Now,* Matthew. Time is of the essence. And bring me a broom."

Matt nodded and went back into the kitchen, returning with a stepladder and the broom he kept in the storage room. Placing them both in front of the dumpster, he held out his arm to help steady his grandfather as the old man climbed up.

Once he reached the top step, Edward said, "Hand me the broom."

Matt did.

It was a painstaking few seconds as the Chief used the broom to move aside the garbage bags that had piled up inside the dumpster over the past few hours. Several restaurants and bars had back doors to this alley, and the dumpster was shared among them.

Edward handed Matt back the broom. "Help me down."

Matt once again offered his grandfather his arm, and when the Chief reached the pavement, he asked, "Well? What do we do now?"

"Nothing." Edward shook his head. "The guy's not in there anymore."

"What?"

The Chief barked a laugh. "I'm kidding. Christ almighty. Of course he's in there. Where the fuck else would he be?"

"Not funny, Chief." Matt detected the faint odor of onions, and realized that his armpits were soaked with perspiration. "I have absolutely no sense of humor right now."

"You're going to have to jump in there and get him out."

Matt looked up at the dumpster. "Chief, there's no way. I sprained something when I threw him in there in the first place. There's no way I can throw him back out."

Feeling the outer walls of the dumpster with a liver-spotted hand, Edward circled the bin, his eyes roaming every inch of the black metal. Matt had never seen his grandfather so focused, so alert.

"Goddammit, there's no door. Sometimes these things have sliding doors in case something goes in accidentally that you need to get out. But . . ." He paused. Leaning against the bin, he positioned himself carefully, then shoved it with his shoulder. The dumpster moved slightly, though not much. "Good. This is good. The whole thing is tilted. See that? It's kind of balancing on that one corner."

"Huh?"

"Pay attention, stupid. The dumpster. It's *tilted*."

Matt still didn't follow.

Edward let out a sigh. "The body is fairly close to the top of the bin and there's only one layer of trash on top of it. The dumpster is already tilted. You can see the part of it that's broken right here." He indicated to a spot at the bottom near the cement that Matt couldn't see, but he nodded anyway. His grandfather shoved against the bin again. "See? A bit wobbly. We might actually be able to tip this thing, and get him to fall out of the top."

"Okay," Matt said. That made sense. "And how do we that?"

"Where's your van?"

"A block away." Nobody was allowed to park in the alley. The city only permitted three minutes for loading and unloading, so Matt had parked it as he usually did down the street, which was about a five-minute walk. Two if he ran.

"Go and get it. And hustle, goddammit. We don't have time to waste."

Six minutes later, Edward was behind the wheel of Matt's supply van, which was bumped up against the dumpster, rear end first.

"Now listen to me. I'm going to try and move the dumpster using the van," Edward said through the open driver's-side window. "But I need you to help, too. Make sure you do everything you can to get it to tilt, and when it does, get the fuck out of the way."

"You want me to help?" Matt said, confused. "Using what? Brute strength?"

"Don't be a smartass. You're a strong man. Do your best to push."

"Are you joking?"

"Am I laughing?"

No, his grandfather wasn't laughing. In fact, Matt couldn't remember the last time he'd seen the old man so serious.

"Okay, I'll try." He took a deep breath and tried not to think about his aching back. "But my back really hurts—"

"Fuck your back," Edward barked. "If you're standing, it's not broken. This is your ass on the line and right now tipping the goddamned dumpster is the only option we got. You want to get the body out or not?"

"Yes, Chief."

"Then do what the fuck I say."

Matt nodded, then determinedly put both hands up against the side of the dumpster.

Edward put the van in reverse and moved the vehicle back slowly. Metal scraped against metal for a few seconds, and with a groan, the dumpster finally tipped. Several bags of garbage fell out of the top, one of them breaking open when it hit the hard cement. His grandfather continued to reverse, and Matt used all his strength to push against the metal, ignoring the screaming pain in his lower back.

A moment later, the dumpster tipped over the entire way. It hit the pavement with a clang that was alarmingly loud, and Matt froze, waiting to see if someone would come running around the corner. Then he realized that was just silly. A noise that loud at this time of night would have people running *away* from it, not toward it. Plus every establishment in Fremont was closed at this time of night.

Garbage bags spilled over onto the pavement, and with them, the body of PJ Wu. Matt was taken aback at the sight of his friend's lifeless form, which already looked different than it had a few hours ago. PJ's skin was ashy, his hair matted down from whatever liquids had soaked him. A few hours ago, PJ could have been sleeping, maybe unconscious. But now? He looked dead. Totally, completely dead.

Shifting the van into drive, his grandfather pulled forward a few feet and then cut the engine. Stepping out, he surveyed the piles of garbage filling up the narrow alleyway and nodded. "Perfect. Exactly what we wanted to happen." Pulling open the van's back doors, he snapped, "Well, don't just stand there. Go get a tarp, something we can wrap him in. We have to get him into the back of the van."

Matt did as he was told, and was back a moment

later with a clear plastic tarp that he'd found in the storage room. He maneuvered his way through the piles of garbage toward PJ, stepping over the mounds of old food and empty coffee cups and God knew what else. The scent of rotting produce was cloying, but adrenaline was pumping through Matt's veins now and his olfactory senses barely registered anything. He helped the Chief roll the body into the tarp, then bent forward and grabbed PJ's foot.

"No, you take his shoulders, I'll take his legs," the Chief said. "I'm no 'spring chicken anymore, goddammit."

Matt didn't argue. Edward took hold of PJ's ankles while Matt grabbed the body under the armpits, and the two of them slowly hoisted the body into the back of the van. It was only a few feet, but they moved slowly, careful not to trip over the bags. Trying to ignore the throbbing pain in his back, Matt hoisted PJ's front end into the back of the van, then jumped inside to pull the body all the way in. Climbing back out, he slammed the doors shut, then leaned against the van to catch his breath.

"Where to now, Chief?"

"Your house," Edward said. He was already pulling open the driver's-side door. "I'll drive the van, you go get the Seville. I parked it across the street in the pay lot." He tossed Matt his keys. "Follow me. And if for some reason I get stopped by the cops, you keep going, you hear me? I don't want you around while I'm answering questions. Not that they'd dare ask me anything. I am the Chief, after all."

Matt nodded, then glanced down at the garbage that was still spilled everywhere. "Do we just leave it like this?"

Edward snorted. "Why, you want to clean it up?"

"I don't know."

"Kid, you have a lot to learn about what to give a shit about and what not to give a shit about. Tomorrow morning Waste Management will show up and they'll just think somebody cut through the alleyway and rammed into the dumpster. They'll haul the garbage into the back of their truck and they'll put the dumpster back upright, and it'll be like it never happened. *Capiche*?"

"I got you."

"Now go get my car. And don't speed. And be careful when shifting; it sticks when you shift it out of drive."

A half hour later, the supply van was parked in Matt's driveway alongside the Chief's Cadillac. The two men were inside the garage with the door down and locked, PJ Wu's body in front of them atop the old work table. The bright white lights overhead made the dead man's skin look even grayer. Edward had lit a cigar, but not even its smoky sweetness could completely mask the smell of garbage emanating from PJ Wu's dead body.

"Aren't you even going to ask me what happened?" Matt asked, his voice small.

"I already know what happened." The Chief blew out a stream of smoke. "You killed him."

"Don't you want to know why?"

Edward snorted. "Not really. Though I'm assuming the little shit mouthed off one too many times and you hit him with something. I saw the wound on the back of his head. But the why doesn't matter, Matthew."

Matt wasn't sure he understood this, but if his grandfather wasn't curious, then Matt wasn't about to force-feed him an explanation. Not that he had one, anyway.

"It was an accident."

"Sure it was," the Chief said.

Matt let out a breath, feeling spacey and light-headed now that the adrenaline had drained from his body. "It was. I swear."

"Enough yakking." Edward stood up and rested his cigar on the ashtray on top of the shelf beside him, where it continued to smolder. "Time to get to work." Reaching behind him, he pulled out a chain saw. "I hope this is still charged."

"Oh fuck. Oh hell." Matt stared at the Chief in horror, the haze in his brain instantly lifting. Reflexively, he backed up a step. "Are you . . . are

148

you going to . . ." He couldn't bring himself to finish the question.

Edward barked a laugh. "I'm not doing a god-damned thing, kid. This is your shit show, dummy. You're doing it." He grinned, shaking the chain saw slightly, and it rattled into the silence of the garage.

"No. No fucking way. I can't."

"Sure you can." The Chief stepped toward him, holding out the saw. "He's already dead, Matthew. You killed him, remember? He won't feel a goddamned thing, trust me on that."

The old man was deadly serious, and there was a light in his eyes that mirrored the one Matt had seen in that horrible video. Recoiling, he shook his head rapidly. "I can't. Chief, please. I can't do this. Maybe . . . maybe I should just turn myself in. It was an accident. They'll believe me, right? I'm your grandson. They won't believe I could do anything bad on purpose."

Edward held out the saw. "You're wasting time. The sooner we dispose of the body, the better."

"Chief." Matt's breath was coming out faster, and he struggled to stay calm. He felt as if he were on the verge of hysteria. "Chief, please. Don't make me do this."

"What the hell did you call me for then?"

"I . . . I don't know."

Edward rested the saw at the edge of the table and took another step forward toward his grandson. "Do you want to go to prison?" he said softly, his dark eyes piercing Matt's face. "Do you want to spend the rest of your life locked up? Because that's what will happen. You'll go to the state pen, where you'll be beaten and raped and God knows what else. Is that what you want? Is that what you want for me, your grandfather, who's now officially an accessory?"

"No," Matt whispered. "That won't happen. It was an accident. You were trying to help me. They'll understand."

"All right," the Chief said, shifting tactics. "Let's say you don't get locked up. Let's say we put the body back where he died, and you somehow convince the jury that it was self-defense and so they don't convict you of anything, not even manslaughter. What kind of publicity would that be for you? Whether you meant to kill him or not, the kid's dead, Matthew. And he's dead because of you. What would that do to your reputation? To your restaurant? To your TV show deal?"

"I . . ." Matt's voice trailed off. He couldn't bring himself to answer.

"It would all go away, wouldn't it? Everything you've dreamed of, everything you've worked for. Is that what you want?"

"Of course not." Matt's voice was thin and shaky. "I don't want to lose everything."

Edward's voice, in contrast, was strong and

firm. "Then don't throw it away. You made one mistake, do you understand me? One goddamned mistake, and now your life is on the line, and if you don't smarten the fuck up and do everything I tell you, you will lose everything that means anything to you. Do you understand me?"

Matt still couldn't seem to speak.

"Do you understand me?" the Chief roared, and Matt jumped.

"Yes, yes, I understand you."

"Then put on that rain poncho. Take the god-damned chain saw. Cut him up. Put him in as many garbage bags as you need to." Edward pushed the saw toward him. "Don't worry about anybody hearing. The garage is soundproofed, remember?"

"I remember," Matt said, his voice practically a squeak. He grabbed the blue plastic poncho hanging from a hook on the garage wall and put it on. He had several; he wore them to Seahawks games when it rained. Then he took the chain saw and turned it on. It roared to life and he cringed, almost dropping it.

"Now concentrate," his grandfather said, plucking his still-lit cigar from the ashtray. Inhaling deeply, the smoke curled around his leathery face and he squinted through it, eyes fixed on the chain saw in Matt's shaking hands. "Remember, you're sawing into bone, and it's gonna get messy. But that's the way it goes, kid."

"God help me."

The Chief blew out a long stream of smoke. "Just pretend he's the spider."

An hour and a half later, it was done.

"What now?" Matt said. The poncho was covered in blood spatter, and his clothing underneath was drenched in sweat. He leaned against the wall, stomach still heaving. On the garage floor to the left of him, in a small pile, were the contents of his stomach. The stench of vomit filled the garage, eliminating any trace of the garbage odors that had been present earlier. Three triple-thick Hefty garbage bags lined the wall, filled with what used to be PJ Wu.

"Now, you put the bags in the van and hand me the keys." Edward was eerily calm, almost cheerful. "I'll take care of it from here."

"Chief, I—"

"You can thank me later. And clean up the vomit. It smells disgusting."

"I was going to ask where you were going."

His grandfather looked at him. "Do you really want to know that?"

No. The truth was, Matt didn't.

"We have three hours before the garbage trucks come," Edward said. "Your job now is to go back to the restaurant and sift through all the waste. Look for anything that might have belonged to your friend and take it with you. The kid was wearing both his shoes, and he had his wallet and phone on him, but he had no keys. Find them."

"He would have them inside his locker at the restaurant." Matt took a breath. "When we went out back to talk, he thought he was going back in."

"Well then, make sure. And spray down the alleyway to get rid of whatever the rain didn't wash away. Use bleach. Then come back and clean this mess up."

"Chief?"

"What is it?"

Matt exhaled. "Thank you."

"You're welcome," Edward said, looking around. "And when you clean up here, be thorough. You'll find a couple of big jugs of bleach on the shelf." His grandfather smiled, his white dentures gleaming in the fluorescent lights. "You know, for times like this."

14

Sam knew what the look on Detective Robert Sanchez's face meant. It meant he had bad news, and she wasn't sure she wanted to hear it.

They sat across from each other at the noisy, crowded Tully's coffee shop in Ballard, sipping their caffeinated beverages—Americano black with three sugars for him, her usual chai latte for herself. She'd paid. She always paid when he was doing her a favor. The detective looked like he always did, dressed in neatly pressed slacks and a button-down shirt, even though he wasn't working today. She hadn't seen him a few months, and she thought his hair looked a little grayer around the temples.

"You think I should dye it?" Sanchez asked, catching her glance. He rubbed his sideburns. "I think I should, but Vanessa says the gray makes me looks distinguished."

"I agree with your wife," Sam said with a smile. "Always listen to your wife."

"It doesn't make me look old?"

"You're fifty-two. You are old."

"Gee, thanks." He laughed and sipped his coffee. "So. I ran the name you gave me." Pushing a folded piece of paper across the table toward her, he said, "Is this her?"

Sam unfolded it, staring down at an enlarged copy of Bonnie Tidwell's California driver's license. It listed her current address in Sacramento. Date of birth was March 17, 1968, making her forty-five. She hadn't wanted to tell Sanchez about Bonnie, as she'd promised the woman she wouldn't, but Bonnie hadn't been at the Sixth Avenue Inn when Sam had stopped in that afternoon. The desk clerk had confirmed that the woman had checked out, leaving Sam high and dry.

So, not sure what else to do, Sam had finally called Sanchez. Not that she felt good about it. She wasn't one to break a confidence.

"Yep, it's definitely her," she said. "Did you run a background check?"

Sanchez's brow furrowed. "You realize I don't work for you, right? I really don't have time to be doing checks on random people I don't know."

"But you do know her," Sam said. "You don't recognize her? You questioned her on a case."

Sanchez took the picture back and examined it. "If I did, I don't remember."

"I thought you'd recognize the name."

"Bonnie Tidwell?" The detective shook his head. "Doesn't ring a bell. Mind you, I'm better with faces than with names."

"She was a friend of my mom's," Sam said. "They were roommates. She was the one watching me when you came to my house the morning after my mother was killed."

Sanchez's eyes widened, then he took a good look at the picture again. "Well, shit. Yeah, okay, I do remember her. But she was just a kid back then. Hell, so was I. But I'm pretty sure Bonnie Tidwell wasn't her name. From what I remember, it was like, Joyce-something." He thought hard for a moment. "I can't remember. I'd have to check my notes, but I'm pretty sure her last name was Polish."

Sam bit her lip. Great. So Bonnie Tidwell wasn't

the woman's real name. Maybe Jason was right, maybe Bonnie wasn't on the up-and-up and did have some weird agenda after all.

"Now for the inevitable next question," Sanchez said, his dark eyes boring into hers. "Why are we talking about this? Has she contacted you?"

Sam avoided the detective's gaze and took a sip of her latte, trying to figure out how to respond.

"Samantha." Sanchez sighed, pushing the piece of paper back to her. "You had me look into this for a reason without telling me why. So I did you a favor and I looked into it, and I didn't ask questions. But now I know that she was a friend of your mom's. What I want to know is why *you* know her, and why she told you her name was Bonnie Tidwell when it's Joyce Kubacki." A grinned crossed over his face. "Ha! See? I knew it would come to me. Joyce Kubacki. There you go."

"I promised her I wouldn't say anything."

"She got in touch with you?" he asked again.

Sam hesitated. "Something like that."

"Okay." Sanchez shrugged. "So what? That doesn't surprise me. You and your mom lived with her for a while and I'm sure she's always wondered how you were doing, and where you ended up. And it's not like it's illegal to change your name. People do it all the time, for lots of reasons. I wouldn't be surprised if the murder spooked her and she decided to leave and start over somewhere else. Bonnie Tidwell has no history prior to 1988, so I'm guessing that's about the time she changed her name."

That made sense to Sam. Bonnie had fled Seattle in 1987 and had probably hid out for a year before assuming a new identity.

"And what did you find out about Bonnie after 1988?" she asked.

Sanchez reached into his pocket and pulled out another piece of paper. Consulting it, he said, "Nothing of note, really. Bonnie—or should I say, Joyce—seems to have lived a pretty boring life, just like the rest of us. Worked steadily at a few different places. Took some courses in photography part-time through an art school. Got married, got divorced, got married again, got divorced again. Now she owns her own studio doing commercial photography. 'Bout it. Nothing too exciting . . . except for the fact that you're asking me to look into her." The detective's stare was unwavering. "So are you going to tell me why now?"

"I told her I wouldn't talk about her with any-one."

"Samantha, my sweet." From the tone of his voice, Sanchez was running out of patience. "I really don't have time to pry it out of you. You might have told her you wouldn't say anything, but here we are, talking about her. Might as well tell me everything."

157

Sam sighed. He was right, as usual. "She didn't exactly contact me. We sort of . . . came across each other." She told him about the website, TheSerialKillerFiles.com, then told him about Bonnie's reaction when the woman first saw her in person.

Sanchez frowned. "Well, isn't that something? The Internet is indeed a strange and wonderful place. And scary as hell, too." He looked at her sternly. "I can't believe you'd go and meet with some perfect stranger you met from a serial killer website. Are you out of your mind?"

"I went during the daytime," Sam said defensively. "And I brought Jason with me."

"Oh really?" The detective raised an eyebrow. "I'm surprised you didn't bring your boyfriend with you."

His words hung in the air. Sam didn't know how to respond to that, either. Frankly, she was tired of making excuses for Matt and how busy he was. He was always busy. So was she. So was everybody. It was starting to get old.

"Anyway," Sanchez said. "So it was a social visit? She just wanted to catch up?"

"Not exactly," Sam said, hesitating again. "She believes my mom was killed by the Butcher, and that she knows the Butcher's real identity. She knows I'm writing a book about it. That's why she wanted to meet in the first place."

"Jesus Christ, now I've heard everything."

Sanchez threw his head back and laughed. "And who is the Butcher? That is, according to our friend Bonnie/Joyce?"

"She hasn't told me yet."

"Of course she hasn't," the detective said, laughing so hard that a patron at the next table glanced over with a smile. "Of course."

"Bobby, she was dead serious." Sam couldn't help but feel annoyed. "I believe she knows exactly who he is."

Sanchez leaned in toward her, his laughter fading. "Have you brilliant conspiracy theorists forgotten that the Butcher is *dead?* And has been since 1985?" He shook his head in frustration, then took a long sip of his coffee. "My sweet, I know you're searching for closure on Sarah's murder, and you know that if I could have solved the case and made an arrest, I would have. Nobody wants her killer found more than me."

Sam gave him a look.

"Other than you, of course," he amended, softening his tone.

"Will you just listen for a minute?" Sam said. "Bonnie knows the identity of the Butcher because he tried to kill her, too. A couple of days after Sarah died, the same guy who was watching Sarah at the McDonald's grabbed Bonnie." Taking a deep breath, she told Sanchez everything that Bonnie had told her, from the chloroform to the bear. "It's why she left town."

"That is definitely a strange story," the detective said. "But it's just that. A story."

"It's true. She even wears a little bear pendant. Around her neck. And she saw the cleaver, Bobby. It was the Butcher."

Sanchez sighed, and it was clear he was no longer amused. "Then why didn't she tell someone? Why didn't she tell me?"

"I don't know, she was scared."

"Fine. She was scared. Understandable." The detective clearly wasn't buying it. "So she leaves the state. Starts a new life under a new name. Makes sense."

"Right . . ." Sam waited for the punch line.

"Then why come back now?" Sanchez said. "Twenty-six years after the fact? Why come back? Why the sudden need to tell her story?"

"I don't know," Sam said, frustrated. "I can only imagine it's because she can't live with what she knows anymore. That she wants the truth to come out once and for all."

"What's in it for her?"

"You sound like Jason."

"I always said that boy was smarter than he looked." Sanchez finished the last of his coffee and then pushed the cup aside. "Samantha, if you want, I'll talk to her. Okay? Would that make you feel better? Maybe she'll tell me the name of who she thinks the Butcher is. I'll run it, we'll see what comes up. Whoever it is that tried to grab her is probably dead by now, but it's worth it to me if it makes you feel better. Is that fair?"

"Yes."

"Where's she staying?"

"Well, that's the thing," Sam said, biting her lip. "She checked out of her motel this morning. I have no idea where she is, and I have no contact information for her."

"OMG." Sanchez shook his head. "That stands for 'Oh my God.' My kids say it all the time. This just keeps getting better and better."

"I know," Sam said, amused. "And please don't say it again. You're about forty years too old for it. So you'll track her down?"

"Why not? It's not like I'm busy or anything." The detective saw the look on her face and softened his tone. "She's probably back in Sacramento. I'll find her. We'll talk."

"You really don't believe me, do you?" Sam said.

"Rufus Wedge was the Butcher, and the Butcher is dead." Sanchez took her hand gently. "That's what I know. Whoever killed your mom was someone else. And whoever grabbed Bonnie/Joyce was someone else. Assuming the woman's even telling the truth. If she is, maybe it was the same guy who killed your mom, and maybe we'll be looking for a different serial killer altogether. But it's *not* the Butcher, okay? You have to let that go. The Butcher was Rufus Wedge, and he's long gone, my sweet."

Sam nodded, allowing the detective to hold her hand. It was a fatherly gesture. Sanchez had always looked out for her. She understood that this wasn't any different, but everything in her gut told her there was more to the story.

"Just promise me you'll keep an open mind," she said.

"Of course I will." Sanchez squeezed her hand. "But you have to promise me the same thing, too."

It was easier said than done.

15

Matt hadn't talked to his grandfather since Monday night, and you know what? That was fine by him. He had no idea what the old man had done with the three Hefty bags full of PJ Wu's body, and you know what? He didn't want to know. So okay, Matt wasn't sleeping well, but it had been a stressful time all around, and you know what? That was life.

There was a light knock on his office door before it opened. Lauryn Kinney poked her head in, her expression tentative. Normally she and Matt got along very well. He offered her a smile, and her whole posture relaxed.

"You look nice," he said. "What's the occasion?"

Lauryn's blond ponytail was sleek and impeccable, and her navy dress fell to her knees. "Thanks. I came straight from the courthouse." She hesitated, clearly not sure whether to say anything more.

Matt forced himself to look interested. "How's that going? It's about custody of your son, right?"

"Yes. It's been hell but my lawyer says not to worry."

"Anything I can do?"

She raised an eyebrow, surprised. "Actually, since you asked, I may need some time off next week. There's another hearing and I need to meet with my lawyer before we go back to court."

Matt nodded. "Say no more. Just let me know the time and we'll do the best we can to work around it."

"I appreciate that, Matt." She smiled, clearly relieved. "I thought it was going to be a problem. Hey, any word from PJ? I tried to call him this morning but his phone is going straight to voice-mail."

Matt's heart skipped a beat and he instantly stiffened. "You, too, huh?" he said, trying to insert the right note of concern into his voice. "Same here."

"I asked around, and none of the staff has seen or spoken to him in the last couple of days," Lauryn said. "I'm a little worried. We both know he hasn't always been the most reliable guy, but he always calls if he's not coming in. Do you have a number for his parents? Maybe they know what's going on."

"They're in San Francisco," Matt said, and that was true. "And he wasn't close to them. But you know what, maybe I should give them a call anyway."

Lauryn frowned. "You don't think anything bad's happened to him, do you?"

"I'm sure he's fine," Matt said. "I've known him a long time. He'd call if he was in trouble."

"Well, that's what I mean. He hasn't called anyone, so what if . . ." She stopped, then shook her head. "You know what, I'm not even going to go there. That's just silly. He's all right, I'm sure. He's probably just being PJ. When you talk to him, make sure you tell him this isn't cool. I know he's your friend and all, but still. We have a business to run."

This time Matt's smile was genuine. "Maybe I should let you ream him out. It would be nice to not be the bad guy for a change."

She laughed. "Anyway, I almost forgot the reason I came back here. The people from the Fresh Network are here. They're waiting for you in the bar."

"Shit, they're early." Matt pushed his chair back and stood up, smoothing the front of his shirt. Opening the drawer, he grabbed a thin silk tie, then paused. "Do I look all right? Tie or no tie?"

"Definitely do the tie."

"What are they like?" he said, wrapping it around his collar and then fumbling with it. "Dammit, I think I need a mirror, I'm not used to doing this blind."

"They seem fine. Here, let me help." Lauryn reached out and helped him with his knot. "There, that's perfect. Don't be nervous," she said with a grin. "They approached you, remember? Just be yourself. You got this. I'll let them know you'll be out in a minute."

She left, closing the door behind her. Matt sat back down in his chair, knees feeling a little wobbly. He was a little nervous about the meeting with the producers, yes, because he really wanted this reality show, and he needed to make a good impression. But it was also the first time anyone had asked about PJ, and lying about it hadn't been as easy as he thought it would be. Taking a deep breath, he ran a hand through his hair. He needed to get a hold of himself. He needed to relax and breathe and focus, and remind himself of what really mattered.

So PJ Wu was dead. Yes, it was a tragedy, and yes, Matt felt terrible. But it had been an accident, okay? Obviously Matt hadn't meant to kill his friend. He'd lost his temper, and had punched the guy, and PJ had fallen, slammed his head into a rock, and died. It was awful and unfortunate, but it had happened, it was done, and nothing could or would bring the guy back to life.

But did that mean Matt's whole life had to stop, too? Did that mean he was no longer entitled to the opportunities he'd worked so hard for? PJ hadn't been close to his family, anyway. His parents were in California, and the rest of his family was in Hong Kong (or was it Taiwan? or Singapore? Matt couldn't remember now). Like Lauryn had just pointed out, PJ hadn't always been the most reliable employee. Nobody even seemed that surprised that he'd missed a couple of days of work without calling.

Besides, bad publicity for Matt would spell bad publicity for the restaurant. He had thirty-five employees and they all depended on him—would it be fair to them if Adobo went downhill?

He'd worked so hard for this, for this opportunity, for this restaurant. Two producers from the Fresh Network were here right now, waiting to speak to him, because of the things he'd accomplished. Because he was somebody important.

So no, there was no way in hell he was about to throw his whole life away over an *accident*. PJ's death didn't seem to bother his grandfather at all . . . so why should it bother Matt?

It doesn't bother Grandpa because Grandpa is a psychopathic serial killer, the little voice in his head whispered.

Matt shook his head hard, forcing the voice to shut up. *Stop with that shit,* he told himself. *That shit won't help.* PJ Wu was gone and there was nothing Matt could do about it. He didn't know what the Chief had done with the body, and frankly, he had absolutely no desire to know. All he could do now was move forward, step up, and take what was rightfully his.

It was showtime.

Smoothing his hair one more time, Matt opened the door and stepped down. "Let's roll," he said under his breath. "You got this."

The female Fresh Network producer was tiny, with wavy dark hair and a dimple on one cheek. Her name was Karen Burgundy, and she looked like a Mini-Me version of Halle Berry with her mocha skin and long-lashed brown eyes. If this was who they sent in to close deals, then Matt couldn't imagine anybody ever saying no.

"The idea is to film a few days' worth of footage, then go back and do the editing before we see what it looks like. Kind of like a trial run," Karen was saying. The tip of her manicured forefinger touched the outer corner of her mouth briefly. Whether she had a habit of doing that, or whether it was a deliberate move on her part to get Matt to look at her lips—which were pouty and full and alluring as hell—he didn't know.

Her skirt was short, red, and flared. Never breaking eye contact with him, she slowly uncrossed one lean leg, then crossed the other over it. It took effort for Matt to not look down.

"So obviously you know that the show will primarily focus on your food trucks, which are just like, super-popular right now." Bernard Vitale was the other producer, and Matt guessed he was gay. He plucked an invisible speck of lint off his fitted cashmere sweater. "But there'll still be a lot of filming here at the restaurant. Either way, we need to see you doing all the actual cooking, serving, and whatever else."

"How many trucks are you featuring?" Matt finally managed to ask, prying his eyes away from Karen. "And how much screen time do I specifically get?"

"It really depends on the rest of your staff. The ones who are good on camera will get a fair chunk of screen time, but you're our star. Expect us to shoot you at least one full day a week, likely a Saturday, when things are busiest." Bernard consulted his iPad. "We were hoping to talk to your assistant head chef, PJ Wu. Is he in today?"

Matt blinked. "Uh, actually, no, he's not." He paused, wondering how much to say. "Actually, guys, I'm not sure he'll be involved. There have been . . . some issues."

"Oh?" Karen said, cocking her head to one side. "What kind of issues? You should know that that's not necessarily a bad thing. Issues can often make for fabulous TV."

Matt smiled. "I'll have to get back to you on that. He's, uh, not exactly the most reliable guy.

Is it a deal breaker if he's not part of the reality show?"

"Hello, it's not a reality show, it's *unscripted television*," Bernard said, immediately annoyed. "I hate that term, *reality show*. We all know that anything on TV isn't exactly reality. I mean, what is?"

"Don't worry too much about it," Karen said, giving Bernard a look. The fingernail was back at the corner of her mouth. "It's you we want, one hundred percent. Whether PJ's available or not."

"But you guys did make a good pair on the Food Truck Challenge last fall." Bernard looked disappointed. "You were like the Nazi, barking orders, and he was rolling his eyes behind your back making the funny one-liners. We'd have to replace him with someone you'd have a similar kind of chemistry with."

"That would probably be anybody here," Matt said with a chuckle. "I'm kind of a hard-ass."

"Hard-asses are hot," Bernard said. "Just look at Gordon Ramsay."

"Exactly," Karen said. "But the difference is, you're actually good-looking. The camera just eats you up. Gordon's not even remotely hot. I can see our female audience falling head over heels in love with you."

"Not to mention gay men," Bernard added.

Matt laughed. He knew they were flattering him, but he didn't mind at all.

"And might I suggest a little tweaking when it comes to your look?" Bernard's tone was delicate. "Don't get me wrong, your hair is fabulous, but I'm betting if you let it grow out a little it would go curly. And curly hair is hot. I actually know someone here in Seattle who could cut it for you properly. I'll give you his number."

"Okay," Matt said, self-consciously running a hand through his hair. "No problem."

"And your clothes . . ." Bernard gave him the once-over, frowning slightly at Matt's tie. "I mean, you obviously look great in a shirt and tie, but you're very dressed up."

"So what am I supposed to wear, a T-shirt?"

"Well . . ." Bernard said. There was a glint in his eyes that made Matt a little uneasy. "Do you work out?"

"Of course I do."

"Mind if I ask you to take your shirt off?"

Matt blinked. "Right now? Are you serious?"

"Trust us," Karen said with a smile.

Looking around the bar, which was empty save for the three of them, Matt got up off his bar stool with a sigh. He quickly removed his shirt and tie, and soon was wearing nothing on top but a black sleeveless undershirt.

"I told you," Bernard said to Karen. "Look at those biceps."

"Oh, I'm looking," Karen said, her eyes

roaming over every inch of Matt's torso. "And so will every other woman in America."

"Now, *this* is your look," Bernard said to Matt. "Sleeveless shirt, pair of jeans. You always show the guns. Always."

Matt was flattered, if a little uncomfortable. "That's fine. Can I put my shirt back on now?"

"If you insist," Karen said with a wink. He felt his face flush.

"But remember, it's a reality show, so while your looks matter, so does your personality." Bernard's tone was prissy but professional. "How you interact with your staff and the customers and the other food trucks owners will make all the difference. The key is to commit to whatever personality you decide to show. Like the whole hard-ass thing? With your looks? Hot," he said. "Very hot."

"I'm fine with all of it," Matt said. "As long as we still focus on the food. And I still have a restaurant to run, don't forget, so I'll need to know what days we're filming way in advance."

"Of course we'll focus on the food." Bernard sounded insulted. "We're the Fresh Network, *hello*. The food is always the focus, but the people are what sells it."

"We'll also need more background on you," Karen said. "Personal stuff. On the Food Truck Challenge, they mentioned that your grandfather is the former chief of police of Seattle and I love the little cameo he gave at the end. He has such a commanding personality. Any chance he'd want to be involved with the show?"

Instantly, Matt tensed. "He's a colorful guy, the Chief. But I highly doubt it."

"The Chief, that's right!" Karen said, clapping her hands together. "I love that. We were thinking he'd be awesome. He's got a very authoritative presence, so alpha male."

"Like you," Bernard said. "But unlike you, he'd be more of a spice instead of the main dish. A little Chief here, a little Chief there."

"He reminds me of someone . . ." Karen paused, thinking. "Oh, what's his name, it's right on the tip of my tongue . . ."

Bernard snapped his fingers. "Clint Eastwood. He's practically a dead ringer, with that square jaw and that steely squint."

"And the cigars," Matt added. "He never goes anywhere without his cherry-flavored cigars."

"Even better," Karen said. "So do you think he'd be interested?"

Matt forced himself to smile, but it felt tight and unnatural. The Chief, a serial killer and now Fresh Network star? How much crazier could things get? "I really don't think so," he said. "It was a fluke that he made an appearance on the Food Truck Challenge at all. I'm not sure he'd want to do a regular thing."

"We'd obviously pay him well," Bernard said. "Worth a shot, right?"

"He definitely doesn't need the money, but I'll talk to him."

"Bring him to dinner tonight," Bernard said. "And I hear you have a girlfriend, right? Who's a published author? Bring her, too."

Caught off guard, Matt paused while he figured out what he wanted to say. "Yeah, I don't know about that, guys. Sam . . . she's not exactly the reality TV type. Sorry, I mean *unscripted television,*" he said when he saw the look on Bernard's face. "And things aren't exactly ideal with us right now."

Karen nodded. Did she look pleased? Matt thought so.

"I understand, Matt, but romantic challenges can add a really great level of drama to the show if that's something you're both willing to be open about." The producer leaned forward, revealing a hint of olive skinned cleavage beneath her crisp white blouse. "We all want the show to be successful, don't we? Just talk to her. Maybe she'd appreciate the publicity it would give her since she's a writer. You never know, she might surprise you."

"Fine, I'll talk to her, too." Matt looked at his watch. "The lunch rush is starting soon. Is there anything else? Or can it wait till dinner tonight?"

"It can wait," Karen said. "But we want you to

know, Matt, that the Fresh Network is really excited about having you on board. You're going to be a big star."

Matt couldn't help but smile. The feeling he had right now was almost impossible to describe. Maybe it was because the producers had been kissing his ass for the past hour, but it felt like every bone in his body was tingling. He could almost hear the clicking of everything he'd ever wanted snapping right into place.

He really was going to be a star. And to think he'd actually considered turning himself in, and throwing it all away.

PJ Wu who?

16

There wasn't a damned thing wrong with Edward's nose, thank you very much.

His eyesight might not be as crisp as it used to be, and his hearing wasn't as sharp, but his nose was still one hundred percent functional at eighty years old. Marisol had always said he had a nose like a wolfhound, and Edward had never disagreed. He was a hunter, and hunters were born with a naturally keen sense of smell.

The only downside was that he couldn't shut it off. He could close his eyes or stick headphones over his ears, but his goddamned nose kept right

174

on working. Which was a real drawback when the whole bus seemed to smell like Bengay lotion and Shalimar perfume.

The sign-up sheet for the day trip to Tulalip had been posted a week earlier, and it filled fast like it always did. The Sweetbay Village Retirement Residence had a full-time activities director, a perky young thing in her early thirties with double-Ds and a mop of curly black hair. Kyla Murray's sole job was to keep the seniors amused several times a week with games of charades and Pictionary (for the old fogies who liked to stand), bingo and gin rummy (for those who didn't), and round robin tennis (for the active folks). And once every two weeks, there was an organized day trip of some sort. When Edward had seen that it was for the big Indian casino north of Seattle, he'd signed up immediately. You had to be quick; the sign-up sheets for day trips were full within a few hours. Village residents liked getting out and about.

Edward enjoyed a good casino once in a while, but that wasn't why he was going.

His seatmate on the bus was a fidgety old fart named Donald Martini, and it was all Edward could do not to break the man's neck. Martini, reeking of Old Spice, had plopped himself down into the aisle seat and had nodded off within sixty seconds. By the time another minute passed, he'd elbowed Edward twice already. When the man's bony elbow dug into his ribs a third time, Edward placed a hand on his seatmate's skinny arm and spoke in a low voice.

"I'll kill you, my friend."

"What's that, Edward?"

"I said try and be still, my friend."

Martini looked instantly apologetic. "Sorry, Edward. I think I need my dosage adjusted. I've been a goddamned spaz all week."

"Probably a good idea."

"Sad about old Greg, huh?"

"Damned shame." Edward spoke in his most agreeable voice. "Terrible accident. A reminder for all of us to be careful. We break too easily nowadays."

The funeral for Greg Bonner had taken place the day before, and a bus had been hired by the Village to take anyone to the funeral home who wanted to pay their respects. Bonner had been found in the kitchen the morning after he died, bright and early, right where Edward had left him. An ambulance had been called, but not the police. It was clear he'd slipped and fallen. No reason to be alarmed.

After all, old folks died in old folks' homes every day.

The bus hummed along and the vibrations weren't unpleasant. The upbeat chatter that had peppered the air for the first twenty minutes of the bus ride was finally beginning to die down.

All around him, gray heads began to loll as his fellow Villagers began to nod off, Donald Martini included.

Looking out the window, Edward watched the traffic go by, then finally closed his own eyes. He was looking forward to Tulalip. It had been thirty years or so since he'd last been there, and it had been fun.

The thing about Indian reservations is that they had an abundance of Indian girls. And Lord knew Edward had never minded Indian girls. He smiled as he recalled the last time he'd been there. It was a fun memory.

AUGUST 1983

He'd spotted her the minute she'd come into the bar. Young with a plain face, the heavy makeup was the only reason she passed for pretty. Cheap clothes showed off her nubile body in all the right spots. The insolent look in her eyes masked her loneliness and need for love. She couldn't have been more than fifteen.

She was perfect.

The bartender eyed her as she sidled up to the bar, but said nothing. She took a seat beside Edward and crossed her legs, her cutoff denim skirt riding up to show her lean, tanned thighs.

"Buy me a drink?" Sweet, husky voice. Dark eyes thickly lined with navy kohl looked up at him. Foundation a shade too light was caked over the blemishes on her forehead and chin, and her lips, coated with a frosty pink lipstick, parted to reveal even, pearly teeth.

"Sure," Edward said. "What'll you have?"

"Shot of Jameson," she said to the bartender.

The man nodded, poured, then placed the shot glass on the counter between them. She tossed it back like a pro. Edward watched carefully for her reaction, but there wasn't one. No grimacing, gagging, or coughing. A solid drinker at fifteen. *Indian girls*. It seemed to be in their DNA.

"Another?" he said, and she nodded. The bartender reappeared and the act was repeated.

She couldn't have been much taller than five two. Maybe a hundred pounds soaking wet. Chipped glitter nail polish on tiny fingers. She had pretty little hands. Four earrings in her right ear, three in her left.

"What's your name?" she said.

"Ed."

"I'm Agatha." Her finger brushed his forearm. "My friends call me Aggie. You can call me that if you want to."

"Okay, Aggie."

"So how come you're here?" Dark eyes were now a tad glazed, whereas a moment ago they'd been clear. The whiskey had kicked in.

"Just passing through."

"Going to Canada?"

"Yep."

"Everybody's always going to Canada. What's so interesting about Canada?"

Edward smiled. "For me, it's where the work is."

She smiled back. "Truck driver?"

"Salesman."

She seemed satisfied with that. "Quarter for the juke box, Ed?"

He fished one out and handed it to her. She took the coin, her fingers grazing his a little longer than was necessary. He felt a small tingle of pleasure. She would do just fine.

A moment later Blondie's "Heart of Glass" came over the loudspeakers. Agatha was back, standing in front of him, swaying hips that still needed time to develop into the curves she was destined to one day have.

But, of course, wouldn't.

"Dance with me, Ed."

He took her hand and eased off his bar stool, allowing her to lead him to the tiny dance floor. There were maybe a dozen people in the bar. Edward had never been here before, and would never come here again after tonight, and so he was pleased he'd picked a good spot. The lighting was extremely dim, the air permeated with cigarette smoke. A man and a woman in their early thirties huddled in the corner, kissing furiously. An affair, clearly. The rest of the patrons were middle-aged men, drinking alone or in pairs, bleary-eyed and world-weary and not paying any attention to the man dancing with a girl who looked young enough to be his granddaughter.

Aggie moved up against him, her narrow hips thrusting against his thighs. She was so petite he could see the top of her head. Her hair was freshly washed and smelled like Head & Shoulders. Her sticky-sweet perfume reminded him of birthday cake. Skinny arms circled his waist. He moved a little to the music. She moved a lot.

A minute later, she looked up. "You like me, don't you, Ed?"

"I most certainly do."

"I can tell." Her flat stomach pressed against his crotch. "I can feel it."

"Can't help it. You're a beautiful girl."

She smiled. "Want to hang out somewhere else?" She pulled him down so her lips were at his ear. "I'm not expensive. I know a place where we can be alone. I do everything. And I mean every-thing." She wiggled her butt, and her hot breath on his neck sent another tingle up his spine.

"How much for a few hours?" he said.

She pulled back to look up into his face, her smile growing wider. "A few hours? Serious?"

He nodded.

"Like . . . gee . . . like . . . two hundred?"

"Okay, let's go."

Her surprise and glee were obvious. She

bounced a little, grabbing his hand again. It was undoubtedly the most money she'd make all week. "We'll take the back way out."

There was a door to the left of the dance floor with a big exit sign overhead. Edward followed her out, sneaking a quick glance over his shoulder before stepping through to the fresh air outside. Nobody was watching them. The bartender was busy chatting up an older woman who'd just come in. The way she was dressed, she could have been Agatha in twenty-five years.

Sorry, he meant *Aggie*. That's what her friends called her, and they were about to become very good friends.

"Hey, Aggie," Edward said once they were outside. "My car's just parked over there. Why don't we go for a drive? It'll be more comfortable."

She hesitated. "There's a motel just—"

"Motel?" Edward frowned. "I don't want to hang out with you in a motel room. Too claustrophobic, and I think I might want you all night now. I was thinking we could go grab some food, go for a drive, find a romantic spot."

She giggled.

"I have plenty of money," he said.

"Lemme see."

He pulled out his wallet, fat with cash, and opened it so she could take a look.

Satisfied, she said, "What kind of food?"

Bingo. "Anything you want. I'm hungry. Aren't you?"

"A little."

"Burgers and fries sound good?"

Her eyes lit up, and in that moment, he saw the little child in her. Something inside him stirred. "Okay."

He drove to a McDonald's twenty minutes away, farther south, closer to Lynnwood. Aggie sat in the front seat with her Big Mac in both small hands. She was eating like she was starving, which she probably was. The burger was polished off in three minutes, and she started to go to work on the fries. One hand fiddled with the radio dial.

"Oh, I love this song," she said. "Mind if I turn it up?"

He shrugged and she jacked up the volume dial. Linda Ronstadt's clear voice melted out of the speakers as she sang about the blue bayou. Aggie joined in, and Edward was surprised to hear that she was a decent singer. Good timing, impressive range, maybe a little thin in the higher registers, but nothing that training wouldn't be able to help. Mind you, it was Marisol who had the real ear—his wife would have been able to confirm whether the girl had any real potential—but Edward thought Aggie did. Her young, sweet voice filled the car and he didn't mind it at all.

Glancing at her sideways, in the dark like this . . . she could almost pass for Lucy.

182

He made a right turn, heading off I-5 and onto a smaller road that at this time of night appeared to lead to nowhere.

"Where are we going?" Aggie had stopped singing. A french fry dangled in one hand. She peered through the windshield, but other than the winding road, there was nothing much to see.

"Taking a shortcut," Edward said.

"But there's nothing out this way. Just forest."

"I know. My friend has a cabin out this way. Hope I can find it. It'll be a bit of a drive, so you should just relax until we get there." Edward smiled sideways at her. "It's pretty, you'll see. Has a fireplace and everything."

"Can't see nothin' right now." She settled back in her seat and popped the french fry into her mouth. "I don't care where we go. I just have to be back before it gets light out, at the latest. I have to get my little brother ready for school."

"I'll make sure you are. I have a camera. You're so beautiful, I was thinking we could take some pictures."

She smiled. "It's extra for pictures, and I'll need the money up front." She placed a hand on his arm as if to soften her words. "But I promise you we'll have a really good time."

"I don't doubt that at all, Aggie. I'll pay you when we get there. I'll even throw in an extra hundred."

"Why?"

"Because I like you," he said. "And I want to help you. Who knows, if this goes well, maybe we can make this a regular thing whenever I pass through every month."

That seemed to please her. "Every month?"

"Yep."

"Wowza!" she said, lifting her arms up over her head. Her french fries spilled over onto her lap. "Oh, oops. I'm so sorry." She started plucking them back up quickly, her eyes darting to his face to gauge his reaction. "I didn't mean to spill. Gosh, I'm so sorry."

Poor little thing. Beaten at home, hooking at fifteen. She really didn't stand a chance.

Really, he was doing her a favor.

"It's okay, Aggie," he said in his most soothing voice. "You'll make it up to me."

"Promise I will. Once we get to the cabin. I'll do anything you want, Ed."

Of course she would. They always did.

Four hours later he was on his way back to Seattle, all traces of Agatha removed from his car.

He turned up the radio, still at the Top 40 station Agatha had left it at. Duran Duran's "Hungry Like the Wolf" came on.

Mouth is alive, with juices like wine
And I'm hungry like the wolf

Fitting.

He opened his eyes when his seatmate drove another elbow into his ribs.

"All right, everyone, we're here." Kyla Murray's sweet voice carried easily from the front of the bus. "Wake up."

Edward sat up straighter and blinked, disappointed to be jolted back to reality. The 1980s had been his favorite decade, by far, and he felt a small sense of loss as the memories of Aggie faded away.

The Sweetbay Village activities director, however, was not a bad consolation prize for being forced back into the present. She was standing at the front of the bus with her clipboard in hand, her bright blue Village golf shirt straining against her ample breasts. Edward felt a stirring in his groin at the sight of her, and looked down, almost hopeful.

Dammit. Nothing today. Not like the other day, with the loose end, Joyce.

"I'll hand you your buffet coupons as you exit the bus. Remember to go and register for a Player's Club card if you don't already have one because you can earn points for your next visit. We'll meet back here at the front entrance at six p.m. You all have my cell phone number if you need me."

Donald Martini was still snoring beside him, and it was finally Edward's turn to drive an elbow into the man's ribs. He did it a little harder than necessary, and the man awoke with a jolt.

Stepping off the bus, Edward took a moment to breathe in the fresh air. Everyone else filed straight into the casino, chattering excitedly like monkeys, the women clutching their purses close as they tended to do.

Edward accepted his coupon from Kyla with a smile and stuffed it into his pocket. He waited until she was busy talking to Donald Martini behind him, who was peppering her with dumb questions, probably just so he could stare at her tits. Not that anyone could blame him.

And then, instead of following the herd into the casino, Edward turned and made a right.

Time to find a girl for some fun.

17

The Green Bean was situated in the heart of Sweetbay, not far from Matt's house. It was probably Sam's favorite coffee shop, because the coffee beans were ground to order and the pastries were made in-house every morning. Since quitting her day job to write full-time, she had become quite the connoisseur of coffee shops.

At the moment, however, her latte and cheese Danish were the last thing on her mind. Pausing her iTunes playlist, she yanked out her earbuds, hardly able to believe what she was reading online. The *Seattle Times* had just uploaded a new article with the headline BODY FOUND IN MARYSVILLE, SECOND BODY FOUND IN SEATTLE AREA.

In the first paragraph, a hiker had discovered the body of a young female in a densely wooded area in north Marysville earlier that morning. The male hiker was Marty Stephanopoulos, age fifty-two, of Marysville. He had veered off the trail to "answer the call of nature," as he put it, and had been shocked to discover a dead female body lying barely three feet away. The young woman's identity had not been released, which told Sam that the victim was likely under the age of eighteen. Stephanopoulos was quoted as saying, "I was midstream when I saw her lying there under a pile of leaves. I totally freaked out." Foul play was "strongly apparent," and the police had ruled it a homicide.

The second paragraph went on to report that another body, also female, was found in a parking lot behind a Mexican restaurant in the Capitol Hill neighborhood in Seattle. The police weren't releasing her identity, as her next of kin had not yet been located, but the article stated she was forty-five years old and a resident of the state of California. The police had also ruled her death a homicide.

Spokespersons for both the Seattle and Marysville police departments confirmed that there was no reason to think the murders were related.

Taking a deep breath, Sam read the article one more time, her brain going a mile a minute.

Was it possible that the second victim, the older female, was Bonnie Tidwell?

Sam hadn't heard from the woman since she'd dropped her off at her motel the other night. Sam had given Bonnie her phone number and mailing address, and had invited her to have dinner at Matt's restaurant if Bonnie was able to make the time before heading back to Sacramento. Things had been tense between them, but Sam was hoping the woman would change her mind about opening up.

But Bonnie had never called. And as Sam had told Sanchez the previous day, the older woman had checked out of the Sixth Avenue Inn that morning.

A shiver passed through her and Sam buttoned up her cardigan, even though the Green Bean was a little warm. She hated to bother the detective, but she didn't see what choice she had but to call him. If she didn't, this would bug her all night. She finished off her Danish and then reached for her phone. But before she could scroll for his number, it rang.

"How weird, I was just about to call you," Sam said. "What timing."

"Bet I know why." Detective Robert Sanchez's

voice was grim. "Is it because you haven't heard from Bonnie Tidwell?"

"Oh shit," Sam said, her heart beginning to race. "Don't even tell me."

"You already know?"

"Just tell me. Is she dead?"

"Yes, she is." Sanchez sounded both surprised and suspicious. "How did you know?"

Sam sighed, taking a moment to process what Sanchez had just confirmed. *Poor, poor Bonnie.* "An article was just uploaded to the *Seattle Times* website. They mentioned a dead body, female, forty-five, from California."

Sanchez grunted. "At least they didn't say her name. Or shit, did they?"

"No, it said you were still trying to locate her family." Sam rubbed her eyes, feeling the onset of a headache. "Bobby, I don't understand. When did this happen? The article said she was stabbed behind some Mexican restaurant? I just saw her two days ago."

"She had a single wound to the chest. Medical examiner thinks it was likely made by an ice pick. Official cause of death is exsanguination."

"So she bled to death." Sam closed her eyes.

"I'm sorry, my sweet."

"Do they know who did it?"

"We're working on it."

Sam's eyes widened. "It's *your* case?"

"Afraid so. When the call came in and they told

me who it was, of course I asked for it. Did she ever tell you if she had kids, or a boyfriend? I can't seem to find anyone, here or in California."

"She never had kids, she said. Just two ex-husbands. If she had a boyfriend, she didn't mention it to me." Taking a few seconds to compose herself, she said, "The other murder isn't related?"

"The one in Marysville? No, I just talked to the detective working the case up there, and it doesn't seem like it. He said that the victim is a seventeen-year-old high school dropout from Everett. She lived in a rental house up in Tulalip, fairly close to the casino, with seven other people, all about her age. Not sure if she was into drugs but it wouldn't surprise me. No record, worked part-time at Walmart, and when she wasn't working, she hung out a lot at the Wheels Go Round truck stop diner off I-5. Her boyfriend works there as a fry cook, and he's older. Like thirty."

"Yikes, that's pretty old to be dating a teenager. Did Marysville PD talk to the boyfriend?"

"Of course, but he was working at the diner the whole day, and multiple witnesses have confirmed it. He definitely didn't do it."

"Okay, and what else did the detective say?"

"Not much. Someone remembers seeing her talking to a homeless man and then leaving with him after a few minutes. She never came back to the diner. Boyfriend called the cops last night when she wouldn't return any of his calls, but they didn't follow up on it because she wasn't considered a missing person yet. They found her body this morning, but she'd been dead for at least fifteen hours. She'd been raped with some kind of blunt object, could have been a baseball bat, but they're not sure. Cause of death was strangula-tion."

"Did he penetrate her, too?"

"The ME says it's hard to tell, but possibly not," Sanchez said. "No fluids were found in or around her vagina or anus."

Sam shuddered. She was a visual person and it took effort not to picture what the detective had just described to her. *That poor, poor girl. Nobody deserved to die like that. Nobody.*

"So they think the homeless man might have done it?" she finally said.

"They're looking for him, but they haven't found him yet. The homeless guy, he's in his fifties, and apparently he's a regular at the truck stop, and around Marysville in general, so they'll catch up to him soon if they haven't already. He does a lot of odd jobs, holds up signs on street corners for some of the local businesses, that kind of thing. Apparently he never bothered anyone, though."

"Maybe he was paid to lure her out."

"That's definitely possible." He hesitated. "Listen, Samantha, there's one other thing, but if I tell you, it stays between you and me. This info hasn't been released yet. I'm not even sure if I should tell you because I know what you're going to say."

"Tell me." Her breath stopped.

"The victim's hand was chopped off. Fairly cleanly, below the wrist."

Sam froze. "The left or the right?"

"The left."

"Oh God. The Butcher—"

"We're not going to have this discussion right now, okay? We can talk about it more later when I see you in person. But yeah, let's just say I'm starting to think you might not be totally off base." Sanchez sounded muffled, as if he was covering the receiver with his mouth, which he probably was.

Holy crap, did he actually believe her? She was almost afraid to hope. "Then when are we seeing each other?"

"At some point you'll have to come in and make an official statement about Bonnie/Joyce. It's possible you were the last person to see her alive other than her killer. But it doesn't have to be today, since we've already talked."

"You don't want me to come now?"

"No, I'm too swamped. I'm working on a couple of different things, and I'm actually going to see your boyfriend in a little bit."

"You're going to see Matt?" Sam was surprised. "About what?"

"The parents of one of his employees filed a missing persons report," Sanchez said. "His name is PJ Wu. You know him?"

"Of course I know PJ." Sam's mouth hung open for a moment. "He's missing? Matt never mentioned it."

"I'm sure he's been busy. I know the feeling. I wouldn't normally do a missing persons case, but the detective who caught it recognized Adobo as Matt's restaurant and knew that I knew you guys. I offered to go talk to the staff there, though I'm now wondering why. I got too much going on."

Sam's head was spinning. She had to agree with Sanchez; it was just all too much. PJ was missing? What the *hell* was going on today? And why wouldn't Matt have mentioned that their friend had disappeared? Surely he knew.

Mind you, her boyfriend had been so busy, all they'd really done the last few days was exchange a handful of text messages. She hadn't seen him since that fight in the restaurant, she realized suddenly.

"I'll call you later, okay?" Sanchez was saying. "Set up a time for you to come in. In the meantime, if you think of anything regarding Bonnie/Joyce, call me."

"Of course."

They disconnected, and Sam closed her eyes again, needing a moment of silence to process

193

everything the detective had just told her. Who had stabbed Bonnie? Who'd even want to? And was it actually possible there was a new Butcher victim? How could the two murders *not* be connected? Sam didn't care if she was a civilian, she was going to figure this out. It was all too coincidental, and she needed answers. And now, of course, the alarming news about PJ Wu. She hoped he was okay.

As sad as Sam was about Bonnie's death—because there was no denying that the woman had been very kind by providing as much information as she could about Sam's mother—Sam had to admit she felt very disappointed. Bonnie was the only person who knew the truth about the Butcher's real identity. And now she was taking it to her grave.

But Bonnie *had* mentioned that the Butcher was still alive. What was it she'd said, exactly? *Monsters like that don't die unless they're killed.*

If they nailed the wrong guy back in 1985, that was almost thirty years ago. Assuming the killer was somewhere between the age of thirty and fifty, as Rufus Wedge had been (and as most serial killers tended to be), then it was entirely possible that Bonnie was right, and that the Butcher was still alive. At his youngest, he'd be sixty. At the oldest, around eighty.

He'd be old, yes, but not necessarily dead.

But was he still killing? That was the thing that

Sam couldn't wrap her mind around. It was one thing to have gone uncaught all these years . . . but to still be killing? At his age? And it was another thing to have continued to kill after 1985 for a few years, as Sam's theory had been all along. But to be silent for the last two decades, only to kill again *now?* What in the world could have triggered that?

Fuck it. She needed to talk to Edward Shank. He'd spent a good chunk of his career catching killers. He would know the answer to this.

18

Matt was not expecting to see the middle-aged detective sitting at the bar chatting with Frankie the bartender when he arrived at Adobo. Though Robert Sanchez was an old friend of Samantha's, Matt had met him only a handful of times, and it certainly wasn't commonplace for the detective to drop by the restaurant. There was only one reason Sanchez would be here, and Matt wasn't sure he was ready. He ducked into his office quickly before the man could spot him.

He needed to compose himself. He was feeling totally off today. He wasn't sure how many glasses of wine he'd had the night before; he'd lost count after four. Karen, the producer from the Fresh Network, had kept him up late and paid the tab. They'd had dinner at the Pink Door, famed in Seattle for their live cabaret and burlesque show, and while the evening had been fun, Matt had realized almost immediately that they were no longer there to discuss business. The low-cut, skintight black dress Karen had shown up in had been the first clue. Bernard begging off early to go back to the hotel and watch *Grey's Anatomy* had been the second clue.

Work clearly hadn't been on Karen's mind. While she'd expressed disappointment at neither Sam nor the Chief being able to make dinner (both of them had declined Matt's invite, citing other plans), the producer's behavior suggested otherwise. She'd greeted him with a kiss on the cheek, her lips lingering on his skin a little longer than necessary. She'd laughed at all his jokes, frequently touched his arm as they spoke, and there hadn't been one word mentioned about the reality show—sorry, *unscripted television series* —all night long.

He hadn't slept with her, but dammit, he'd come very close. He wasn't proud of how far he'd let things get, but Christ, he and Sam were so emotionally and physically disconnected that it almost didn't feel like cheating.

Even though he knew damn well it was.

Taking a deep breath, Matt left his office and made his way toward the bar, willing himself to stay relaxed.

"I thought that was you, Bob." Matt extended a hand, and Sanchez slid off his bar stool to shake it. "Nice to see you. Sam send you here for an early lunch?"

"Nice to see you again, too, Matt. No, I'm actually here on official police business."

Here we go. Heart lurching, Matt forced himself to react with surprise, careful not to overdo it. "Well, that's not something I hear every day. Happy to help with whatever I can. Beer? Glass of wine?"

"I'm on the clock. But a Coke would be great."

"Frankie, two Cokes, please, and an order of *lumpia*," Matt said to the bartender. "Bob, why don't we sit over there? A bit more privacy."

They took seats across from each other in a corner booth, and Frankie arrived with their Cokes. "Food will be right up, guys."

Sanchez smiled at the bartender, then took a long sip of his soda. "I'm sure you're a busy guy, so I won't take up too much of your time. I'm here about PJ Wu. He works for you, yes?"

"He does, and has been for seven years now." Matt frowned. "Why do I get the feeling you're about to tell me something horrible?"

The detective's expression remained neutral. "When's the last time you saw him?"

"Three days ago. He was scheduled to work the last two days, but he never showed."

"Is that unusual?"

"It's . . . happened before," Matt said with the just the right amount of hesitation. "He's had some personal issues."

"And what can you tell me about those personal issues?"

Before they could answer, Jimmy was back with a steaming plate of fried *lumpia*. "Fresh out of the pan, gentlemen," the bartender said. "I'd give it a minute to cool."

"Thanks, Frankie," Matt said.

"That smells delicious." Sanchez leaned forward and inhaled. "What are they?"

"Minced pork, onion, garlic, and a few other top-secret ingredients, in a thin flour wrap and pan fried. Try it with the homemade sweet chili sauce," Matt said, moving the plate closer to the detective. "If you don't love them, I'll take it personally. It's my grandmother's recipe."

"Do I use my fingers?"

"Of course you do. You're in a Filipino restaurant. Only way to go."

Smiling, Sanchez dipped a *lumpia* into the sweet chili sauce and took a bite. Chewing slowly, he closed his eyes. "Oh hell. That's good. I mean really good. Kind of like spring rolls, but . . ."

"So much better."

"Yes," Sanchez said, and the two men shared a laugh. "I need to come in more often." He popped another *lumpia* into his mouth.

"So long as you bring your family and friends."

"So about PJ . . ." the detective said, his mouth full.

"Right. You were asking about his personal life," Matt said. "I honestly don't know too much about it. We're not that close."

"Really?" Sanchez swallowed his food. He looked surprised as he dusted his fingers off and reached for his Coke. "Frankie the bartender said you guys go back a long way."

"We were friends in college, but we don't really socialize much anymore," Matt said, silently cursing Frankie. "Mainly it's just a business relationship these days. Not his fault, I'm just so busy with the restaurant and food trucks. And there's a TV show on the Fresh Network in the works. Did Sam tell you?"

"No, she didn't, but congrats. That's great news." The detective cleared his throat. "I spoke to PJ's wife this morning. Sharon. Well, I guess she's his soon-to-be ex-wife. She said PJ has a gambling addiction."

Matt nodded. "That's true."

"How much did you know about it?"

"Not too much," Matt said ruefully. "I think he mainly bet on sports. Sometimes he'd do an all-night poker thing. He'd sometimes ask for an advance on his pay. He seemed to be more down than up."

"Most gamblers are." Sanchez sighed. "Anyway, his soon-to-be ex-wife filed the missing persons report. He missed a court appearance. Since nobody's heard from him in twenty-four hours, we have to look into it."

Matt frowned. "Well, I hate to say it, Bob, but PJ hasn't been the most reliable employee lately. He's been late a few times, and I've had to speak to him about his attitude."

"Frankie mentioned that the two of you had it out the other day."

Goddamn you, Frankie. "We had a disagreement, yeah. About his lack of punctuality, mainly. If he wasn't such a good cook, I probably would have fired him a long time ago."

"But you didn't fire him? The other day?"

"No," Matt said. "I told him to go home. I dismissed him for the day because he wasn't in the right frame of mind to work."

"And that was the last time you saw him."

"Yes. I can ask the staff if anyone's spoken to him, but I doubt it. They would have told me."

The detective leaned in slightly. "Between you and me, Matt, you think PJ blew town?"

Inside, Matt cheered, but outwardly he made sure to continue to seem concerned. "I honestly don't know what to think, but I'd have to say it's totally possible. He was always owing people money, and he knew a lot of shady folks. It wouldn't surprise me if it all caught up to him and he decided to split. He and Sharon didn't get along."

"She made that very clear." Sanchez's phone buzzed and he checked it quickly before slipping it back into his breast pocket. "Mind if I hang out here a little while, talk to some of the other employees? Maybe he mentioned something to someone about where he might be going."

"Of course." It took a huge amount of effort for Matt not to sigh with relief. "Stay as long as you want, and please finish the *lumpia*. If you want anything else, just let Frankie know, and it's on the house."

"Considering how good it is, maybe I will order something more. What's good?"

Matt laughed, slipping out of the booth. "What kind of question is that? Everything's good. Tell you what, I'll surprise you. I'll even make it myself."

Sanchez grinned. "Your girlfriend says you don't have much time to cook these days."

"Sam's right. I miss it."

Sanchez's dark eyes appraised him. "She's a good girl, isn't she?"

Matt nodded.

"Make sure you take care of her, Matt."

Matt forced a smile. "Of course. I'd better get cooking, Bob. Nice seeing you, and keep me posted about PJ."

It was a relief to escape to the kitchen and away from the detective's prying eyes. He'd survived the questioning (*interrogation*), but as he prepared the man's meal, he couldn't help but wonder.

What had the Chief done with the body?

Or, he should say, body *parts?*

19

The male nurse at Sweetbay Village escorted Sam right to Edward's room even though she hadn't asked, smiling at her the whole way. Miguel was really good-looking, she had to admit, and she snuck a few peeks at his biceps, clearly visible under the dark blue scrubs he wore. She was very aware that it had been a while since she'd last had sex, and she felt her cheeks burn at the thought.

Was Matt having sex with someone else? Her stomach churned. She couldn't let herself think about that right now.

In the hallway, they were passed by a couple of paramedics, who nodded to Miguel and then gave her the once-over.

"Mrs. Barney's going to be okay," the taller one said, slowing down. He was speaking to Miguel but looking at Sam. "BP was a little high but nothing serious. She says she's trying to wean herself off her blood pressure meds, but she never talked to her doctor about it. She had a small scratch on her arm from the fall, but that's it."

"Thanks, Chris. We'll keep an eye on her."

"We'll probably see you tomorrow," the other paramedic said, winking at Sam, and the three men shared a laugh.

"The ambulance must be here all the time," Sam said to the nurse as they continued down the hallway. "I'm sure there are all kinds of medical emergencies."

"Not just medical emergencies, but death." Miguel placed a hand lightly on her back and steered her around the corner. "One of the residents croaked last week. Old guy fell in the kitchen while getting his usual midnight snack, hit his head on the way down. Head wound, lots of blood."

"Wow, thanks for the visual."

"Come on, I know you can handle it. You write about true crime."

She glanced at him. "How did you know that?"

"The Chief told me. He's quite proud of you."

Sam laughed. "Is he? He never tells me that."

"He tells everyone, and I can see why." The smile was back on Miguel's face, and it brought out the dimple in his left cheek. He lifted an arm to scratch the back of his head, and his biceps flexed. "You know, I don't think you visit your grandfather often enough."

Sam laughed again. "The Chief isn't my grandfather. I'm actually dating his grandson."

They stopped in front of room 214. "Lucky guy."

"Which one?"

"Both of them," Miguel said with a wink before walking away. "Don't be a stranger."

Edward opened the door before she could even knock, and Sam blinked at the sight of the old man. He looked tired, exhausted even, and his sour expression caused Sam to take a half step back.

"That pretty boy nurse making a pass at you, Samantha?" The Chief poked his head out, peering down the hallway. Thankfully Miguel had already rounded the corner and was out of sight. "I could hear the two of you from behind the door. You tell me if he's harassing you, and I'll put a boot up his ass."

"Nothing to worry about, Chief," Sam said. "I'm sure he flirts with all the girls here, young and old."

"Probably, but he shouldn't be. I don't give a shit how good-looking he is, you're Matthew's lady, and that's disrespectful to me."

"So glad you're making it about you," Sam said dryly. "Now, are you going to invite me in so we can eat, or am I going to stand in the hallway all afternoon?"

"You brought food?" Looking down at the Green Bean box in her hand, he finally grinned and shooed her inside. "Why didn't you say that?"

"What's got your panties all in a bunch?" Sam asked, handing Edward the bakery box and shaking off her coat. Throwing it on the sofa, she appraised him. "You seem awfully wound up today. And you don't look so great. You feeling okay?"

"I'm fine. I've just been a little bored, I suppose. Not much going on here."

"No gin rummy? Or bingo? Or what's that other one that old people like to play . . ." Sam snapped her fingers. "Backgammon?"

"Ha!" He gestured to the sofa. "Sit where you like, and I'll make tea."

"I guess I should have called first. How's your hip?"

"Hip's fine. I may have overdid it on my walk the other day but it's all right. And by the way, you never have to call first if you're bringing me cannolis from the Green Bean."

"How'd you know they were cannolis? You haven't even looked inside the box."

"Don't need to, I can smell them." Edward moved slowly around the kitchenette, opening cabinets. "Did I ever tell you I dated Marie Cossetto?"

"The owner of the Green Bean? No," Sam said, settling into the couch. "When was this?"

"Oh, a lifetime ago. She was Marie Beaudreau back then." Edward plugged in the kettle and came back around. "We were just kids, really. This was before I even went to the police academy."

"What happened?"

"She dumped me for Paulie Cossetto." He chuckled at the memory. "I was heartbroken. But then I met Marisol, and the world was right again."

"Didn't Paulie end up in prison? For some kind of white-collar crime thing?"

"Yeah, he was an investment guy. Swindled his clients out of millions, went away for twenty years. He's out now, though, living in Puyallup, and of course they're divorced." The kettle whistled and he headed back to the kitchenette. "I knew Paulie. He really wasn't a bad guy."

"We'll have to disagree on that," Sam said. "He obviously was if he bankrupted the people that trusted him with their money."

"It's never that black-and-white, Samantha," Edward said, returning with her tea. "Not everyone is all bad or all good. Good people do bad things every day, and bad people do good things every day."

It seemed an odd thing to say for someone who'd spent a lifetime catching criminals. Sam waited for him to elaborate, but the Chief seemed content to let his words hang in the air, and the two sipped their tea in silence for a moment.

"So the reason I'm here," she finally said, "is I wanted to pick your brain. There've been two murders in the last day. Middle-aged woman and a teenage girl."

"Saw it on the news a little while ago," Edward said. "The middle-aged woman was stabbed behind Las Cucarachas. That's too bad, I like that place. They have good *carne asada*."

"I knew the woman." Sam sipped her tea. "Her name was Bonnie Tidwell. She was a friend of my mother's. She came into town to see me, to . . ." She paused. "To tell me what she could about my mother."

"Jesus Christ." Edward looked at her with concern. "I'm sorry, Samantha. That's a damn shame."

"Spoke to Robert Sanchez a little while ago. He's working the case."

The Chief nodded. "Good. I like Bobby, he was always a hard worker. Did he give any information that wasn't in the news?"

She shook her head. "He's working on it."

"You said there were two murders?"

"The other one was a seventeen-year-old. Happened in Marysville, not far from the big casino. She was raped and strangled, and her hand was cut off."

The Chief's face was hard to read. Sam supposed it was hard for the man to feel emotion when it came to murder, having been in homicide for almost forty years. "Is that so? That wasn't in the papers."

"Bobby told me. He talked to the detective at Marysville PD who caught the case. I imagine they're keeping it quiet for now."

The old man nodded. "Of course they are. And you're here because it reminds you of something."

"The Butcher." Sam leaned forward. "Chief, her hand was chopped off. Likely with a cleaver, just below the wrist bone. Her *left* hand."

Edward smiled, but there was no humor in it, only indulgence. "That always was the Butcher's signature move. Someone obviously copied it."

"What if someone didn't?"

The Chief barked a laugh. "You're still on that track, eh? Rufus Wedge is dead, my dear. I was there, remember?"

Sam took a deep breath. "Yes, but what if Rufus Wedge wasn't the Butcher?"

Edward sighed and took a sip of his tea. "We've been over this before, Samantha. Many times. You know I'm always interested in your theories, but I don't know what more insight I can offer. Wedge was our best suspect. Maybe the case wouldn't have held up at trial, but that doesn't mean he didn't do it."

"Well, things are different now," Sam said. "Technology has come a long way. If there's a trace of anything on her body left behind from her killer, they'll find it. You can't just kill someone and get away with it anymore."

Edward laughed again, and this time he seemed genuinely amused. "Sure you can," he said. "Happens every goddamned day. Now what do you say we break open that box of cannolis? I've been patient long enough."

20

Even though the rest of the house was dark, the lights were on in the bedroom, and that meant Matt was home. Sam was perfectly positioned under the magnolia tree in the corner of his back-yard, the full moon behind the clouds providing just enough light for her to see her surroundings while still remaining in the shadows. The deck he was building was almost finished and it provided a bit of cover as well. Looking up at his lit bedroom window, she waited.

So okay, she was totally spying on her boy-friend. And yes, it was ridiculous and humiliating, and she wasn't proud of herself. People did stupid things to get answers. Matt had been pulling away for a long time now, although if Sam was really honest with herself, he'd never been completely available. And something had to change.

A rustling noise made her jump, and she turned to see a squirrel paused nearby, sitting on its haunches, watching her with suspicious, glinting eyes. If the squirrel could actually think, it would probably be wondering what in the hell this woman was doing hiding under a tree at midnight.

And if the squirrel could actually talk, it would have been a fair question. The answer was, she needed to catch him red-handed. She needed a concrete reason—an inarguable, tangible, very strong reason—to walk away from this relationship, because otherwise, she wasn't sure she ever could. Or would.

Sam didn't know for certain whether Matt had actually had sex with the slutty female producer from the Fresh Network (which, let's be real here, didn't come close to being as classy as the Food Network, even on its best day). But everything in her gut told her he had, and might still be.

Oh yeah, she knew all about Karen Burgundy. Though Sam had initially turned down Matt's invitation to dinner at the Pink Door with the Fresh Network producers, she'd changed her mind. She might not be interested on appearing on her boyfriend's reality show, but that didn't mean she couldn't be at the dinner to support him. She loved him, despite how difficult things had been lately. And frankly, she wasn't sure why they were so disconnected now, and why Matt could never seem to make time for her, and why he'd become so strangely private ever since moving into the Chief's old house.

Sam had arrived at the Pink Door thirty minutes late, well after the burlesque show had started, and she'd rushed inside, apologies for her tardiness on the tip of her tongue. That's when she'd seen them. They were seated at a table right by the stage, huddled close and whispering like lovers. The image of that slutty producer's hand on her boyfriend's leg, leaning in to shove her desperate cleavage in his face, was burned in Sam's brain. It had taken all her willpower not to grab the woman by her hair extensions and punch her. She had never felt so angry, so insulted, and so hurt, all at the same time.

Still, though, the public display of inappropriateness wasn't quite enough to convict Matt. Flirting with and being attracted to another woman were one thing, but it didn't mean he had necessarily crossed the line into Cheaterville. If he had, though, they were over. Sam knew she could never forgive him, and either way, she needed to know.

The lit bedroom wasn't telling her much. She thought she could make out Matt's silhouette behind the curtains, but she couldn't confirm whether or not he was actually alone. *Dammit.*

Clenching her teeth, she began to creep through Matt's backyard. Within a few seconds she had crossed the nearly finished deck and was at his back door. She paused, deciding what to do. The house had never had an alarm system. The Chief had always believed that security alarms were essentially useless, because if someone was determined to murder you, then no alarm system in the world was going to stop them from doing it. And if someone was going to rob you, well then, let 'em. That's what insurance companies were for.

She tried the door handle, but of course the back door was locked. No surprise there. Where did he keep that spare key? After a minute of searching, she found it hiding in the planter a few feet away.

Inserting the key, she held her breath, listening for the click that told her the door was unlocked. Twisting the doorknob, she pushed the door open slowly, then paused again before stepping inside. Elmo, Matt's cat, immediately came to greet her, and she knelt down to pet him. The Abyssinian purred and nudged her hand, but thankfully that was the only sound he made.

She closed the door behind her as quietly as she could, and stepped farther into the kitchen. The main floor of the house was completely dark, but Sam had been here enough times when Edward had owned it that she knew the house well.

Moving silently through the kitchen and down the hallway, she navigated her way toward the steep staircase. She took the steps as quickly as she could, knowing a few of them would creak, and reached the top of the landing in record time. She paused again. Matt's bedroom was at the end of the hall, his door open just a smidge.

She stood still, cocking her head toward the bedroom. At first she couldn't hear anything over her own breathing, but then all of sudden, there it was.

He wasn't alone, goddammit. Sam could totally *hear* them.

Oh God, it was really happening. Matt and that slut were in his room, right now, fucking like a couple of dogs in heat, and the confirmation of this hit Sam like a sledgehammer to the gut. Yes, she had wanted to catch him, and yes, she needed to see it for herself, but never could she have anticipated a pain like the one that was stabbing her in the chest like an ice pick, making it impossible to breathe.

They weren't being overly loud, but there was no mistaking that her boyfriend was in his bedroom and *totally having sex with someone else.* That fucking slutty producer with Sam's boyfriend of three goddamned years? It was unconscionable, and Sam felt the rage build up inside her. Willing herself to remain some semblance of calm, she moved closer to the door, every inch of her body tense. She could hear sounds of a bed squeaking, and Matt grunting, and that Halle Berry clone moaning like the disgusting whore she so obviously was.

How could he do this to her? How could Matt have actually brought that witch home? They were really in there, fucking each other as if they had the goddamned right to do it, as if there wasn't someone else in the picture who loved him, that they'd be *hurting.* What gave them the goddamned *right?* Who the hell did they think they *were?*

The pain would come later. Right now, Sam was so mad she could stab them both.

213

Striding toward the bedroom, she pushed the door open before she could overthink it.

And got an eyeful, all right.

Matt was on the bed, but he wasn't naked. He was wearing a T-shirt and a pair of basketball shorts that had been pulled down to his knees. His erect penis was in one hand, and he appeared to be alone.

Yes, totally and completely alone . . . unless the two people having sex in the porn movie on the wall-mounted TV counted.

"Holy fuck!" Matt shrieked, his face a mask of shock and horror at the sight of her. Scrambling, he pulled his shorts up over his erection, swearing when the elastic band snagged his penis. Grabbing the remote, he thrust it toward the TV in an attempt to stop the movie, but all he managed to do was hit the fast-forward button. The two people having sex onscreen were now on warp speed, and if Sam hadn't been so surprised by the entire thing, she might have laughed.

Her boyfriend's face was a flaming shade of red that Sam couldn't recall ever having seen before. He glared at her, chest heaving. "What the fuck? What are you . . . how the hell did you get in? Why didn't you call first? Oh Jesus Christ."

He was almost shaking from embarrassment. His legs were jammed together on the bed, and he sat with his arms crossed over his chest, his expression a blend of guilt and indignation as he continued to glare at her.

Sam bit her lip. The relief she was now feeling was so palpable she thought she might crumple. As she tried to figure out what to say to her boyfriend, the DVD decided to resume regular play again. Onscreen, the girl with the big fake boobs looked up at the man mounted on top of her and moaned, "Yeah, harder! Fuck me! Just like that! Harder!"

Matt finally managed to mute the sound, staring at her, and Sam spoke into the strained silence.

"Oops."

Because really, what else could she say?

21

Edward's new family physician didn't look old enough to drink, let alone prescribe medication, and he eyed the young doctor suspiciously as the man took his blood pressure. He supposed the doctor seemed proficient enough, and so far was quite amiable, at least as far as doctors went. "I didn't realize Dr. Kleinberg retired. Nobody told me," he said, feeling grumpy.

"Sorry about that. They should have sent you a letter." Dr. Brian Ross unstrapped the blood pressure cuff from Edward's arm. "Did you move recently?"

"Yep. Old folks' home. Sweetbay Village."

"I'm familiar with Sweetbay," Ross said. "Don't see a lot of patients from there, though. Don't they have their own doctors?"

"That's the problem," Edward said, shifting his weight a little. He was sitting on the patient table, feeling exposed and chilly in the thin green smock they had made him wear for the appointment. "They have a few different doctors that rotate in and out. Hard to see the same person twice, and I'm not fond of inconsistency. Plus they only see patients on Tuesdays and Thursdays."

"And today is Monday." Ross grinned. Picking up his iPad, he made a few notes, then grabbed his stethoscope. "I'm going to listen to your heart now."

"What happened to my folder?" Edward asked.

Holding up a finger, Ross pressed the stethoscope against Edward's chest and listened for a few moments. Nodding, he said, "What's a folder? Some archaic thing? Everything I need to know about you is in the computer now. Welcome to the year 2014."

Edward grunted. "I don't trust those tablet things. Hit one wrong key and next thing you know, everything's gone."

"That's the beauty of it. The iPad has no keys." Ross laughed. "But I get what you're saying, and my grandfather would share the same sentiment. He thinks computers and the Internet are everything that's wrong with the world nowadays. He still writes letters. By hand. I can't even imagine." The doctor shuddered as he typed a few more notes into his tablet. "Your heart sounds good, by the way. Nice and strong. You seem to be in great shape for eighty years old. Do you still exercise?"

"I walk a lot. And if my hands and hip aren't bothering me I'll play a little tennis, do a few sit-ups, that kind of thing."

"That's more than what I do," Ross said with a grin. "Keep it up. Whatever you're doing, it's working. You have the blood pressure of a man half your age. Wish mine was as good."

"I've always had good blood pressure." Edward was pleased at the compliment. "I don't let things get to me, know what I'm talking about? Stress is not healthy. I've never been one to stress."

"So tell me about Sweetbay Village," Ross said, putting aside his iPad. "We were thinking of sending my wife's mother there, but my cyes almost fell out of my head when I found out how damned expensive it is. You think it's worth the money? Mind you, it's either that or she lives with us, and I'm not sure you can put a price on the freedom of not having your mother-in-law move in. She's just, how do I put it . . . a difficult woman. If she moves in, I'm going to need blood pressure medication for sure. Do you like it there?"

Dr. Ross had to be the chattiest doctor Edward had ever met with. And yep, just a kid. He'd learn soon enough, as all doctors did, that time was money.

"It's fine." Edward waved a hand. "Food's pretty good and there's lots of stuff to do. I wasn't crazy about moving out of my house, but my hip had been bothering me and I took a fall, scared my grandson. You ever heard of Matthew Shank? He's a chef here in Seattle, owns a restaurant called Adobo. Lots of his recipes are from his grandmother, may God rest her soul."

"I'm sorry for your loss, Mr. Shank. I've heard of Adobo, been meaning to stop in. I heard the food is terrific." Ross smiled again. "How does the grandson of the chief of police end up a chef, anyway?"

"Call me the Chief, everybody does." Edward felt a tingle of pleasure at the recognition. The doctor might be young, but he obviously wasn't ignorant. "And that's a question for Matthew, though I can say he never really expressed an interest in following in my footsteps. He was very close to his grandmother. I used to worry he might be a pansy, because you know, a little boy in an apron, following his grandmother around in the kitchen? A bit queer, right? But I'm told cooking is a perfectly acceptable male profession nowadays. Plus he's always liked girls, thank sweet Jesus."

Ross laughed out loud. "Well, I can say that ladies do love a man who can cook. I'm pretty good in the kitchen myself, and a good home-cooked meal never fails to win me bonus points with the wife."

"If you want to keep your marriage intact, I recommend sending the mother-in-law someplace that isn't your house. Sweetbay Village is as good as it gets."

"I appreciate the recommendation."

"You're welcome. How old are you, anyway?"

"I'll be thirty next month."

"Christ. I got whiskey on my shelf that's older than you."

"I have to confess, I was looking forward to meeting you when I saw your name on my schedule this morning. I'm kind of a fan." Ross leaned back in his chair and smiled. "You were a guest lecturer for one of my psychology classes."

Edward raised an eyebrow. "That so? Which college?"

"Puget Sound State."

"What was the professor's name again?" Edward frowned, trying to remember. "Pretty little thing. Chinese, I think, but not fresh off the boat, spoke perfect English."

Ross chuckled and shook his head. "Dr. Tao. Sheila Tao."

"That's it," Edward said. "I remember her well. She hounded me for a year to come and guest lecture, but public speaking was never my thing. Finally gave in, though. She was fascinated with the psychology of serial killers."

"Aren't we all?"

"And to think she almost got killed by one herself."

"I read about that," Ross said. "That was a messed-up story."

"That's what happens when you fuck with crazy."

"You were great, by the way." The doctor smiled. "Your presentation, I mean. It was cool to hear about Rufus Wedge from the perspective of the cop who caught him. And killed him. That ever keep you awake at night?"

"Not even a little bit."

"You also talked about the other serial killers from the area, like Ted Bundy, Robert Lee Yates, Ethan Wolfe, et cetera. I think you even nick-named the Northwest 'Butcherville.' I always thought that'd make a cool name for a book or something."

"You have a good memory," Edward said, impressed. "And hopefully it does. My grandson's girlfriend is an author, and she's writing a book about Rufus Wedge. *Butcherville* is actually the title she's using."

Ross glanced up at the clock. "Wish we had more time. God knows I could talk about this stuff all day." He reached for his iPad and swiped the screen. "So. Back to the boring medical crap. You appear to be in good health, and your prostate looks good, but we'll see if the lab tests show anything in your blood. You mentioned the arthritis in your hip. How bad is the pain? Your file says that you've been offered prescriptions for pain meds in the past, but have always declined."

"Well, I'm not declining this time. Go ahead and write it up. Be generous."

"Really." Ross's eyebrows shot up. Consulting his tablet, he said, "Are you aware that there's a note in your file that says—and I'll read it to you word for word—'Do not offer this patient pain meds as he will bite your head off.' " He turned the tablet around so Edward could see it.

Edward saw the notation and chuckled. "I may have done that once or twice. I've got my pride, you know. But I would definitely like some now. The hip is bothering me more than usual, and it's beginning to interfere with my—" He stopped himself. He'd almost said *plans*. "My quality of life," he finished. "I need to be able to get around quickly, and I need to be able to bend and twist and lift things."

"I can certainly appreciate that, and I have a couple of different ones I'll let you try. One will reduce inflammation and take the edge off, and the other is a pretty good painkiller for the days when it's extra bad." The doctor tapped on his iPad, then looked up again. "Is there anything else we can address while you're here?"

"Yes." Edward cleared his throat. "I'd also like a prescription for Viagra."

Ross didn't miss a beat. "Don't see why not. I assume you're sexually active?"

"Not yet, but I plan to be."

"Good to know that age doesn't kill the urge," the doctor said with a grin. "Is she cute?"

"Of course she is, and so is her friend."

Brian Ross laughed. "That's awesome. Okay, I'll fax your prescriptions over to the Village pharmacy. In fact, I can do that from my iPad right now. Unless . . ." He paused. "Unless you want to pick up them up at the pharmacy downstairs?"

"That would be good," Edward said. "I'll just grab them on my way out. Everybody knows who I am at the Village, and I don't need anybody knowing my private business."

"Understandable, though you have nothing to be ashamed of. I know guys my age who use Viagra." Another few taps on the iPad, and then Ross stood up. "All set. You can go ahead and get dressed, Chief. Let me know if you have concerns about any of the drugs. The painkillers can cause stomach upset, but the most common side effect for Viagra is a wicked headache. Hopefully that won't happen to you. If it does, let me know. We have other options, though Viagra does tend to be the most effective."

Edward maneuvered off the table slowly. The younger man offered him a hand but he ignored it. "You'd be surprised at the goings-on at Sweetbay Village, son. There's more sex going on there than a college dorm."

"Really?"

"No, not really." Edward winked. "But it's close. Lots of widows and widowers looking for a bump and tickle."

"Huh." A thoughtful look passed over the doctor's face. "Maybe we *should* send my mother-in-law there. What better way than sex to remove the stick out of her butt?" Ross shuddered. "That's an unpleasant thought. Mind you, she's pretty good-looking for seventy years old. You inter-ested?"

"Not even a little bit."

The prescription would take thirty minutes to fill, but that was no problem. At his age, all Edward had was time, and he settled into a chair near the pharmacist's counter with his pager in his lap. He picked up the newspaper in front of him, interested to see if there'd been any updates on the homicide investigation of the teen found dead in Marysville.

Jamie. He couldn't help but smile when he thought of her. What a delicious little thing she'd been, with her bleached blond hair and black roots, the cubic zirconia nose stud, the way she'd cried once she finally figured out she was going to die, so wonderfully lithe and squirmy.

They always cried. And they always squirmed.

He just wished he'd been able to penetrate her. He'd been forced to use a tree branch, which could be fun sometimes, but he'd been hoping to *feel* her, goddammit. And his eighty-year-old equipment had failed.

Skimming through the newspaper, he saw that the media reports had nothing new to add from the day before. So far no mention had been made of the missing hand on Jamie Chavez, and Edward assumed there wouldn't be, at least for a while until they figured out what it meant. Marysville PD had obviously elected to keep that tidbit under wraps, perhaps to avoid premature comparison to the Butcher. Police had to be careful about what information they released nowadays, what with all that social media crap and things going "viral." It was important to manage the flow of information, and to reassure the public that everything was under control. Like ducks on the water, it was all smooth sailing on top and paddling like mad underneath. He was certain Marysville PD was scrambling to make sense of the crime.

Which they never would. Edward had been careful. He was always careful. There was a reason he'd cut off Jamie Chavez's hand, and there was a reason he'd left Bonnie Tidwell's intact.

That being said, there was nothing significant about human hands for Edward. But serial killers had to have a signature, and severed hands and a cleaver had seemed as good as any. He needed the cops to believe that a serial killer was at work with Jamie. However, he didn't want them thinking that at all with Bonnie.

Nothing was spontaneous, and nothing happened accidentally. And nothing hyped the media and the bloodthirsty public into a frenzy more than a serial killer at large.

At first, creating the Butcher had been a strategic career move. Catch a serial killer, get famous, get promoted. Edward had planned it all from the start. You didn't make chief of police by catching small-time criminals nobody remembered.

But then . . . he'd gotten to like it.

More so than that even, he'd started to crave it. And that's when he knew he needed to stop.

Stopping had not been easy. There'd been a few slips, but it had been easy to make those killings seem random. Nobody's hand had been chopped off in any of Edward's post-1985 kills, because Edward didn't personally give a rat's ass about hands.

He did, however, have a thing for hair. He liked the way it smelled, especially when freshly washed. It reminded him of brushing Lucy's hair when she was little, something he always did before putting her to bed. Maybe the urges had started then . . . he didn't know, and it didn't much matter. Edward had never been a "why" person. He never questioned motivation—his, or anyone else's.

And now the urges were back. Rather than fight them, he had decided that the Butcher would come out of retirement. He was never meant to go peacefully into the night, to die and then never be remembered. He had plans. One more kill, and soon the media would be contacting Edward for the former chief of police's thoughts on the matter. Was he ready for his close-up once again?

Why yes. Yes, he was.

The pager in his lap buzzed, and the sensation wasn't unpleasant. His prescription was ready.

The pharmacist, a woman in her mid-forties and quite attractive, smiled at him as she handed him the white paper bag with his Viagra and painkillers inside.

"Have you taken these medications before?" she asked, and the glint in her eye made Edward wonder if it was more than just a professional question. He liked to think it was, even if he was more than three decades her senior. Her name tag read NANCY.

"No, I haven't, Nancy. Never needed it before."

A smile wrestled the corners of her lips upward, but she fought to control it. "The Celebrex can cause skin reactions and stomach ulcers, so make sure you let your doctor know right away if you experience either of these. As for the Viagra, you're on the lowest dose at twenty-five milligrams, so hopefully you won't experience too many side effects. I'm sure your doctor mentioned headaches, flushing, and stomach upset. Sometimes, and this is not very common, your eyes will get a little weird and colors won't look quite right."

"I'll be sure to watch out for that." Edward couldn't tell for sure, but he thought the pharmacist had nice tits under her white coat.

"There's more information in the packet." She leaned forward a little and dropped her voice. "Also, sometimes men experience erections that last a long time, as in more than four hours. If that happens to you, don't try to wait it out. Go to the ER right away, or else you could, you know, do permanent damage."

Edward smiled. "Noted."

She returned the smile. "Have a great day, Mr. Shank."

He left the pharmacy and climbed into his Cadillac. The retirement home was a good twenty minutes away, and he certainly could have saved himself some time and a little gas if he'd just allowed the young doctor to call in his prescription to the pharmacy on-site at Sweetbay Village, as the man had originally offered. But Dr. Ross had been correct in assuming that

Edward didn't want anyone there to know he was using Viagra. Men could get embarrassed about that type of thing.

The doctor was half right. Edward didn't want anyone there to know he had a prescription for Viagra . . . because the Viagra wasn't for him.

It was for someone else. The guy just didn't know it yet.

22

All Matt wanted to do was forget the past week had ever happened. Between his near fling with the Fresh Network producer and the awkward-as-hell night where Sam had caught him masturbating, he wanted to press the backspace button on his life and delete everything that had happened over the past little while. And let's not forget that he had accidentally killed his friend, PJ Wu. And then dismembered the guy's body . . . not so accidentally.

It was horrific. All of it. And he knew that if he let himself think about it too long, he might lose it completely.

Karen, the sexy TV producer, was becoming less and less sexy with every annoying text message and voicemail she sent. She'd been back in San Francisco for a few days, but even from eight hundred miles away, she was nearing bunny boiler territory. Matt was half expecting her to show up at any moment with a knife, screaming, "I will not be ignored!"

And Sam . . . that was another story. The two of them were barely speaking, and the argument they'd had the other night had spiraled into a giant clusterfuck. Yeah, it was totally embarrassing to be caught red-handed (*har dee har har*), but goddammit, the reason his girlfriend had felt the need to spy was even worse. She had seen him with Karen that night at the Pink Door, and had assumed he was sleeping with the producer. She wasn't totally off base, but he'd gotten defensive anyway, and they'd shouted at each other until she'd left in tears.

And to compound matters, Matt did feel like a dick. Deep down, everything his girlfriend had yelled at him was true. He was emotionally unavailable and unwilling to commit. He never put their relationship first. His career mattered more to him than anything, and yes, he probably would end up alone if he didn't get his priorities straight.

And he had done so many things—so many awful, horrific things—that he wasn't proud of. He knew he had to change. He just didn't know how. Add to that the pressure of the TV deal and the angst over PJ being labeled as missing . . . it was so overwhelming, Matt didn't know where to start.

Matt could tell that the restaurant was controlled chaos outside his office door, but he chose to remain holed up at his desk. There was too much to catch up on, and he wasn't in the mood to talk to anyone. He wondered, and not for the first time, how he'd managed to get so far away from the reason he'd become a chef in the first place. Other than the day he'd cooked a meal for Detective Sanchez and the cooking they made him do for the TV show, when was the last time he'd truly been an artist in the kitchen? He crunched numbers all day, told people what to do, and signed paychecks. He hadn't gone into this business so he could cook his grandmother's food on television wearing a tank top that probably made him look like a douche bag.

What he wouldn't give for his *lola* to still be alive. She'd always been a calming presence in his life.

His phone vibrated and he checked it quickly. Another text from Karen. It was her fourth message of the morning and it was barely 10 a.m. If he didn't text back, this would continue the rest of the day, so he finally responded with a smiley face emoticon. That ought to shut her up, for a little while, anyway. He then deleted the entire text chat.

There was no denying that Matt's personal life was in the shitter.

A knock on his door caused him to swivel

around in his chair. One of his new hires, Sara, poked her head in.

"Matt? There's someone here to see you. Says he's a friend of yours? But he's wearing a badge, so I think he's a cop."

He sat upright. "Sanchez?"

"Yes, I think so."

"Tell him I'll be there in a minute, I just have to finish something up."

She nodded and closed the door behind her.

Matt took a deep breath and fought off the panic that had instantly arose. What did Sanchez want now? He'd already told the man everything, and he couldn't imagine what other questions the detective could possibly have. Picking up his phone, he wondered if he should call the Chief before speaking to Sanchez. He hadn't talked to his grandfather in days, and still had no idea what the old man had done with the body. It was probably best he didn't know, but now Matt was nervous.

He made the call, and it went straight to voice-mail. *Shit*.

Heading out of the office and into the bar area, he found Sanchez standing even though there were several bar stools available.

"Bob," Matt said, extending his hand. "You must have liked the food. Two visits in one week."

"Sorry to bother you, Matt." Sanchez didn't smile. "I'll be quick. I just wanted to let you know that I have an update on PJ Wu."

"Do you want to talk in my office?"

Matt led him back to the small office, which now seemed even tinier with the two men in it. He took a seat at the desk and Sanchez eased himself into the small chair Matt had in the corner.

"I'll get right to the point," the detective said. "We found PJ's body."

Matt blinked, unsure how to respond, and his mind immediately whirled through the last few episodes of *Law & Order: SVU* he'd seen. How would a person who *wasn't* PJ's killer react to what the detective had just said?

"You said body," Matt finally said. "That means he's dead?"

"Yes. I'm very sorry."

"Well, shit." Matt exhaled and leaned back in his chair. His heart was racing a mile a minute, and there was nothing he could do to help that, but he imagined that a reaction like that would probably be okay in a situation like this. "What the fuck happened?"

"It's a homicide."

"He was murdered?" Matt couldn't tell if Sanchez was trying to gauge Matt's reaction for any sign of guilt, or whether the man always stared this intensely while he was in work mode. Matt maintained eye contact with the detective and tried not to squirm in his chair. "When? How?"

"He's been dead for a few days, it looks like. His body was found at the dump."

"Someone killed him and left him at the dump? I don't understand."

"Well, that's the thing." Sanchez's tone was casual but his eyes remained focused on Matt's face. "We're ruling it a homicide because of the way he was found. But we still haven't determined the specific cause of death."

"The way he was found?" Matt knew he was repeating everything the detective was saying, but that somehow also seemed the appropriate thing to do for a person in shock. "I'm sorry, Bob. I still don't understand."

"His body was not . . . intact."

Matt winced.

"Sorry, Matt. I know that must be hard to hear."

"Just tell me the whole thing."

Sanchez seemed a bit more relaxed now, and he crossed one leg over the other. "We found his head, a foot, and part of his torso. We're still looking for the rest."

"Holy. Shit."

"As I said, we haven't determined the actual cause of death, but there appears to be some type of trauma to the head consistent with a fall."

"Which . . . which could have been accidental."

"What makes you say that?"

"Because I can't imagine anyone killing PJ," Matt said, and it was the truth. "He was a nice guy. A regular guy. It wasn't like he had enemies." That was also the truth.

"Well, that may be, but people who die accidentally don't then end up dismembered at the city dump."

Why had the Chief put him in the dump? Why not just Dexter him and dump him in the Sound, weighted down with rocks?

Because the Chief doesn't have a boat, you idiot, his mind replied.

Matt cleared his throat. "I don't know what to say. This is absolutely horrible. Has his family been notified?"

"We told them this morning. If there's any friends you'd like to tell, or if you'd like to tell the staff yourself, that's fine."

"What do I tell them?" Matt's voice was dull, and again, it was a genuine reaction. "Do I say he was murdered?"

"You can say whatever you feel comfortable saying. I'd wait, though, until the end of the day. This kind of news can be really upsetting."

"Yeah." Matt shifted in his seat. "Yeah, it is."

"Is there anything new you'd like to tell me?"

"What do you mean?" Matt stiffened. "I don't know anything more than what I already told you."

The detective smiled slightly. "I just meant, is there anything that might have occurred to you that you maybe didn't think of the last time we talked? Memory is a funny thing."

Matt shook his head. "No, I'm sorry. I wish I had something that could help you."

"You said he had no enemies, that he was a regular guy."

"Yes, that's true."

"But everybody knew he had a gambling problem."

"Well, yeah, like I said last time, that was no secret. He was into sports betting. Got in over his head a few times, but it didn't seem to be anything an advance check couldn't cover. As least so far as I was aware."

"We checked into his cell phone records going back six months. He'd been receiving regular texts from a bookie who works for Keyser Wong." Matt's face must have been blank, because Sanchez continued. "He's a well-known member of one of the Chinese gangs around here."

"I had no idea." Again, a truthful statement.

"Oh yeah," Sanchez said. "And they're nasty pieces of work. They've been known to dismember their victims once they've been killed, to make . . . how you say . . . a point. Your friend isn't the first one to end up at the dump."

Matt exhaled. It all made sense. Obviously the Chief had known about the gang, which is why he'd disposed of the body the way he had. "You think that's who killed him?"

"It's a definite possibility." Sanchez stood up, stretching briefly. "Just wanted to let you know. This actually isn't my case anymore, as it's been funneled over to the guys who work organized crime. I told them I'd come back to talk to you, since I know you personally and had already spoken to you before."

Matt nodded slowly and he stood up, too, his legs feeling like jelly. He knew it was because of the relief that was flooding through him. "I appreciate that, Bobby."

"Of course. How's Sam?"

"She's good," Matt said. "We, uh, haven't really seen a lot of each other lately. The restaurant's been kicking my ass and she's got some stuff going on."

"She's pretty obsessed about her current book."

"Yeah."

"Tell her I said hello. I was expecting her to pester me more lately, and she hasn't been." Sanchez smiled. "Not that I'm complaining, but when she heard about the body that turned up in Marysville the other day, she was all over me like white on rice for information, even though that's not my jurisdiction."

"Body? Marysville?"

Sanchez grimaced and opened the door to Matt's office. The noise from the restaurant flooded in. "Yeah, teenage girl. Raped and murdered. Sam, bless her heart, wanted to know if it was somehow related to the Butcher."

"What?" Matt almost fell over and he grabbed the edge of his desk for support. "The Butcher, as in *the* Butcher? Why would she think that? The Butcher's dead."

"She's got a theory that he might not be, and I will admit, it's sounding more and more intriguing." The detective looked at him closely. "She doesn't talk to you about her work?"

"We don't really talk about our jobs."

"Ah. Probably a good idea. Not just for you two, but for any couple." Sanchez shook his head. "The Butcher's always been personal to her. Because she thinks he killed her mom."

"What?" Matt's mouth hung open in genuine surprise. "I didn't know that."

Sanchez looked surprised. "Yikes, then I probably shouldn't have said anything. I just . . . shit, I just assumed she'd told you about her theories."

"Sam's always had her secrets." Uneasy, Matt wondered what else he didn't know about his girlfriend of three years. "That's her theory? That a dead serial killer murdered her mother?"

Misreading Matt's reaction, Sanchez said, "I know. I think it's absolutely crazy, too, and that's probably why she never mentioned it to you. But we can't underestimate grief, my friend. She's always craved answers, and when they don't come . . . well, it's human nature to start inventing our own."

Matt's mind raced. He needed to find out what Sanchez knew. "But didn't the Butcher die before her mother was murdered?"

237

Sanchez nodded. "Yeah, but she thinks the real Butcher was never caught. But you didn't hear that from me, okay? Let her tell you."

The two men shook hands again, and Sanchez left. Closing the office door behind him, Matt slumped into a chair, unable to process what the detective had just let slip.

Sam thought the Butcher killed her mother?

But the Butcher was the Chief.

Matt felt the blood drain out of his face as the realization sank in. His grandfather murdered his girlfriend's mother.

This was no longer a clusterfuck. This was a living nightmare.

23

Sam didn't know exactly when everything had begun to fall apart, but things with Matt were a mess, and she didn't have the slightest clue how to start fixing it. She wasn't even sure if she wanted to fix it.

It almost didn't matter whether or not he had cheated on her with that producer. Sneaking into her boyfriend's house to try to catch him in the act had been stupid, because she didn't need to see him having sex with someone else to know that their relationship was in trouble. If he really had cheated, it was only a symptom of everything else that was wrong. Things hadn't been great between them for a long time now.

Had they ever been great? her mind whispered, and she winced at the thought. She knew she was forcing it, and had been for months. Maybe longer, if she was being totally honest with herself. In comparison to Jason, her boyfriend knew so little about her. Half the time she forgot to tell him things, and the other half of the time she didn't tell him because she was pretty sure he wouldn't care.

She was parked in the visitors' lot in front of Jason's building, needing a minute to compose herself before seeing her oldest friend. She didn't want to get into a discussion with Jason about Matt—after all, Jason was his friend, too. He'd introduced them to each other three years ago, and she hated putting her childhood friend in the middle. Smoothing her hair, she took a few deep breaths and forced herself to calm down before getting out of the car.

The doorman recognized her and let her in. His face was almost as dark as his uniform, and he smiled at her, his glimmering white teeth sparkling under the bright halogen lights of the lobby.

"He already said he was expecting you," the doorman said, accompanying her to the elevator. Holding the door open for her, he used his key card to swipe for access to the penthouse. "Go right on up."

"Thanks, Ronnie."

"Nice to see you again, Sam."

"You, too."

Sam smiled at the doorman as the elevators doors closed. Though Jason had never said specifically what his condo was worth, Sam knew it had to be a lot. He'd been living here for a long time, back from his Seahawks days, and even though the market had dropped, it still had to be worth at least a couple of million.

The elevator opened and she stepped into the private lobby. The top floor was divided in half. Jason was in penthouse A. Some former professional basketball player (Sam couldn't remember who, but the guy had apparently played for the Lakers for years before retiring with the Sonics in 2006) was Jason's neighbor in penthouse B.

She pressed the penthouse a buzzer and waited.

A moment later, a blonde—not Jason, but almost his height—answered the door. She was leggy with big boobs, clad in nothing but a pair of Lululemon yoga shorts that barely covered her ass, and a neon sports bra that did a nice job of showing off her ample cleavage. She instantly made Sam feel short and frumpy.

"Uh, hi." Sam leaned back, checking the letter above the buzzer again. Yes, she had the right penthouse. "Is Jason home?"

"You must be Sam." The blonde smiled and stepped forward. Before Sam could move away or even protest, she was wrapped inside toned arms, her face pressed against a tanned chest. The girl had to have about seven inches of height on Sam, yet they probably weighed close to the same. "I'm Lilac."

"Ah," Sam said, politely disengaging. She wasn't really a fan of physical contact with strange women. "I've heard a lot about you. Nice to meet you."

"Likewise. Come on in. We were just making tea. Would you like some? We have chamomile, we have oolong, and we picked up this lovely roasted organic dandelion tea from Pike Place the other day. That's what I'm having. I really recommend it."

We? Since when was Jason part of a *we?* And since when did he drink herbal tea?

"I'm good, thanks," Sam said, trying to look past her. "Sorry, where did you say Jason was?"

"Are you sure? The dandelion's really good." Lilac's eyes flicked over Sam's body and then she patted her own flat stomach. "I'm bloated today, and it's great for water retention."

"I'll keep that in mind for when I'm bloated," Sam said, but she found herself sucking her stomach in anyway.

"Jay!" Lilac called in a singsong voice, padding barefoot back toward the bedroom, where Sam heard her say, "Your *friend* is here."

Sam did not like the way she said the word

friend. And since when was Jason a *Jay?* He'd always been a *Jase*. Always.

Jason stepped out of the bedroom, wearing blue jeans and a white V-neck T-shirt, hair still wet from a recent shower. His lopsided grin broadened when he saw how irritated Sam looked. He gave her a rough hug and a quick peck on the cheek. "Be nice," he said in her ear. "She's not that bad."

Dammit, he smelled good, and Sam was dismayed she even noticed.

"Was I interrupting something?" she asked him. "I'm a little early, I know."

"Of course not," Jason said, heading to the kitchen. He grabbed a beer from the massive stainless steel refrigerator and popped it open. "We had just finished up." He saw the look on Sam's face. "*Yoga*. We just finished yoga. Lilac gives me private instruction."

"Bet she does," Sam said under her breath.

"I'm heading out." Lilac came out of the bedroom dressed in jeans so tight Sam wondered how she didn't have cameltoe. She'd thrown a sheer knit top over her sports bra, but her cleavage was still clearly visible through the semitransparent fabric. "Call me to say good night, baby."

"Of course."

She snuggled up to him and gave him a long, lingering kiss on the lips. Sam thought she might hurl. "It was nice meeting you," she said, presumably to Sam, then flounced out, leaving nothing but the faint trace of her floral perfume behind.

When the door was closed, Sam turned to Jason. "Seriously?"

"Beer?"

"Yes. And . . . seriously?"

"Come on," Jason said with a laugh, opening Sam's beer. He poured it into a glass before handing it to her. "She's a sweet girl."

"Is *sweet* the new word for hot and dumb?"

Jason rolled his eyes. "I will never get girls. You're so instantly competitive, always assuming the worst about each other."

"First of all," Sam said, settling into Jason's leather sofa, "you've never had a problem getting girls."

"You know what I meant."

"Second of all, I didn't assume the worst. She's just . . . a bit of a bubblehead."

"She is not." Jason plopped down beside her and took another swig of his beer. "She has a master's degree."

"In what?"

"Finance."

"You're fucking with me. You can't be serious."

Jason grinned. "As cancer. She used to be a trader, worked for Bindle Brothers."

"And then decided to become a yoga instructor?" Sam still couldn't tell if he was joking.

"She owns her own studio. Sorry, studios. Plural."

"Which one?"

"Yogalicious. There's eight locations now, I think."

"Oh." Sam felt even smaller than she did before. "Well, that's good for her. Maybe I should take a class. God knows I could lose five pounds." She looked down at herself, feeling dumpy and soft.

"Nah," Jason said, and he reached over and tweaked her nose between his fore- and middle finger. "You're good the way you are. Curvy girls are better."

"I think Lily would disagree."

"It's Lilac."

"You know what I meant."

They smiled at each other and sipped their beers for a few minutes, feeling no particular need to talk.

Finally Jason said, "So I don't know if Matt told you yet, but PJ's dead."

"What?" Sam almost spit out her beer. "What happened?"

"They found his body in a dump." Her friend grimaced. "Funeral is this Saturday. His folks are flying in tomorrow to make the identification, and they're bringing the body back to San Francisco for the service."

Sam sat still, her head spinning. "This is so

crazy. It feels like I just saw him. I knew he was missing, but I can't believe he's dead. Do they know how he died? Was he killed?"

Jason shrugged. "I don't know the details, but I think it had something to do with his gambling and getting involved with the wrong people. Ask your friend Sanchez, he's the one who worked the case. I'm surprised he didn't tell you already." He looked at her closely. "Actually, scratch that. I'm surprised *Matt* didn't tell you."

"He's . . . he's had a lot on his mind," Sam said, her voice faint. She still couldn't believe PJ was dead. "Are you going to the funeral?"

Jason shook his head. "No, I can't, I have a meeting in Portland I can't postpone. But I'll send flowers."

"I guess you weren't really that close to him anyway," Sam said. "But Matt was. Do you know if he's going to the funeral?"

"In San Francisco? You're asking me? I doubt it. And hey, if it makes you feel better, I didn't hear it from Matt, either. I saw it on fucking Facebook from one of his other friends."

Sam slumped into the sofa. "Oh."

They sat in silence another moment, each processing their own thoughts, and then finally Jason patted her leg. "Anything new with Butcher two-point-oh?"

Butcher 2.0. That's what she'd dubbed him. Sam

had called Jason right after she'd read the news report about the murder in Marysville and spoke to Robert Sanchez.

"Nothing. Bobby said he'd call if he heard anything new but I haven't heard from him."

"Still no mention of the missing hand in the papers?"

"Nada."

"Hmmm." Jason finished off his beer and placed the empty bottle on the side table. "You know, even if this new guy isn't the old guy but instead is someone entirely different who's copying the Butcher, that would make a nice ending to your book."

"What do you mean?"

"It's like . . . how can I put it . . ." Jason paused, searching for the right words. "It's like the full circle. You could start with the Butcher's murders, and then finish with these new ones."

"Assuming there are any more."

"Assuming, yeah." He sipped his beer. "What did the Chief say when you floated your theory past him?"

"Not a whole lot." Sam sighed, kicking her shoes off and tucking her legs under her. "We didn't really get into it. I think he's getting tired of me talking about how he might have gotten the wrong guy, and I suppose I can't blame him. Besides that, he didn't look like he was feeling too well the last time I saw him."

"What are you talking about? The Chief never gets sick."

"He wasn't sick. More like, he's been coned."

"You've lost me."

Sam laughed. "Okay, you remember that cat you used to have? Bugsy? Remember when she got clipped by that crazy kid on a bike? Oh, what was his name . . ." She frowned. "Kenny. Kenny Perkins."

"Oh God. I remember him," Jason said with a snort. "He had that giant Schwinn that was twice the size he was. What were we, twelve?"

"I was twelve, you were fourteen."

"Right."

"And remember how we took Bugsy to the vet, and after they patched her up, they put one of those cones on her?"

"Yeah, and she was all depressed. For the whole two weeks she had to wear it, she just moped around, wouldn't play, wouldn't chase her toys, nothing. It's like her little spirit was crushed."

"Right," Sam said. "That's the Chief right now. Coned. Bored. Uninspired. Like someone's crushed his spirit. It's hard to see him like that." She bit her lip.

"There's a very simple solution for that," Jason said. "The old man needs to get laid."

Sam paused for a moment, then made a face. "Okay, that's totally gross. Now I have a visual in my head of the Chief having sex. Thanks so much for that."

"I'm just saying. And it shouldn't be hard for him to find someone to have some fun with. Those old folks' homes are dens of sin."

It was Sam's turn to laugh. "Dens of sin? You sound like Father Patrick, lecturing us about why we should never, ever have sex before marriage and why we should live at home with our parents for as long as possible. Because college dorms are dens of sin."

"Well, not for you, Miss 'I Was a Virgin Until I Turned Twenty-Two.' You wouldn't know anything about it."

"Shut up."

"So what does Matt think about the Chief's new sex life? He was really close to his grandmother, and it hasn't been that long since she passed away."

"I would tell you if I knew, but we don't talk about Edward," Sam said. "We barely talk at all these days, actually, except for the really fun argument we had the other night."

Jason raised an eyebrow, and reluctantly Sam recounted the details of what happened, from her hiding in the bushes, to sneaking into Matt's house, to catching him watching a porn movie.

Jason had to put his beer down, he was laughing so hard. He seemed equal parts tickled and horrified. "Oh shit, that's awesome. And horrible. What the hell were you thinking?"

"I thought he was cheating on me."

"Come on, he would never do that."

"Really?" Sam stared at Jason, turning serious. "Would you tell me if he was?"

"Yes, I would."

"But that would be a violation of bro code."

Jason shrugged and sipped his beer again. "What can I say? You come first. You always have. You know that."

Sam closed her eyes. In three years, Matt had never come close to uttering those words to her, and it was nice to hear, even if it was from a man who wasn't her boyfriend.

"Don't get me wrong, you're both my friends," Jason said. "But I've known you practically my whole life. You and I grew up together. I swear to God, if he ever hurt you . . ." He trailed off and looked away, but Sam noticed his hands had bunched up into fists.

"Things haven't been good for a long time with us, Jase," Sam said. "I don't think we're going to make it."

Jason nodded, not saying anything. He didn't need to.

"And lately he's just been . . . difficult. I mean, more so than usual." She stared into her beer glass. "So quick to fly off the handle. Defensive. Angry. And yet everything is going his way. He's this huge success, but it never seems like it's enough. And that's how he makes me feel."

"Then end it. You deserve better."

Her eyes welled up, and Jason pulled her into a bear hug.

"You'll be okay," he said in her ear, his breath warm and comforting. "You have me, and I'm not going anywhere."

She opened her eyes and looked at Jason. All she saw in his face was compassion and concern, and in the soft light of the penthouse, he had never looked more beautiful.

"Will you kiss me?" she asked softly.

He stared intently at her. He didn't seem surprised by the question. His eyes took in her face, her lips, her hair. He smoothed a dark strand away from her cheek, and with his other hand, he stroked her jawline.

"No," he said. "Because you're not asking for the right reasons. When you do, I will."

24

Edward couldn't do it the way he used to anymore, not unless he drugged them. And that, of course, took all the fun out of it. It was only truly enjoyable when they were conscious of their fear, knowing death was imminent.

It was the look in their eyes that turned him on. That look, the moment they understood that they were going to die, was what Edward craved.

Did this make him a psychopath? He didn't think it was that simple. People killed other people for lots of reasons. It was just that *psychopath* was such a trendy word, something folks liked to bandy around as a way to explain why people did bad things. But Edward knew better. Some folks just *liked* doing bad things. In his opinion, there was no need to question it. It was why he'd stayed a cop and had never been interested in working for the FBI when they'd come calling after he'd brought Rufus Wedge down. Edward had never had any interest in analyzing the whys . . . because the whys really weren't that fascinating.

Besides, everybody had hobbies. Some people golfed. Some people fished. Some people hunted deer. Edward killed. Because he liked it, goddammit. It was really that fucking simple. And the kills had helped his career. He'd felt great satisfaction in creating the Butcher, and almost as much satisfaction when he accepted his promotion to chief of police.

The recreation room at Sweetbay Village was loud as always, filled with the usual bunch of residents engaged in various activities. Dinner wasn't for another hour and this was the time of day when the rec room was at its fullest. Around him, old fogies were watching TV, playing board games, sitting and chatting. There was old Cecilia in the corner with her two closest friends, Esther and Deb, and the three of them were working on a quilt. In the other corner was old Millie, holding that annoying bastard Jack Shaw's hand and laughing at every word he said.

Edward sat across from old Donald Martini, who looked like he was falling asleep on the other side of their chess board. "Your move, Don."

"Eh?"

Edward spoke louder. "Your move."

"Oh, right. Sorry, Edward."

He knew it would take Donald at least five minutes to decide whether to sacrifice his rook (and in the end he wouldn't, which would win Edward the game—he'd played Don several times in chess over the past month and the old guy's moves had become predictable), so he swiveled in his chair slightly to get a better of view of the TV mounted on the far wall. The King5 evening news was on, and there was an update about Matthew's friend.

"The identity of the man found in the dump has been released," the anchorwoman was saying, a beautifully exotic lady who would have been described as "Oriental" back in Edward's day, but now was known as Asian, thanks to the politically correct pundits. "Patrick Jason Wu, age thirty-one, was a Seattle resident originally from San Francisco. He worked at Adobo, a popular eatery in Fremont. Our sources tell us that Wu, whose dismembered body was discovered yesterday morning, might be the victim of the Wong crime family, as he had known affiliations with several of its members. Sources tell King5 that his death might be part of a turf war between the Wong and Chang families." The news cut to an interview of the guy working at the dump site where Wu's body had been found.

Ha. It had been too easy, really.

It hadn't taken Edward long to find out exactly who PJ Wu was and what his weaknesses had been. He hadn't even had to run a background check to know the kid was in deep debt—all he'd done was glance through Wu's phone and he'd seen several texts about owing money, bets placed, and the like. Kids put everything in those goddamned smartphones nowadays.

Edward normally never worried about covering up, as half the fun of killing was the discovery of the body and the flurry of investigation that ensued. But in this case, he'd had no choice but to put a fictional spin on PJ's death. After all, he didn't want Matthew to go to prison.

He felt eyes on him and turned his attention to the next table, where Gloria Marsh was sitting across from Helena Rubenstein. The two women were playing gin rummy, and the rumor was that these two ladies were a little on the slutty side. Edward liked them both. They were fun.

Gloria, in particular, was a perky little thing with a face full of makeup that seeped into her wrinkles. Even in her late seventies, she still wiggled when she walked and giggled when she talked, and hell yes, Edward could appreciate that. It wasn't her fault she was getting old. She'd shown Edward a picture of herself back in the day once. She'd been beautiful in her prime. Movie star looks, pinup girl body, dark brown hair that offset red Cupid's bow lips perfectly.

Now she looked as if someone had deflated her, and all that was left were the wrinkles and hair dye where her youth used to be. Getting old sucked donkey's balls, and he couldn't blame her for fighting it as best she could. But age was winning the battle, as it always did.

She smiled at him, her blue eyes still clear and twinkly even at the age of seventy-eight. It wasn't hard to see that she had a thing for him, and Edward didn't mind the attention. Not at all. In fact, it was time to do something about it. Lord knew it had been a long time . . . there'd been nobody since Marisol.

He was ready.

Returning her smile, Edward said, "Who's winning, Gloria?"

"Helena," Gloria said with a girlish giggle. "As usual. I think she stacks the deck."

Helena, eighty-one years old, didn't appear to hear her name mentioned and so she didn't turn around. Edward winked at Gloria, who winked back.

"By the way, have you ever tasted salted chocolate, Edward?" Gloria asked.

"Can't say that I have, Gloria."

"It's quite lovely. My granddaughter brought me some the other day. The sea salt enhances the flavor of the dark chocolate, making it taste richer and sweeter."

"I do have a sweet tooth," Edward said with a grin. "My grandson's sweetheart brought me some cannolis the other day from the bakery, and they certainly didn't last long."

"And you didn't share any with me?" Gloria feigned a pout, then giggled again.

"What was I thinking? Next time, my dear."

"Maybe later, after supper, you'd like to try some of my chocolate?" Gloria said, and her lips stayed parted just long enough for Edward to read her invitation loud and clear. "Around eight, perhaps?"

"That sounds fine. I would love to."

They exchanged smiles again, and Edward turned his attention back to his chess opponent, who was still contemplating his next move. Don Martini was leaning forward, his chin resting in a liver-spotted hand, and he glanced at Edward with a sly grin. "Looks like somebody's got a hot date."

"Ha," Edward said. "Listen, Don, you going to be a few more minutes? I think I need to run to the john. Gotta drop some kids in the pool."

"Yeah, you go ahead, Edward," Don said. "At

least you're regular. They got me on some new medication now for my heart, and I've hadn't a decent shit all week. Maybe I'll make a hot cup of tea and ponder my next move while you're gone, so you take your time."

Both men stood up but they headed in opposite directions. Edward headed straight for his room. There was a restroom inside the recreation area, but of course Edward didn't really have to use the toilet.

He entered his room and locked the door behind him. Opening the closet door, he reached into his jacket pocket and found the small prescription bottle of Viagra he'd picked up at the pharmacy the other day. He shook out four pills and placed them on the small coffee table, then retrieved a knife from the kitchenette so he could grind them up into powder. Then he ripped a little chunk of paper from the Village newsletter that was lying on the coffee table and carefully placed the powder inside it, folding it up neatly.

He couldn't kill the way he used to anymore, and he had to admit, he was bummed about that. It was why he didn't bother going to his cabin in Raymond anymore. He owned over two hundred acres in a densely wooded area, but if he couldn't really kill like before, what was the point of driving down there?

He'd always been a strong man, and in a lot of ways still was, but after Jamie Chavez and Bonnie

Tidwell, he'd been exhausted. The pain meds Dr. Ross had prescribed helped considerably, but he didn't have the body of a fifty-year-old and he had to accept that. The urge to kill was back in full force and he had no desire to stop it . . . but that didn't mean he could physically keep up with it. Adjustments were necessary.

Jamie, especially, had worn him out. She'd been a squirmy little thing, and he'd had to stun her several times with the tree branch in order to keep her subdued. It had really taken the fun out of it, because then she'd been too out of it to fight anymore. Back in his prime, he'd been able to hold them down with one arm while doing whatever he'd wanted to them with the other.

He had to acknowledge that it couldn't be that way now. But that didn't mean he couldn't work around it. And old Donald Martini had always been on his nerves.

He headed back to the recreation room, where Don was waiting with his mug of hot, steaming tea. He was currently flirting with Helena, and between the two of them and their bad hearing, the conversation was a few decibels louder than it needed to be. Gloria was nowhere to be found, but there was a small folded slip of paper on the table on Edward's side of the chess board. It was a note.

HOW ABOUT SIX P.M. INSTEAD?
I'LL COOK DINNER. GLORIA.

Edward grinned, and stuck the note in his pocket. *Perfect.* Deftly, while Don's back was still turned, he withdrew the paper filled with Viagra powder into his opponent's mug, where it dissolved quickly. The taste might be a little bitter, but he doubted Don would notice with all the honey he put into his tea. Finally, Helena left, waving at them both.

Chuckling, Don turned back around to face the table. "We still got our charm, don't we, Edward?" he said with a wink. "The ladies just love us. Wish my pecker still worked. They said I can't take nothin' right now with my heart condition, but boy do I miss a good go-round."

"Helena definitely likes you." Edward grinned. "But I thought you and Millie had a thing. What's she doing over there with that bastard Jack Shaw?"

"Apparently he's quite the ladies' man," Don said, reaching for his tea. "She dumped me when she found out the pecker don't work."

"For that geezer? He looks like a retired midget wrestler."

"But he's got more money than a rich Jew and he promised to take her to Europe this summer. And apparently the ding-dong still works without any help. That's the rumor, anyway."

"Started by who, Jack Shaw?"

The two men shared a laugh. Don shrugged good-naturedly. "She let me feel her tits, so I don't mind. On to the next."

Edward watched as Don sipped his tea. Making a face, Don said, "Bitter. I didn't put enough honey in it."

"I'm going to get a snack anyway. I'll grab you some."

"Appreciate that, Edward."

He was back in two minutes with a slice of cheese and a few crackers, and a few packets of honey for Don's tea. The old guy stirred all of it in, then sipped again. "There, that's better. It's your move, by the way."

Edward moved his knight and the two men continued to play. After about twenty minutes or so, he said, "Don, you're looking a little flushed, my friend."

"You know what, I do have a headache." Don squinted and rubbed his temples. "Oh boy. Haven't had pain like this in a while."

"You want to call it a day?"

"No, I'll manage, let's just finish. You've won four in a row, I gotta try and win one this week, at least." He picked up his mug again and drained the last of his tea.

A few minutes later, Don said, "You know what, Edward, maybe I will lie down."

"Are you all right?"

"I—" Don reeled back in his chair, clutching his chest, his eyes wide with panic. Then he fell over, onto the floor, landing on the carpet soundlessly.

"Nurse," Edward said, his voice raised just a little. "We need a nurse."

The recreation room was a loud place—the volumes on the televisions were always turned up, and since half the Village residents were deaf, everyone talked loud as well. Nobody moved. Nobody was paying attention. Edward waited another few seconds while Don lay on the floor, his hand over his heart. The man's eyes finally closed. He was losing consciousness.

Edward waited an extra beat before finally shouting, "Nurse! We need help here!"

It was loud enough that there was a momentary pause of silence before the whole room exploded in commotion.

Edward backed away, letting the two nurses on staff—there were always two, usually a female and a male—do their job.

He knew they wouldn't be able to save him. One hundred milligrams of Viagra combined with all the medications for his heart and blood pressure that Don was already taking . . . the old guy didn't stand a chance.

By the time the paramedics arrived, old Don was dead.

Edward soaked up every moment of the exhilaration. He watched as the ambulance carted Don away, his face appropriately somber, but his insides brimming with pleasure.

"He's already gone," said the male nurse to the

female nurse. Miguel, his name was. "Damn. Poor guy."

"I can't believe it," someone beside Edward was saying. He turned. It was Helena, mascara staining her cheeks. "We were just talking. He seemed fine."

She turned to him for a hug, but Edward moved away. He didn't want her feeling what just sprouted up in his pants.

"There now," he said instead, reaching out and patting her shoulder "It's terrible, but to be expected. Don wasn't in the best health. He was on so many medications."

She nodded, dabbing at her eyes with a lace handkerchief.

He turned away from her, heading quickly down the hallway toward the elevators. Checking his watch, he saw that it was five minutes to six. Perfect timing. Like Don had commented earlier, Edward had a hot date.

By the time Gloria opened the door, his cock was throbbing.

"Oh my," she said, when she saw the look on his face. Edward reached for her, kissing her hard, before shutting the door behind him.

A moment later, when he pulled down his pants, she said even louder, "Oh my!"

"Oh my, indeed," Edward said. "Now stop talking. Don't make me gag you."

Who needed Viagra?

25

It was the third reported death at the Sweetbay Village Retirement Residence, and Sam couldn't help but wonder if Matt's grandfather knew something about it. How could Edward Shank not know? You'd think that if anyone would be suspicious about three deaths so close together, he would be.

According to a news report she'd read online, three Village residents had died in the past month. The first was Greg Bonner, age eighty-eight, who'd fallen and hit his head in the middle of the night while hunting for a snack in the kitchen, something he was known to do. Ruled accidental.

The second death was Donald Martini, age seventy-nine. Martini hadn't been in the greatest health and he'd suffered a massive heart attack while playing chess with another resident. The article suggested he'd suffered complications from all the medications he'd been taking. Ruled accidental.

The third death, which happened just last night, was Gloria Marsh, a once-divorced, once-widowed seventy-eight-year-old who'd been found dead in her bed. Cause of death was still unknown, but Village staffers had confirmed that Marsh had been in excellent health and was still very physically active up till the day of her death. The police were conducting an investigation.

Sam pulled up to the retirement home and cut the engine. She hadn't visited the Chief since their last awkward conversation about the Butcher and she was worried that the old man was annoyed with her. She also wanted his advice about Matt.

Her phone buzzed as she was reaching for her purse, and she saw she had a text message from Jason.

What are you up to?

Sighing, she switched her phone to silent. She still hadn't fully processed what had happened between the two of them the night before, and she couldn't let herself think about it right now. Not until she made some decisions about Matt. She and Jason hadn't even kissed, but somehow every-thing was . . . different.

She hadn't called Edward to let him know she was stopping in, but he always seemed pleased to see her. Hopefully today would be no different. Entering the elegant, warm reception area of the Village, she nodded to the male nurse she'd chatted with the last two times she'd visited.

"Well well, look who just walked in and made my day. Hello, sunshine. Here to see me?" Miguel said with a grin.

"Careful," Sam said, returning the smile. "If the Chief hears you, he won't be pleased."

"I know, he's protective of you. Can't say I blame him. It's nice to see you again."

"Likewise." Sam signed in with the receptionist. "Say, what's going on over here? I saw something online about three deaths in the past couple of weeks? Is that normal?"

Glancing at the receptionist, Miguel placed a hand on her shoulder and steered her away from the front desk. "It depends. We do have some special care residents here but not too many, as we're really not equipped for it. This is supposed to be a retirement home for *active* seniors, remember, not sick seniors."

"That's what I thought," Sam said with a frown. "That's why I was surprised to read the article this morning about you guys losing three people. One of the deaths is under investigation?"

The nurse gave her a look. "Someone has her journalist hat on today."

"No, not at all. You know I'm not a journalist. Just a writer with an overactive imagination, fortunately or unfortunately."

"It's definitely under investigation, as the cops were here and everything. I was the one who found Mrs. Marsh." Miguel grimaced. "She'd missed breakfast and her friends were worried, so they had me unlock the door to check on her. She was dead, lying naked on her bed. Wasn't pretty, let me tell you. You ever seen someone who died from asphyxiation? It was gross, and I'm not even that squeamish." He shuddered.

"Asphyxiation?" Sam stared at him, not sure she'd heard correctly. "As in strangled?"

"Yep. They're not confirming it, but I know strangled when I see it. You could see the bruises around her neck, clear as day."

"What the hell? So she was murdered? Wow." Sam was quiet for a moment.

"Well now, nobody said anything about that."

"You just said she was strangled."

"She was, but she wasn't necessarily murdered." Miguel leaned closer to her and she got a whiff of his musky aftershave. "Mrs. Marsh, she was . . . how do I put this delicately? She was quite sexually active. She might not have been killed on purpose, know what I'm saying?"

"Oh jeez. You're kidding me." Sam knew exactly what he was saying, though death by sexual asphyxiation was hard to imagine considering the woman's age. "But wasn't she in her seventies?"

"Seventy-eight," Miguel said. "And age doesn't matter anyway, not when you have Viagra. Which, as coincidence would have it, is what the other resident died of."

Sam looked at him, not comprehending.

"Mr. Martini overdosed on the little blue pill." Miguel's tone was somber. "He shouldn't have even been on it in the first place. He had heart issues and was taking way too many medications."

"So why did his doctor prescribe it?"

"I highly doubt his doctor did, unless he wanted to lose his license, as would the pharmacist who would have dispensed it. No, Mr. Martini probably got the Viagra from one of the other residents here. Or he ordered it online from Mexico or some other country where you don't need a prescription. Nothing surprises me about old folks anymore, especially not Mrs. Marsh. That lady used to look at me like I was a steak and she was starving." Miguel shuddered slightly at the memory. "Anyway, whoever she was with before she died used a condom. I have a friend who works with the medical examiner, and he confirmed it." He paused, waiting for her reaction.

"Uh . . ." Sam wasn't sure how to respond.

"Nobody at their age uses condoms," Miguel explained earnestly. "Seniors can't get pregnant, so they never think it's necessary."

"Oh, right," Sam said. "A benefit of having geriatric sex."

"Yeah, but they *should* use protection. The senior population is rampant with STDs. It's pretty disgusting, when you think about it. God knows everybody here is doing it with everybody else. That's a lot of bodily fluids being exchanged."

"Okay, that's seriously gross. Thanks for that."

Sam wrinkled her nose. "Any idea who the Chief's doing it with?"

Miguel laughed. "You'd have to ask the Chief. He's one of the few I haven't heard rumors about. If he's fooling around with anyone here, he's been pretty discreet about it."

"Hmmm." Sam thought hard. She couldn't help but be intrigued by everything Miguel was saying. "So if Mrs. Marsh had sex right before she died, then you guys can probably figure out who she was with. What did the visitors' log say?"

"It said nothing. Nobody signed in to see her yesterday. Which would suggest that whoever it was is from here."

Sam shook her head in disbelief. "Who would have thought something like that could happen here? Maybe we should get the Chief to investigate. He'd probably find out who it was in two minutes."

"No kidding. Whoever her lover was, he hasn't come forward. Probably too scared. Maybe we'll never know."

Sam smiled at Miguel and squeezed his arm before stepping back. "Anyhow, I should go see Edward. But thank you for satisfying my curiosity."

"Anytime. Don't be a stranger."

"You said that last time."

He winked. "And I'll mean it every time."

Sam caught the elevator to Edward's floor. The

receptionist had obviously called up, as the Chief's door was already open when she arrived. Entering his small room, Sam's mouth dropped open when she caught sight of Matt's grandfather, who was in the kitchenette boiling water for tea.

She blinked to make sure her contact lenses weren't foggy. The Chief looked completely different than the last time she'd seen him, which had only been a couple of days earlier. She could hardly believe her eyes as she took him in. He was moving around the kitchen easily, no trace of any hip pain, and he was rosy-faced and relaxed. It seemed impossible, but somehow, the Chief looked . . . younger.

"Okay, not to gush, but you look *great*," Sam said, shrugging out of her coat. She took a seat at the bar stool by the counter. "What's going on with you? Have you been drinking water from the fountain of youth? If so, can I have some?"

The Chief chuckled, his eyes twinkling as he poured hot water into two mugs. "I must be extra handsome, the way you're staring at me. And two visits this week? You must like me a little."

"Seriously, Chief, you look awesome." Sam couldn't stop staring. "What have you been doing? New skin cream? New diet? New girlfriend?"

"Maybe all of the above." He winked and dropped a tea bag into her mug, pushing it toward her. "I wish it was as exciting as that, my dear, but I'm afraid it's not. My new doctor prescribed some pain meds for my hip."

"And you're actually taking them?"

"I know. I can hardly believe it myself. Somewhere, pigs are flying." Edward took a sip of his tea and took a seat beside her at the counter. "But really, though, that's all it is. It's amazing how much better I feel now that I'm not in pain all the time. I'm moving better, I'm eating better, and I'm sleeping better."

"I'm glad to hear it. You certainly look terrific."

"Maybe you could tell my grandson that. I haven't seen him in a while." He frowned at her. "It took you a while to get up here. You must have enjoyed your little chat with Miguel?"

"Uh . . ." Sam took a sip of her tea. She hadn't been expecting that comment. "It was interesting. He was just telling me about the woman who died here last night."

"Any excuse to keep talking to you, obviously. His goddamned eyes are always more on your tits than your face."

"Don't be crude, please." Sam pursed her lips. "We were talking about the woman who died. That's all."

"That would be Gloria." Edward reached for the sugar bowl. "Poor lady. There was a lot of activity here this morning after she was found. I liked her. She was a friend."

Sam looked at him closely. "A good friend?"

"You might say that."

"I'm so sorry. You must be so upset." Though he didn't look upset at all.

"She wasn't my only lady friend," the Chief said with a small shrug. "And I certainly wasn't her only male companion, either. But she was fun, and she'll be missed."

"Do you know what happened to her?"

"The rumor mill is saying it was a sex thing." He raised an eyebrow and took another sip of tea.

"And what do you think?"

He shrugged again. "Not to speak ill of the dearly departed, but it wouldn't surprise me. Gloria was quite . . . frisky." A small smile played at his lips.

"And what does the rumor mill say about who she was with last night?"

"Nobody seems to know. But I'm sure PD will investigate and get it sorted out. Anyhow." Edward waved a hand. "I don't smell cannolis. Is that because you didn't bring me any?"

"Crap, I forgot."

"So then what brings you by?" He looked at her expectantly. "As much as I'd like to believe that you're here to watch *Wheel of Fortune* with me, Samantha, I can tell you have something on your mind. Out with it."

Sam hesitated. "I don't quite know how to start . . ."

"The beginning usually works for me."

She stirred more sugar into her tea, trying to figure out the right words. Finally, taking a deep breath, she said, "Matt and I . . . we're having problems."

"What, he screw around on you?" The Chief didn't miss a beat. He looked at her sternly. "You tell me if he did, Samantha, and I'll have a talk with him."

"No, he . . ." Flustered, Sam suddenly didn't know what to say. "I actually don't know. We haven't been close lately."

"Well, whether he did or didn't, it doesn't have to be a deal breaker, you know." Edward softened his tone. "Matthew's a good kid. His worst flaw is that he thinks he's got it all figured out, when in truth, he's got a lot to learn. Like how to prioritize."

"I can't disagree with that."

"And he's arrogant."

"I can't disagree with that, either."

"He probably gets that from me."

Sam smiled, wisely not saying anything.

Edward chuckled. "Listen, sweetheart. A man like Matthew is hard to tie down. He's bright, he's ambitious, he works hard, and he's goddamn successful at what he does. That's who he is, and while those things are attractive qualities to a woman like yourself, they also make it difficult to have a relationship."

Sam nodded. The Chief had nailed it. She waited for the advice she knew was about to come.

"You either accept it or you don't," Edward said. "But you won't change him. That drive . . . it's in his DNA. He's not going to slow down. Not for you, not for me, not for anybody."

"I don't want to change him," Sam said. "But it's Matt who's changing."

"In what way?"

"He's different these days, Chief." She bit her lip, unsure how to explain. "He's always been ambitious, I've known that since the day we met. And he's always been a busy guy, and that's never bothered me. I knew that from the beginning, and I honestly don't mind scheduling time with him in advance if that's what it takes. But lately, he's been really tightly wound. Tense. Distracted. Angry. It's not just me who's noticed it. His staff has complained about it, too. I'm not sure if it's just stress, but right now he's not the Matt I know. He's not the guy I fell in love with."

"You know he's always had issues with anger." Edward's dark eyes were impossible to read. "We've dealt with that before. It doesn't make him a bad person."

Sam knew the Chief was referring to Matt's arrest for assault last year. She'd been with her boyfriend when it happened. They'd been at a bar in downtown Seattle, watching the Seahawks game with a bunch of friends, when some drunken guy who was rooting for the other team had gotten a little too friendly with her. Matt had told him to quit it, and the two had exchanged heated words until things had come to blows. Her boyfriend ended up breaking the other man's nose and wrist, and if Edward hadn't intervened after Matt's arrest, he might have landed in jail.

"I know," Sam said. "But then he took those anger management classes, started seeing a therapist, and he calmed down. And he was better. Up until a few weeks ago. And now it's like he's backslid. He's worse than ever."

"Has he hit you?" Edward stared hard at her. "You tell me if he's laid a hand on you, Samantha."

"No, it's nothing like that," she said quickly. "Of course he hasn't. But I feel like he's a ticking time bomb. Not just with me. With everyone."

"So he hasn't hit you, and he hasn't cheated on you. He's just been . . . busy. Working hard. Becoming successful." Edward frowned. "I'm not sure I follow."

Sam was close to tears. This was hard enough to talk about without having to explain it to Matt's old-school grandfather. Maybe talking about this with the Chief wasn't such a good idea after all. "It's just . . . I feel like we're not going to make it, Chief. I don't know how to be in this relationship with him anymore."

Edward snorted. "Then maybe you shouldn't

be, Samantha. Maybe you're not the right girl for him. Nobody would blame you if you walked away. It's your decision. Though I doubt you'll ever meet another man like him."

An awkward silence fell between them. That wasn't the advice she'd been hoping to get. She hadn't known what to expect by coming here to discuss Matt, but this certainly wasn't it. Now she felt downright stupid. Sipping her tea, Sam stayed quiet, not knowing what else to say.

"How's the book coming along?" the Chief finally asked. "Any new theories you want to run by me since you're here?"

Sam shook her head, still feeling like an idiot. "Just the same one I had last time."

"You think the Butcher was someone other than Rufus Wedge," Edward said. "And that the Butcher, whoever he really is, killed your mother."

"I wasn't going to bring it up again. You seemed annoyed with me the last time I was here."

"Annoyed?" The Chief laughed. "My darling, I wasn't annoyed. The fact that you think I killed an innocent man is not annoying, sweetheart."

Sam felt a wave of relief. "I'm so glad. I certainly wasn't trying to insinuate that you didn't do your job properly."

"Oh come off it."

She blinked, not sure how to take that. "Um . . . what?"

"That's exactly what you were trying to

274

insinuate." The Chief's voice turned to ice. "And let me tell you, it's fucking insulting. I'm not annoyed, I'm pissed-off. You have a pretty head on your shoulders, my dear, but I wonder about the size of your brain sometimes. I really do."

Sam froze. "I . . . I'm sorry, Chief. I—"

"You know what, I have things to do today." Edward got up off his bar stool. He reached for Sam's mug and put it in the sink, even though she wasn't finished. "Why don't you run along now? And tell Miguel downstairs that I said hello. If that pretty boy male nurse is the kind of man you like spending time with, then maybe you shouldn't be with Matthew at all."

Sam's mouth dropped open. She was ushered out, the door slamming behind her, before she could even think of a response.

26

PJ Wu stood at the edge of the bed, looking down at Matt, eyes like black holes in his pallid face. PJ wasn't happy. Ghosts never were.

"How could you do it to me, man?" PJ's voice was pleading as he reached forward to touch the blanket covering Matt's feet. Matt tried to move away in time but couldn't, because of course he was paralyzed. He could feel PJ's cold fingers through the thin sheet. "I thought we were friends."

"We are," Matt said. "We were."

Obviously he was dreaming, and none of this was real. But lucid or not, it didn't make it any less real, or any less terrifying. He couldn't seem to wake up. He would have to ride it out, like he had every night for the past week.

"We were friends, man. I never wanted you to die. It was an accident. I'm sorry. I am so sorry."

"Then make it right. You're not the Chief. You can make it right."

"It's too late." Matt felt the tears running down his face, hot and salty and full of guilt. "It's too late. I can't change it now, buddy. I'm sorry. I'm so sorry."

"You cut me up." PJ's face darkened and his voice became accusing. Suddenly he was at the side of the bed, only inches away from Matt, and again there was nowhere to run. In Matt's mind, he was squirming, but in reality, his body was frozen. "You chopped me into little pieces and now I can't have an open casket. Do you know what that's doing to my mom? They don't believe in cremation, Matt. They think they've been cursed. My mom cries every day. Every day, Matt. She thinks I was a bad son, that I got killed because I did something bad."

"You weren't, you were a good son, and you

were a good friend." Matt was somehow speaking even though he couldn't feel his lips moving. "It was me. I lost my temper, I wasn't thinking. I didn't mean for it to happen."

"But it happened, and you need to make it right."

"I can't. If I say anything, I'll lose everything."

"But it's not fair!" PJ yelled. "It's not fair, don't you understand that? I'm dead and it's because of you and it's not fair! It's not fair! It's not fair!"

"I'm sorry!" Matt cried. Please God, he wanted to wake up, he wanted to wake up so PJ would stop yelling, so he could breathe, because he couldn't breathe, because the blankets were twisted around his neck and he was choking and PJ was so angry, so angry, and shouting awful things. "PJ, I'm sorry! I'm sorry, please, man, I'm so sorry!"

Matt woke up.

His eyes flew open and he took a giant gasp of air, hands clawing at his throat to remove the twisted bedsheet that wasn't there. It took a few seconds to remember that it was a dream, a god-damned awful dream, and that there was nobody in the bedroom but him, because PJ was dead and gone and not really here to torment him.

He was safe.

His pillow was drenched in sweat and his face was salty from the tears he'd really cried. Matt sat up, rubbing his eyes with his hands, trying to shake it off. But like all nightmares, it clung. The awful dream was still there, and it had felt totally real.

The clock told him it was 3:52 a.m. Every night was like this. It would be an hour or two before he'd be able to fall back asleep.

How did the Chief do it? How did he sleep?

Grandpa sleeps just fine because Grandpa is a psychopath, that little inner voice whispered, and Matt lay back down, taking deep breaths to try to restore his heart rate to normal.

Eventually, blessedly, he slept.

The men's bathroom mirror showed every line, crease, and wrinkle on Matt's sleep-deprived face. Cold water helped a little to reduce the puffiness around his eyes, but there was nothing to be done about the dark circles. He looked five years older than he had two weeks ago, and felt about twenty years older than that.

And, of course, today was the first day the camera crew would be here.

It wasn't officially show footage, more like a trial run, according to Karen, who was back in town. So far he'd successfully managed to keep all of their conversations to restaurant-related matters, and she seemed to finally be getting the hint that he wasn't interested in anything more than that. At least he hoped so.

Bernard was waiting for him when he exited the bathroom.

"Oh no. No no no," the producer said, looking up at Matt. He stood with a hand on one skinny hip, dressed head to toe in black save for the flashy white leather belt around his waist. A black cross-body bag (a "man bag," as Matt often thought of them) completed the producer's look. "Honey. What happened? Pardon my bluntness, but you look like absolute shit."

"Exactly what I needed to hear, Bernard. Thank you."

"I'm not trying to be an asshole, although I know I probably sound like one, but honey." The producer's face was twisted into a frown. "Welcome to the world of high-definition TV, where the cameras pick up on everything. Back into the restroom. Quick quick." He snapped his fingers and shooed Matt back into the men's room.

"Over there," Bernard said, pointing to the middle of the long counter where the sinks were. "That's where the lighting is best." The producer whipped out a small black kit from his man bag.

"What's that?" Matt said, suspicious. "That better not be makeup."

"That's exactly what it is, and you will stand still while I apply it, and thank me when I'm done."

"Hell, no."

Bernard gave him a look. "Don't be ridiculous. You're going to be on television. The lights are incredibly bright, and did you hear me when I said 'high definition'? Everybody needs a little help. Trust me."

Matt sighed. He decided he didn't have the strength to argue. "Fine, do what you want. I don't care."

"You will when I'm finished," Bernard said in a singsong voice.

He closed his eyes and felt Bernard's fingers on his face, dotting God knows what onto his cheeks and under his eyes. He felt a powder puff and then a brush, and then some kind of balm being applied to his lips. A few stray eyebrow hairs were tweezed, and then his brows were combed. Then he felt Bernard's fingers in his hair, and there was some kind of spray applied.

"Okay, open your eyes," Bernard said, and Matt did as he was instructed. "Look up." Standing on his toes, the producer put some Visine into Matt's eyes and he blinked in reflex. "Good. That's better."

Matt looked into the mirror once again and was surprised. Goddammit, he did look a lot better. His skin was glowing and the hollows in his cheeks weren't as prominent. His eyes were clear. Wow. He could see why girls liked makeup so much. What a difference.

"How'd you get the puffiness to go away?"

he said, touching the area under his eyelashes that had been swollen only moments ago. "That's amazing."

"Hemorrhoid cream. Works like a charm."

"Dude. That's totally gross."

"You askcd." Bernard dug through his man bag again. "Your energy is still for shit, though. You need to pep up, and you have two options." He held up a small bottle of 5-hour Energy in one hand, and a tiny vial of what could only be cocaine in the other. "Pick one."

"Are you shitting me?" Matt stared at him. "I'm not taking drugs to be on a fucking reality show."

"Unscripted television, for the love of God," Bernard said, thrusting the 5-hour Energy drink toward him. He slipped the vial of coke into his pocket. "Drink up, quick quick. Everybody's waiting for us."

Matt downed the energy shot in one gulp. He was starting to think that maybe the rumors were true about the Fresh Network. These people were definitely more than a little suspect. In his wildest imagination, he couldn't imagine being offered cocaine by anybody who worked at the *Food* Network.

"Ready?" Bernard said, heading back toward the door.

"As I'll ever be," Matt said.

As soon as he stepped out, the camera was right

in his face. Bernard was right, the lights were insanely bright.

"You look fantastic." It was Karen's voice, and Matt squinted. He hadn't noticed her standing behind the camera guy and could barely make out her outline. "Okay, so we're going to film you for a little bit here, then follow you to your food truck out in Kirkland and do a few hours of filming there."

"Got it."

"Tip number one—don't ever look directly at the camera." Karen stepped forward, and Matt felt her fingers in his hair as she smoothed it. "Tip number two—act natural. Be yourself."

"Okay," Matt said with a grin. "But just remember, you told me to."

27

Sam sat in an interrogation room at the East Precinct, the fluorescent lights bright above her head. The table was metal and rectangular and there were four chairs. It had been ten minutes since she'd been ushered in, but she was in no particular hurry. She couldn't deny she was a little tickled to be here, and that it was kind of cool that Sanchez had asked her to come to the precinct immediately. Fingering the visitor's badge clipped to her shirt, she wondered if they'd let her keep it.

A small camera was mounted up in the corner

of the room, and its light was flashing green. She didn't know if that meant she was being recorded, or just watched. Reflexively, she smoothed her hair, tucking a loose tendril behind her ear.

The door to the interrogation room opened and Detective Robert Sanchez finally entered, armed with two Starbucks coffee cups.

"And here I was expecting a generic Styrofoam cup filled with whatever that sludge is you call coffee," Sam said with a smile. "Starbucks doesn't fit with the image I had in my head of making an official statement at a police precinct."

"Ha." Sanchez took a seat across from her and slid her cup across the table. He was dressed in a dark gray suit, one of his better ones, and his tie was actually knotted, albeit loosely. "You've been watching too much *Law & Order*, my sweet. One of the detectives was going for a Starbucks run so I put in an order. Soy chai latte, right?"

"Aw, you remembered." Sam took a sip.

"Okay." The detective took a long sip of his coffee, then lcaned back in his chair. He looked tired. "Let's get this over with because I'm sure you're a busy girl, and God knows I'm a busy guy. When was the last time you talked to Bonnie Tidwell, otherwise known as Joyce Kubacki? I need you to be specific, Samantha. I need an exact time frame."

Sam's eyes wandered up to the camera again. "Are we being recorded?"

"Yes."

"Who's watching us right now?"

The detective sighed. "A couple of really experienced police officers. Actually, I have no idea. Wave if you want to."

Sam lifted a hand and wiggled a few fingers. "I last saw Bonnie six days ago," she said. "I drove her back to her motel and we said our goodbyes."

"Did you walk her inside?"

"No, I just dropped her off out front."

Sanchez took another sip of his coffee. "And how did you leave things with her?"

"Uh . . ." Sam had to think for a moment. "We talked for a few minutes in the car before she got out. She promised to get in touch with me when she got back to Sacramento. Then she double-checked that she had my address because she was going to send me a box of photos that she had of my mother and me. We hugged. I thanked her for meeting me, asked her to reconsider telling me the Butcher's name. She said she'd think about it, and would let me know if she had time for dinner before she headed back home. Then we said goodbye."

Sanchez looked up. "What do you mean by 'get in touch'? Was she going to call you? Email you? What?"

"Actually, I never gave her my cell phone number. All the communication we'd had up till then was done through the online forum, and I started kicking myself the next day when I realized I had no other way of getting in touch with her. That's why I stopped by the motel again, and that's when the clerk told me she checked out. I just assumed she decided to head home early, and I won't lie, I was pissed. I was hoping she'd talk to me."

"What was the name of the website again?"

"TheSerialKillerFiles-dot-com."

Sanchez nodded. "So after you dropped her off at the motel, you never communicated with her again?"

"Nope. I did try, " she added, as if this somehow made a difference. "I sent her a whole bunch of messages through the forum, but she never responded."

"I'm going to need a copy of all the exchanges you had with her on the forum. From the time you first met. Better yet, give me your login info and I'll print it out myself."

"No problem."

"Anything else that you can think of that I should know about?"

"Nothing comes to mind." Sam slumped a little in her chair. "This isn't much help, is it?"

Sanchez waved a hand. "Don't worry about it, I didn't think it necessarily would be. If you'd have thought of anything you would have called, so we're just crossing *i*'s and dotting *t*'s."

"You said that backwards."

The detective was quiet for a moment. "Did Bonnie/Joyce tell you she had cancer?"

Sam sat up straighter. "No. Did she?"

Sanchez nodded. "The medical examiner confirmed it. We subpoenaed her medical records from Sacramento. Looks like she was stage four pancreatic. Nothing anyone could have done for her. That kind of cancer works quickly."

"Oh God." Sam put a hand over her mouth. "Bonnie never said a word. Do you think that's why she came up here?"

The detective shrugged. "I can't even begin to guess what her motivations were, but it's as good an assumption as any. She probably figured she had nothing to lose by telling everything she knew, whatever that might have been."

"She knew the Butcher's real identity."

"So she said."

"You still don't believe that, do you?" Sam frowned, frustrated. "When we talked the other day you sounded like you weren't ruling out my theory after all. Because that girl from Marysville was missing her left hand. Come on, Bobby, I thought you were finally with me on this."

Sanchez turned and looked right into the camera. He made some sort of hand signal and waited. A few seconds later, the green light stopped flashing. Then the light was red. And then it went out entirely.

"What's going on?" she asked. "You turned off the camera?"

"That's because we're about to have a personal conversation, and I don't want anyone listening." The detective's expression was serious. He laced his fingers together on top of the table. "There's something I need to tell you. About the Butcher."

"Okay."

"First, the disclaimer." Sanchez's eyes bored into hers. "What I'm about to say, I shouldn't be telling you. You're a civilian, you're too close to the situation, and you're going to freak out. All good reasons I should keep my mouth shut, but I'm not going to, because after everything you've been through, I feel you need to know. I believe you've earned it. But that's me being a friend, not me being a cop."

"Okay," Sam said. She had absolutely no idea what Sanchez was about to say, but that was certainly one hell of a disclaimer. "I understand. I won't say anything to anyone, Bobby."

" 'Anyone' includes Matt. And the Chief. And whoever else you might be tempted to tell."

"I understand." She refrained from mentioning the argument she'd had with the Chief earlier, and the fact that Matt's grandfather might not ever speak to her again.

"Disclaimer number two," Sanchez said. "It was agreed at the very highest level that this information was not to be made public. When you freak out, I want you to keep that in mind, okay? I only found out myself this morning, by accident."

"I hear you. You're killin' me, Smalls," she said, quoting *The Sandlot*. She reached for her latte, then changed her mind. She was now too wound up to drink anything. "Just tell me before I pass out."

"The Butcher had another element to his signature." Sanchez took a breath. "It wasn't just the hands."

"What?"

"The Butcher kept hair," Sanchez said. "From the victims. A small swatch of it, near the nape of the neck. But not all the way under. It was like he parted the hair through the middle and snipped a piece off, as if he didn't want us to know he did it. Which he probably didn't. But all the Butcher victims had a swatch of hair snipped off. Every single one."

"Including my mother?" Sam held her breath.

"Yes."

She sat back in her chair, trying to process this new information. Her head began to pound. "Let me make sure I understand what you're saying because you know I'm about to freak out. You're telling me that the Butcher kept hair from his victims? And you're confirming that my mother was a Butcher victim?"

"The answer to your first question is yes. The

answer to your second questions is, it's a definite possibility."

"And you found out about the hair how?" Sam paused. "Or maybe an equally important question is, how the *hell* did you not know about the hair before?"

Sanchez was prepared for the question. "The detective who's working the Jamie Chavez murder case in Marysville asked for the Butcher files to be sent over right away. Her missing left hand flagged him, which was understandable, but he thought he was probably looking for a copycat. That's what we all assumed as soon as we heard about it. He didn't think anything would come of it, but he wanted to see the old Butcher files anyway, just to compare the notes from those murders to Chavez. No problem, right? It's his case, he can investigate it however he wants. So we boxed up all the files and sent them over. He then called me this morning. Asked me if I was aware that the medical examiner's files from the Butcher cases were all missing."

"Medical examiner's files are missing how?"

"They're gone," Sanchez said. "He said none of the ME's reports are in the files. I have no idea where they went; I just assumed everything would be in there. I asked Records, and they have no idea, either. Nobody can even verify *when* the ME's files went missing. Back in the eighties, there was no backup system. So if the hard copy reports are gone, they're gone."

"Okay," Sam said, confused. "So what does that mean?"

"Well, it was bugging me, so I decided to track down the ME, the one who worked the original Butcher cases. His name is Cam Bradbury. He's in his early seventies, retired, and lives in Portland now."

"Okay."

"He wasn't even surprised when I called asking about the missing files, said he figured that somebody, eventually, would notice. What he told me was that the Butcher had another element to his signature. Everybody knew about the hands, of course, because that was made public. But nobody knew about the hair."

"Why?"

"Because he was advised to leave that part out."

"Okay," Sam said, her mind working. "But that happens, right? The police don't always release everything to the media. For lots of reasons."

"That's true. But internally, the missing hair should absolutely have been in the autopsy reports."

"So why wasn't it?"

"Like I said. Bradbury was instructed to leave it out."

"By who?" Sam said, still confused. "And . . . why?"

"By Captain Edward Shank, lead detective on

the case." Sanchez grimaced. "Bradbury said that Edward Shank made it very clear he didn't want the hair mentioned anywhere, that it was to be kept secret. Nobody on the task force even knew; it was only Shank and Bradbury. The ME said that at the time, the Chief wanted to minimize leaks, to help distinguish the real Butcher murders from the copycats. And back then, leaks were rampant at Seattle PD. Stuff was always getting out."

"Yes, and there were two copycat murders already." Sam rubbed her temples. "Okay, so I get why Edward wanted that kept out of the reports during the investigation, but once Wedge was shot, shouldn't there be full disclosure?"

"That's an excellent question, and one we'll have to ask the Chief. It's possible he might have forgotten he'd had that info redacted earlier, what with all the media coverage after Wedge was shot. But whatever the reason, the reports are missing. And while Bradbury has no reason to lie, I can't actually confirm if what he's saying is true. Because the reports are just gone."

"And you can't exhume the bodies because hair decays after a year or so," Sam said, recalling what she'd read in her homicide investigations textbook. The same textbook, ironically, that had been a Christmas gift from Edward Shank.

"Right."

Sam leaned back in her chair and stared at the

detective. "So what about Jamie Chavez? Was she missing a swatch of hair?"

"Yes."

"And what about Bonnie Tidwell?"

"Yes. Her, too."

Sam closed her eyes as the weight of it finally hit her. "So you're looking for the Butcher. Holy shit."

"We could very well be." Sanchez wrung his hands. "I personally think so, but we'll have to be very careful about how we present this to the public. It's one thing to be searching for a new Butcher. It's a whole other thing to be searching for the *old* one."

"Because that means Rufus Wedge didn't do it," Sam said, her voice faint. "Which means Seattle PD shot the wrong guy."

"Yes. And yes." The detective leaned forward. "And there's deeper ramifications than even that. I ran a query on female murder victims between the ages of fourteen to nineteen, who were missing swatches of hair. Other than your mother, there were two, one in 1989, and another in 1993. Both teenagers, both brunette, both missing hair from the same spot. Hands intact, though, which is why it didn't flag. And two wasn't enough to point to a serial killer, especially since the murders were four years apart. One was found in southern Oregon, and the other in northern Washington."

"And it also didn't flag because the hair from

the Butcher cases was never reported," Sam said, horrified. "Oh God, this just keeps getting worse and worse. If the Chief hadn't decided to keep that information quiet, three more women, including my mother, wouldn't have died." Her voice was bordering on hysterical.

The detective grimaced. "In Edward Shank's defense, he did the best he could under the circumstances. You were too young to remember what it was like back then, Samantha. The city was *freaking out,* to borrow an expression from my kids. The body count was piling up, and there were already two copycat murders. The whole investigation was becoming a nightmare. Seattle PD was under a tremendous amount of pressure to find the Butcher, and I can understand why Shank thought he was doing the right thing by withholding certain bits of information. But now, in hindsight? This is a fucking mess."

"Are you going to do a press conference?"

"Eventually, but not until we know exactly what we're looking for. Connie Lombard wants this quiet until we know just what we're dealing with."

Sam nodded. That made sense. Constance Lombard was the current chief of police.

"Right now the official tagline is that we're looking for a *new* serial killer with similarities to the Butcher," Sanchez said. "We're not going to say anything about Rufus Wedge being the wrong guy until we're absolutely fucking sure."

Sam sat back, her eyes welling up with tears. On the one hand, she felt vindicated. Her theory about Wedge being the wrong man all along was about to be proven true. But all she felt inside was . . . empty. Her mother was still dead. It really didn't change anything at all.

"You okay?" Sanchez asked softly.

"I don't know."

"When this comes out, you'd better believe it's going to be a media frenzy." The detective closed his eyes for a moment and swore under his breath. "You say nothing, you understand? I told you because I know you need the closure. But this goes nowhere outside this room. You don't tell your boyfriend. Nobody. Tell me you hear me."

"Loud and clear, Bobby." Sam wasn't about to argue. "So then who the hell is the Butcher?"

"I don't know, but we'll catch him."

"And who's going to tell Edward?"

"That he headed up a task force that killed an innocent man?" Sanchez laughed, but there was not one trace of amusement in it. "I don't know, but it sure as shit isn't going to be me."

28

Matt tried calling Sam again, but her phone went straight to voicemail, which meant one of two things: either her phone was off, or she was hitting the ignore button as soon as she saw his name and picture pop up on her iPhone.

Pretty easy to guess which one it was, since Sam's phone was never off.

He knew things had been distant between them, and yeah, he'd definitely been a shit to her lately. Okay, if he was forcing himself to be totally honest, he'd been a shit to her for a lot longer than "lately." He'd always put his career before his relationship with Sam, but could anyone blame him? He'd had an incredible wave of success for someone so young.

But here was the thing . . . he missed her. He missed her in a way he didn't think was possible. He missed her laugh, he missed her smile, he missed her face.

Sam had always been there for him, always doting on him, always so proactive about making sure they had plans to see each other, always thinking up fun things for them to do. But in the last few weeks, she had stopped all that. She hadn't been around at all. She wasn't interested in his reality show. She'd stopped coming by the restaurant to say hello. She hadn't slept over at his place in weeks, not since he'd moved into the Chief's old house. Other than that weird night when she'd snuck into his house only to catch him watching a porno, she seemed completely uninterested in his life.

And he hated it. Because he realized now that he'd been taking her for granted, and that his life seemed *less* somehow without her in it.

The camera crew was packing up their equipment and Matt stifled a yawn. He thought the first couple of tapings had gone well. There'd been some drama between himself and one of the servers. One of his bartenders was a charismatic dude and he'd had some funny, candid moments. A baseball player for the Seattle Mariners had come in to have dinner with a few of his buddies (arranged by the good folks at the Fresh Network, of course), and that had been completely entertaining because one of the guys in the group hit on a waitress that he'd already slept with but had forgotten about. It had been fun.

Karen was in front of him suddenly, and Matt blinked.

"That could not have gone better today. You're a star in the making, Matt." The producer's voice lowered to a purr and she put a hand on his arm. "Why don't we go somewhere and decompress? Change of scenery and some drinks? We can talk about just how far your star can . . . rise."

He stepped back, refraining from rolling his eyes at her cheesy come-on. What the hell had he ever seen in her? He honestly couldn't remember now what it was about her that he'd found so attractive initially. What a colossal mistake she had been, and as far as he was concerned, it would never happen again. With her or with anyone.

"I'm sorry, Karen, I can't. I have plans with Sam."

"Bring him along." The producer winked. "I don't mind."

"Sam. As in Samantha. My girlfriend."

"Oh." Karen's body language immediately shifted from hot to cool. "Gotcha. Okay, well I'll see you tomorrow. We'll have one more day of shooting, then we'll do an edit and see what we've got."

"Sounds good," Matt said. "Have a nice night."

She left, her step a little quicker than usual, and Matt waited around until the camera crew finished packing up their gear. It had felt a little strange to lie to Karen about having plans with Sam, because obviously they had no plans. He tried calling her again, and again it went straight to voicemail. Where the hell was she?

Matt said a quick goodbye to the Fresh Network crew, and then locked the door behind them after they left the restaurant. Clicking lights off, he headed back to his office to get his things so he could exit out the back way as he always did.

Maybe Jason would know where Sam was. Jase always seemed to know. Matt tried calling his friend, but Jason's phone, which was also never turned off, also went to straight to voicemail.

Okay, for real now, what the *hell* was going on? Why wasn't either of them answering?

And come to think of it, Matt hadn't seen or heard from Jason in a while, either. Scrolling quickly through his phone, Matt located the last text message he'd received from his friend.

Well over a week ago. *Huh.*

The little seed of suspicion that had been in Matt's brain for a long time was finally beginning to sprout. Clenching his fists, he felt himself begin to swell with an anger so intense, it couldn't possibly be rational.

So help me God, he thought, the rage seeping into his pores. *If they're fucking each other, I will kill them both.*

29

Trying to get into Jason's condominium was like trying to break into Fort Knox. There was a doorman and a security guard on staff at all times, but if Matt was going to catch his friend fucking his girlfriend, then he didn't exactly want them calling the ex–Seahawks quarterback upstairs to let them know he was coming up.

Matt was parked in his utility van across the busy city street in Jason's neighborhood off Denny Way, the engine idling, staring into the well-lit lobby of his friend's building. It was a fancy-ass place, filled with people who had money. Mind you, Matt wasn't resentful of his friend's success in the NFL—if you could make millions of dollars playing any sport professionally, why the hell wouldn't you?—but at times he did resent Jason's *face*. It was handsome, recog-nizable, and it opened a lot of metaphorical doors, something Matt was still working on.

Well, not the handsome part.

Once upon a time Matt had thought about living in a building like this, but then his grandfather had announced that he was giving Matt the house. Which, at the time, had seemed like the greatest gift ever. But now he wished it hadn't played out that way. Because if Matt had moved into a building like this, he would never have dug up that goddamned crate in the backyard, he wouldn't know his grandfather was a serial killer, and he wouldn't be having nightmares about PJ Wu.

Continuing to stare into Jason's building, Matt considered his options. He could either shift the van into drive and head back home to leftover stew and whatever was recorded on his DVR, or he could let the doorman announce his arrival to Jason, which would then give Sam a chance to hustle out as he was riding the elevator up to the penthouse.

Unless . . .

He killed the engine.

Didn't he have the code to Jason's side door entrance somewhere? He couldn't remember the reason Jason had given it to him, but Matt could remember using it at one point. Grabbing his iPhone, Matt clicked through it, opening a note labeled "Miscellaneous" where he stored bits of random information. It took him a few seconds of scrolling to find it, but yes, there it was, aptly titled "Jason's side door code." It was 131313. No surprise there; thirteen had been Jason's Seahawks number.

Matt stuck his phone in his pocket and locked the van door behind him. The damp chill caused him to shiver a little as he made his way across the busy street and around the building to the other side, where there was a glass door and a keypad. Punching in the code, he waited, and a second later the door opened.

Yeah, baby. It was almost too easy.

He made his way down the softly lit hallway to the elevators, which were located just off the lobby. A quick punch of the button and he'd be in the elevator before anyone saw him. But before he came close to reaching the doors, the uniformed doorman appeared in front of him. *Shit*.

"Good evening, sir." The doorman smiled, his

300

shiny white teeth contrasting against his dark skin. Though pleasant and polite, his eyes were sharp, and the man was built like a pit bull. Likely ex-military. "May I ask to see your ID?"

"I'm just going up to see a friend." Matt's heart rate picked up, but he managed to sound calm and confident. "He gave me the side door code to make things quicker." He stepped to the side, a lame attempt to get around the doorman. Behind him, Matt could see the security guard, who was also built like a pit bull but with paler skin, watching them both.

Pit Bull One's smile seemed genuine, but he didn't budge. "I totally understand, sir, but building policy is that the side door code is for residents only. All guests do need to be signed in. Which apartment are you visiting?"

"Is this really necessary?" Matt did his best to sound put out. "Clearly if he gave me the code, he doesn't mind me coming up to see him."

The doorman's smile never wavered, but it did tighten, and he turned back to glance at the bored security guard, who suddenly didn't seem to so bored. *Jesus Christ, put guys in uniforms and they automatically think they're in control of the universe.*

"I do understand, sir, but I still need to check your ID and notify the tenant that you've arrived. Otherwise, I can't let you up." Pit Bull One looked pointedly at the phone in Matt's hand. "You're welcome to call your friend to check that I'm giving you the correct information. I'm sure he'll understand, too. The residents all know the drill."

You've got to be fucking kidding me. "No, that's fine, if anyone's going to call, it might as well be you."

"Which guest did you say you were visiting?" the doorman said as he headed back to the lobby desk to where the security guard was seated. Pit Bull Two picked up the phone, finger poised above the number pad, appraising Matt from behind the desk.

"I'm here to see Jason Sullivan. Tell him it's Matt Shank."

"Mr. Sullivan, in penthouse A," the doorman said to the security guard, who nodded and punched in a code. "I assume then, that you have a key for the elevator?" he said to Matt. "The penthouse floor is only accessible with a key."

"I don't." *Shit. Forgot about that.*

"Then it's a good thing we're here to call for you." Big smile.

Matt didn't smile back.

The security guard cleared his throat and spoke into the phone. "Good evening, Mr. Sullivan, it's Troy from downstairs. You have a friend here to see you?" He listened a moment and then said, "He said his name is Matt Shank." A nod. "I will. You're welcome, Mr. Sullivan." He nodded to Pit Bull One.

The doorman accompanied Matt to the elevators and pushed the button. When it opened, he stepped inside, one hand holding the door open for Matt to follow. He inserted his key card into the slot and then pushed P for penthouse. "You're all set, sir. Have a good evening."

"Thanks," Matt muttered. When the elevator door finally closed and he was alone, he looked up at the camera mounted in the corner and said, "Blowhards," as clearly as he could enunciate.

Yes, it was immature, but whatever. Did these yahoos in polyester uniforms actually think he was a stalker or some kind of criminal?

But you are a criminal, his mind whispered. *You're a murderer.*

He caught a glimpse of himself in the elevator's mirrored walls, and had to admit, he'd seen better days. His dark circles were getting worse, and his face was looking craggier. He needed sleep.

The elevator chimed softly as it flew upward to the thirty-fourth floor. When he stepped out, the door to Jason's apartment was open slightly. He took a deep breath and knocked before pushing it open. "Jase?"

The penthouse hadn't changed much at all since Matt had last been here, though he still couldn't remember exactly when that had been. Twelve-foot ceilings, light walls, dark furniture, all very simple and all very expensive. Way above Matt's current pay grade.

"Matt!" Jason came out from the kitchen area, open bottle of beer in hand. He offered it to Matt immediately, seeming surprised to see his friend, but not particularly nervous. Matt noticed a woman's purse sitting on the kitchen counter, but it wasn't one he recognized. Had Sam bought a new purse, or was it someone else's? "Good to see you, buddy. Were you in the neighborhood?"

"Sorry for just dropping in. I tried calling you but your phone's been going straight to voicemail all evening."

"Oh, shit. Yeah." Jason looked over his shoulder quickly and lowered his voice. "Lilac's here. She hates it when I get calls during 'our time.'" He used his fingers to make exaggerated air quotes, his lips pursed in displeasure. "I fucking hate having it off, but I'm trying to be respectful of what she wants, you know? We don't get a lot of time alone together. I mean, you know how it is."

"Lilac's here?" Matt suddenly felt very uncomfortable, and okay, more than a little bit foolish. He'd come primed for a fight and wasn't expecting that the reason he hadn't been able to get a hold of Jason was that he was actually with his *own* girlfriend, and not Matt's. "Sorry, I didn't mean to interrupt. Shit, I should go." He moved to put his untouched beer on the breakfast bar.

"No!" Jason said, his voice filled with good-humored urgency. "Stay. Please. We've been together all afternoon. All. Afternoon. So please, just stay. Hang out. For me."

Matt finally allowed himself to laugh, and immediately felt his whole body relax. "Okay, okay. I'll hang out. Nice to see you, my friend. Got any food?"

"Yes I do," Jason said promptly. "And I love how you own your own restaurant, and yet you're always hungry. There's leftover pizza. I ordered it before Lilac got here." His voice dropped and he leaned closer. "Totally forgot she was a vegan and I had them, like, *pile* it with sausage. She picked it all off, but she was so grossed out." He chuckled with glee. "I'll pop it in the oven; there's still half of it left."

"Jay? Baby?" An unequivocally girly voice floated out from the bedroom. "Did you say something? Who's here, honey bear?"

Jason looked at Matt, stricken, and Matt lost it. He burst into laughter, trying to hold it back, unsuccessfully, behind his hand. "Oh shit, dude. She actually calls you *Jay?* And *baby?* And . . . *honey bear?*"

"Yes, and you know I hate it, and don't you say a fucking word," Jason hissed.

"Are you kidding? I'm going to record this for ESPN."

"Bite me."

A second later, Lilac appeared from the bedroom. As she crossed the living room floor

305

toward them, Matt felt his mouth drop open slightly. Tall, maybe five foot ten, she was barefoot, wearing a simple cream dress that hung down to her ankles but was cut very low up top, showing her ample and well-defined cleavage. Her platinum hair was swept into a topknot that was designed to look casual, but still looked totally sexy. Her cheekbones were high, her eyelashes were long, and her lips were full. If she was wearing any makeup, Matt couldn't detect it.

She was smoking hot. So *this* was what had been keeping Jason busy the past little while. It all made sense now. Until she spoke.

"I'm sorry, we haven't met," Lilac cooed in a little-girl voice, stepping toward Matt. "I'm Jay's girlfriend, Lilac Sills."

Matt held out a hand, but she ignored it, instead wrapping her long, slender arms around him. He felt her breasts press against his chest, and wondered if they were real; they felt a tad too firm. He made a mental note to ask Jason about that later. "Matt Shank," he said into her topknot. "Nice to meet you."

He glanced over at Jason, who shrugged apologetically. Lilac pressed against him for a few seconds longer than was necessary before pulling away.

"Oh, wait. You're Matt Shank. I know you, Jay talked about you. The Food Network guy?"

"Fresh Network," Matt and Jason said in unison.

"Huh?" Lilac said, looking back and forth between them. "What's that?"

"There's two different networks," Matt said. "The Food Network's the big one. The Fresh Network is . . ." He paused, searching for the right words, feeling stupid.

"The other one," Jason finished.

"Oh." Lilac seemed mildly confused, and Matt couldn't help wonder if that was a common thing for her. "Well, at least you're on TV. You could be the next Naked Chef."

"Sam would love that, I'm sure," Jason said with a chuckle.

"Oh." Lilac's face changed, her warm expression cooling. "You're *that* Matt. You're Sam's boyfriend. I met her the other day, right, Jay? She's . . . nice." The last word rolled off her tongue dubiously.

"Is that right?" Matt said, and just like that, he felt his whole body stiffen again. "What, did you guys all go for drinks and forget to invite me?" He kept his tone light.

"No, we didn't go anywhere," Lilac said, giving Jason a look. "She came by to hang out with Jay as I was *leaving*."

Jason suddenly looked uncomfortable. Matt forced himself to smile. "Well, that's typical with those two. They've been friends a long time. Better get used to it. They're like brother and sister."

Lilac's smile was frosty. "Not like any brother and sister I know, but if you say so."

"Hey now," Jason said, stepping in. "We've *all* been friends for a long time. Since grade school for me and Sam, and college for me and my boy here."

"Sounds a little incestuous." Lilac's pout was equal parts childish and sexy. "I feel left out."

"So do I," Matt muttered.

"Anyway, I'll be on my way." Slipping into her shoes, Lilac reached up and pulled out the elastic band holding her topknot in place. Long blond hair tumbled over her shoulders in waves and she tousled it lightly. Damn if she didn't look like a Victoria's Secret model. Matt knew he was staring, but there didn't seem to be any way not to, and it didn't seem to bother her a bit. In fact, she seemed to expect it. "I'll see you boys later?"

"I'll call you tomorrow." Jason leaned over and pecked her on the lips. In heels, she was almost his height so he didn't have to bend down. "Have fun tonight at the yoga thing."

Lilac wiggled her fingers at Matt before walking out the door. He didn't know if she always walked like that, but it was hard not to notice her perfect ass cheeks under the clingy fabric of the dress. Once she was gone, Jason breathed a sigh that sounded a lot like relief.

"*That's* Lilac?" Matt said, turning to his friend.

"You never said anything about her looking like that. She's the yoga instructor?"

"Why do you diminish it?" Jason reached into his fridge and pulled out a beer for himself. "She's not just a teacher, she actually owns a bunch of studios. I know she doesn't seem like it, but she's actually pretty smart. When she's not being completely jealous and annoying and smothering the shit out of me, that is."

"If she looks like that, who gives a shit if she smothers you? You poor, rich, ex-football player. If it's too much for you, she can smother me instead. Be happy to take one for the team."

Jason smiled and shook his head. "Don't be deceived. It gets old after a while."

"I feel your pain and suffering. Jackass."

The two sipped their beers in silence for a moment.

"So what brings you by?" Jason finally said. "Oh hey, I guess I can turn on my phone now. Hooray."

There was no way Matt could admit that he'd come by to try to catch Jason alone with Sam. Because—and this was no way a knock on his girlfriend—what would Jason want with good old Sam, when he clearly had his hands full with Lilac? Who looked like *that?* Not that Sam wasn't pretty, because she was a beautiful girl in her own right, but let's be real here. Sam wasn't five foot ten with legs from here to China.

And there was something to be said about legs from here to China.

Goddammit, Matt really needed to get his shit together. Some days it felt like he was losing his mind.

"I just wanted to see how you were doing," he finally said. "I wasn't able to get a hold of you today. Your phone didn't ring."

"Aw, you missed me." Jason was scrolling through his phone, which was pinging with all the texts and emails that had accumulated over the day. "Yeah, sorry, man. Lilac and her rules. We're going to have to talk about this later, she and I, because I'm not sure I like this particular rule. I missed three business calls, one of which I really needed to take. Shit. Oh, and it looks like Sam's sent a bunch of texts . . ." Jason's voice trailed off, his eyes widening. He put the phone up to his ear.

"What is it?" Matt said.

Jason held up a finger while he listened.

Matt pulled out his phone, beginning to seethe again. Nope, there was still nothing from Sam. So his girlfriend had called Jason at some point today but not Matt, her actual boyfriend? And they weren't sleeping together? Right.

"She called me as she was heading to the police station," Jason said, putting his phone down. "Apparently they called her in to give a witness statement."

"For what?" Matt's mind flew to PJ Wu, but it

couldn't possibly be about PJ. He wasn't even sure Sam knew what had happened to PJ.

"They wanted to ask her about that lady who came into town, the one who knew her mother," Jason said. "They found her body the other day. She was murdered."

"What lady?" Matt had no idea what Jason was talking about.

"From the forum, that serial killers website."

"What website? I have no fucking idea what you're talking about."

"She didn't tell you about it?" Jason looked just as confused as Matt felt. "About meeting Bonnie?"

"Who's Bonnie?" Matt could hear himself getting loud but he couldn't help it. He had no idea what Jason was referring to, which was bad enough, but what he hated more was that his friend knew things about Sam that he didn't know. It wasn't right, and it was making him angry. Gritting his teeth, he said, "Obviously she didn't say anything to me about any of this, Jase, or I would know what the fuck you're talking about. So could you please just explain before my brain explodes?"

Jason rubbed his temple, something his friend did when he was stressed. "Sam met a woman online who claimed to know the identity of the Butcher."

"The Butcher? As in the Beacon Hill Butcher?"

311

That was the last thing Matt had expected to hear, and his blood pressure immediately rose. "She's still on that?"

Jason gave him a dirty look. "It's personal to her, and you know that. She's not going to give up until she proves the Butcher really killed her mother. You know how obsessed she is. She's writing a book about it, for Christ's sake."

Matt swallowed, willing himself to stay calm even though his head was spinning. *Does she know? So help me God, does she fucking know?*

"Anyway," Jason continued, "this woman, Bonnie, said she wanted to come to Seattle to talk to Sam. That she had information for her about the Butcher that nobody else had."

"And Sam agreed?" Matt was struggling to process all of it. "Why in the *hell* would she agree to meet a perfect stranger? From some serial killers website, no less?"

"Because the woman sent her a picture of her mother." Jason sighed heavily. "It was the freakiest thing, man. Apparently Bonnie and Sarah were close friends back in the eighties. She had no idea Sam was Sarah's daughter. When Sam saw the picture, she knew she had to meet the woman. Don't worry, though, she didn't go alone. I went with her. Didn't want her to get ice-picked." He made a stabbing motion with his hand, accompanied by a squawking sound.

Matt didn't laugh. He couldn't; he felt like he'd

just been hit with a sledgehammer. Putting his beer down on the kitchen counter, he forced himself to speak in a normal tone of voice. "And this all happened when?"

"The past couple of weeks." Jason said this casually, but his facial expression was tense. "You've been busy, man."

Somehow those four words sounded worse to Matt than anything else his friend had just said. It was hard not to take it as criticism. "Yeah, well, I would have gone with her had I known. She didn't tell me any of it."

"You've been busy," Jason said again. "And let's be real here, you don't like hearing about this stuff, anyway. You think it's stupid."

"And you don't?" Matt's jaw clenched. "She thinks a dead serial killer murdered her mother. It's bad enough you indulge her, but the Chief does, too."

"Because it's important to her." Jason looked at him. "That's what friends do. They care about the things their friends care about."

Matt returned the stare. "You've been getting pretty close to her lately."

"I've always been close to her." Jason, who'd been leaning against the granite breakfast bar, straightened up to his full height of six three. Reflexively, Matt straightened up, too, putting him an inch above Jason. "She's a good friend."

"How good?"

"Don't start. That shit's getting old, and you know it."

"You've always had a thing for her."

"I've always cared about her, yes," Jason said evenly, his jaw working. The phone on the kitchen counter rang—not Jason's cell, it was his home phone line, but he ignored it. "And I always will care about her. I did before you came along, and I will long after you're gone."

"The fuck that's supposed to mean?"

"Don't pretend like you've been a good boyfriend, Matt. You've been a shit to her, and your relationship's going nowhere." Jason's ears were turning pink, and his words were coming faster. "First with the whole house thing, not wanting her to live with you even though you have four fucking bedrooms and you knew all she wanted was to make a home with you. Then with this reality show thing. She thinks you fucked the producer. Did you?"

"I don't know what the fuck you're talking about." Matt's mind reeled as he tried to absorb everything Jason was saying, while at the same time figure out what to say back that wouldn't get him nailed. "She thinks I fucked Bernard? Bernard's gay."

"The other one. The Halle Berry look-alike. And don't be a dick, you know what I meant." Jason's stare was unwavering. "She saw you two, okay? At the Pink Door. She showed up a few minutes late, feeling bad because she knew you'd invited her to the dinner and she turned you down. Well, she ended up going, and she saw the two of you."

"There was nothing to see."

"That's not what she said. She said Halle Berry was all over you, and you were loving every second of it. You call that being a good boyfriend? Should I go on?"

"Fuck you," Matt said, and he could feel the anger and hate rising up inside him. Jason Sullivan better not push him, or God help him, he'd smash the beer bottle he was holding right into his friend's face. "Get off your sanctimonious high horse, asshole. Like you're ever a good boyfriend to any of the women you've been with?"

"None of those women are Sam, and we're not talking about me."

"So now we get to the truth." Matt crossed his arms over his chest and moved forward an inch. "Why don't you just admit that you want her, Jase? You've always wanted her, and you've been right here in the middle of our relationship like a fucking fungus that won't go away, whispering in her ear about how lousy I am for her, and how I'll never give her what she wants. Why did you even introduce me to her if you've wanted her for yourself all along?"

"I've never said any of those things to her, buddy, but they're true, and you and I both know it. And trust me when I say that I wish I'd never introduced you." Jason's home phone rang again. This time he glanced at it, but made no move to answer it.

"Right," Matt said. "So tell me, have you fucked her? Is that the reason I haven't been able to get a hold of either of you all week?"

"And you say *I'm* the sanctimonious son of a bitch?" Jason stepped forward, fists clenched. "Where do you get off, man? This whole sense of entitlement thing is getting really old. You think the whole world revolves around you? You think you can just be with her when you need her, and then blow her off when you decide you're too busy?"

"So you'd be better for her, then?" Matt said with a sneer, well aware of Jason's hands. He couldn't help but hope that his friend would hit him. Hell, it might feel good to take the punch . . . and then rally back with a big one of his own. Unlike PJ Wu, Jason Sullivan would actually put up a fight, and Matt was ready for it. "You think you can make her happier than I can?"

"Anybody could." Jason's voice was low and menacing. "That's what you don't get, my friend. *Anybody could.*"

"Anybody could what?" A female voice came from the doorway, and both men turned to see Sam watching them. Her dark eyes were as wide as saucers as she took in the two of them, both big guys, standing with their fists clenched, squaring off against each other. "What the hell is wrong with you two? Are you seriously fighting right now? I could hear you guys before the elevator doors even opened."

"What are you doing here?" Matt and Jason said, again in unison.

"Ronnie let me up." Sam stared at Matt, then at Jason, and then her eyes focused on Matt again. "He tried calling up, nobody answered, but he knows me so he let me in."

"Oh, that's perfect," Matt said with a bitter laugh, looking at Jason. "Just perfect. He lets her up, but I have your side door code and I get the Spanish Inquisition?" He turned to Sam. "No doubt you're here all the time."

"What the hell has gotten into you?" Sam was looking at him with an expression he'd never seen before. It was a mix of disgust and wonderment. "Who *are* you?"

"I'm your boyfriend, or so I thought—"

"You know what, I don't care." Sam held up both hands, her tone clipped. "I don't give a shit what you two are fighting about, because I've had a crazy day, okay? A crazy, awful, horrible day. I finally get confirmation that my mother was murdered by the Butcher, but instead of it making me feel better, instead of it making me feel vindicated because it means I'm not crazy, it makes me feel worse, because now I know that *my mother was killed by the Butcher.* Isn't that awesome? Go figure." Her voice had gotten louder.

"What?" Jason said, his mouth dropping open. "Are you sure?"

Sam turned to him. "I can't talk about the details, but yes. They're taking another look at the Butcher's cases. Bobby told me himself today." She stared at Matt. "Imagine the poor sucker who has to tell the Chief he got the wrong guy? I'd love to be a fly on the wall for that conversation."

The oven chimed, causing them all to jump.

"Pizza's ready," Jason said.

30

Edward hadn't felt this good in years.

No. Scratch that. He hadn't felt this good in two decades.

His intention wasn't to kill Gloria, but, much like urination and sex, killing could be hard to stop once you started. At least in his experience.

His groin twitched at the memory, and he smiled. Gloria had been a hot little thing, firmer than he'd expected underneath her clothing. Muscle tone could have been a little better, perhaps, but what else could you expect from a woman in her seventies? Her tits had been the biggest surprise. Good size, good shape, and firm. She'd giggled when he'd complimented her, admitting to having breast implants put in when she was in her sixties, "more as a way to lift them than to make them bigger." Hey now, he'd said, no need to explain. They'd looked good and he'd stayed hard, so there was nothing to complain about.

Until she started getting on his nerves. Women never changed.

They were lying side by side on the bed, watching the smoke from Edward's cherry-flavored cigar circle above them. There was a strict no-smoking policy at the Village, but he knew Gloria wouldn't say anything. All Edward wanted was to be still for a while and enjoy the afterglow of having pleasured a female for the first time in over ten years without the help of pharmaceuticals. Was that too much to ask? Apparently it was.

"I like you, Edward," Gloria had said, rolling over on her side to look at him. Her mascara was smudged around her eyes and there was not a trace of coral lipstick left on her mouth. Her ash-blond hair was mussed. She wasn't unattractive. "Do you like me?"

"I like you fine." He patted her bare knee with his hand.

"Maybe this weekend we could go out to dinner. Somewhere nice. You still drive, don't you?"

He nodded and took another drag on his cigar.

"My daughter is having a birthday party in

two weeks. She lives down in Tukwila close to the airport. You should come, she'd love to meet you."

"We'll see."

"It's been a long time since I've been with a man." She looked up at him through her eye-lashes. "I'm very choosy."

He grunted. "That's not what I heard."

Propping herself up on her elbow, Gloria stared at him. "What did you hear?"

Edward grinned. "Just that you're not that choosy." He patted her knee again. "Don't get your panties in a bunch. I'm not judging. I don't care."

"No man likes a loose woman," she said, her face flushing. "I am not a loose woman."

"Okay."

She lay back down. "I'm enjoying your company, is all. I would like to get to know you better. I've been alone for a couple of years now, and frankly, it's hard to be alone. My kids all have their own lives, and I don't drive that much anymore, and while I have a lot of friends here, I miss having a man to do things with, to take care of. How long have you been a widower, Edward?"

"Four months," he replied, puffing on his cigar.

"I suppose it hasn't been that long for you. But a man of your stature and reputation must have his pick of women. You should know I'm well-off. I have money and I'm very comfortable."

"I would assume that, since you live here. The Village ain't cheap."

"But it would be nice to have someone to travel with, and there are still places I haven't been that I'd like to see. Do you like to travel, Edward?"

He sighed. "What I like is quiet. Anybody ever tell you that you talk too fucking much?"

She recoiled, pulling the blanket over her bare torso. "Language, Edward," she said, frowning. "If we're going to spend time together, I can't have that language used. I have grandchildren. They hear enough of that nonsense on TV, and oh my goodness, the music they listen to nowadays? It's so vulgar, so profane."

"You're so ironic," Edward said, amused. "You'll fuck like a jackrabbit in heat, but you get offended at the word *fuck*. Makes no sense to me."

"*Language,*" she said, pursing her colorless lips.

And that's when he'd lost it. Turning to face her, punched her square in the face.

It stunned her for a few seconds, and he used the time to carefully stub out his cigar in the water glass sitting on the bedside table. Putting a hand to her face, she began to cry. Before she could say anything, he was on top of her, pinning her down with his size and weight. It wasn't hard to do. He was six four and 180 pounds, and she was maybe five two and 110 pounds soaking wet. His fingers wrapped around her neck and squeezed. Her eyes bulged, and as the life drained out of her, he felt his cock grow hard again.

Just like with Marisol. And just like with Marisol, he'd clean up when he was finished.

FOUR MONTHS EARLIER

His dinner was late. That had been happening a lot lately. Once wasn't a big deal, twice was annoying as hell, but three times? In one week? Unaccept-able.

He poked his head into the kitchen and saw Marisol sitting at the table, staring into space, Bicycle playing cards laid out in front of her for Solitaire. She'd also been doing that a lot lately —not the Solitaire, but the staring—and he didn't particularly mind or care, unless his dinner was late. Something was simmering in a pot on the stove. He walked over to it, lifted the lid, and peeked inside. *Adobo*. It smelled good, but he couldn't tell whether it was even close to being done or not. She was the cook. He paid the bills. That's how things worked in the Shank house-hold. He put the lid back down.

"Marisol," he said, turning to her, keeping his voice neutral.

She didn't respond. She just sat staring, her face not making any specific expression. Edward believed she had heard him, though it was clear she wasn't processing. Which to him, felt the same as being ignored.

"Marisol. I'm starving. When will dinner be ready?"

Again, nothing.

He walked over to her and checked out her Solitaire game. Moving a red queen underneath a black king, he then bent down and moved her hair away from her ear. He touched her gently, lovingly, and then said, in a volume three times louder than it needed to be, "Marisol! Where the hell is my damned dinner?"

She blinked, his loud voice snapping her out of whatever reverie or daydream she'd been immersed in. Her eyes widened, and she looked up at him, her face morphing into an expression of clarity. "What did you say, Edward? I'm sorry, I must not have been paying attention."

"It's six twenty," Edward said. "What time do we eat dinner, Marisol?"

She looked up at the clock mounted on the kitchen wall. It took her about two seconds to process what time it really was, and he watched as the fear seeped into her body. Her posture stiffened and her glance turned skittish. She pushed back from the kitchen table, her wooden chair scraping the tiled floor.

"I'm so sorry, my dear. I don't know how I lost track of the time." She stood up and headed right to the stove. Checking under the lid of the pot, she stirred and then tasted. "It's ready. It's perfect. I'll serve you. Do you want a beer?"

He nodded, but he was not to be appeased. Three times late was simply ridiculous. He knew it and she knew it. He didn't think he would hit her—the hitting had stopped decades ago, before Matthew was born, and he had other outlets if he felt the need to get physical—but he definitely needed to think of a way to help his wife not forget.

As he ate her cooking, which was of course delicious (*adobo* was her specialty), he stewed.

Later that evening, they sat side by side on the sofa in the living room in front of the television watching *Jeopardy!* Edward smoked a cigar. Marisol knitted. This was their usual routine. And in keeping with their routine, Marisol had called out the answers (or questions, as they were on *Jeopardy!*), usually getting them right about half the time. But then she stopped. And then she sat, once again staring into space, the knitting needles in her hands not moving.

"Marisol," he said.

"You hurt Lucy," she said, her voice faint but clear, her eyes blank. Her slight Filipino accent was barely discernible when she spoke softly like this. "You hurt our daughter. You're the reason she's dead."

It was not the response he'd been expecting. She was really out of it. She was never allowed to talk about their daughter. Ever. He'd taught her that lesson a long time ago.

"Marisol," he said, forcing himself to be patient. "Snap out of it."

She didn't move. She didn't acknowledge that she'd heard him. He felt his blood begin to boil. Again, he was being ignored.

He reached over and touched her breast. Gently. They hadn't had sex in over ten years, and surely this unfamiliar touch would wake her up.

It didn't. She didn't move. But she did start knitting again.

He frowned. He didn't know what this bullshit was, but he didn't like that she wasn't talking to him, and he snapped his fingers in front of her face.

"Marisol. *Marisol*. Stop ignoring me. I am speaking to you."

Her fingers moved faster. He stared at her hands weaving the orange yarn together. He had no idea what she was making. He never did, because he never asked, and she never talked about it because she knew he didn't give a shit. She wasn't doing this on purpose.

Or was she?

He touched her breast again, this time pinching her nipple beneath the soft cotton of her sweater. He pinched hard. Her mouth opened and a little moan escaped her lips. Sitting this close to her, something he usually didn't do, he could smell the *adobo* on her breath. Somehow it only angered him more.

He took the yarn and needles away. She didn't protest. Standing up, he grabbed her by the hand and pulled her up to her full height of five foot three. Again, she didn't protest. She was standing just fine, not swaying or leaning or doing anything to show she was disoriented or dizzy or confused. What the *hell* was wrong with her?

"Marisol," he said again.

Nothing. And it was infuriating.

He glanced at the piano in the corner. It was an 1890 Mathushek upright, the piano he'd probably paid too much for thirty-something years earlier, but she'd loved it, and at least he hadn't forked out the megabucks for a baby grand. He led her to it, and she walked slowly, but her posture was perfect. Her eyes stared at nothing. Pulling out the piano bench, he guided her around it, then pushed down on her shoulders until she was seated.

Opening the book of sheet music in front of her, he selected a piece he knew she knew from memory. *Moonlight Sonata* by Ludwig van Beethoven.

"Play this," he said, tapping the page.

She didn't move. He didn't think she would, since she hadn't responded to any of his other verbal commands.

He placed her hands on the ivory keyboard,

chipped and worn in places. Who knew how many hands over the years had touched these keys? Who knew exactly where this piano had been, and what it had seen?

"Play," he said again, pushing the A-flat key, which he knew was the first note for the right hand in *Moonlight Sonata*. He was a competent piano player himself, and knew more than enough to get by if someone wanted to sing a Christmas carol or two and Marisol was busy in the kitchen, but he was by no means in his wife's league.

At the sound of the A-flat key, her hands flexed. Long fingers—wrinkled now, the nails not so perfectly manicured anymore—were still full of dexterity. She began to play. The haunting notes filled the room and he sat back and watched. She was playing perfectly, with the right speed and the right dynamics, and it sounded beautiful, as it always did.

She was either losing her mind or she was messing with him.

Either way, it was unacceptable.

He waited a few minutes until she got to the end of the song, ending softly on a quiet note, and then placed his hand on hers and stood her up. She looked at him, her eyes clearing once again, as they had before dinner.

"Edward?" she said. "Was I playing?"

"Yes, you were, my dear. And it sounded wonderful as it always did."

She smiled, and he leaned down and kissed the tip of her nose. She laughed and moved to put her arms around him.

He allowed her to hold him for a moment, but just a moment.

Then, turning her around so she faced away from him, he bashed her head into the corner of the Mathushek as hard as he could.

Once was all it took. She was a small woman, and it hadn't even taken that much effort. She fell to the floor, Edward making no attempt to catch her. She lay on the hardwood floor, looking up at him with dark eyes that understood.

She had to have known that this moment was coming at some point.

She had to have known, because she'd known for a long time exactly who, and what, her husband was. Even though he'd promised her that he'd stopped. Which he had. Until now.

The wound gaped open, and the blood flowed freely. Edward dragged her slowly to the foot of the stairs, only a few feet away, and sat with her there until she died.

Afterward, he cleaned up the blood on the piano, using a Q-tip to remove the blood from the carved roses, along with the little trail she'd left behind that led to the stairs. He then smeared blood in the spot where he wanted them to find it, and then he called 9-1-1.

Marisol had slipped down the stairs, he said.

She'd fallen and hit her head on a stone gargoyle that lay at the base of the last step, something they'd bought together when they'd toured Italy for their anniversary years ago.

Nobody questioned it. He was the goddamned former chief of police of Seattle, for Christ's sake, the man who'd brought down the Beacon Hill Butcher in a cinematic shoot-out outside Rufus Wedge's apartment building. His wife was seventy-nine, only a year younger than Edward, and she hadn't been in the greatest health. She'd been disoriented lately. He hadn't been diligent enough about watching her. They should have sold the house years ago and moved into a rambler, or a retirement home, or someplace just plain safer.

There there, the pretty paramedic had said. Accidents happened. The police were called, but since the young officers who showed up were too in awe of Edward's presence, very few questions had been asked.

More than three hundred people showed up for Marisol's funeral. Most of them were Edward's friends and former colleagues. Marisol, though a sweet, gentle woman, had never had many of her own friends, and what family she had was in the Philippines. A few of her old piano students came by to pay their respects, but that was all.

When the excitement died down a few days

after the funeral, Edward was left with a kitchen full of pies and casseroles and lot of remorse at his lack of impulse control.

He would never taste his wife's *adobo* again.

31

Matt was acting so strange.

He offered Sam more tea, and she held out her mug so he could fill it. He was fanatical about his tea, having purchased some fancy kettle from Teavana a little while back that had cost more than her monthly car payment. She had never had the heart to tell him that she couldn't tell the difference.

They had left Jason's together, and she'd been prepared to go back home, by herself. Until tonight, she and Matt hadn't even spoken since that awkward night she'd snuck into his house. So when he'd asked her to follow him back to the house in Sweetbay so they could talk, she was surprised.

This was it. This was the end. And she couldn't say she was surprised.

"I don't know why I'm so nervous," Matt said, and as if on cue, he spilled a drop of tea on his kitchen counter. He wiped it away with a dish towel and then handed Sam her mug. "I guess it's that we haven't really talked in a while. Not counting arguments, that is. I guess I feel a bit weird."

Sam accepted the tea with a small smile, but didn't feel the need to say anything. Of course it was weird with the two of them now. How could it not be? They were so disconnected, so removed from each other's daily lives. She was fairly certain that, despite his hot denials, he had done something inappropriate with that slutty producer from the Fresh Network. And she hadn't been perfect, either—she'd asked Jason to kiss her. Her relationship with Matt, which probably should never have started in the first place, had been on thin ice for a while. And that was probably understating it.

Why was it always so hard with Matt, and so easy with Jason?

Stop it, she told herself. This wasn't the time to think about Jason. Her feelings for him were too complex, too confusing. She needed to focus on the man in front of her, which was Matt.

Pulling out a chair, he sat perpendicular from her at the kitchen table. For a moment, they sipped their tea in silence, both of them wrapping their fingers around their mugs for warmth. Sam glanced around the kitchen, still so filled with Matt's grandmother's presence. The giant wood fork and spoon that she'd brought over from Manila was still hanging on the wall above Matt's head.

"You must miss her," she said. "Lola, I mean."

Matt smiled, but it was filled with sadness. "I do. Every day. Sometimes I come home from work half expecting to see her in the kitchen making *torta*."

"What's *torta* again?"

"The ground beef with egg. You like it."

Sam nodded. "Right. I do."

"I should make it for you sometime," Matt said. He looked at her, his eyes red and moist. "I should cook for you. I can't remember the last time I did that."

Sam looked down into her tea mug. "I can't, either."

"She loved you, you know." Matt smiled again, his eyes flickering away. He seemed to be having a hard time making eye contact. "You were the granddaughter she never had. You know, some-times I wonder if I have a brother or a sister somewhere out there. Sometimes I think I should try looking. Lola always said they never knew who my father was, but I think she was just trying to protect me. I mean, come on, the Chief could find anybody. Sometimes I wonder why he never tried to find my dad."

Sam was surprised. Matt never made references to his parents, ever. His mother had given birth to him when she was sixteen, and according to Edward, even Lucy herself didn't know who Matt's father was. Shortly after Matt was born,

Lucy had died of a drug overdose, as drug addicts tended to do.

"Have you been thinking about that lately?" she said, her voice soft. This had been the last thing she'd been expecting to discuss, but she couldn't imagine not talking about it if this was something he truly needed to talk about. She did still care about him, after all.

"Sort of." He sipped his tea, swallowed, and finally focused his gaze on her. "I've been thinking a lot about family, and about the way I live my life, and my priorities. I've been thinking about whether or not I'm happy."

"Are you?"

He paused. "I should be, but . . . no."

She had no idea where this was going.

"Sam, do you ever wonder what your life would have been like if your mother hadn't died?"

It was an easy question to answer. "All the time. I'd be a different person, that's for sure."

"In what way?"

"I wouldn't want the things I want so much. Or maybe I would, but I'd be willing to be patient. Something like this . . ." She gestured at their surroundings. "A house, a family . . . maybe those things wouldn't be so critical to me now because I would have had them growing up. I know I've put a lot of pressure on you over the past year."

Matt shook his head. "You really haven't. You've been completely normal, actually. It's me.

I'm the one who doesn't know how to do this."

"Do what?"

"Be happy. With you. With us."

She looked at him. Here it was. The breakup. She braced herself for what was about to come.

"I have this thing in me, always wanting to be better, always wanting more," Matt said. "No matter how much I do, no matter how much I achieve—"

"It's never enough," Sam finished. "But that's who you are, Matt. That's exactly why you've had so much success. Because you're driven. Because you want more."

"But what's the point?" Matt said, his voice cracking. "What's the point of the food trucks, of the restaurant, of the TV show, of this house, if I have nobody to share it with? If there's nobody to come home to? What's the point of it all if I'm going to end up dying alone?"

Sam stared at him. She wasn't sure what she was supposed to say. What he had just said was the same thing she'd been telling him for the past year.

"I've had a terrible few weeks," Matt said, and Sam watched in shock as tears began to seep from the corners of his eyes. "A terrible, awful few weeks. I have done things . . ." His hands shook, and he wrapped them around his mug tighter to steady them. "I don't like who I've become. This is not who I want to be."

"I thought everything was going well for you." Sam reached over and squeezed his hand. Despite everything that that happened, it was hard not to comfort him. After three years together, it was still her default setting. "You've been so busy."

"When we were at Jase's tonight, and you were talking about your mom, and that lady you met who died, I realized how much I don't know about you," Matt said. "And I know it's my fault. Because I don't ask. Because I don't show interest. Because I'm selfish. And I shouldn't be. If anyone should understand what it's like to have questions, what it's like to need answers about your mother, it should be me."

"Matt—"

"Just please let me finish." He took another deep breath. "I have not been a good boyfriend to you. I know that. But I can change, Sam. And I want to. And if you let me, I will spend the rest of my life being a good husband to you, in all the ways I wasn't as your boyfriend."

Sam was speechless. That had definitely *not* been what she'd expected him to say.

Reaching into his pocket, Matt pulled out a small, dark blue jewelry box. A ring box. Sam stared at it, then stared at Matt. She opened her mouth to speak, but no words came out.

"Open it," he said.

She did, and her breath caught in her throat. It was a diamond ring. A beautiful diamond ring in a vintage setting, with a center stone that had to be close to two carats. She recognized it immediately.

"It was my grandmother's," Matt said. "You don't have to wear it if you don't want to, we can get you something else, but you always said you liked it. No matter what, I want you to have it. She would have wanted you to have it."

"I . . . you're giving me Lola's ring?" Sam's mind couldn't seem to keep up.

"Yes. I want to marry you."

Sam's hand flew to her mouth. "Oh, Matt . . ."

In a flash he was out of his chair and kneeling in front of her. "I love you, Sam. I really do. I know I have a horrible way of showing it, but I can't lose you. I need you in my life. You make me want to be better. And I can be better. I promise."

"Matt . . ." Sam's eyes welled up with hot tears. Leaving the ring inside the box, she pushed it away. It was all so confusing. How many times had she dreamed of this moment, of Matt down on his knees, asking her to spend forever with him? "Matt, I can't. It's too late. This isn't right, and you know that. All you're doing right now is throwing out a Hail Mary. We both know this isn't working."

"I don't want this to end."

She touched his face, her heart breaking. "But it already has."

He shook his head, too overcome with his own

emotions to speak. Both of them were full out crying now. Standing up, she pulled him to his feet, and they held each other. She felt his lips at the top of her head, and she lifted her face up to his, her eyes closed. His lips touched her forehead, her eyelids, her nose, and then her mouth. The heat was still there. Oh yes. It didn't change anything between them, but it was still there, and Sam felt it surge through her body. Passion had never been their issue.

But she knew then, even as his lips covered hers and she responded, that she wasn't in love with him anymore. Not the way she used to be. Not the way she should be.

He kissed her deeply, his tongue searching hers, holding her tighter than she could ever remember being held. It felt good. She kissed him back, their tongues intertwining, her hands slipping under his shirt, lifting it up so she could caress the small of his back. He kept one hand on the back of her neck while his other hand slid down to her buttocks, rubbing, squeezing.

Unzipping his pants, she pulled his jeans down past his knees, then pulled his boxer briefs down as well. Placing both arms underneath her armpits, he lifted her up, hoisting her with ease onto the kitchen table, pushing aside their empty tea mugs. He pulled off her jeans, never breaking eye contact with her, and she couldn't remember the last time she'd felt so wanted.

Her panties were on the floor a second later, and he entered her in one smooth motion. Neither of them spoke. The only sound that could be heard in the kitchen was their mutual moaning. What they had was over, but somehow this moment, this one last time, felt right.

As he thrust deep into her, she looked up into his eyes. "I'm sorry, Matt."

His face was full of pleasure and pain. "Shhh. Don't say that. It doesn't have to be over. We can start again. We can try harder."

"You don't love me."

"Yes, I do. I know that now. I was stupid . . ." He closed his eyes, groaned, panted, and then continued thrusting. "I love you. I've always loved you. I always will love you."

"But I don't love you," she said softly. "Not the way I should."

"I can change."

"I don't want you to."

"I can change," he said, his breath coming faster. Beads of sweat appeared at his hairline. "I want to change. I don't want to be this person. I'm a bad person, Sam. I don't want this anymore. I want you, I want a life with you . . ."

"No, you don't," she said, and suddenly, this didn't feel right anymore. In fact, this was starting to feel very, very wrong. "Matt, stop."

"I can be your everything." His eyes were closed, and he showed no signs of slowing down.

Sam wasn't even sure if he'd heard her. "Just give it a little time. You'll feel it again, I know you will. Just don't leave me, okay? Please don't leave me."

"Matt, stop. I mean it." Sam pushed against him, trying to wriggle away, but her ass was sticking to the wood table and it was difficult to move at all. "I don't want to do this anymore. I changed my mind. Stop."

"I love you." His eyes were still squeezed shut.

She pushed on his chest some more. Still, he continued. Beginning to feel panic, Sam started punching him in the chest.

His eyes flew open and he grabbed both her hands, squeezing her wrists, still continuing to plow into her. Now it was beginning to hurt. She was drying up, and he wasn't stopping, and it was painful. He was hurting her.

"Stop. Matt, stop. Please!"

He let go of her hands and grabbed her by the throat, squeezing so hard, she couldn't breathe. He was cutting off her air supply, and in sheer panic Sam pummeled at him, using her fingernails, raking them over his chest, but still, he didn't stop.

Her vision began to darken, and then it was over.

32

The news reports really didn't have much to say, but the headlines screaming BUTCHER 2.0! were enough to work Seattleites into a frenzy. The story hadn't yet made its way to CNN or any of the other national media outlets, but Edward knew it was just a matter of time. He'd already had several reporters call that morning asking for his opinion, and so far all he'd said was, "I'm confident Seattle PD will do their job, like they always do."

He was watching the latest update on KIRO-7 while sitting in the recreation room playing a boring game of checkers with Johnny Langston. Langston was a skinny, potbellied, seventy-three-year-old widower who had just moved into the Village the previous week. Plagued with health problems, he'd already spent twenty minutes telling Edward about all the medications he was taking.

Edward had managed to tune out the running commentary, focusing instead on the anchorman on the TV screen, who seemed very concerned about the "new" serial killer at large. "In an announcement made last night by Police Chief Constance Lombard," KIRO-7's Jeff Walsh was saying in his deep baritone, "we've learned that the Seattle Police Department is searching for a new serial killer terrorizing the city of Seattle, referred to as the Butcher two-point-oh."

Edward thought *terrorizing* was a fantastic word. Very dramatic, and so effective.

"Your move, Ed," Langston said from across the table, pulling his attention away from the TV.

"It's Edward, Johnny." How many times had he corrected the idiot today? He'd lost count. Tearing his eyes away from the news, Edward focused on the checkerboard in front of him. What a stupid game. Checkers was a game for children and retards, but Langston didn't know how to play chess. "Or you can call me the Chief like everybody else does."

"And what are you Chief of?" Langston said with a snort. "You don't look like an Injun."

Edward sighed, using one finger to slide his red checker into the appropriate spot. "I told you. I was a police officer for over forty years. Retired as chief of police."

"Chief of police of what?"

How was it possible that anyone could live this long being this stupid?

"Of the Seattle Police Department," Edward said, forcing himself to stay polite. *Idiot.*

"Oh, okay. Like what the lady does on the TV right now? She's pretty good-looking. Bet she's got nice tits under that suit," Langston said. "You know her?"

"Yes, I know Connie. She was a rookie when I was Chief. Good woman."

"I've only been in Seattle for the past twelve years, so I don't know nothin' about what happened before I moved here, you know what I'm saying?" Johnny stared at the board, contemplating his next move. "I woulda rather retired to Florida, that's where it's at, the weather's good and housing is cheap, but my kids and grandkids all live here now and I don't wanna have to travel to see them every year at Christmas . . ."

He was still talking but Edward had stopped listening, once again focused on the TV mounted on the wall.

"Police Chief Lombard has confirmed that they are reopening the old Butcher cases from the seventies and eighties, as these new murders closely resemble those allegedly committed by Rufus Wedge," the anchorman intoned. "Former Police Chief Edward Shank, who headed up the task force that shot and killed Butcher suspect Rufus Wedge in 1985, declined to comment."

Edward tried to stifle a chuckle, but he obviously didn't try hard enough.

Langston looked up. "You find this stuff amusing, Ed? You got like, a thing for death and murder and all? Yeah, I s'pose I can see that, being in the line of work you were in."

Edward turned back to his checkers opponent,

wishing he had a mute button for the man who couldn't seem to shut up to save his life. "It's Edward. And it's not amusing, Johnny. It's fascinating. There's a very distinct difference. There's a serial killer at large in Seattle, you know. It's big news."

Kyla Murray, the Sweetbay Village activities director, passed their table with a smile. Her blue golf shirt and dowdy khaki slacks did nothing to conceal her double-D curves, and immediately Edward was picturing her in a lace bra and panties. Red. With a garter belt. Johnny Langston was feasting on her, too, but his approach was less subtle as his eyes scanned her body from head to toe.

"What I wouldn't give for a piece of that ass," Langston said under his breath.

Edward chuckled. Glancing down at the checkerboard, he moved one of his red pieces, jumping it over two of Langston's black pieces. "Your move. And be careful, my friend. Kyla's a nice girl. Don't be disrespectful."

"Don't tell me you're on this whole 'women are equals' thing, Ed." Johnny moved a black piece across the board. "Women are not our equals. I'm not saying we're better, okay? But they're not our equals."

Secretly, Edward agreed, but no way would he ever admit that to a retard like Johnny Langston, who wasn't his equal, either. "Friend, you won't like it here if you don't make an effort to get along with the staff," he said. "Don't make it hard on yourself by being a dick."

"*Friend,* for what I'm paying, I can be a dick if I want to be."

Edward sighed. "Your move already. Quit stalling."

"I can see why you were the chief of police," Johnny said, moving his checkers piece. "You're a bossy guy, you know what I'm saying?"

Edward turned his gaze back to the TV, where they had just cut to an interview with Detective Robert Sanchez. Edward had seen the interview twice already, but he still found it amusing to watch the lead detective's awkward responses to the reporter's questions. Had it really been that long ago when Bobby had been just a rookie in uniform, the first officer on the scene when Sarah's body was discovered?

Edward's mouth twitched up into the smallest of smiles. *Sarah.* He would never forget the lovely Sarah Marquez, nor would he ever want to.

JUNE 1987

He watched her scrub down tables, and thought she couldn't be more than seventeen. Her long dark hair was pulled back in a low ponytail that trailed down the back of her brown and beige polyester uniform. The plastic name tag pinned above her small breast read SARAH. Despite the ugly fast-food dress code, she was still pretty, and he'd noticed her as soon as he'd walked in the door.

He'd been in this McDonald's twice over the past week, and had learned a lot about Sarah just by watching. It didn't take a genius to see that she was a hard worker, well liked by her coworkers, and pleasant to the customers. She'd checked twice on the homeless man wearing the ratty clothes sitting quietly in the corner, and had even snuck him some french fries. She knew all the words to the ABBA song currently playing softly throughout the restaurant. Her daughter's name was Samantha.

Edward sat in the corner opposite the homeless man, on his second order of french fries himself, content in knowing he was invisible to the kids who hung out here. Which was fine by him. It was important that nobody remember him at all.

It had been two years since his last kill, and the urges, for the most part, had passed. He no longer allowed himself to look at the mementos he'd kept—videos, hands, locks of hair, panties— because all they did was stir his desires up again. He'd buried everything in the backyard one weekend when Marisol was away on a church retreat because he couldn't bear to throw anything away just yet.

The memories were all he had left, and while

they were wonderful, nothing compared to the real thing.

The last person he'd killed had been Rufus Wedge, but there hadn't been much satisfaction in it because the kill had been too quick. There had been no fear and no begging, just the fast death of a man nobody gave a shit about, anyway. Wedge had been the perfect Butcher; Edward had hand-picked the guy out of a dozen possibilities. He was a lifelong career criminal with a history of sexual assault and a tendency to never stay in one place longer than a few months, and it had been easy for Edward to choose victims in whatever city Wedge was currently living in.

It had been a long time since his last *real* kill, and Edward missed it. And, fortunately or unfortunately, this pretty young girl with the dark hair was stirring up all those old cravings he thought he'd buried two years ago along with the crate.

Sarah was back behind the counter now, manning the french fry station. Edward enjoyed looking at her. Her face was smooth and unlined, the skin supple and unmarred by the pimples that other girls her age were often plagued with.

Good skin was always a bonus. Good skin was more fun to burn.

Edward left the restaurant and sat in his car, parked a few feet away from the bus stop. Her shift ended at 10 p.m. and he assumed that she would be catching the bus home. The last time he'd waited for her she'd been with a friend, and there had been no opportunity to talk to her. He hoped this time she'd be alone.

She exited the restaurant at exactly 10:08 p.m., giggling as she called goodbye to someone over her shoulder. Walking quickly, she kept her head down as she crossed the parking lot toward the curb where the bus stop was, and that's when Edward made his move. She looked up as he got out of his car.

Her eyes were instantly wary, and Edward pulled out his badge, holding it up so she could get a clear look.

"I'm wondering if you could help me," he said. "My car won't start. I need someone to rev the engine while I look under the hood. Will only take a second."

She stepped back slightly. "You're a cop?"

"Detective, actually." He clipped the badge to his outside pocket. "You've probably seen me eat here before, I usually stop in when I work nights. Any chance you can give me a hand?"

"My bus will be here any minute," she said, her gaze flickering back and forth between his face and his badge. "Maybe one of the boys inside can help you?"

"I already asked around, but nobody has a break, and the manager won't let anyone leave unless they do."

She rolled her eyes. "Ugh, that's Alvin. He's such a hard-ass. He's only two years older than me and he thinks he rules the universe."

"If you miss your bus I can drop you wherever you want to go. I just don't want to have to call roadside assistance. They'll probably get it started in two seconds and then charge me fifty bucks just for coming out. Heck, I'd rather give that money to you."

The mention of money piqued her interest. "Fifty bucks? I could sure use that money. All you want me to do is rev the engine?"

"That's it."

"What if you can't get it started?"

He laughed. "You can still keep the money, I promise. I'll just be waiting for the bus with you."

She shifted her weight, thinking for a moment, and then her eyes focused on his badge once again. Finally she said , "Okay, let's do it. Do you, uh . . . can I have the money up front?"

He pulled out his wallet and fished out two twenties and a ten. "Hop into the front seat. I already popped the hood and the keys are in the ignition. Don't run me over, please."

She giggled and got into the car, placing her purse on her lap. Edward lifted the hood.

"All right, start the engine, and then give me the gas," he called, poking his head around to look at her. She nodded and the engine roared to life. "Keep stepping on it until I say stop."

She obliged, and he pretended to muck around under the hood for another minute.

Finally, he came around to the driver's side, shaking his head. The window was rolled down and from inside the car, Sarah looked up at him expectantly. "I don't get it," he said, infusing his voice with just the right mix of annoyance and confusion. "It's just making an awful rattling sound. I may have to leave it here, take it in to the mechanic tomorrow. I don't want to drive it and then it breaks down on me and I'm stuck in the middle of nowhere."

"It sounded okay to me," she said. "Want to try again?"

"Yeah, we'll have to. But first let me just tinker around with the alternator. Hey, can you pop open the glove compartment? There should be a small tool kit in there, and I'll need that."

"Of course." She reached over and popped it open, digging through the mess of papers inside. "You know what, I don't see anything—"

His hand shot through the window and was around her throat before she could scream. His other hand, filled with cloth and chloroform, knocked her out before she could even register what was happening.

He pushed her straight over onto the passenger side, where she slumped. Then he quickly went around front and slammed down the car's hood, hopped behind the steering wheel, and started driving. Looking over his shoulder, he confirmed there was nothing behind him. Nobody was in the parking lot, nobody had seen anything. Perfect.

Entering the on-ramp for the freeway, he kept the window rolled down, enjoying the warm summer breeze. At this time of night, it would be less than a two-hour drive to his little cabin in Raymond, and she would be waking up by then. The cabin was one of his favorite places on earth. It was in the middle of nowhere, nestled in the midst of two hundred acres of untouched forest that he'd owned for the past twenty years. Sarah would be able to scream all she wanted. Nobody would ever hear her.

Catching someone new, Edward had to admit, was always delightfully sweet, but the best part was always what came after.

The best part was the burn.

"It's your move, Ed." Johnny was looking at him closely. "Where did you go just now? Thinking about Big Tits Kyla, I'll bet. I do that too sometimes. Just space out, you know what I'm saying? Happens more and more the older I get. One minute I'm concentrating on something important, the next minute I'm forgetting what I'm doing. Sometimes I go into a store and forget what I went in there for. Don't you hate that? This one time I went into the hardware store and I . . ."

Edward stopped listening, but not before he

decided that Johnny Langston was officially a waste of space. Who would miss him if he died? Not Kyla, he was certain of that.

There was still some Viagra left. He already knew Langston was on three different heart medications. The drugs would interact nicely . . . or terribly, depending which way you looked at it.

The thought filled him with pleasure. Moving his red checker piece across the board, he jumped over three of Langston's black pieces until he reached the opposite end of the board. He offered his opponent a grin.

"King me," Edward said.

33

It wasn't rape, okay?

She'd been totally into it. She was turned on, she kissed him back, she'd helped him take his goddamned shirt off. So maybe he'd pushed things a little too far, and yes, maybe at the end he'd hurt her, but she'd been into it, and it wasn't on purpose, and it wasn't his fault that she'd let it go too far and that he couldn't stop after that.

Sam put her face in her hands and slumped into the sofa, pulling the knit blanket tighter around herself. God, she sounded exactly like a rape victim. How many episodes of *Law & Order:*

Special Victims Unit had she watched where the characters who lived in the Land of Denial sounded just like she did right now? But this wasn't television. This was Matt, *her* Matt, and in all the years they'd been together, he had never once physically hurt her. He certainly would never rape her. Things had gone too far, that was all, and it had nothing to do with the fact that their relationship was dissolving and that they both knew it was over. For Christ's sake, they still loved each other; *that* part didn't dissolve overnight. Matt was a lot of things, but he was *not* a rapist.

Or . . . was he? He didn't stop when she'd said stop. If anything, he'd gone harder, wrapping his fingers around her throat, causing her to lose consciousness for a few seconds.

She was so confused.

Forcing it out of her mind for now, Sam grabbed her laptop and clicked on the *Seattle Times* home-page, craving some kind of distraction. It worked. As soon as she saw the headline, she grimaced—it was clearly designed to shock.

BUTCHER 2.0?

The Seattle Police Department, in conjunction with Marysville PD, confirmed this morning that they are now hunting for a serial killer responsible for the deaths of two women in the greater Seattle area this past week. Both women were raped and murdered in similar ways, prompting Seattle PD lead detective and spokesperson Detective Robert Sanchez to announce that the city now has a new serial killer at large, dubbed "Butcher 2.0" by the media.

While specific details of both crimes have not been released, a source from the police department has confirmed that the murders bear a strong resemblance to those committed by the serial killer popularly known as "The Butcher" back in the late '70s and early '80s. Rufus Wedge, age 37, was the prime suspect in those murders. Wedge was shot to death outside his apartment building in Beacon Hill by a task force headed up by former Chief of Police Edward Shank, who at the time was a captain and the lead detective on the case.

The article went on to give what little background information there was on Wedge.

Edward Shank was appointed the chief of police in 1985, having received a commendation from the mayor for the Butcher case. It is the duty of the Times to mention, however, that Rufus Wedge was never arrested, tried, or convicted for his crimes. However, the murders did appear to stop after Wedge's death, and these most recent two murders are the first to resemble the crimes Wedge was accused of committing.

Detective Sanchez would not confirm whether Seattle PD is searching for the original Butcher, or the Butcher 2.0, a copycat serial killer.

Former Chief of Police Edward Shank, who retired from the police department in 1998, could not be reached for comment.

Sam reached for her phone and tried calling Sanchez. He didn't answer. Instead, a robotic voice said, "The mailbox you are calling is full. Please try your call again later."

Shit. She tried a different number.

"Hello?" Another female voice, not robotic, was in her ear.

"Hi, Vanessa, it's Sam. How are you?"

"Oh, hello, my dear." Sanchez's wife seemed pleased to hear from her. Sam could make out the sounds of video games being played in the background. "I'm pretty good. You know, busy with the kids and all. They need to go off to college already, because Lord, I'm due for a break."

Forcing herself to be patient, Sam asked how the kids were doing, and the two women made small talk for several minutes. Yes, Jacob had started high school, Christian was on the soccer team, and Dominic had a girlfriend who seemed a little slutty. Yes, Sam's new book was going well, Matt was working hard at the restaurant, of course she'd pass along a hello.

Unable to stand it any longer, Sam finally said, "Vanessa, do you know where Bobby is? I tried calling him a few minutes ago on his cell but he didn't pick up, and his voicemail box is full. He's also not answering his phone at the station."

"Oh honey, I've given up tracking my husband's whereabouts ages ago." Vanessa didn't sound the least bit concerned. "I know him, though. He always calls when he can. Did you try texting him?"

"I did."

"Well, I'm afraid that's about all you can do. But hey . . ." Vanessa paused, muffling the phone. She yelled something into the background, and when she came back on the line, the volume of the video game being played was considerably lower. "He did mention he was meeting with Matt's grandfather this afternoon."

"The Chief?"

"The one and only. I believe they're going to ask him to consult on the new Butcher cases. After all, nobody knows the old Butcher better than Edward Shank. I'm sure Bobby will call you back as soon as he's done. Say, anything new with you and Matthew? That boy put a ring on it yet? I'm waiting for my wedding invitation. It would be a great excuse to buy a new dress."

"Matt, uh . . ." Sam swallowed, unprepared for

the questions. "We're actually not together anymore, Vanessa. It ended . . . it ended recently. We're still friends, though." Instantly her mind flew back to the night before on Matt's kitchen table, and she shook her head, trying to force the images out of her head.

Vanessa must have heard the catch in Sam's throat because she said, "Oh, dear. Oh, sweetheart. Relationships are so tough, aren't they? You know what, I think we definitely need to have dinner. Just us girls, what do you say? I'm not taking no for an answer. How's next week for you?"

They quickly set a date and then Sam hung up, grateful to get off the phone so she wouldn't have to talk about Matt anymore.

Because it hurt. It really did.

34

If they needed Edward's help on the new Butcher cases, then they could damn well come to him. That was how it worked.

Edward had received a phone call from a younger female detective at Seattle PD, someone who sounded very blond over the phone, and who'd turned out to look exactly the way he'd imagined she would when she showed up at the Village a half hour later. Detective Kim Kellogg had been sent to bring Edward back to the police precinct to consult on the Butcher 2.0, but he'd shooed her away, and not so politely. He wasn't interesting in going anywhere. Frankly, it was goddamned insulting that they'd sent that bubblegum blonde to retrieve him. He was the former chief of police, for Christ's sake. Whatever happened to respect?

An hour later, Detective Robert Sanchez knocked on his door.

Bobby Sanchez was no longer the skinny little rookie Edward remembered. In his early fifties now, the man had grown into a smart, confident, and tenacious cop, and these qualities were the reason the detective had built a solid reputation over the years. Sanchez's solve rate was impressive, and Edward could see why Bobby had been chosen to head up the newly formed task force to catch the new Butcher.

The younger man stood in the doorway, looking tired but dapper in his suit, a box of cannolis from the Green Bean in one hand and two steaming coffees in the other. Two blue Seattle PD file folders were wedged under one armpit.

"You really do need my help," Edward said with a grin. "Nice to see you again, Bobby. You're looking good. Come on in."

"I heard this is the way to butter you up." Sanchez stepped into Edward's room, handing the former police chief the box of pastries. "Seems like a small price to pay for your expertise. You should charge more. Your time is valuable."

"That why you sent Froot Loops over to come get me?"

Sanchez winced. "Sorry about that. I was tied up in a meeting, and she volunteered. Kim Kellogg's actually a good cop, though, I promise."

Pointing the detective toward the sofa, Edward retrieved two plates from the kitchenette and served them each a cannoli. Sanchez dug into his, and in three bites his pastry was gone.

"Man, I haven't had anything that sweet in a long time," the detective said, sighing. "My wife would kill me if she knew I was indulging. She's put me on a diet."

"If a man works hard, then a man should eat what he wants." Edward took a bite of his own cannoli, not remotely interested in what the younger man's wife thought of her husband's eating habits. "Have another."

"Wish I could, but I'm watching my blood sugar. Diabetes runs in the family."

"More for me, then. So. Why are you here? The perky blonde said you were thinking of asking me to consult?"

"I'm not just thinking of asking, I'm asking." Sanchez's face clouded as he dusted powdered sugar off his hands. "It's a mess, Chief. We're reopening all the old Butcher cases and comparing them to the two murders from the past week."

"So then who are you looking for?" Edward said. "The old Butcher or a new Butcher?"

"Officially, the Butcher two-point-oh." The detective rubbed his face. "But between you and me, I'm pretty sure they're one and the same. It's a giant mess."

"That's not a mess, Bobby." Edward snorted. "That's a clusterfuck. I don't envy Connie when she has to answer questions about that."

"I don't, either. She mentioned getting in touch with you in the next couple of days. Your phone's probably going to start ringing, too."

"Already has."

"Chief . . ." Sanchez shifted on the sofa. "Whatever happens, I hope you don't think anyone over at PD looks at you any differently. You did the best job you could back then. Wedge was a good suspect. It was a good shoot."

"Do I look like it's keeping me up at night?" Edward said, and then offered the detective a grin. "I'm fine, Bobby. I can handle the heat."

"Damn right you can." With that awkwardness out of the way, Sanchez leaned back, visibly more relaxed than he'd seemed a moment ago. "When word gets out, though, I'm sure it'll just be a matter of time before somebody from Rufus Wedge's family comes forward to file suit on his death."

"Don't you worry about that." Edward waved a hand. "Wedge had no family." *I made sure of that before I chose him.*

The detective nodded. "Anyway, any input you have on these current murders would be appreciated. Don't worry. You'll be an official consultant. We'll pay you an hourly rate."

"Goddamned right you will, but I'll donate it to the Police Kids charity. I don't need the money."

Sanchez smiled.

"Those the files on Tidwell and Chavez?" Edward asked, gesturing toward the blue folders Sanchez had placed on the coffee table.

The detective nodded and pushed them over. "Everything we have so far is in there. Take a look, let me know what you think."

Edward looked down at the files, making no move to open them. He didn't trust himself to look at the photographs he knew would be inside, not while was Sanchez was watching him. He didn't trust himself to contain his excitement at the sight of their dead bodies. "Can I keep these?"

"Yes, those are your copies."

"I'll need some time to read through it all. Why don't I give you a call later?" Edward stood up.

Surprised, Sanchez stood up as well, understanding that he'd just been dismissed. "Of course. I look forward to hearing from you. Thanks, Chief." Reaching for his coffee cup, he paused before taking a sip. "Actually, before I leave, there is something I wanted to ask you about."

"Certainly." Edward glanced at the folders again. "Make it quick, though. I got somewhere to be."

Sanchez stood beside the door but made no effort to reach for the handle. "Back in the day, when you were investigating the Butcher, you opted to keep some things from the media."

"Sure. Standard police investigation tactic."

"Right, I understand that." Sipping from his coffee cup, the detective shifted his weight again, which meant he was feeling uncomfortable again. "But I'm wondering why you left the hair out of the reports."

"What hair?"

"The missing hair from the back of each of the victims' heads." Sanchez cleared his throat. "I know it was a long time ago, but do you recall telling the medical examiner not to put that information into his reports? Cam Bradbury was his name."

"I remember Cam," Edward said, appraising the detective coolly. "Good ME, very thorough. We worked together on a lot of cases. But I can't say I remember anything about that."

"I spoke to him yesterday." Sanchez's face was neutral, but his eyes were fixed on Edward, not missing anything. "He said that each of the Butcher victims had a lock of hair missing. He said you advised him to leave that out of reports, because you were concerned about leaks. You

361

were already dealing with two copycats and the media was creating a frenzy."

"If I did, then I did." Edward shrugged. "Like you said, it was a long time ago. What's your question?"

"I guess what I'm confused about is why." Sanchez cleared his throat again. "I mean, after the cases were closed, why wasn't the missing hair included in the reports?"

Edward stared at the younger man. "Check the reports, Bobby. I'm sure it was. Cam was an excellent medical examiner. He wouldn't have missed a detail like that."

"He didn't miss it. He left it out. On purpose, at your request."

"Okay then." Edward frowned. "So then it was added afterward."

"Was it?" Sanchez sipped his coffee. "We can't confirm whether it was, because the ME's reports are all missing from the Butcher files."

"I wouldn't know anything about that," Edward said. "My job was to catch criminals, not ensure the files of closed cases were complete. Why don't you ask Records what happened? Though I'm sure you already did."

"I did."

"Can't help you, son." Edward shrugged again. "Like you said, it was a long time ago."

"It's just . . ." The detective met his gaze with a cool one of his own. "That information was pretty important. The hair was part of the Butcher's signature, which nobody other than you and Bradbury knew about. If we had known, we might have been able to link future murders to the Butcher. Such as the murder of Sarah Marquez."

"Who?"

"Samantha's mother. She was missing a swatch of hair, too. We're looking at her as another Butcher victim. Had we known about the hair, we would have figured out that Wedge was the wrong man."

"Samantha's mother was murdered two years after Rufus Wedge was killed," Edward said. "What would we have done, Bobby? Raised that piece of shit from the dead so we could apologize to him?"

"No, but Sarah's murder would have told us that the Butcher was still out there. Which would have prevented two more murders, one in eighty-eight, and one in ninety-three. Not to mention the two that just happened this past week."

Edward narrowed his eyes and stood up straighter. "I'm not sure what you're getting at, son, but I sure as shit don't like your tone. Are you suggesting I fucked up?"

"Not at all, Chief," Sanchez said, and while the younger man seemed tense, his voice remained calm. "I'm just saying it's unfortunate that the information we had on the Butcher was incomplete. I know you're close to Samantha. I

363

am, too. I just feel bad that it's taken her this long to get closure, something we could have given her a long time ago had we known everything about the Butcher that we should have. Plus, Wedge was innocent."

Edward sighed. "You still have a lot to learn, son, and you'll understand what I mean by that by the time this is all done. Police investigations are never perfect. You're working with very little evidence, limited resources, unreliable witnesses, and a ridiculous amount of pressure from the public to solve the case. Things get missed, things fall through the cracks. We thought Wedge was our guy. If it turns out he's not, then that's too goddamned bad. But am I sorry he was shot? Hell, no. He was still a piece of shit, still a career criminal, still a pus-filled pimple on the ass of society. Nobody cried over his death, and it's nobody's loss that he's gone. I won't be losing any sleep over it, and I suggest you don't, either. Now if you can find the real Butcher"—Edward crooked his fingers, making air quotes—"then fantastic. I'll be the first one to congratulate you. But I did my job back then. We did the best we could with what we had. And all you need to worry about, son, is doing your job *now*. Do I make myself clear?"

"Crystal."

"I'll call you if I have any insights. Thanks for the cannolis."

Edward showed the younger man out, closing and locking the door behind him. When he heard Sanchez's footsteps retreat down the hallway, he let out a long breath and leaned against the door.

Condescending little shit. But a good detective, certainly.

It was all coming together.

35

It was time to end the charade. It was time to do the right thing.

Matt took a deep breath and cut the engine to the utility van. The clock on the dashboard showed 6:16 p.m., and he should have been at the restaurant for prime dinner hour, because the place would be hopping. Nothing that his well-trained staff couldn't handle without him, of course, but he knew the Fresh Network crew was there right now. Being on camera was the last thing Matt wanted to do today.

Except for this.

His phone pinged again and he glanced down. It was another text from Bernard the producer, who had to be the pushiest guy Matt had ever known. He'd already told the man twice that he had an urgent personal matter to attend to—what the fuck more did they want from him? They produced reality shows, for fuck's sake. This was reality. Shit, maybe he should have invited them all to come along. What he was about to do would undoubtedly make for great television drama.

Leaving his phone on the front seat, Matt got out of the van and headed toward the building. He hadn't been here in years, not since he was very young, and it looked much different than he remembered. It had clearly been renovated since the early nineties, and everything was gleaming and polished.

Kind of swanky for a police station.

Squaring his shoulders, he stepped through the glass doors and into the bright lights of the East Precinct.

The overweight uniformed officer manning the front desk looked up. Matt wondered randomly if the man's weight was why he was stuck manning the front desk, then he shook the pointless thought out of his head. He needed to focus. Willing himself not to shake, he stepped forward.

"Can I help you?" The officer's name tag identified him as a SGT M. COSTA. He was munching on a leftover slice of pizza that looked cold and dry.

"I'm looking for Detective Robert Sanchez." Matt's voice cracked a little on the last word.

"He expecting you?"

"No, but I'm here on a police matter. I'm also a . . . friend." Matt was stumbling over his words and he knew it. Shit, he should have rehearsed or something before he'd come inside.

The officer narrowed his eyes. "Detective Sanchez is extremely busy today. I can try calling his extension but if he's not expecting you . . ." He picked up the desk phone. "Your name?"

"Matthew Shank." Matt waited a beat, then added, "My grandfather is Edward Shank."

"Oh." The desk sergeant blinked. "Well, Jesus. That practically makes you royalty around here." He punched in a few numbers and waited. There was obviously no answer, but he tried another extension and said, "I have someone here to see Sanchez, and I'm gonna go ahead and send him up. Name's Matthew Shank, the former chief's grandson. Can you take care of him? Thanks."

He hung up and crooked a sausage-sized finger at Matt, who stepped forward until his chest hit the counter.

"You'll need a visitor's tag," the sergeant said, clipping a white badge the size of a credit card to Matt's collar. "Elevators are that way. Sanchez is on the fifth floor; make a right when you leave the elevator. And, uh . . ."

"Yes?"

"Tell your grandfather that Mikey Costa says hi." The sergeant's chubby face flushed slightly. "He was my training officer back in the day. Taught me everything I know. I got injured, so I'm on desk now. Tell him we miss him and that he should stop in sometime."

Matt gave him a small smile. "Sure, I'll tell him."

The lobby was fairly quiet and the elevator doors opened immediately when Matt pushed the button. His knees felt like Jell-O and he stuffed his hands in his pockets to keep them from trembling. Marvin Gaye's "Let's Get It On," the instrumental version, was playing in the elevator, and Matt was forced to listen to an entire verse before he reached the fifth floor. The cheesy song did nothing to quell his nerves.

When the elevator doors finally opened, it was total chaos.

The floor was packed with moving bodies, people talking over other people, the conversations melding into one other, making it impossible to understand what anybody was saying. Like the lobby, the fifth floor had been recently renovated. The room was modern, filled with windows and stainless steel, nothing at all like the dreary space he'd pictured in his mind from watching too many crime shows on TV.

Craning his neck for any sign of Robert Sanchez, Matt thought he spotted the detective in the back corner of the room, but he couldn't be certain. A moment later, a petite officer in a tailored pantsuit was at his side.

"Matt Shank?" she said, tossing her blond ponytail from one side of her shoulder to the other. "I'm Detective Kim Kellogg. The desk sergeant called up from downstairs, said to make sure you didn't get lost in the shuffle."

"Hey." Matt shook the hand she offered, and she squeezed his palm so hard he almost winced.

"Follow me." Detective Kellogg took his elbow and navigated him through the pulsing room toward the back corner. She motioned him toward a desk cluttered with papers. The computer monitor was on, and the screen saver was an aquarium scene with brightly colored fish swimming across it. Matt took a seat, wondering for the seventeenth time in as many minutes whether or not he was really doing the right thing.

Sanchez was standing in front of a whiteboard filled with photographs. All of them were colored eight-by-tens of women's faces. There were two lines drawn down the whiteboard in black marker, and on the left side, the largest side, the title read "BUTCHER." There were fourteen photographs underneath it by Matt's count. In the middle section, the title was "BUTCHER?" with a bright red question mark. Under it were three photo-graphs. And on the right side, the smallest side, the title read "BUTCHER 2.0." This section contained only two photographs.

Sanchez glanced over at him and held up an index finger. After a few more minutes of conver-sation with his team, he caught Matt's eye and jerked his head toward a door. Matt stood up and followed the detective through the door and down a hallway.

A moment later they were seated in Interrogation Room 4. It was small with a table, four chairs, and no windows. Once the door was shut behind them, Matt immediately felt claustrophobic.

"This is a bit intense," Matt said, looking around. He noticed a camera mounted to the ceiling, but it appeared to be off.

Sanchez waved a hand. In the harsh light of the interrogation room, every line in his face seemed deeper. The man looked both wound-up and exhausted at the same time, a feeling Matt knew all too well. "Don't be concerned, I just wanted us to have a quiet place to chat. I didn't think you'd want to talk out in the main area. It's a zoo." He glanced up at the camera. "That thing's not on."

"What's going on?" Matt asked, though he already knew the answer. The whiteboard had made it pretty damned clear. "This place is crazy."

"Well, it's not public yet, but it will be as of . . ." Sanchez checked his watch. "Two hours from now. The chief of police will be giving a press conference."

"To say what?" Despite his nerves, Matt couldn't help but be curious.

"To officially confirm to the public that we're looking for the Butcher."

"You mean the Butcher two-point-oh?" Matt

said. Sanchez looked surprised, and Matt explained, "I saw it on the whiteboard."

"Right. No. Not the Butcher two-point-oh. There is no Butcher two-point-oh. We're looking for the actual Butcher."

"I don't understand." Matt felt his heart stop. "What about Rufus Wedge? Are you saying he didn't do it?"

"I've already talked to your grandfather, Matt. He knows what we're going to say."

"Holy shit," Matt said, and his shock wasn't completely feigned. "That's going to be a . . ."

"Operation Clusterfuck," Sanchez finished. "That's what we're calling it internally, but don't you repeat that outside of here. How's Sam?"

"I . . . she . . ." Matt stopped, not sure what to say. His mind was still reeling, and he hadn't had time to figure out how to answer questions about Sam.

"Spend some time with her if you can. She needs you right now." Misreading Matt's expression, Sanchez added, "Because of her mother being one of the Butcher's victims."

"Oh. Right," Matt said.

A silence fell over the two of them and Matt wasn't sure how to fill it. His intention when he'd come to the precinct to talk to Sanchez had been to discuss PJ Wu, not the Butcher. He'd been planning to turn himself in. But now . . .

Now it seemed kind of pointless. Seattle PD

clearly had bigger fish to fry. They were looking for the Butcher, for Christ's sake—the *real* Butcher. And his grandfather, the former chief of police of Seattle, was the man they were hunting. Which meant the Chief had murdered those two women from the past week, one of whom was Sam's mother's friend.

Because, of course, the Chief had also killed Sam's mother.

Operation Clusterfuck, indeed.

Matt made an instant decision. He wasn't going to say anything about PJ Wu. Because it didn't matter anymore. If they caught the Chief and nailed him for the Butcher murders—*all* of the Butcher murders—then Matt's life as he knew it would be over, anyway. His career and everything he'd worked for would be gone. Why the hell would he want to speed that up?

"So what brings you by?" Sanchez was rubbing his eyes. "Man, there might not be enough coffee in the precinct to get me through the next few days."

"I actually just stopped in to, uh . . ." Matt frantically searched for a reason. "I have a supplier in the area, and I was just picking some things up. I thought I'd stop by and talk to you about Sam. She and I . . . we broke up last night."

"Oh shit." Sanchez seemed genuinely dismayed. "I didn't know that, I haven't talked to her. I haven't even been home since yesterday morning.

I'm so sorry to hear that, Matt. What happened?"

"I think . . . it's like you said. The stuff with her mother. It's kind of intense. I think she wants to be on her own for a while."

"Yeah." The detective chewed on his lower lip as he considered his next words. "But you know what, give her some time. When all of this is done and life gets back to normal, she may have a change of heart. She loves you. She always has."

"I haven't been the best boyfriend to her."

"Please," Sanchez said with a shrug. "All men feel that way. We always think we could be better, and you know what, that's a good thing. So you're a workaholic. There are worse things, trust me. Give her a few days, then revisit the conversation."

"You think?" Matt couldn't keep the hope out of his voice. He hadn't come here expecting advice on his love life from the detective, but God knew he needed it.

Sanchez stood up, the chair scraping against the concrete floors. It was a terrible sound, like nails on a chalkboard, and both men winced. "I do think so. Our Samantha, she's a loyal girl at heart. She'll give you a second chance. Just make sure that when she does, you follow it up with actions. Show her what's different. It's not about words. From now on, it's about what you do."

Matt stood up, too, and followed the older man out of the room. "I think I can do that."

The detective clapped him on the back. "Give her my best. I'll be swamped for a while with the investigation. Hey, if you see your grandfather, tell him I look forward to his input."

"His input?"

"We've brought him in as a consultant."

Matt was taken aback, though why he was surprised, he didn't know. Of course the Chief would want in on this. "How he'd take the news when you told him that he'd caught the wrong guy?"

"Pretty good, actually," Sanchez said. "Didn't really have much to say. Makes me wonder if the Chief already suspected . . ." He stopped, as if remembering who he was speaking to. "Anyway, I gotta get back to work. Good to see you, kid. Don't be a stranger. And remember what I said about Samantha."

Matt left the station, waving goodbye to the overweight desk sergeant, who now appeared to regard him with a new respect.

He'd come very close to turning himself in. Thank God he hadn't. What he'd done to PJ was a terrible thing, but it really had been an accident. He would find a way, short of going to prison, to make it up to PJ's family somehow.

He was also going to win Sam back, no matter what it took. There was nothing he couldn't accomplish if he put his mind to it—hadn't he proved that already? He wanted what was rightfully his.

Which was everything.

Enough with the whining. Enough with the guilt. Maybe there was no rewind button for life, but surely Matt could change the channel.

36

The Chief's Cadillac was in Matt's driveway when he pulled up, and he groaned. He was in no mood to see his serial killer grandfather today, or any day, for that matter. He'd managed to avoid the Chief for the past few days. The man was bad news.

The front door was closed but unlocked.

"In the kitchen," an authoritative voice called out.

Matt closed the door behind him and headed toward the sound. "Wasn't expecting you to drop by," he said as he entered the kitchen. He tensed as soon as he saw his grandfather; he couldn't help it. "I need you to call first, Chief."

"I suppose you want me to give you my key then, too." Edward Shank was standing by the stove, stirring something in a pot that smelled pretty good. "Staking claim over what's yours, are we?"

"You gave me the house." It was weird to see the old man cooking. In his whole life, Matt had never seen his grandfather cook anything other than hot dogs, steaks, and hamburgers on the grill. "If you want the house back, just say so. Otherwise, yes, I would like the extra key."

The Chief snorted. "Relax. I don't want it back. And the key's right there." He pointed to the counter where three keys lay, one for the front door, one for the back door, and one for the garage. "All yours, kid."

"What are you making?" Matt asked, although he already knew the answer.

"*Champorado*. I had a craving."

"I didn't realize you knew how to make it." *Champorado* was a chocolate rice porridge, typically eaten for breakfast. "Need help?"

"I've watched your *lola* make it enough times. I think I can handle it. Besides, I like her version better than yours."

"My version *is* her version," Matt said, his tone clipped. "Who do you think taught me?"

"Easy." The Chief gave him a look. "So testy today. Your grandmother makes it best. I'm sure you can't disagree with that."

"It's the same recipe, Chief. Even Sam can make it."

"You gave Samantha the recipe?" His grandfather frowned. "You shouldn't have done that. It's a family recipe. Samantha isn't family."

That annoyed Matt even more. "Stop it. Lola loved Sam."

"Love has nothing to do with it, my boy,"

Edward said. He stirred some more, then dipped the spoon in and tasted it. Satisfied, he placed the lid on the pot and turned back to Matt. "If Marisol had wanted Sam to have the recipe, don't you think she would have given it to her at some point?"

"I think she would have, but she died so suddenly."

"That's true, she did." The Chief was quiet for a moment. "Those stairs . . . you oughta think about putting carpet on those stairs, Matthew. They're very slippery. I never got around to doing that and look what happened to your grandmother."

"Did you kill her too, Chief?"

Edward turned back to the stove. "That's a helluva thing for a grandson to ask his grandfather, kid. What's gotten into you today?"

"It would be a crazy question," Matt said. "Except for the tiny little fact that you're a serial killer."

Edward turned the heat all the way down, and then finally took a seat at the kitchen table. Reaching into his breast pocket, he pulled out a cherry-flavored cigar. Biting the tip off, he motioned for Matt to sit beside him.

"You can't smoke in my house, Chief."

"Now it bothers you? So arrest me." The Chief lit up, and immediately the aroma of sweet cherry smoke filled the air. "Are you going to tell me what's got your panties in a twist? Come on, sit down and talk to me. You and Samantha having problems?"

Matt didn't move. "Did you kill Lola? Yes or no?"

"Your grandmother's dead." A flicker of pain crossed his grandfather's face. "Leave it alone."

"After everything I already know, you're not going to answer me?" Matt's laugh was harsh and unfeeling. "Well, I guess that tells me everything I need to know."

"She was sick," Edward said, releasing a thin stream of cigar smoke through his nostrils. "Her mind was starting to go. It was just a matter of time before we'd have to put her in some kind of round-the-clock care facility, and you know she would have hated that."

"*That's* why you killed her?" Matt couldn't believe what he was hearing. "Because she was sick?"

"I put her down, yes. It was time."

"Lola wasn't a sick cat, Chief." Matt slammed his hands down on the counter, shaking so hard he thought he might pass out. A faint buzzing started up in his head, and his temples were pulsing so hard it felt like someone was hammering on them. "She was your wife. She was my grandmother. How could you have done that?"

"It wasn't that hard." The Chief saw the look on Matt's face and sighed. "You weren't there, kid. You didn't see her. I could never leave her alone. She might have fallen, drowned in the bathtub, or burned herself. Or the house. She was seventy-nine years old, for Christ's sake. Do you know what her quality of life would have been? I was doing her a favor."

"You were doing yourself a favor."

"Same difference."

"How did you do it?" Matt said. The buzzing was growing louder now, like a swarm of bees was inside his head, frantic to get out. "Paint a picture for me. You said she fell down the stairs, hit her head. What really happened?"

"She hit her head."

"On what?"

"The piano."

"The piano that's still in the living room?"

"Yes."

Matt's fists were clenched. "You slammed my grandmother's head into the fucking piano?"

Edward didn't answer. Instead he took another long drag on his cigar.

"Fuck you!" Matt screamed, stepping closer to the old man. "Fuck you, Chief! I fucking hate you. I hope they catch you and I hope they give you the death penalty." He tried to breathe, tried to calm down, but he couldn't. The rage he felt was so intense, all he wanted to do was lash out. "I hope you fucking die, and I hope you go to hell, where you belong, you son of a bitch."

"We're all going to die someday," Edward said, looking up at him. His expression was calm, almost peaceful.

Stepping forward, Matt grabbed his grand-father by the hair with his left hand and yanked his head back. Cocking his right arm, he prepared to strike. He'd never wanted to hit anyone so badly in his life. He wanted to punch the living daylights out of this man, the man who'd raised him, the man who'd killed Sam's mother, the man they called the Butcher.

The Chief smiled. In his eyes, there was no resistance, no remorse, no sadness, no fear, no pain. Nothing. There was no soul inside Edward Shank. Matt saw that now.

"Go ahead," his grandfather said softly. "Go ahead, kid. It will make you feel better, and it will stop that buzzing I know is in your head right now. It's getting louder and louder, isn't it? So make it stop. Go ahead. Put me down like the goddamned animal you think I am."

"I wish you were dead," Matt said, tears streaming down his face. "You're a monster, Chief. I hope they get you and I hope they kill you."

"Oh, they will," Edward said. "But do you really want me dead before I can tell you all about your mother?"

"What?" Matt dropped his arm and let go of his grandfather's hair. "What about my mother?"

"I'm not going to be around much longer,

Matthew." Edward took another hit of the cigar, allowing the smoke to trail out of his lips slowly. "So if you want to know about your mother, now's the time."

"You son of a bitch." All the fight went out of Matt then, and he slumped into a chair across from his grandfather. The Chief had him by the balls and he knew it. Matt needed to know. "You asshole. Okay, then. Fine. Tell me. I want to hear it. I want to hear everything."

"First, go get me a bowl of *champorado*," the Chief said. "And then you can ask me whatever the hell you want."

37

Sam tried calling Bobby again, and the third time was a charm. She had seen the press conference a couple of hours before and had no doubt he was swamped, and of course he'd managed to call her back during the exact three minutes she'd left her phone in the car while grabbing takeout sushi.

"Hey," he said, picking up on the last ring. "Sorry, it's been a crazy day. Can you hear me okay? I'm driving."

"What's going on?" she asked. "Did you catch him?"

"Ha." The word came out like a bark, short and snappy. "I wish. I'm good, my sweet, but I'm not that good. No, I just thought you'd want to know something interesting. Again, this is on the down low."

"Goes without saying."

"We got DNA on the killer. There were skin cells under Bonnie/Joyce's fingernail we were able to retrieve. Which would suggest she scratched the Butcher, but he didn't bleed."

"You're kidding. That's great!"

"Yeah, it would be, but we ran it through CODIS and there was no name attached." Bobby gave her a moment to digest this piece of information before continuing. "Which means we still don't know who he is."

Sam knew that CODIS stood for Combined DNA Index System, but she knew almost nothing about DNA. "Well, that sucks."

"But here's something weird. The DNA of Tidwell's killer? It might not be attached to a name, but it does match the DNA we found on PJ Wu."

"I . . . what?" Sam frowned, trying to understand what Sanchez had just told her. "What are you saying? The Butcher killed PJ? Why would he do that?"

"No, he didn't kill PJ," the detective said. "I didn't say it was an *exact* match. But there is family relationship between whoever killed PJ and whoever killed Bonnie/Joyce. The lab tech discovered it by accident—he thought he'd mixed the samples up. Turns out both sets of DNA share certain markers that prove they're father and son. The father killed Bonnie/Joyce. The son killed PJ Wu."

"Holy shit." Sam let out a breath, trying to process it all. "Are you sure?"

"DNA doesn't lie," Sanchez said. "It's definitcly father and son. Not uncle and nephew, not brother and brother. Father and son."

"Do you think they're working together?"

"No idea, but trust me, I'm still trying to figure what the hell this all means, too. I don't see this every day." Sanchez honked his horn and swore under his breath. "Anyway, I'm heading to the airport to catch a flight to Sacramento. I've been in touch with their PD and I have a warrant to search Bonnie/Joyce's house."

"Okay, good luck." Sam's head was still spinning. "Bobby, before you go . . ."

"What is it?"

"Why do I feel we're missing something here? I don't know how to articulate it, but it feels like . . ." Her voice trailed off. She wasn't exactly sure what she was trying to say. All she knew was that something didn't feel quite right.

"Actually, I know what you mean." Sanchez sounded as frustrated as Sam felt. "It feels like there's a huge piece of the puzzle we're missing, and it's right there. If I could just find it, everything would make complete sense. Because right now nothing does."

383

"Exactly."

"I'm trying to get a hold of the Chief, but he isn't returning my calls. I've left him five messages. Have you heard from him?"

"No, I haven't." Sam wasn't sure whether or not to tell the detective that she wasn't exactly on the Chief's good side anymore. "But if you're desperate, I guess I can try calling him. He usually calls me back."

"I'd appreciate that. You can go ahead and tell him what I told you, too. Whatever it takes to get him to call me. Tell him it's urgent."

Sam nodded even though Sanchez couldn't see her. "When are you back from Sacramento?"

"Late tonight. I'll only be there for a few hours. Vanessa mentioned the two of you were having dinner soon? I know she's looking forward to it. She misses you."

"Yeah, we're supposed to," Sam said, gritting her teeth. *Shit.* She loved Vanessa almost as much as she loved Bobby, but the last thing she wanted to do was discuss her love life when a huge manhunt for the Butcher was going on. "I'll give her a call after I talk to Edward."

"You do that. Tomorrow all the kids are with their friends, so she'll have a night to herself. See that she stays out of trouble, you hear?"

Sam managed a small laugh. "If anything, Bobby, she'll keep me out of trouble."

38

"I never liked the name Lucy," Edward said, the smoke from his cigar circling his face. He squinted at Matt. "I always thought it sounded too little-girlish, but your grandmother always liked it. I was hoping for a boy, so when she popped out a girl, I let her pick the name."

Matt could still see the red marks around the old man's throat from where his fingers had pushed too hard. Maybe it should have made him feel bad, but Edward didn't appear to be angry about it. "Lucy is a family name."

"Yes, it is. Your grandmother's mother's name was Lucilla."

Edward stubbed out his cigar, then stood up and went to the stove, helping himself to another bowl of *champorado*. "She was a beautiful baby, your mother. Almost never cried. Was so easy to take care of, until about eight or nine years old, and then her rebellious streak came out."

Matt allowed a small smile. "I guess that's where I got it from."

"She was never a bad girl, you understand. But she did require a heavier hand. She acted out a lot. Misbehaved. Didn't listen. Then when she turned thirteen, she started with the marijuana. By fourteen, she was addicted to painkillers.

Skipping school. And there were a lot of boys."

"One of whom was my father."

Edward returned to the table, spooning *champorado* into his mouth, his gaze drifting to some place faraway. "When she got pregnant, we were devastated. Obviously. And embarrassed. To have a teenage daughter plagued with drug problems, and now a pregnancy? It made me seem like a terrible father.

"She wanted an abortion," Edward said. "I would have allowed it. Lucy was in no shape to take care of herself, let alone an infant. But your grandmother wouldn't hear of it, and she insisted she have the baby. Pretty much locked Lucy in her room the whole time to make sure she didn't use drugs while she was pregnant. Then you were born. You were healthy, thank God."

"You and my mother would have aborted me?" Matt said in disbelief. It was probably the most hurtful and insensitive thing anyone had ever said to his face. "So if it wasn't for Lola, I wouldn't even exist?"

"Oh please." The old man waved a hand dismissively. "Don't be such a drama queen. You would have wanted the same thing had it been your knocked-up, Vicodin-addicted child. And, anyway, it's water under the bridge. You're here, aren't you?"

Matt slumped in his chair. His grandfather's logic was horrifying. "Why wouldn't she name the father?"

386

"Wasn't so much that she wouldn't. She couldn't. She didn't know who she'd been with."

"You never tried to find him?" On the one hand, Matt couldn't believe his grandfather was finally opening up to him about his mother, but on the other hand, this was more painful a conversation than he'd anticipated, and he wasn't sure how much he could handle. "You were the chief of police. If anyone could find him, you could."

"Sure I looked." Edward finally finished his bowl of *champorado* and pushed it away. "But what did it matter? You were fine with me and your grandmother; you had everything you needed. Sure, I asked around, but nobody owned up. She never really had a boyfriend, but she was around a lot of boys. If I knew who he was, I'd have told you. I have never lied to you, Matthew."

"Except about the part where you're a serial killer everyone calls the Butcher," Matt said, his voice flat. "Or are you conveniently getting dementia and forgetting that part?"

"Mind isn't quite the steel trap it used to be, but I remember most things." His grandfather relit his cigar and inhaled. "But sure, sometimes I can't remember. Sometimes a memory pops into my head and it feels like it happened yesterday, when it really happened twenty years ago."

"So what happened to her? To Lucy?"

"She committed suicide."

"You told me she died of a drug overdose." Matt couldn't believe what he was hearing. "You just said you never lied to me, you asshole."

"That was what your grandmother wanted you to think." Edward seemed oblivious to Matt's name-calling. "Lucy was a junkie; she could easily have died that way. But she didn't. She hung herself. Here, in this house. In her room, which then became your room. You were three months old. She was high on pills and whatever shit she'd shot into her veins, and your grandmother came home from church and found her, hanging in her closet. She used one of my neckties."

"Oh God," Matt said, putting his head in his hands. "Oh God oh God oh God."

"You said you wanted to know."

"I . . . I don't know. I don't know what I want." He looked at up his grandfather. "How many people have you killed?"

"More than twenty. Less than thirty."

Matt's head hurt. "How many victims as the Butcher?"

"Seventeen. I think. I had to change my MO after Wedge was shot, so that's actually a complicated question to answer."

"Try. Because none of this makes sense to me."

"You understand this more than you think you do," the Chief said, squinting at him through the cigar smoke. "You're a lot like me, Matthew.

From the time you were little, I saw things in you. Your discipline. Your drive. But also your anger. Your penchant for violence. Dark things."

Matt refused to take the bait. What the old man said was total bullshit. He wasn't like the Chief. He couldn't be. "I want to talk more about Lucy. Why did she get into drugs? What did you do to her, you sick fuck?"

It was Edward's turn to pause. "There's nothing more to tell," he finally said. "She was a troubled girl. It happens. But like I said, she stopped doing the drugs when she was pregnant with you, which is why you weren't born a retard. She went back on them after she gave birth. You weren't breastfed, but you turned out fine."

"I'd agree with that," a voice said from the hallway, and both men turned to see Sam walking toward them. "Sorry to interrupt. The front door was unlocked and the doorbell doesn't seem to be working. I tried calling you both, but neither of you were answering your phones."

Matt's heart leapt into his throat at the site of her. Had she heard anything? She wasn't acting like it.

"I don't even have mine with me," Edward said. "Must have left it in the car."

Matt's was on the kitchen table in front him, but it was turned facedown, and set to silent. "Sam, this isn't a good time . . ."

"Nonsense," the Chief said. "It's lovely to see

389

you, my dear, despite how we last left things. Bowl of *champorado*? Made it myself."

"I thought I smelled something good," Sam said with a smile. She looked at Matt. "Is that okay?"

"Sure," Matt said, frustrated. He wanted to finish his conversation with the Chief. "Help yourself."

Sam grabbed a bowl from the cabinet and scooped out a portion of porridge. "You guys are talking about your mom, huh?"

"Yeah."

"I guess that's the one thing you kids had in common," Edward said. "Both of you grew up without mothers. Explains why you get along so well."

"We—" Sam said, but Matt shook his head slightly. "That's true," Sam said, changing gears. "It did bond us when we first met. I've learned a lot about my own mom lately, too."

"Is that right?" Edward said.

"Actually, that's why I'm here." Sam put her spoon down and licked the chocolate off her lips. "Did Matt tell you about Bonnie Tidwell?"

The Chief shook his head. "I didn't hear about her from Matthew. I know who she is because I have her file back in my room."

Matt sighed. "Sam, *I* didn't even know about Bonnie Tidwell until Jason told me."

"Oh right," she said. "Well, I just talked to Bobby. Chief, he's been trying to get a hold of you the past couple of hours. There's been a development he wanted to run by you."

"I'll call him when I leave here," Edward said. "But I take it he gave you an update?"

"Yes." Sam shifted her gaze between the two men. "Bonnie Tidwell's killer shares DNA with PJ Wu's killer. Isn't that crazy?"

Matt felt the blood drain out of his face. *Oh God. Oh God they were going to find out.* The cops had the Chief's DNA, and once they put it together that the Chief was the Butcher, they would know that Matt had killed PJ Wu. Forget his career falling apart, forget the restaurant and the TV deal and the food trucks disappearing, Matt was going to be sent to *prison*. For the rest of his life. Trying to sound normal, he managed to say, "That is crazy."

"They ran the DNA from both murders, and the killers share genetic markers," Sam said. "Whoever killed PJ Wu is the son of whoever killed Bonnie Tidwell."

Matt froze. "What? *Son?* What the fuck are you talking about?"

"It's true," Sam said, misinterpreting Matt's strong reaction. "They're father and son. Not uncle and nephew, not brother and brother. As Sanchez said, DNA doesn't lie. They're definitely father and son."

Matt's heart was pounding so hard in his chest, he almost couldn't hear her. Teeth clenched, he turned to the Chief. "You raped my mother?"

"Shut up, Matthew." Edward's face was like stone. "Just shut up."

"You—"

"Shut up!" Edward roared, standing up. "Just shut the fuck up. Do you want her to know?"

Sam's face was twisted into a frown, and her head was bobbing left and right. "What are you guys talking about it? What am I missing here?"

"Oh God, I'm going to be sick," Matt said, his stomach churning. His head felt like it was about to explode. The buzzing was louder now, louder than it had ever been, and he really thought he might throw up. "Sam, the Chief is my father. *My fucking father.* Oh my God. Oh my God."

"Matt, I don't understand."

They were staring at each other, but Matt didn't know how to explain further. Matt's head was reeling. Sam seemed confused. Neither of them noticed the Chief moving toward her with something shiny and rectangular in his hand.

"Matt, what—"

It was all Sam got a chance to say before a cleaver struck her in the chest.

39

Matt watched in horror as Sam dropped to the floor, looking down at herself with as much shock as he was feeling. There was surprisingly little blood. The cleaver was wedged inside her, almost dead between her breasts, at least two inches deep. She looked up at him, her eyes huge and round. Opening her mouth to speak, all that came out was a moan. The whole awful scene seemed to be unfolding in slow motion, and his legs felt stuck, although his brain was screaming at him to do something, anything, to help her.

He stepped toward her but before he could reach her, there was a hand on his arm. He turned to see his grandfather looking at him with an expression that terrified him.

The old man's cheeks were flushed, the rich red color spreading to his chin and forehead, and then his throat. His dark eyes were alight with excitement, and in that moment, the Chief seemed almost twenty years younger.

"Leave her be, Matthew."

Matt shook him off and crouched down over Sam. She was slumped against the lower kitchen cabinets, her feet splayed in front of her. She was conscious but her eyes were glazed, her face pale, her lips parted slightly. Reaching forward, he touched the handle of the cleaver, and she cried out.

"Don't," she said, gasping. "Don't touch it. Just leave it. Just leave it in, in case . . ." Her eyes rolled back and it took her a second to focus on him again. "It hurts. Call . . . call an ambulance."

She was about to pass out, and Matt was terrified that if she did, she might never wake up. He took her hand and was alarmed. It was cool and clammy, and her skin was becoming paler. She was going into shock.

Matt reached into his pocket to feel for his iPhone, but of course it wasn't there. It was on the kitchen table where he'd left it, behind his grandfather, who stood above them watching the entire scene with avid interest. And there was no other phone in the house. Matt had canceled the landline when he'd moved in. He didn't think he would need it, since he was hardly ever home anyway.

"Hand me my phone, Chief," Matt said, his voice ringing out clear in the kitchen, surprising even himself. "I have to call nine-one-one."

Edward turned and reached for Matt's iPhone. He slipped it into his pocket. "Leave her be, Matthew. Or better yet, drive the cleaver all the way in. Put her out of her misery. Put her down. You must have thought about it. Don't fight it. Unleash it."

"Give me my fucking phone!" Matt screamed,

and on the floor, Sam jolted. His grandfather, on the other hand, didn't even flinch. "I will fucking kill you, you fucking son of a bitch!"

He stood and faced the old man. The two of them were the exact same height. Same build. Same eyes. Same square jaw.

Jesus Christ. How had Matt not seen it? How had he not known? All this time, Edward had insisted that they never knew who his father was. And yet, all along, it was the Chief who was his father.

It was sickening. It was horrific. It was beyond comprehension.

"Give me my phone, or I'll take it from you," Matt said.

"Then take it," Edward said. He smiled.

Matt lunged.

40

Detective Robert Sanchez checked his phone, frowning at the text message he'd just received from Kim Kellogg that was insisting he call her on her cell phone. He was finally checking his messages after making it through the slow security lineup at Sea-Tac Airport, but her message confused him. She was scheduled to be at the precinct all night and he'd told her not to go anywhere. Why was he calling her cell phone?

"It's Sanchez," he said. "Why aren't you at the precinct?"

"I am at the precinct," the younger detective said. Sanchez turned up the volume on his phone. It was loud at the airport and he could barely hear her. "Something just came through on the DNA found on PJ Wu."

"We already know it shares genetic markers with the Butcher." Sanchez hustled his way to the gate, checking his watch. His stomach growled as he passed the food court, but his flight was boarding in a few minutes and there wasn't time to grab anything.

"Yeah, but we got a match in CODIS."

Sanchez stopped. He could see his gate from where he was, but they hadn't started boarding yet. Moving closer to the wall, he narrowly avoided being trampled by a frantic mother and her four kids who blasted by. "Shit, that's fantastic. Send me the report. If we know who killed PJ Wu, we'll be able to find out in two shakes who the Butcher is."

"That's the thing . . ." Kellogg hesitated. "Bobby, this is crazy. What you're going to see is absolutely bonkers. I wouldn't believe it myself if I wasn't staring at it with my own eyes right now. I suggest you be sitting down when you read it."

Sanchez rolled his eyes. He didn't have time for Kellogg's melodrama. "Kim, just send it. I'm almost at my gate. I'll read it on my iPhone while I'm boarding."

He disconnected and a moment later, he got the email. Clicking on it, he pulled up the PDF of the CODIS report.

And almost lost his balance.

Enlarging the image, he stared at the name.

CODIS had matched the DNA found on PJ Wu's body to one Matthew Shank. Current address: 1789 Poppy Lane in the Sweetbay neighborhood of Seattle. Owner of Adobo, located in Fremont.

What the *fuck?*

He called Kim back. "Are you shitting me?" he said when she picked up, again on the first ring. "Tell them to run it again. That can't be right. I know Matt Shank, he's a good kid."

"I know, I met him the other day. He's Edward Shank's grandson."

"This is not happening," Sanchez said, trying to make sense of it. "Are you seriously telling me that Edward Shank, the former chief of police of Seattle, has a grandson who's about to be arrested for murder? And that his grandson's father, whoever the hell *he* might be, is our Butcher?"

"I can't wrap my mind around it, either," Kellogg said, her voice still hushed. "I did try to look for Matthew Shank's father, but there isn't one listed on his birth certificate."

Sanchez frowned, trying to remember what

Sam had told him about Matt's parents. "As far as I know, he doesn't know who his father is. His grandparents said they didn't know, either. This just keeps getting worse and worse. This really is Operation Clusterfuck." A voice came over the loudspeakers, announcing that his flight was now boarding. "Shit."

"Are you getting on the plane now? You want me go pick up Matt Shank?"

Sanchez stood for a minute, debating what to do. "No," he finally said, turning around. "No, I can't let you do it. The Chief would flip. I'll do it myself. This has to be handled delicately. Don't say anything to anyone until I call you, you understand? This can't get out until we figure out how the hell we're going to handle it."

"That's why I told you to call my cell," Kellogg said. "I knew you wouldn't want anyone here to know."

"Smart girl."

"Who's telling Shank? Not the one who killed Wu. The older one, the one you used to work for."

"Guess that would be me." Sanchez gritted his teeth as he walked back the same way he'd just come. "How do my kids say it nowadays? FML. Fuck my life."

41

His grandfather—his *father,* goddammit—wasn't as strong as Matt was, but that didn't matter, not when the Chief had a gun in one hand, and Matt's iPhone in the other.

Behind him on the floor, Sam wasn't moaning and he could no longer hear her wheezing, but he didn't dare turn to look to see if she was still conscious. He didn't want to take his eyes off the Chief for a second, despite how much he wanted to go to Sam, and comfort her, and save her.

But he couldn't think about that now. He couldn't do anything until he got his goddamned iPhone out of the Chief's hand. Sam had a fucking cleaver stuck in her chest, and there was no way to help her without calling 9-1-1. Getting rid of the house's landline, which at the time had been a cost-saving decision, now seemed like the worst idea in the world. His cell phone was the only link he had to the outside world, and if he couldn't get his phone back, Sam would die.

How had it come to this? He couldn't be sure Sam wasn't already dead on the floor behind him. He couldn't be sure about anything anymore, because nothing made sense. The only thing he did know for sure was that his grandfather, the man who'd raised him and given him everything, was now standing in front of him with a gun pointed at his head.

"I don't want it to be like this," Matt said. "Please, Chief. I don't give a shit who you really are or what you did, okay? I just want to call nine-one-one for Sam. She won't make it if I don't. Please, Chief. Give me my phone."

"Have you ever thought about how you wanted to die, Matthew?" Edward said. His cheeks were rosy, his eyes shining with excitement. The gun, something small and black, rested in his liver-spotted hand easily. Matt hadn't even been aware that his grandfather was carrying it. "Because I know I think about it all the time."

"Please. Chief, please." Beads of sweat were dripping down Matt's temples and he swiped them away. "I will do anything you want, okay? Anything. Just give me the phone so I can call for help."

"There's no point, because there isn't enough time." Edward said this pleasantly, as if the words weren't completely horrific. "She hasn't got much longer, Matthew. There isn't a lot of blood on the outside, but I heard and felt something break, so I know she's bleeding internally. Do you want to say your goodbyes? I don't mind. I'll wait."

"No!" Matt felt nothing but sheer panic. "No, I'm not saying goodbye to her, Chief. I love her. She is the love of my life."

"You certainly have a strange way of showing it." Edward looked down. "Doesn't he, Samantha? Didn't you just tell me the other day that Matthew was a lousy boyfriend to you? Or did I misinterpret?"

Behind him, Matt heard nothing, because of course Sam didn't respond to the question.

"See?" his grandfather said. "We're losing her. Sorry about that, kid."

"Why?" Matt said. It seemed like a pointless question but it was all he could think of to say, and he needed to buy time. "Why hurt her? Why the gun? I'm your . . . son, for Christ's sake. If I wanted to turn you in, don't you think I would have done it by now?"

"You were going to turn me in. You thought about it, don't lie. It was just a matter of time." Edward sighed deeply. "And that's not how I want to die, Matthew. I don't want to die in prison. Have you ever seen the inside of a men's prison? It's inhumane. That's not how I want to die. But neither do I want to die in an old folks' home, rotting away like yesterday's discarded supermarket produce."

"So then how do you want to die?" Matt asked.

"Spectacularly," the Chief said with a smile. "In a blaze of glory."

Matt couldn't even begin to understand what the hell that meant.

"Tell me, would you kill me to get the phone

to save Samantha's life?" his grandfather said.

"I . . ." Matt stopped. Oh God. Oh God what a horrible question. How could the Chief ask a question like that? What kind of answer was he expecting to hear? Taking a deep breath, he said the first thing that came to mind. "Yes. I would."

"Even though I'm your father and she's just a girl you never wanted to marry?"

Goddamn him. "Yes."

"Why?" Edward asked. His grandfather's eyes bored into him. "Explain it to me."

"Because you're old," Matt said. "And you're a fucking monster. Sam's young. And a good person. She deserves to live." His eyes welled up with hot tears, but he blinked them back. He didn't want to show weakness around the Chief.

Edward nodded. The satisfied look on the old man's face told Matt that he'd just said the right answer, whatever "right" was in this scenario. "So you're saying it's time to put me down."

"Chief, please. Just give me the gun." Matt's tone stayed even. "Please. If you don't, I'll have no choice but to take it from you."

"I expect nothing less from you, Matthew."

Matt took a step forward. Edward gave him a small smile and raised the gun higher.

"You want me to shoot you in the face or in the heart, kid?"

"You won't shoot me, Chief."

Matt reached forward and grabbed Edward's

arm. His grandfather resisted a little, but not nearly as much as Matt expected him to, and a few seconds later he got a hold of it. He forced it out of the Chief's iron grip, fully expecting the gun to go off.

It didn't.

Matt pointed the gun at his grandfather. "Give me my phone, Chief."

"Kill me first, kid. Then you can take it."

"What?" Matt said, not sure he heard the old man correctly. "What did you just say?"

Edward sighed again, and this time it was heavier. "Put me down like the dog I am, kid. I'm tired. And this is how I want to go. Go on. You can do it. One shot. It'll be over in a second. The safety's off. All you have to do is pull the trigger. You can say it was self-defense. It's my gun, registered to me. My prints are on it, just like they are on the cleaver. They'll believe you."

"I . . ." Matt didn't know what to think, how to feel. "What? No. That's ridiculous. I can't do that."

"You're not getting your phone unless you do it." Edward's voice was steel. "So you have no choice but to do it. Do it to save her."

Matt squeezed the trigger ever so gently, but he couldn't bring himself to press it all the way.

"One quick squeeze and it's done," the Chief said, somehow managing to sound reasonable. "Come on now, don't be a pansy. Think of all the people I've killed. Think about how much you hate me."

"Shut up," Matt said. "I can't think."

"You don't have time to think. Come on, hurry now. Samantha's still breathing, but she doesn't have long. You need this phone, don't you? So go on. Do it. Shoot me. Remember, I raped your mother."

Matt squeezed the trigger and the bang was louder than he expected.

42

Sanchez heard a sound ring out from inside the house as he was about to get out of his car, and there was no mistaking what it was.

"Christ," he swore under his breath, pulling out his phone. He dialed 9-1-1. "This is Detective Robert Sanchez," he said when the dispatcher asked him what his emergency was. "Badge three-two-four-two-seven. I've got shots fired at one-seven-eight-nine Poppy Lane in Sweetbay."

"Roger that, Detective, we're sending backup."

Stepping out of his car—his own Nissan, as he'd headed straight here from the airport—Sanchez drew his weapon from his holster. The gun felt a little foreign in his hand, even though he carried it every day. Despite what those shows on TV claimed, homicide detectives rarely had cause to draw their weapons, because usually by the time they arrived at the scene, everybody was dead. The only time he ever handled his gun was when he practiced at the gun range or cleaned it. He'd certainly never been in a situation like this before. Grimacing, he moved quickly up the porch steps of Matt Shank's house.

Peeking through the side window, he could see that the kitchen lights were on. He detected movement. Trying the doorknob, he found the front door unlocked. Sanchez entered the house quietly.

Reaching the kitchen a few seconds later, he froze at the scene before him.

Samantha was sitting propped up against the kitchen cabinet, jean-clad legs splayed in front of her. Her head was lolling to the side at an awkward, uncomfortable angle, and her eyes were partially open, her lips parted. Sanchez couldn't tell if she was breathing, and wouldn't be surprised if she wasn't, considering the huge stainless steel chef's cleaver stuck dead in the middle of her chest.

Matt Shank was crouched beside her, and he looked up at Sanchez. "Oh, thank God," he said, his voice cracking. His eyes were wild, and he was shaking violently all over. "Thank God you're here. I don't—"

"Step away from her." Sanchez aimed his gun at Matt's chest. "Step away from her, Matt."

"But it wasn't me. I didn't do this. I—"

"Step the fuck away from her right now, Matt," Sanchez said, his voice only one decibel lower than a shriek. "Don't make me ask you again."

Matt stood up and moved a few feet away from Sam, closer to the opposite wall.

"Now face the wall," Sanchez said. "Kneel down. Put your hands up over your head."

The younger man did as he was instructed, and Sanchez stepped closer to Sam. Not taking his eyes off Matt, he reached down and pressed two fingers to her throat. There was a pulse, thank God, but it was extremely faint. Keeping the gun directed at Matt's back, he called 9-1-1 again from his phone.

"This is Detective Sanchez at one-seven-eight-nine Poppy Lane. I'm waiting for backup on shots fired. I need an ambulance. Female, age twenty-nine, chest wound. Hurry."

He disconnected and stood back up. "Turn around," he said to Matt.

Shuffling on his knees, Matt turned back around, facing Sanchez with this hands still up in the air.

"What the fuck happened?"

"Do you think she's going to be okay?" Tears were streaming down Matt's face. "I couldn't call for help, but I couldn't leave, and I didn't know what to do—"

In the distance, the screech of sirens could be

heard. "The ambulance is coming. So are the police. Matt, what happened here?"

"It was the Chief," Matt said, his voice choked. "My grandfather. He—he stabbed her."

Of course that made no sense to Sanchez, but he barked, "Then where is he?"

"He ran. I had the gun. His gun. I shot at him but I missed." He tried to slow down, to breathe. "I couldn't do it, Bob. I couldn't kill him. I wanted to, so badly, but . . . it would mean I'm like *him*. And I can't be like him, okay? I just wanted to get him away from Sam."

Sanchez squeezed his eyes shut for a second, trying to decipher everything the younger man had just said. "Why in God's name would the Chief stab Samantha, Matt?"

From the kitchen floor, Matt looked up at the detective with bloodshot eyes. The younger man's entire body was still trembling, his armpits were soaked with sweat, and he looked much older than his thirty-two years. "Because he's the Butcher," Matt said. "And he's a fucking psychopath."

Sanchez stared at him as the words slowly processed. What Matthew Shank had just said was absolutely insane. Edward Shank, the former chief of police of Seattle, was the serial killer known as the Butcher? Of course he wasn't.

A tingle ran up Sanchez's spine then.

Holy shit. Holy mother of God.

It was insane, yes, but somehow, it fit. It fucking fit.

On the floor, Sam moaned. Forgetting that he was supposed to keep his hands up in the air, Matt got up off his knees and rushed over to her. He cradled her head in his hands. "It's okay, baby," he whispered, tears streaming down his face. "You hang on, okay? You hang on. Help is coming, and you're going to be fine. I promise. Just hang on. Please hang on."

Sanchez lowered the gun. "Keep talking to her, okay?" Grabbing his phone again, he made another call. "Kim, this is Sanchez. I need a BOLO on Edward Shank . . . yes, *that* Edward Shank. We need to find him and bring him in immediately. He's our guy." Covering the phone, he said to Matt, "What's he driving?"

"If you didn't see his Cadillac in the driveway, then he's in it," Matt said. "But he knows how to hot-wire a car, so he's probably ditched it by now."

Sanchez repeated this information to Kim Kellogg, and then summed up what Matt had said about the Chief.

"You're kidding, right?" the female detective said on the other line. "Please tell me you're joking, Bobby. I'm not putting it out there that the Chief is the Butcher. That's im—"

"*Now,* Kim."

Sanchez disconnected and headed to the front door. He opened it to see the ambulance arriving, along with the fire department, four squad cars, and about two dozen neighbors milling around to see what all the excitement was about. A minute later it was chaos inside the Shank house as the paramedics started working on Sam, and the officers secured the scene. He grabbed Matt's arm.

"I need to know where your grandfather would have gone, Matt."

"I have no idea." The younger man seemed dazed. The adrenaline was leaving his body, and soon he'd be so exhausted he'd probably be unable to answer any questions coherently. "He didn't tell me."

"Think." Sanchez squeezed Matt's arm for emphasis. "The Butcher . . . he liked to leave his victims in wooded areas. The Chief liked to hunt. Did he have a favorite spot?"

Matt frowned, trying to concentrate. "Yes. Yes, he had a cabin. I don't know if he goes there much anymore, and I've only been there a couple of times myself. It's out in Raymond, about two hours from here. As far as I know, he still owns the land it's on."

"Okay." The detective hesitated, choosing his next words carefully. "I'd appreciate it if you didn't let him know we were coming."

Matt looked at him, his eyes suddenly clear. "No fucking chance in hell. That son of a bitch hurt Sam." Both men watched as Sam was lifted

409

into a gurney. "And I wouldn't need to tell him, anyway."

It was the detective's turn to frown. "What do you mean?"

"He knows you're coming." Matt's tone was flat and fierce. "All of this? It's exactly what the Chief wants. So I hope you give it to him. Do what I couldn't do. Send the fucker to hell."

43

The one-room cabin in Raymond, Washington, hadn't been used in a while as Edward didn't hunt much anymore. But the generator had gas, and so he had lights and hot water, at least for now. They weren't far behind him, he knew that, but it would take them a while to find his exact location.

He owned two hundred acres of undeveloped land out here, and the cabin was smack in the middle of it. There were no roads leading directly to it, and unless you knew exactly where you were going, it wouldn't take much to get lost. The woods were dense, and the huge trees above the cabin provided ample coverage should they decide to send out helicopters.

Oh, how he hoped they would send out helicopters.

He figured he had about an hour.

Standing at the old rusty kitchen sink, Edward

stared at his reflection in the little locker-sized mirror he'd tacked up above it. The face staring back at him was that of a stranger. When had he gotten so old? His face was lined deeply, the jaw slacker, the eyes more sunken, the lips thinner. He was still a reasonably handsome man, but getting older sucked donkey's balls.

He'd lived much longer than he'd ever expected.

He'd nearly been caught in 1985. It had been sheer luck that had finally allowed him to pin the murders on that loser Rufus Wedge.

Ah, Rufus. Had Rufus been just a little bit smarter, or a little bit stupider, Edward might never have had to stop being the Butcher. The dumb shit had ruined it for both of them.

APRIL 21, 1985

"Do you understand what needs to happen here?" Edward said.

The dim bulb of the storage room light swung slightly, casting moving shadows over Wedge's slack, pockmarked face. Wedge had worked at the U-Store-It for almost four months now, which was the longest amount of time he'd ever held down a job. They were standing inside a locker that had gone unpaid for three months, and Wedge was responsible for clearing out its contents.

"Yeah." Wedge kicked at a box with his boot. "You're gonna arrest me. I go peacefully."

"I'll make sure you get the best public defender. There are some good ones. The prosecution will try and indict you, but it won't stand, because there's not enough evidence. But we need to show the public that we're working hard on this case. There's so much heat."

"And then I get the hundred grand?"

"No, Rufus, you get seventy-five," Edward said, trying to be patient. "You already got twenty-five. The rest will be wired to the offshore account we'll set up after the trial. You'll be in jail for a few months, okay? But nothing you can't handle. You're the Butcher. Nobody's going to fuck with you."

"How do I know you'll give me the money?"

Edward smiled. "You'll have to trust me." He leaned in. "I could have had you arrested for shit you really did, don't forget. That would put you away for ten years, maybe more. This is a good deal."

Wedge still looked doubtful, but then again, that wasn't far off from his normal expression. "So why do you do it?" he finally asked, chewing on his lower lip. His teeth were stained brown. "Why do you kill them?"

"Because I need to. And because I can."

The urges had been terrible lately. Whenever he had one, he'd drive over to whatever shit town Wedge was currently living in, and find a girl with brown hair.

A girl who looked like Lucy.

He'd slipped with his daughter. He'd gone too far, and once Matt was born, he promised never again. Rufus Wedge would be taking the fall for him tomorrow. The public would calm down. And then it would all be over. Fortunately, or unfortunately.

It would be the end of this chapter, and the beginning of something new.

Edward snapped out of his reverie when he heard the helicopters circling above.

He took one last look at the old man staring back at him in the cheap plastic mirror and nodded, smoothing his hair into place.

Reaching down, he picked up the Remington that was leaning against the side of the sink, lifted it, and cocked it. He loved holding the rifle. It was so solid, so wonderfully heavy.

"Showtime," he said.

44

It had taken them more than an hour to find the cabin, but they found it.

Sanchez was dressed head-to-toe in tactical gear, as were the others in the unmarked police van that pulled up to the front of the cabin. The gear weighed a good thirty pounds, and while

Sanchez wasn't considered a big guy, the adrenaline coursing through his veins made the heavy attire feel feather light. Five guys dressed in the same tactical gear looked at him, waiting for the order. They all seem slightly stunned, as if they couldn't really believe they were here.

Frankly, Sanchez could hardly believe it, either. Edward Shank was the Butcher?

What kind of terrible joke was this?

But it wasn't a joke.

Sanchez nodded to the team, and the rear doors of the van were pushed open. Everybody spilled out, spreading out and away from each other as they moved silently across the dirt and grass toward the cabin, weapons drawn.

The cabin was small, all right, and not exactly picturesque. The wood exterior was dirty and decaying, and the entire area smelled faintly of rot. There were two windows at the front, and both were so crusted over with dirt that it was hard to tell if any lights were on inside. The front door wasn't much more than a thick sheet of plywood.

They shone their lights at the house. Taking a deep breath, Sanchez said loudly into the stillness, "Edward Shank! Police!"

The front door swung open immediately.

Shank stood there, tall and erect, his eyes bright as he surveyed the scene. He was wearing his formal dress blues. Gold tassels framed his broad shoulders, brass buttons ran straight down his chest, and there was a satin stripe running down each pant leg. At his side was a rifle. Buckshot. Sanchez blinked. Nothing about this picture was right.

"I was expecting you boys a half hour ago," the Chief said with a grin. Putting a hand over his eyes to shield it from the bright lights, he said, "Robert? That you, my little Mexican friend?"

Sanchez was Chilean, not that it mattered now, and he wasn't about to correct the former chief of police–slash–serial killer. "Stand down, Chief," he said instead. "Put your weapon down and get on your knees, hands in the air. You're under arrest."

"For what, specifically?"

"Seventeen counts of first-degree murder."

Shank nodded, seeming satisfied with the answer. Then he squinted. "Any chance you can kill those lights? I can't see a goddamned thing."

Sanchez made a motion with his hand and the bright spotlights were reduced to two beams from two different Maglites.

"Better, thank you," Shank said. Then he stepped forward, rifle still at his side.

"Don't move!" Sanchez shouted. Around him, his team raised their guns higher. "We're here to bring you in, Chief. You know how this goes."

"I certainly do, and this was fairly close to

how I imagined it would be." The Chief sounded calm, almost eerily so. His authoritative voice rang out in the quiet area. "Is Matthew with you?"

"No, he's not."

"How's Samantha?"

Sanchez hesitated, then finally said, "I'm told she's going to pull through." He knew no such thing. On the way over he'd heard that Sam's vitals were worsening, but he had no intention of repeating that out loud. He couldn't even think about Sam right now.

"That's good," Edward said. "I was neutral on Samantha. Didn't particularly want anything bad to happen to her, but she was getting on my nerves. Felt good to stick that cleaver in her chest and shut her up."

"Chief, put your weapon down and get on your knees."

Shank laughed. "That's not going to happen. I'm eighty years old now, and I can't remember the last time I kneeled. Come on, Robert. We all know how this is going to end."

"And how's that, Chief?"

"I'm going to raise my rifle. When I do, you'll shoot me."

Sanchez sucked in a breath. "Please don't do that, sir. Please."

"Too late," Shank said, raising his rifle quickly.

Within a second, multiple shots rang out,

peppering the still night air with their staccato and bright sparks. The smoke from the guns was strong. Acrid.

From his stance thirty feet away, Sanchez heard the thud when the Butcher hit the soft, damp ground.

He pulled off his helmet and sighed deeply. Regretfully.

"No more now," the detective said quietly. "No more now, you goddamned son of a bitch."

Epilogue

FIVE DAYS LATER . . .

Sam watched the news from her hospital bed. The Butcher had made national and even international headlines, and she'd had countless calls from every major media outlet asking for her story. Not to mention three calls from publishers offering her a better book deal than the one she'd originally been contracted to write.

She didn't want any of it. Not anymore.

Her mother had been murdered by a serial killer, and the time had come to grieve for Sarah Marquez properly. Then, and only then, would she be able to move on.

Her phone pinged and she reached for it,

wincing as the bandages strained against the wound on her chest. She saw that she had an email from Miguel, the nurse from Sweetbay Village, asking how she was doing. She put the phone back on her side table without responding.

Matt had been arrested for the murder of PJ Wu. The cops had searched the inside and outside of Adobo thoroughly, and traces of PJ's blood had been found in the alleyway behind the restaurant, and also inside the dumpster. From what Sam had heard, he'd confessed everything once they'd brought him into the station. It had been an accident, he said. He'd panicked, he said. He'd only dismembered the body because the Chief had told him to, he said.

Sam had cringed when she'd heard that. Not in a million years would she have believed him capable of something so sickening, so gory.

Her ex-boyfriend would be going to prison for a long time. As soon as she was released from the hospital, she planned to visit him. Regardless of what he'd done, Matt had saved her life. She needed to make sure he was okay.

There was a knock on her open door and she looked up.

Jason was watching her from the doorway, holding a bag of greasy fast-food tacos. After two days of hospital food, nothing could possibly have smelled better.

"Miss me?" he said, putting the bag down on the table beside the bed.

"Yeah." She smiled up at him, at the man she'd known almost her whole life. They'd been kids when they met, and looking at him now, she could still see traces of the boy she'd always loved.

And not like a brother.

"You have a funny look on your face," he said with a knowing grin. "I think you want to kiss me."

"Shut up. No I don't." Pausing, she looked at him out of the corner of her eye. "But, hypothetically, what if I did?"

"I would then ask, hypothetically, if you brushed your teeth."

Sam rolled her eyes. God, he could be so infuriating. She reached for the tacos, trying to ignore the burning pain where she'd been stabbed. She was healing, but she would have a scar. "Just forget it."

He took a seat at the edge of the hospital bed, laughing. His finger brushed a lock of hair away from her face, his expression turning serious.

"Okay," he said. "Ask me."

"Nope, don't want to."

Jason moved closer. Dammit, he smelled good, like soap and water. "Ask me," he said again.

Why did he have to be goddamned cocky? Except . . . his hand was shaking. Just a little.

"Fine," she said. She met his gaze, faking a confidence she didn't quite feel yet. "Will you kiss me?"

He grinned. "You didn't say please."

She smacked him. He kissed her anyway.

Acknowledgments

I am forever grateful to do what I do, which is invent fictional people and make them do horrible things that I could never do myself in real life. I certainly could not murder people fictionally—and with great glee—without the help of my rock star agent, Victoria Skurnick, who is so supportive and always has my back. It's also been a pleasure working with my new editor, Natasha Simons, whose fresh input has made this book so much better. I owe a very special thank-you to Kathy Sagan for believing in me, and this story, from the beginning.

I'm so happy to continue to be part of the Gallery Books team. Huge thanks to Jennifer Bergstrom, Louise Burke, Karen Kosztolnyik, and my publicist, Stephanie DeLuca, for supporting this book, and all my books.

I will always be thankful to Steve Hillier, who didn't laugh six years ago when I announced I wanted to write a book, and who instead let me write as much as I wanted to and then bragged about me to everyone he knew.

My girlfriends do a stellar job of making me feel talented and important, even when I don't. So much love goes out to Dawn Robertson, Annabella Wong, Lori Cossetto, Shellon Baptiste,

Micheleen Beaudreau, Jessica Szucs, Nancy Thompson, Jennifer Baum, Jennifer Bailey, Teri Orell, and Scott Kubacki (who's not a girl, but who is my counterpart in all things darkly funny).

I'm also grateful for my supportive family, especially my mom, Nida Allan (who'll read this book in one sitting), and my dad, Roberto Pestaño (who won't read it at all because of the sex scenes). My big brother John Perez also won't read this book, but he'll cheer me on anyway and hopefully listen to the audio version if he's bored at work.

Lastly, I'd like to thank Darren Blohowiak, the newest member of the family, my best friend, and my love. Thank you for not running the other way when I told you what I do for a living, and for only being mildly uncomfortable whenever you see me with a knife in my hand. I promise never to cut you. I love you too much.

About the Author

Jennifer Hillier is the author of two previous novels, *Creep* and *Freak*. She is a member of the International Writers Organization, International Association of Crime Writers, and Mystery Writers of America. Originally from Canada, she now lives in the Pacific Northwest. Visit her online at www.jenniferhillier.org, follow her on Twitter, and read her blog, The Serial Killer Files, at www.jeniferhillier.org.

Center Point Large Print
600 Brooks Road / PO Box 1
Thorndike, ME 04986-0001 USA

(207) 568-3717

US & Canada:
1 800 929-9108
www.centerpointlargeprint.com